W9-AKI-654

PAOLA SANTIAGO
AND THE
RIVER OF TEARS

PAOLA SANTIAGO
AND THE
RIVER OF TEARS

TEHLOR KAY MEJIA

RICK RIORDAN PRESENTS

DISNEY • HYPERION   LOS ANGELES NEW YORK

If you purchased this book without a cover, you should be aware that this book is stolen property. It was reported as "unsold and destroyed" to the publisher, and neither the author nor the publisher has received any payment for this "stripped" book.

Copyright © 2020 by Tehlor Kay Mejia

Introduction copyright © 2020 by Rick Riordan

All rights reserved. Published by Disney • Hyperion, an imprint of Buena Vista Books, Inc. No part of this book may be reproduced or transmitted in any form or by any means, electronic or mechanical, including photocopying, recording, or by any information storage and retrieval system, without written permission from the publisher. For information address Disney • Hyperion, 77 West 66th Street, New York, New York 10023.

First Hardcover Edition, August 2020

First Paperback Edition, May 2021

10 9 8 7 6 5 4 3 2 1

FAC-025438-21078

Printed in the United States of America

This book is set in Janet Antiqua Std/Monotype

Designed by Jamie Alloy

Library of Congress Cataloging-in-Publication Control Number for Hardcover Edition: 2019038724

ISBN 978-1-368-04933-7

Visit www.DisneyBooks.com

Follow @ReadRiordan

SUSTAINABLE FORESTRY INITIATIVE

Certified Chain of Custody

Promoting Sustainable Forestry

www.sfiprogram.org

SFI-01054

The SFI label applies to the text stock

To all the women (here and gone)
whose stories, myths, and superstitions
have shaped my world

CONTENTS

DON'T GO NEAR THE WATER

When I was a kid growing up in Texas, I was terrified of going into deep water. That wasn't just because the movie *Jaws* had freaked me out. (Although, yes, that giant robotic shark had scared the Twizzlers out of me.)

Worse: I had grown up listening to campfire stories about La Llorona, the weeping ghost who had drowned her own children in a river and was condemned to wander the riverbanks for eternity, looking for their bodies. If she happened to come across a living child at the river, well . . . she might claim you as her own and pull you under.

Whenever my family camped near the river, I would hear strange wailing sounds at night. I'd huddle deeper inside my sleeping bag. The next morning, I sometimes found heavy tracks in the mud, as if made by dragging, shuffling zombie feet. I was sure La Llorona had been on the prowl, looking for someone like me to drag into the cold, murky depths. Yeah, I had a fun childhood. Thanks for asking.

That's one reason I'm so excited to share Tehlor Kay Mejia's *Paola Santiago and the River of Tears* with you. She gives us a brand-new take on the ancient folktale of La Llorona, and I want you to read it so you can be as terrified as I was!

To be fair, our hero, Paola Santiago, is a lot braver than I was at her age. She's got a scientific mind, and she doesn't believe in old folk legends like La Llorona . . . despite the fact that she has suffered from horrible nightmares about the nearby Gila River her whole life, and even though her mom is always warning her about evil spirits and lighting velita candles to keep her safe. Ghosts aren't real. Are they? Her mom is just spouting silly superstitions. Right?

Then, when something terrible happens at the river—something that could shatter Pao's entire life and the lives of her two best friends—Paola starts to wonder if science will be enough to figure out the mystery.

This story is chock-full of suspense and fantastical elements, but it's more than just a page-turner. I love *Paola Santiago* because the characters are so relatable. Have you ever struggled with loving your parents while also being mortally embarrassed by them? Have you ever been jealous of a best friend? Have you ever secretly *crushed* on a friend? Paola's got *all* these problems and more. She's smart and courageous, but she's also a bubbling stew pot of conflicting emotions about herself, her friends, and her family. Does she have what it takes to handle all that *and* confront the truth about the strange disappearances that have been happening around town? You're about to find out!

I'm really envious of you, reading this book for the first time. You're going to make some lifelong friends in Paola, Emma, Dante, and the rest of the marvelous characters. So put another log on the campfire, guys. Roast some s'mores. Get ready to laugh and enjoy and maybe even shiver in fear at the story you're about to hear. But whatever you do ... don't go near the water.

Rick Riordan

ONE

Algae *Again*

It was 118 degrees in Silver Springs, Arizona, and the Gila River was thick with algae. But Paola was careful to keep that observation to herself. The last time she'd mentioned algae in front of her best friend Dante, he'd shoved a gummy worm up her nose.

Algae was green and slimy. It stuck to your feet when you stepped into the wrong part of the swimming hole. It smelled awful. It made the river look weird and alien when the water got too low. But when processed and extracted and purified, an acre of it could create ten thousand gallons of usable biofuel.

And wasn't that awesome enough to make up for its general ickiness?

Aware of Dante and her other best friend, Emma, sitting on the picnic blanket on either side of her, Pao didn't speak aloud the wonders of algae. Sometimes she thought there were still granules of sour sugar from that gummy worm slowly making their way to her brain through her nasal cavity. There was a lot of candy spread out before them today, and Pao didn't want to find out what other varieties would feel like in her nostrils.

Shuddering, she kept her daydreams private for now.

In Silver Springs, the place where Pao was unfortunate enough to have lived since she was four years old, there wasn't much to do *but* daydream. In fact, she had become somewhat of a pro.

Sometimes she pondered algae or other fuel experiments, sometimes which kind of robot could best handle the unpredictable topography of Mars, sometimes the latest rocket launch and where it was headed. But Pao's spacey-ness didn't discriminate. She'd also been caught drifting off about her favorite graphic novel series, double-chocolate sundaes, and how unfair it was that her mom wouldn't let her get a dog. (Spoiler alert: It was really, really unfair.)

The thought of dogs had her pondering the specifics of certain breeds again, and she was barely aware of Dante and Emma's banter beside her until it was too late.

"Earth to Pao!" said Dante on her left, his hand inching dangerously close to a bag of Milk Duds, like he could tell she was silently breaking their no-algae agreement.

"You might have better luck with '*Mars* to Pao.'" Emma giggled on her right.

Pao let today's gloopy green daydreams float away into the sherbet-colored sky and sat up to face her two friends, smiling in an *I know I'm weird but you love me anyway, right?* kind of way.

"What did I miss?" she asked.

"Best superhero weapons," Emma said. "We were debating Captain America's shield versus Thor's hammer."

"Ah, sorry," Pao said. "But either way, you know I don't like weapons that defy physics. It's cheating."

Emma smiled and shook her head, her freckles standing out against her pink cheeks, her hair sandy and glossy, hanging in two curtains on either side of her face. Beside her, Dante rolled his eyes and huffed, his black hair flopping into his eyes. He tossed it off his face with a flick of his head, a move he'd learned from the older boys on his soccer team, and Pao was feeling so magnanimous she didn't even tease him for doing it.

"Not everything has to be scientifically accurate, Pao," he said, making her regret her mercy. "It's summer—can we just forget about school stuff for, like, three seconds?"

"We can't afford to. The polar ice caps are melting, Dante," Pao said witheringly. "Coral reefs are dying by the acre. The ozone—"

"Okay, okay, I get it," he said. "All science, no fun."

He saluted, and Pao, feeling bad for being a stick-in-the-mud, tossed a Cheeto at him and stuck out her tongue.

It feels like it's always been the three of us, Pao thought as Dante ate the Cheeto and then Emma began trying to toss Skittles into his mouth. But it had been Dante and Pao first, long before Emma moved into town two years ago.

Dante had been Pao's neighbor since they were four, when her dad (whom Pao barely remembered) had left for good and her mom had been forced to move them into a run-down apartment complex at the edge of the desert.

Aside from sporadic birthday cards from her father (never with money inside, and only sometimes *on* her actual birthday), it had been just Pao and her mom for the past eight years.

In the beginning, her mom had tried to put up a brave front, but on several occasions, Pao had spied her crying out on the patio. One time Dante's abuela heard the sobbing, and she immediately insisted on having Pao and her mom over for dinner that night. And then the next night. And the next. Every evening for weeks Señora Mata had made rib-sticking feasts while Dante and Pao eyed each other warily across the shag-carpeted living room.

But then came the day when, as the kitchen filled with the smell of arroz con pollo, Dante held out a die-cast metal space-ship for Pao to play with, keeping the astronaut action figure for himself. The shag carpet had turned into the terrain of an alien planet, and they'd been inseparable ever since.

Well, at least until the beginning of sixth grade, when Dante had joined the soccer team and started putting gel in his hair. All this past year he'd felt half-in, half-out to Pao, like he was always thinking about being somewhere else when they were together.

Pao had been grateful for the end of soccer and school and, with the start of summer, the return of the Dante she'd always known. But she couldn't help worrying about what seventh grade would bring for the three of them.

"It's getting late," Pao said, cutting off her own space-out for once and shifting gears, picking up the candy wrappers and chip bags. She was (probably unsurprisingly) a stickler about litter. When you had researched the effect of trash on the world's bodies of water, it felt criminal to leave plastic behind.

Dante grabbed the last empty M&M's bag as the sun began to sink in the sky, signaling the approach of the when-the-streetlights-come-on curfew they'd all been given. "Hand 'em over," he said to Pao. "I'll go to the trash can."

Pao could see it in silhouette, up near the graffitied sign that marked the beginning of the river hiking trail. The city rarely emptied the can, but using it was better than littering.

"Hurry," Emma said, and Dante saluted again.

They were always careful to get back home on time. No

one wanted their parents to come looking for them because then they'd have to explain where they'd been. They'd all been expressly prohibited from going anywhere near the river after Marisa Martínez had drowned last year, sending all the middle school parents into a panic.

Pao was deeply offended by the restriction. She was a *scientist*. She knew about cold pockets in rivers that could cause hypothermia even when the air temperature was shattering thermometers, and currents that could grab you in water six inches deep, and other invisible traps and hazards beneath the surface that were a one-way ticket to drowning.

Not that she was *afraid* of the water or anything.

Not at all.

And even if she was understandably *wary* of it, there was no way she would admit that to her mom. Because Pao had already heard more than enough lectures in her young life about the dumbest reason ever to be afraid of anything:

A ghost.

That's right. Pao's mom had forbidden her from going anywhere near the Gila years ago, well before Marisa's tragic accident. The reason Pao had missed out on birthday parties, riverside barbecues, and anything else water-related had a different name: La Llorona, or the Weeping Woman—the spirit of a mother who, according to a centuries-old legend, had murdered her own children. And who was also supposedly super active in this region.

And no, her mom's belief in the story was not a joke, or an exaggeration. Just a complete and total embarrassment.

La Llorona is the most terrifying of all our ghosts, her mom would say. *She drowned her children in a fit of rage and was cursed to wander the riverbank forever, calling their names . . . and looking for her next young victim.*

Her mom was a gifted storyteller. Pao didn't like to admit it, but back when she was eight years old, the stories had given her nightmares. Nightmares she'd erased with good old-fashioned research. The ghosts and wailing and disembodied hands had been replaced with sneaky currents, hypothermia, sunken tree branches that could snag an ankle. . . . Those things were legitimately scary.

But ghosts? There was no scientific basis for them. No evidence at all that their existence was even possible, let alone likely. An old folktale was definitely not a valid reason to change one's plans.

Especially when the plans happened to be the first boy-girl river-tubing party one had ever been invited to.

Not that Pao was still bitter about that or anything.

Dante took off for the trash can, but not before stuffing the last half of a Snickers in his mouth, his cheeks bulging around it.

"Gross, Dante," Emma said. As he jogged toward the trailhead, she turned to pull one of Pao's shoulder-length braids. They hadn't talked about it, but Pao wondered if Emma was as glad as she was to have the old Dante back.

"Seriously, though," Emma said to Pao, "you're extra out-there today. What are we obsessing about?" Her blue eyes were bright and curious, like she was brainstorming a list of topics for a group project at school. "The potential habitability of Europa?" she guessed first. "Or why they don't make whole sleeves of pink Starbursts? Ooh, is it the dog thing again? What's this week's breed?"

Pao smiled back, grateful that her mom's fixation on all things supernatural hadn't made the list.

Emma Lockwood was more interested in comics than the solar system, and she liked cats more than dogs (the horror!), but she was the kind of person who took the time to learn about what *you* loved. She cared about what you cared about. Pao had moved on from thinking about Europa months ago, but she didn't mind the question—she knew she was lucky to have a friend like Emma.

Plus, seriously, why *didn't* they make whole sleeves of pink Starbursts? They were by far the best flavor.

Even though Emma's family lived on the golf-course side of town, far from the sagging roofs and peeling walls of Dante and Pao's apartment complex, their twosome had effortlessly become a threesome the day Emma had pulled out her America Chavez comic in homeroom.

"I'm not allowed to talk about today's obsession anymore," Pao said under her breath with a resigned look at Dante, who had just reached the can and was tossing their junk-food detritus into it.

"Oh, right," Emma whispered, a mischievous twinkle in her eye. "Dante doesn't like *algae*."

Pao giggled, but Emma wasn't done. As Dante turned to make his way back, Emma pulled Pao to the river's edge and scooped up a handful of the forbidden green stuff.

That was another thing Pao loved about Emma. Even with her sparkly purple nail polish (she went for manicures with her mom every two weeks), she was still willing to get her hands messy for the sake of a good prank.

Pao scooped a satisfying blob of algae for herself as Emma hid behind the scrub bushes near their blanket. Pao was just about to follow, when a splash at the center of the river drew her eye.

It had been too large to be one of the fish that leaped up for water striders, but strangely, the surface of the river was now still. No ripples. You didn't even have to be a scientist to know that ripples formed in water at any point of disturbance.

Had Pao's ghost ruminations caused her imagination to kick into overdrive?

Goose bumps erupted across her arms.

"Pao! He's coming back!" Emma whisper-shouted from the bushes, and Pao shook her silly fears out of her head. She had imagined it. Or it had just been a trick of the light. There was an explanation for everything, even if it wasn't immediately obvious.

She slid in beside Emma, the scrub hiding them from Dante, who approached looking confused.

"Guys?" he asked, and Pao suppressed a giggle, algae still dripping from her hands.

"Now!" Emma shouted, exploding out of the bush and running toward Dante, Pao right behind her.

For a minute, Pao was worried that too-cool Dante would return. That he'd roll his eyes or do that weird new hair-flip thing and say they were being dumb.

But he screamed, turning on his heel and running like the swamp creature was behind him. "Oh, no you don't!" he shrieked, his recently lower voice jumping three octaves.

They chased him until they were breathless and cracking up, then finally dropped the offensive substance before rinsing their slimy hands in the shallows.

Emma's cell phone rang while she was shaking her hands

dry. She always turned away when she answered it, Pao had noticed, covering as much of the Wonder Woman case as she could, like it might offend her and Dante by being so shiny and expensive-looking.

Pao didn't have a phone of her own. It was just sort of understood that her mom couldn't afford anything but the army-green landline that hung on the kitchen wall, and Pao didn't dare ask—even though there was a constellation-tracking app she would have *loved* to try. . . .

At least Dante could relate. His abuela probably didn't even know what a smartphone *was*, much less appreciate the benefits of having one. And it wasn't like she was rolling in money either.

"Dinnertime," Emma said with a grimace when she hung up. She swung her leg over her purple mountain bike that, according to Dante, "screamed Colorado."

"See you tomorrow?" Pao asked her. "You're bringing the telescope, right?"

"And you're bringing the snacks," Emma replied. "*Don't* eat all the pink Starbursts this time." She pedaled off, kicking up dust on her way west, away from the swampy smell of the summer-low river.

Pao tried not to envy her too much.

She and Dante walked away from the lingering glow of the sunset that gilded Emma's side of town like a blessing. After a mile or so, their own dilapidated apartment complex loomed ahead in silhouette.

The sun always bails on us first, Pao thought. And wasn't that fitting?

The fifteen units of the Riverside Palace apartments (the irony of the name was not lost on Pao) looked like the kind of motel people drove right by. There were two stories, with one sagging staircase right in the middle.

At one point, there had been sixteen units, but apartment F's roof had caved in three summers ago and no one had bothered to fix it. F was unoccupied now, of course, but sometimes high schoolers smoked cigarettes in it at night. Whenever Dante's abuela caught those kids there, she chased them off with her house slipper, yelling curses in Spanish while they sped away laughing on those low-to-the-ground bikes Pao secretly coveted.

Unit B was empty, too, its dark windows drawing Pao's eye as always. A boy and his parents had lived there until six months ago, when uniformed men had come in a van and arrested them. Pao, Emma, and Dante had witnessed the whole thing while taking turns on Emma's bike in the parking lot.

Pao had tried to ask her mom about it, but she had only hugged her tightly and said something about "privilege" that Pao didn't quite understand.

No one had rented the apartment since, and Pao often wondered what had happened to the people who had been taken from it.

The Palace's stairs, with their peeling sea-green paint and warped railing, were where Pao and Dante always said good night, before he went up and she stayed down. Their apartments, C and K, were stacked on top of each other, separated only by Pao's ceiling and Dante's floor.

Tonight, when they reached the stairs, Pao lifted her hand for their usual high five. Dante slapped it automatically, but he didn't go up right away. Instead he lingered, gazing down at Pao's feet until she was all too aware of the mud on her Kmart Converse knockoffs and the chocolate smudge on his chin.

He's taller than me, Pao realized. When had that happened?

"Hey, so I wanted to say . . ." he began, still looking at her scuffed sneaker toes.

"Yeah?"

"Well, your algae and stuff? I know I give you crap, but I actually think it's pretty cool. I mean, not the algae," he clarified quickly. "But, like, just how much you know about it and stuff. That's cool. So."

"Okay," she said, her cheeks heating up. "Um. Thanks." Dante had never acted this way with her before. She wasn't entirely sure she hated it.

"But seriously, if you ever try to put that gross stuff in my hair again"—he met her eyes, sounding more like his usual self—"I'll think of something way worse than a gummy worm to stick up your nose."

When he smiled, his teeth were bright white against his summer-browned skin. He bumped her shoulder with his as he headed for the stairs, acting all casual and laid-back.

But the tops of his ears were flushed purple—she could see it as the parking-lot lights flared to life.

Pao's curiosity crackled in the wake of Dante's blush. She wished she could stay outside to mull it over while the evening air cooled around her. But her mom was waiting. As always, Pao lifted her chin and steeled herself before she went inside.

Time to face the ghost stories.

TWO
Tarot Cards Never Tell You What's for Dinner

When Pao opened the door to apartment C, the smell of incense was overwhelming. That meant her mom was reading tarot. Pao's steeliness started to buckle. Her mother only consulted the cards when things weren't going well.

"Mom! I'm home!" Pao called, dropping her backpack on the living room floor. There had to be fifteen candles burning on the shelf above the serape-covered couch. Green candles, Pao noted. She only burned those when they needed money.

Well, more than usual, anyway.

"In here, mijita!" her mom called from the dining room/ kitchen, which only took about five steps to reach in their tiny apartment. Pao pasted on a smile as she crossed the threshold, hoping not to notice any other signs of bad news.

Her mom sat cross-legged in the paisley-upholstered dining chair, her dark hair in a messy bun held with a single chopstick. Her eyes were narrowed at a tarot spread on the weathered kitchen table, incense smoke swirling around her.

"You know," Pao said, "if we had a *dog*, he could bark for help when you pass out from all this incense and one of the candles sets the house on fire."

The smoke alarm had stopped working a year ago, but the manager of the Riverside Palace hadn't responded to multiple requests (from Pao, of course) to replace it.

Pao's mom smiled back from the tiny table, but her eyes were tired. "My old-souled baby," she said, reaching out to squeeze Pao's hand. "You've always been the adult around here."

A sadness settled in Pao's chest. Mom had said it lightly, like a joke, but Pao didn't think it was funny. They were always speaking to each other in a kind of code, disguising important facts. Pao wished that, for once, they could just *talk*. That not everything had to be signs and candles and old souls and too-real jokes.

"Do those cards say anything about what's for dinner?" Pao asked, trying to hold on to her smile even though the incense smoke was giving her a headache.

"Oh no," her mom said. "Is it that time already?" She pushed aside her too-long bangs and looked in disbelief out the glass door to the patio. Twilight was settling over the crowded terracotta pots where Pao's mom grew herbs and flowers.

Pao tried to quash a feeling of irritation. Had her mom really been so wrapped up in the cards that she didn't notice the time? It wasn't like the whole sky-changing-colors thing was easy to miss.

But of course, her mom didn't allow clocks anywhere she did divination work. She always said, along with cell phones and microwaves, clocks "messed with the vibe." Apparently, the ancestors couldn't get to her through all that "noise."

And the ancestors, among other things, protected them from the ghosts.

Too bad they can't also protect us from the rent going up, Pao thought. Her mom tried to hide that kind of stuff from her, but

Pao trained her observational powers constantly. She didn't miss the notices with red rectangles around the past-due amounts.

Pao never would have admitted it out loud, but her mind went immediately to Emma, who was probably sitting down to a meal consisting of multiple food groups right now. Meat and potatoes and something green that her parents would bribe her with ice cream to finish. At Emma's house, they didn't have to joke about fire hazards, or who the real adult was.

As quickly as the thought landed, Pao swatted it away. It wasn't fair. *Mom's doing the best she can.* Plus, they were a team, and Pao didn't want to know what would happen if either of them believed otherwise. Even for a minute.

Pao's mom got up and rummaged in the freezer until she found a Ziploc bag full of Señora Mata's cheese-and-jalapeño tamales. "I forgot we had these!" she said, turning around and preheating the oven before Pao could check the leftovers closely for freezer burn. "It'll only be forty-five minutes, okay? Some brain food for your experiments!"

On her way back to her seat in front of the tarot cards, her mom kissed her on the forehead, which only made Pao feel worse.

"You know, I'm actually not that hungry anymore," Pao said, even though she was. Right then, the urge to get out of the incense-filled kitchen and be alone with her guilty thoughts was stronger than the urge to eat.

Plus, leftover tamales always got all dry and rubbery when they were reheated in the oven, and the cheese ones were her least favorite kind.

"We ate a lot of junk food this afternoon—I think I feel a stomachache coming on."

"Let me get you some peppermint tincture!" her mom offered, turning too fast. Two tarot cards fluttered down like dry leaves in a wind gust.

"It's okay, really," Pao said quickly. "I'm just gonna go lie down."

"You sure?" her mom asked. "You know, El Cuco can hear a growling stomach from miles away. . . . And I'm working late at the bar—I won't be here to chase him out of your room tonight."

Her mom's face was somber, but the bogeyman story was so juvenile it only made Pao more eager to escape. She hated pitying her own mother—it felt like wearing a shirt that didn't fit right.

"That doesn't even make sense," Pao said. "What kind of monster would want to eat a skinny kid?"

Pao didn't know why she had posed that question. It wasn't like she wanted to hear her mom's rebuttal. . . .

But none came. Her mom's eyes were glued to the floor, probably already drawing some significance from the way the cards had landed under the table.

On another day, Pao might have jokingly asked if the Tower and the Fool cards meant they could get a dog. But today, for a reason she didn't fully understand, she just left the room without saying good night.

Emma's mom would follow her daughter into the hallway at a time like this. Pao would've bet her Celestron beginner's microscope kit on it. And not just because the microscope was totally inadequate for someone at her skill level.

But Pao sat on her bed alone, surrounded by the pictures of the SpaceX and Blue Origin launches she'd printed out at the library, the colored ink streaky and dull. Taped to the wall above her desk (which was her grandma's old sewing table, so it didn't have any drawers) was last year's science project on algae farming. She'd won first place without even mentioning the organism's potential to power rockets.

Meanwhile, her mom burned candles in search of money to pay bills and thought the right card layout could keep ghosts and monsters away.

Maybe, Pao thought sleepily, if she had enough algae, she could blast herself right out of this place. . . .

In her dream that night, Pao walked along the river, and above her was a darkness so absolute it made her shudder.

A green glow emanated from the water, and as she made her way toward it, she saw silhouetted shapes beneath, passing back and forth in a haunting kind of dance.

She knelt on the bank, sensing the fabric of the dream bending and shimmering around her. But even as she recognized the surreality, she was excited about finding bioluminescent creatures this close to home. Would they stay still long enough to let her get a good look?

One of the creatures broke the surface, and Pao leaned closer, mesmerized by the pale grace of it, the long, fingerlike tentacles reaching for the sky.

But was one of those tentacles wearing Emma's ring? Heart-shaped and set with a real ruby, it was kind of hard to mistake, even from a distance. . . .

That's when Pao realized they weren't tentacles. It was a hand. A human hand. With fingernails painted a sparkly purple.

She tried to scramble back from the river's edge, but the hand grabbed her by the wrist, the ruby ring glinting in the green glow from the water. Pao screamed, a high, hollow sound drowned out almost instantly by an unearthly wailing that kicked up all around her like a gust of wind.

Pao was pulled farther toward the water's terrifying depths, her shoes and socks getting soaked as she fought futilely against the hand's inexorable grip. The crying grew louder.

It grew louder still as she stumbled and fell to her knees.

But somehow it was loudest of all when the hand pulled her under the water's surface.

Pao woke in a panic, half off her mattress, a scream lodged in her throat.

It was a dream, she told herself. *Just a dream.*

The weird splash she'd seen yesterday—and its weirder lack of ripples—came to mind. It must have seeped into her subconscious.

Pao pulled out the clandestine, taped-together alarm clock that she kept under her bed. It read 1:15 a.m. A grumble erupted from her stomach, making her think of El Cuco and her mother's warning. She'd fallen asleep in her clothes—even her shoes.

Pao breathed deeply, trying to calm her racing heart, focusing on the glow-in-the-dark stars on her ceiling as the dream's images slowly faded.

It had been a long time since she'd dreamed of drowning.

She'd had her first riverbank dream when she was nine. Nothing much had happened in it. But for third-grade Pao, that terrible, utterly dark sky had been enough to make her wake up screaming, drenched in sweat, and send her running to her mother's room for comfort.

Throughout the rest of elementary school, she'd had the

dreams at least once a week. Her mom had been at a loss. She'd invited curandera friends and other healers to try to purge whatever was haunting Pao, but nothing worked.

After that, they'd gone to a real doctor's office, where nurses attached things to Pao's head and screened her for all kinds of conditions she didn't have.

Eventually, Pao was referred to a child psychiatrist—one her mom would never have been able to afford. Pao was midway through fourth grade by then, and even at that age, she noticed the dark circles under her mom's eyes from being awakened so often, the wrinkles that appeared on her forehead every time the doctor suggested a new treatment or a test their insurance didn't cover.

So Pao had stopped running to her mom. She pretended that the dreams had gone away on their own. Over time, they became just another strange part of her life, one she hardly thought about beyond the first few terrifying minutes after she woke up.

But she'd never dreamed of a disembodied hand before. And definitely not one wearing Emma's ring . . .

When her pulse had returned to its normal resting rate (more or less), Pao shook herself mentally, cursing her mom for telling her scary stories at such a young age.

There's no such thing as ghosts, she told her reflection in the window as she kicked off her shoes, even though she looked a little like a spirit herself, pale in the warped glass.

Hypothermia, cold pockets, submerged branches, invisible currents. Pao recited the true dangers of the river like a mantra. They were a mile away, no threat to her in this quiet apartment. *Hypothermia, cold pockets . . .*

The hallway was empty, the apartment quiet as Pao headed for the kitchen. Her mom always left for her waitressing job at eight thirty, and she didn't come home until closing time, around two a.m. If anyone asked, Pao was supposed to say that Dante's abuela watched her at night, and she had for a while. But when she turned ten, Pao petitioned to be allowed to sleep in her own bed, tired of the stiff, uncomfortable sofa at Dante's.

Her mom, so concerned with supernatural threats, had been less concerned with real-world things like home invasions and electrical fires and Child Protective Services, and Pao had gotten her wish.

Strange as her mom's priorities were, Pao knew she was grown-up enough to keep herself safe. As if to prove the point, she walked through the living room, checking all the incense burners and candle glasses to make sure everything had been extinguished. Tonight, she noted gratefully, they had. Her mom had even remembered to lock the door behind her, though Pao wasn't sure why. She was pretty sure La Llorona wouldn't be deterred by anything as pedestrian as a dead bolt.

Pao didn't let herself think of the ghostly hand from her dream. Or the wailing. The memories were already starting to fade.

"If we had a dog, we wouldn't need to worry about monsters and ghosts," Pao grumbled, even though there was no one around to hear her perfectly sound argument.

The Moscow watchdog was widely considered the best breed for home protection, but their large size made them impractical for apartments. Staffordshire terriers were more sensible size-wise, but apartment managers didn't love their resemblance to the pit bull. There was a perfect breed out there somewhere, Pao knew. She just had to keep looking.

In the kitchen, she planned to eat cereal from the box until her stomach quieted down, but she found a plate covered by a pot lid. It held two of the three cheese tamales and a note:

In case you get worried about El Cuco. I love you.

This time Pao made a conscious decision not to compare the note, or the cold chewy tamales, to what was probably happening at Emma's house. But even so, disappointment in her own life took up more space in her stomach than the food.

THREE
Cold Pizza and Cold Cases

Pao woke up for the day at ten, her body adjusting to summer vacation much faster than it had ever adjusted to the school-year schedule.

No more dreams, she noted, satisfied by her brain's return to reason.

Her mom would still be asleep, and Pao probably had an hour before Mrs. Chavez showed up for her weekly remedio. Mrs. Chavez had arthritis, and she paid Pao's mom to ease her pain with tea and salves made from the herbs on the patio.

The mystery of how her mom always got up on time without a clock was one Pao had accepted she would never solve with science.

Pao was under strict orders not to be on the premises during tarot readings or curos, which her mom did for extra money. Her mom never said it directly, but Pao knew she was supposed to stay away because her skepticism "interfered with the vibe." Like she was a microwave oven and not a twelve-year-old who got sick of wandering the neighborhood in record-breaking heat while her mom pretended to do magic.

Hopefully, Mom will get real money this time, Pao thought.

Sometimes she let clients pay with books or eggs or massages—or, worst of all, IOUs. The refrigerator door was plastered with blue Post-it Notes from Mrs. Jacobs, who always brought one with a dollar sign on it in lieu of cash.

Pao's mom never turned anyone away. She said healing was a "calling."

On the kitchen table was a plate with two pieces of cold pizza from the bar where her mom worked, along with another note:

If we had a dog, you would have been up four hours ago to walk him. Plus, he would have eaten your breakfast. See you after the curo. XO Mom

"It would be so worth it," Pao told the neighborhood cat, Charlie, who was prowling around on the patio. Pao ate the first piece of pizza in two bites, slid open the door, and tossed the crust to him. He sniffed it suspiciously before deciding it was a prize worth carrying away.

Pao was (obviously) a dog person, and you'd never catch her cuddling a cat. But the Riverside Palace had its own ecosystem, and Pao had a grudging respect for Charlie and the other wild cats for keeping roof rats and scorpions away.

After a quick shower and the daily hunt for her notebook and pen (in case of any brilliant ideas, obviously), Pao barely made it out of the house before her mom woke up. She heard her door open just as the front door was closing. It was a dance they'd been doing all summer—avoiding each other as their differences became too big for their tiny space to hold.

The heat outside was oppressive even at eleven, and though she'd planned to spend the day doing scientific research on the library computer with occasional breaks to look up dog breeds her mom couldn't possibly refuse (Maybe a hypoallergenic breed like the West Highland white terrier? Or a Border collie, which rescued people from natural disasters?) Pao calculated her personal temperature-to-distance-to-motivation ratio and muttered, "Forget it," to the Riverside Palace's resident sprawling, dusty cactus.

Sighing, she turned up the stairs to Dante's apartment instead and knocked, barely waiting for Señora Mata's "¡Adelante!" before walking in.

"Good morning, señora," Pao said to Dante's abuela, who was sitting in front of what had to be the third broadcast of the morning news. "Okay if I hide out here again today? My mom has a client."

Señora Mata muttered something in Spanish before crossing herself. When she looked back up at Pao, there was pity in her eyes. Pao knew it meant she was welcome, as always, but that Pao's mom could use some assistance from heaven.

"Well, I'll just be in Dante's room," Pao said, loud enough for him to hear in case he was doing any weird boy stuff in there. Even so, she waited outside the door for as long as she could stand before knocking.

Dante answered looking normal, though—his hair sticking up at weird angles, no styling gel in sight. As usual, his room smelled like dirty socks and his abuela's Florida Water, which she used for cleaning despite its distinct lack of antibacterial properties. Pao's mom was obsessed with the stuff, too. It was one of the many things the two of them had in common, including devotional candles and questionable taste in tamale fillings.

As she walked into the room behind him, Pao remembered

Dante's blush and her own fizzy feelings of curiosity last night, and she wondered if things would be awkward between them today. But apparently the weirdness was like bioluminescence: harder to spot in the daylight.

Well, that was one hypothesis, anyway. She'd have to keep working on it as more data came in.

Dante tossed her a lukewarm can of Coke and a PlayStation controller before flopping down into his nest of twisted blankets and changing the racing game to two-player. Just like always.

"Emma coming by?" Dante asked.

"Nah," said Pao as she selected the pinkest car and the driver with the nineties high ponytail, just so it would be more annoying when she beat him. "She has a piano lesson today, then lunch with her parents *at the club.*"

Dante nodded, and Pao immediately felt bad for using her phony posh voice. Emma never sounded like that. That was her life, the same way this one was Pao's. It just felt strange that they were so far apart sometimes, like Emma was in a world Pao couldn't reach.

Case in point: The only time Pao had ever eaten lunch with the Lockwoods at the country club, she had accidentally ordered duck—which was called something fancy and French she'd been embarrassed to ask about. Then she'd used the wrong fork, as Emma had gently informed her in a whisper. Pao hadn't had the guts to go back there since, and she still apologized under her breath every time she saw a live duck.

In the too-small bedroom, which was already heating up, Pao won the first two races without even trying. They talked sparingly as they continued the tournament, Dante managing to get by her in one round and doing a horrifying victory dance.

When Señora Mata called "¡Almuerzo!" an hour or so later, Pao was grateful for the break. It was only a matter of time before Dante would get sulky about losing.

Pao knew some girls let boys win just to keep them interested, but beating Dante was one of the great joys of her life. No amount of new nocturnal boy-girl strangeness was going to replace that.

Dante's arm brushed hers as he stood up. Pao's stomach and all the organs around it seemed to swoop.

I'm still not letting him win, she told her stupid body.

The layout of Dante's apartment was identical to Pao's, but while Pao's mom had left their main room open to hold all her bookshelves and small altars, Señora Mata had divided hers into a living room and dining area.

In this house, we don't eat in front of the TV like heathens, the señora liked to say, ignoring the fact that the only thing that separated the table from the TV in question was a floral-print couch. Not to mention the fact that the TV was always on.

During lunch, Pao had to use a lot of brainpower to keep her elbow from touching Dante's. Unfortunately, it wasn't distracting enough to block out the news broadcast. Pao always found the local news depressing, and today was no exception.

According to the anchor, it was the one-year anniversary of Marisa Martínez's drowning in the Gila River. Her body had never been found.

"Such a shame," the señora said, in accented English for Pao's Spanish-challenged benefit. "She was so beautiful."

Pao hated it when people talked about Marisa, though she did her best to hide it. Marisa had been the town darling. Latina, but blond and barely sun-kissed, so everyone could feel good about loving her. She'd been popular in school, while Pao was the weirdo with only two friends and the I NEED MORE SPACE T-shirt.

Regrettably, Pao had been the butt of one too many of Marisa's jokes. Two years older, Marisa had always made fun of Pao's obsession with "goofy space stuff," and her tendency to "smell like hierbas." She also mocked Pao's mom for looking "out of it" at fundraisers and school programs.

It was strange when someone you didn't like died prematurely. Pao was sorry about what had happened to Marisa, of course, but she always had a squirming guilty feeling when anyone brought it up.

Today, though, the guilt was second to the reminder of Pao's strange experience at the river yesterday. The ripple-less splash. The nightmare that had followed . . .

The news moved on, reporting on a string of child abductions up north, near Mesa. As the anchor talked excitedly about a possible suspect in the kidnappings, grainy security-camera footage showed a tall, lanky figure with dark hair and pixelated features. A shiver traveled down Pao's spine. The guy in the video didn't look much older than the teenage boys who hung out in apartment F. Pao knew he couldn't be one of them, though—Mesa was too far away.

She tried to listen to this story, but Señora Mata was still clucking about beautiful Marisa.

"Yeah, it was a tragedy," Pao said, irritation buzzing in her chest like a swarm of yellow jackets. "But *not* because she was blond and pretty. Because she was a *person*, and people's lives are valuable whether they're beautiful or not."

Señora Mata's mouth fell open, revealing a piece of green pepper stuck to her dentures. The air in the room seemed to evaporate, and Pao felt an entirely different kind of swoop in her stomach—fear, this time. But the angry buzzing was still there, too.

"Well, I think that's enough lunch!" Dante said, grabbing Pao's plate and standing up between his abuela and his friend before either one could get seriously injured. "Pao was just leaving, weren't you, Pao? Good-bye! See you next time!" He nudged her toward the door with his foot, still holding both of their plates, three-quarters of Pao's meal untouched.

At the door, he said in a sharp whisper, "You can't talk to her like that! She's just old. She doesn't know any better."

"That's no excuse," Pao said, her own brown skin and dark hair glaring at her from the mirror that Señora Mata had hung by the door to ward off bad energy. "If we don't talk about our messed-up beauty standards, how will they ever change?"

As Dante's expression hardened, Pao knew she would take all the boy-girl weirdness in the world over the storm clouds gathering between them. But she wasn't wrong, so she didn't apologize.

Some things are worth standing up for, she told herself, even though her chest ached.

"Not every fight is your fight!" he said, still clearly frustrated as she opened the door.

"Oh yeah?" she asked, her temper flaring. "And what's *your* fight, Dante?"

He rolled his eyes. "*You're* my fight, Pao."

Pao wasn't sure what he meant by that, so she didn't answer before he shut the door behind her. Through the open window, she could hear his abuela berating him in Spanish. Probably asking why he bothered with such a loudmouthed girl when he could be searching for a silent blond supermodel girlfriend who did nothing but cook.

If I had a dog, Pao thought, *I'd train it to pee on her doormat.*

All afternoon, Pao tried to forget what had happened at lunch by brainstorming natural sources for rocket fuel and eating what had to be her body weight in Starbursts. When she ran out of pinks, she just kept going—reds, oranges, even a dreaded yellow.

A sign of emotional distress if there ever was one.

All she managed to put in her notebook was a sugar-smudged sketch of the river. If she unfocused her eyes, she could almost see a ghostly hand rising out of the water, like in her dream.

When a knock sounded on her apartment door at five forty-five, Pao tried to beat her mom to it, in case it was Dante. She didn't quite make it in time, so all three of them ended up in the living room together, their eyes watering from candle smoke and incense.

"What are you two up to tonight?" Pao's mom asked, sliding in a hoop earring as she prepared for an early shift.

"Nothing much," said Pao quickly.

Too quickly. Her mom's face lost its dreaminess and focused in on her immediately. "Paola . . ."

"We're using Emma's new telescope, okay? It's practically homework."

"As long as you're not going anywhere near the river."

"No, ma'am." Pao put on her best innocent act and willed Dante to do the same. It wasn't her fault the riverbank was the only place where it was cool enough to hang out *and* dark enough for stargazing.

"Good," said her mom, now distractedly searching the living room for her other high heel. "Because you know La Llorona haunts the Gila. There have been sightings. You don't want to get caught out when she's searching for her lost children—"

"*Mom!*" Pao snapped, embarrassment making her cheeks hot.

"I know, I know, you don't believe in ghosts," she said, like she hadn't just humiliated her only daughter. "But they're saying there's a *murderer* in Mesa, so you stick close to home, you hear me?"

"Mesa is miles from here," Pao said dismissively. "And, according to the news, those kids are being *abducted*, not murdered."

But her mom didn't hear—she was too busy digging out her other shoe from under a couch cushion. "Aha! Found it!" She slid the low-heeled shoe onto one foot while hopping on the other, her purse strap in her mouth. When she finally had herself together, she swooped in, smelling like rose oil, to kiss Pao on the cheek. "I love you, mija," she said. "Be responsible, and no river—I'm serious."

"I love you, too, Mom," Pao said, discreetly wiping lipstick off her cheek.

"Make sure she stays out of trouble, okay?" her mom said to Dante and, to Pao's infinite embarrassment, kissed him on the cheek, too. And then, at last, she was gone.

"She's still going on about La Llorona, huh?" Dante asked when they were alone, his tone forced, their earlier argument still looming between them. "Even my abuela stopped with that one when I turned ten. Now she just threatens me with the chancla. Much scarier."

Pao had only been on the business end of the chancla—Señora

Mata's petrified old slipper—once, when she'd accidentally set fire to a macramé plant holder while trying to prove that you couldn't put out an oil fire with water. But she privately agreed that La Llorona was child's play in comparison.

"I just can't believe my mom actually accepts that junk as reality." Pao's embarrassment was making her mean, she could tell. But she couldn't stop. "Spirits haunting the riverbank? At least the maybe-kidnapper is an actual person, even if he is, like, three counties away." She circled the room, blowing out candles. Her mom would have been furious that she didn't thank the ancestors first. "She says she's 'more in tune with ghosts and spirits' because of her tarot and healing work," Pao said. "Which is just—"

Dante was getting this glazed-over look. After all their years of friendship, he could recognize a mom rant coming from a mile away.

"Sorry," she said, grabbing her shoulder bag. "I hope you brought snacks, because there's nothing here, as usual, and I ate all the Starbursts."

Dante patted his backpack reassuringly. "Rode my bike to Seven-Eleven earlier. Abuela let me have the couch change."

Pao nodded her appreciation, glancing up at him and finding him looking back. Their gaze lasted a beat too long, sending Pao's stomach swooping again as she looked away.

Dante shifted uncomfortably and pushed his hair out of his eyes.

Pao's stomach swooped yet again.

She told it to knock it off.

"Hey," he finally said. "About what happened at lunch . . ."

"No, it's okay," Pao said. "She's your grandma. I know it's hard to—"

"I talked to her," Dante said. "After you left. Told her that stuff you said about beauty standards or whatever. I don't know if she got it for sure, but . . ."

Maybe it was the seven thousand milligrams of sugar coursing through her veins, or the promise of the telescope, but Pao didn't let him finish. She stepped forward and hugged him for a long time, his backpack awkwardly knocking into her shoulder bag.

"Thanks," she said when she finally let go.

Dante was blushing again. "Um, yeah. Sure. No big deal."

They walked to the river in silence, but it was a comfortable one. Considering the roller coaster their friendship had been lately, Pao held on tight to the feeling.

When they reached their usual spot near an ancient, twisted juniper, Emma wasn't there yet. Pao pulled the blanket from her bag and spread it on the rocky sand. The water looked almost still, the surface deceptively mild as dangerous currents flowed underneath. Pao shuddered when she thought of her dream—the hand with Emma's ring, the depths of the river. She pushed the memory away.

Dante and Pao sat with their backs against a rock, Dante flipping through a comic, Pao doodling in her notebook, the comfortable silence persisting. Pao didn't want to break it. After twenty minutes of waiting, Dante opened his backpack and started shoving peanut butter crackers into his mouth. For once, snacking was the last thing on Pao's mind. "Emma's always on time," she said, more to the ground than to Dante. He wasn't a worrier.

"Chill," he said, holding out the sleeve of crackers. "Have one."

But food didn't quell the uneasy feeling in Pao's stomach. Emma was never late. She should have been there already.

"Okay, this is officially weird," Pao said when it had been an hour and the light was beginning to fade in the sky.

"She probably forgot," Dante said, but even he was pacing now, his dark eyes darting around the riverbank and to the cactus field in the east.

They both knew that was unlikely, but it was comforting to hope, so Pao played along.

"Yeah, maybe she lost track of time reading comics or something. We can try again tomorrow."

Dante rubbed the back of his neck self-consciously, not meeting Pao's eyes.

"What?" she asked, a little more snappily than she'd meant to.

"Nothing," Dante said. "It's just . . . I'm supposed to play soccer with the guys at the park tomorrow."

Pao tried not to react. Because of Dante's new soccer friends, Emma and Pao had eaten lunch without him more often than not this past year. Pao had thought summer would be a safe time, when they could hang out with Dante like they always had and not worry about him getting too cool for them.

"You guys could come?" Dante offered, but she could tell he didn't really want them to.

For the next ten minutes, they sat in silence, Pao trying to pretend that this summer would be just like all the past ones they'd spent together. Yet she knew it wouldn't. Seventh grade was looming, and everything was changing too fast.

"Let's go back home and call Emma," Pao said, her alternating worries about her two best friends making tears spring to her eyes. She folded the blanket to give her nervous hands something to do. "Maybe her parents wouldn't let her go out and she couldn't get ahold of us to say."

"I bet that's it," Dante said. He didn't tease her about over-thinking it, and he picked up the cracker wrappers without Pao having to lecture him about the river's delicate ecosystem, so she knew he was worried, too.

It almost made her feel better.

They were just turning their backs on the river when Pao saw it: a shadow on the opposite bank. Only a silhouette against the sunset from here, but definitely a person lurking behind some reeds. *Is it Emma?* Pao wondered, squinting. Maybe she just hadn't spotted them. But Pao stayed quiet as she pondered, some instinct stopping her from calling out.

It didn't take long for her to realize that the shape was larger than Emma, and it wasn't a girl, either. What was the guy doing? She would have assumed he was fishing if the pesticides in the river hadn't given all the fish three heads. (Not literally, of course. The toxins in runoff hurt fish by depleting oxygen in the water, but genetic manipulation was, as far as Pao knew, a fantasy.)

If this were one of her graphic novels, Pao and Dante would go up to the guy and follow him into some surreal situation that would end up with them magically finding their missing friend.

But this wasn't a book, and Pao had to admit she was a little freaked by the prospect of talking to a random stranger, even though Dante was with her. "Should we . . . go find out if he's seen Emma?" she asked him, wanting to appear braver than she felt.

"Yeah, right," Dante said, taking her arm and pulling her

away as quietly as possible. "Are you nuts? We're going home to call her."

"Fine," Pao said, pretending to be irritated. But deep down she was glad he'd given her an excuse to walk away.

Just before they were out of sight, Pao turned back to look. The sunset was fading, the reeds were still, and the figure was nowhere to be seen.

FOUR

Things You Can't Take Back

Emma's smartphone went straight to voice mail, but when Pao called her home number, Mrs. Lockwood picked up right away.

"Emma? Is that you?" her mother demanded. "I've been calling your cell for half an hour!"

Pao's heart sank as she wrapped the kitchen phone cord around her pinkie, cutting off the circulation. "Mrs. Lockwood?" she said, her voice thin and high. "It's Pao . . . Paola. Santiago."

Emma's mom hesitated, and Pao thought she could feel her heart sinking across the line. "What's wrong, Pao? Is Emma all right?"

"She . . . never showed up tonight," Pao said. "We were calling to see if she was there. We hung around our meeting spot for a while, but . . ."

"Oh my God." There was a muffled *"Arthur!"*

Pao waited, her heart racing, as she listened to the sounds of Emma's parents' frantic conversation.

"You never saw her at all?" Mrs. Lockwood asked Pao, her voice suddenly clear.

"Not since last night," Pao said.

"Where was she meeting you? She said you were going to be looking at the stars from your balcony."

Pao almost laughed. Only the Lockwoods would believe that Pao's apartment had a balcony. "We . . ." She hesitated. They had a pact never to tell their parents about their frequent visits to the river. But Emma was missing. All bets were off, right? Pao exhaled. "We were supposed to meet at the river at six."

Dante's glowing watch face read 7:28, and Pao quickly did the math. If Emma had left her house on time—say, fifteen minutes before the meeting time—she would already have been missing for almost two hours.

The pause on the other end of the line was louder than any words Emma's mother had spoken so far. "We're going to the police station," Mrs. Lockwood said at last. "Can you join us there?"

Pao and Dante lived half a mile from the town's only police station, but neither had ever been inside. There was an unspoken rule in their families: Never involve the cops. Emma's parents, Pao realized, wouldn't have to abide by the same rule. They didn't have to worry about things like authorities doubting their citizenship.

The two friends tried to look casual as they entered the lobby to wait for the Lockwoods, but they were soon approached by an officer in uniform, his chest puffed out, demanding to know their reason for loitering.

"We're meeting someone here," Pao said, with all the authority she could muster.

"Uh-huh," said the mustachioed man, scanning them with

watery blue eyes set too close together. "Let me guess. Your dead-beat dad? Or is it your gangster brother?"

"No, sir," Pao said as calmly as she could. When Pao and Dante turned ten, her mom had talked to both of them about never, under any circumstances, escalating interactions with the police. Pao was more scared than she'd been at the riverbank, but she stood up straight. "We're just waiting for our friend's parents."

"Listen to me," said the officer, pushing closer, backing Pao against the wall. He stared down at them like they were hardened criminals and not a couple of almost seventh graders. "We've seen your kind in here before. Trouble, all of you. Now, if you don't have business with us, you need to get out."

"Don't talk to her like that!" said Dante, stepping forward. "She's telling the truth!"

The look in the officer's eyes went from suspicious to furious, and Pao put up her hands instinctively, drawing his attention back to her. "I'm sorry," she said quickly. "It's just . . . our friend—she's missing, and her parents asked us to meet them at the station to help file the report or something. We don't want to cause trouble."

Miraculously, the officer took a step back, still scowling but no longer so aggressive.

Pao's breathing slowed.

"Where did your friend go missing?" he asked, his eyes darting to Dante more often than necessary.

"We're not sure," Pao said. "We were supposed to meet her by the river tonight, and she never showed up." She couldn't help but notice he wasn't taking any notes.

"Tonight?" His tone made it clear he was dismissing her

already. "It's too soon to file a report. Why don't you try her boyfriend's house?" He sneered.

"We're *twelve!*" Pao said, wondering whether he would have said the same thing if he knew who Emma was, what she looked like. "She doesn't *have* a boyfriend! We were supposed to use her telescope to look at the stars! And we saw someone out there . . . someone kind of suspicious—"

"Oh, yeah, yeah," said the officer. "I know—a weird crying lady on the riverbank, right? Or maybe it was the bogeyman. Or one of those chupacabra things people are always calling in. *¡Dios mío!*" He said this last part in an exaggerated Mexican accent, putting his hands on his cheeks in fake dismay. *"I'd like to report a ghost estealing my chili peppers."*

Pao's hands shook with rage. "It wasn't a ghost!" she said, trying to keep her tone even. "It was a—"

But the officer was already turning around. "Have her guardian come in tomorrow morning if your friend hasn't shown up yet," he said over his shoulder. "And leave the spooky stuff at home. We have enough going on without being asked to chase *ghosts*. Now get on out of here."

"We never mentioned a ghost!" Pao called after him, but it was too late.

They had only been in the station for a few minutes, but Pao felt like it had been a year. She walked out into the heat of the night with a thousand thoughts crowding her head. She was worried about Emma. She was frustrated that the cop hadn't listened to her. But bubbling underneath it all was something worse than the anger she felt toward that police officer:

Shame.

Pao stormed toward home, and Dante followed.

"What about the Lockwoods?" he asked.

"What are we supposed to do?" Pao asked. "Lurk outside until the cops accuse us of loitering or trespassing? The Lockwoods know everything we know, and nobody cares what we have to say."

"But what about that person we—"

"Dante!" Pao said, her worry colliding with her anger like the ice crystals inside two thunderheads. "Drop it!"

And he did.

Once they reached Riverside Palace, she barely said good night to him, ignoring his concerned looks and declining his offer to wait with her until her mom got back from work.

Inside, she couldn't settle down, the apartment seeming too small and too large all at once. She paced, calculating the time since Emma's disappearance and the distance she could have traveled by now. If someone had taken her into his car somewhere between her house and the river, and driven off at thirty-five miles an hour, Emma could be anywhere from . . .

"Is there a map around here?" Pao asked no one, heading into the kitchen to tear through the drawers. Clogging them were boxes of incense, empty candle glasses, and matches of all shapes and sizes, but of course, no map. Just superstitious garbage that didn't work, getting in the way, offering no solutions.

Pao felt powerless. The cop had made a fanciful ghost story out of her straightforward information. He had assumed she was superstitious because of how she looked, who she was.

And here was all the evidence of her mom's beliefs. The stories and ghosts and folktales that had given Pao nightmares and made the police officer dismiss her at a critical time.

The tension that had been simmering between Pao and her

mom lately overflowed in her brain now, roiling and boiling and bursting into flame. Pao paced again, glaring at every tall glass veladora—the saint candles her mom broke out when things were really going sideways. Pao resented every string of beads that wasn't just a necklace, every corner where her mom claimed a spirit had sat while she communed with the tarot cards or tea leaves.

On the smallest altar stood a glass jar with a white candle inside that was often lit for Pao's protection. As a little kid, Pao had loved striking the match herself, holding it up to the wick, and imagining a bubble of white light around her, shielding her from anything that could cause harm.

Pao glared at the offending object, totally devoid of magical properties. It was only a hunk of wax with a string wick. Lighting it was just another way her mom pretended to control the chaos of their lives, and Pao was tired of being the one who didn't play make-believe.

Barely breathing, she picked up the jar, the candle's hopeful wick just waiting for her mom to get home and give it meaning. But there was no meaning in stories, and magic wasn't any more real than ghosts. What had any of it ever done for them?

Pao took the candle into the kitchen, where the linoleum floor was scuffed and in need of mopping. She raised her arm, which seemed like it belonged to someone else, and let every heated thought about her mom's beliefs buzz through her blood before she dropped the jar, watching it shatter satisfyingly at her feet.

But breaking the candleholder seemed to have broken something in Pao, too, and she was suddenly more exhausted than she'd ever been. She lay down on the couch without sweeping up the pieces of glass.

In moments, the dark water of her subconscious overtook her, her last dream continuing like she'd never left it behind.

The river glowed green again, but this time, Pao knew better than to go closer. There was the hand sticking out of the surface, tension in every reaching finger, the ruby ring glinting in the moonlight. Pao's fear felt so real—a flip-flopping in her stomach—and yet part of her realized it was just a dream as she watched from the shore.

A silhouette approached—the guy they'd seen at the riverbank, she somehow understood. His face was obscured, blurry even at close range, and when he knelt at the water's edge, all the bioluminescence seemed to gather in his hands.

He laughed, an unearthly sound that made the hair rise on the back of Pao's neck, and though she felt invisible, he turned toward her, his hair dark and pixels where his facial features should have been.

Just like the Mesa kidnapper. On the news, his hazy, indefinite features had been a result of poor picture quality, but in the dream, it was something else.

Something . . . supernatural.

He held up his palms, and the green glow flared from them, coming toward her in a wave.

Pao screamed just before the light engulfed everything.

She woke with a start to the sound of a key in the door. Pao's heart was pounding, and the green still seemed to radiate all around her. Was she in the living room or at the river?

Then she remembered everything—Emma, the police officer, the smashed candle, the anger she'd finally let loose.

Her mom looked exhausted in the cool light of the streetlamp shining through the open door, and, for a moment, Pao's familiar guilt came back. The feeling that she should love her mom for who she was and not constantly wish she were someone else. But the frustration was there, too, now tinged with fear.

The desire for her mom to be the grown-up for once was stronger than ever.

"What are you doing up, mijita? And what—" She stopped as her gaze traveled to the kitchen. "Are you okay?" Panic replaced the exhaustion on her mom's face, and Pao saw what she must be seeing: her daughter, groggy and laid out on the couch; the glass on the floor. "What happened in here? Did someone break in?"

"No," Pao said, sitting up and trying to gather her thoughts, to turn them into something her mom could handle. But she was too tired, and too scared for Emma, so everything she tried to grab just scattered.

"Paola," her mom said, her voice going from concerned to stern alarmingly fast. "Tell me what's going on right now."

"First I gotta check the answering machine," Pao said, waking up fully. She'd been asleep for hours. Maybe Emma had been found by now.

Pao darted into the kitchen, carefully avoiding the shards of glass. Her mom shouted behind her, "Young lady, you better start explaining yourself right this—"

But Pao was already returning to the living room, dejected. The light on the answering machine was disappointingly green, not blinking red like it would have been if the Lockwoods had called to say Emma was safe.

"Paola! Start talking!"

"Emma's missing," Pao said, looking at the ground. "She disappeared tonight. I tried to go to the police, but"—she sighed—"they didn't believe a word I said."

"Querida, what do you mean? The *police*? Disappeared from where?"

"Do you want to know why they didn't believe me, Mom?" Pao's voice was louder now. Her frustration was winning against her desire to keep the peace.

"What I want to *know* is—"

"Because they think I'm just another superstitious small-town kid raised on El Cuco and La Llorona! Because they think I don't know what I saw. Because people . . ." Pao took a deep breath. Was she really going to say it? But Emma was gone and everything was falling apart and something inside Pao was falling apart, too. "Because people like you talk about ghosts and old folk stories like they're real. And everyone thinks we're all like that."

It hurt more than she thought it would, voicing this separation between them, putting it out there instead of hiding it in jokes or simply avoiding each other. Pao didn't want them to be at odds—her mom was all she had. But there was no denying that their perspectives on life were very, very different.

And unless something changed in a big way, they probably always would be.

"Paola . . ." Her mom's shoulders were slumped, her eyes exhausted, her black T-shirt stained with bar patrons' food and drink. Her hair was escaping its bun. Pao felt sorry for her.

But not enough to stop herself.

"I'm tired of it, Mom," Pao said, a small part of her watching in horror as it all came spilling out. "The superstitions, the stories, the rituals. They make people think we're crazy and backward." She gestured around at the green candles that couldn't always keep the lights on, at the tarot cards that brought comfort to everyone but them. "It makes everyone feel sorry for us or make fun of us and . . . not take us seriously when we really need them to." She stopped then, but the damage was already done. The words she'd been holding back for weeks, maybe months, had been released, and there was no taking them back.

"If you think my candles and cards are responsible for all the prejudice against Latinx people in this world, Paola Santiago, you have a lot more to learn about the people in it," her mom said. She was angry—Pao could tell by the deeper crease between her eyebrows. "Now, I understand that you're upset," she continued, calmer now. "You must be terrified for your friend, and furious that the police didn't listen to your story. But to blame all this on me and my beliefs would be a big mistake."

Pao felt like someone had punctured a balloon inside her chest. She wanted to cry, but she didn't feel she had the right. Not after the things she'd said. She had drawn a line, and now they were on opposite sides of it. Pao crossed her arms, trying to hold everything in.

"I've had a long night at work," her mom said, crossing her own arms, a mirror image of Pao. "I'll call the Lockwoods first thing to see if I can help. In the meantime, we both need some sleep. We'll talk in the morning—*after* you've cleaned up this mess."

As her mom walked past the kitchen, Pao wondered if this mess *could* be cleaned up. Glass and wax could be swept up, and the new scratch in the linoleum floor would barely show, but what about all the frustrations that had caused her to lose it in the first place? Pao's anger was ebbing, but the toothy thing beneath it stubbornly refused to budge.

And perhaps most bothersome of all, practical Pao couldn't stop seeing that pale, long-fingered hand creeping closer and closer. . . .

FIVE

Not Blood

The next morning, Pao woke early to the smell of coffee, which her mom didn't drink, and the sound of adult male voices, which Pao hadn't heard in this apartment in living memory.

Wearing her slightly too-small space pajamas, Pao walked out into the living room to find her mom addressing Dante, his abuela, and two uniformed police officers.

Her heart sank. If there were police at her house, that meant Emma still hadn't been found. Pao's brain calculated quickly. It was seven thirty, which meant Emma had been missing for thirteen hours and forty-five minutes. A car could have traveled almost a thousand miles by now. . . .

But Pao didn't even know if Emma was in a car. She didn't know anything. The variables were too many—and multiplying exponentially every additional moment her friend stayed missing.

"I'm afraid I don't have any cream," Pao's mom was saying. She wore a silky robe over a camisole and striped pajama pants. "But you're all welcome to coffee." Pao noticed that the mug her mom clutched was shaking slightly.

Normally, Pao would have stood beside her for support, or at least given her a look across the room to make sure she knew they were in this together. But this morning, Pao's mom avoided her gaze, the tension between them too great even with all these other people around.

"Is this Ms. Santiago?" asked one of the officers. Neither of them was the cop she'd met at the station, and Pao wasn't sure if that made her feel better or worse. At least she knew what to expect from Mustache Man.

"I'm Pao," she said, not offering her hand.

"Officer James." This guy was all business, with none of the sneering prejudice of the man from the night before, but still Pao didn't trust him. Bigotry wore a lot of different faces—she knew that well, even though she hadn't started seventh grade yet.

"This is Officer Tyler," the first cop said, introducing his partner. "We've discussed things extensively with Mr. and Mrs. Lockwood, but what we need from you two"—he gestured between Pao and Dante—"is to show us exactly where your meeting place was. We'd like to search the area, and canvass the route between there and the Lockwoods' house to see if anyone saw the girl."

"Have you found *anything*?" Dante asked before Pao could.

Señora Mata looked chastisingly at Dante, and Pao could almost hear her thinking that children should be seen and not heard.

Officer Tyler, on the other hand, considered him speculatively. "Last night's patrol didn't turn up any clues. We're hoping daylight will improve our chances."

"What are we waiting for?" Pao asked, marching toward the door without bothering to get dressed.

Señora Mata hung back, clearly not up for the mile-and-a-half trek across the desert, and Pao thawed a little when her mom said, "No se preocupe, Carmela. You go on upstairs. I'll look after Dante." Pao felt a rush of gratitude toward her mom for hurrying the process along, but then of course she delayed them by insisting on getting dressed first.

Two steps forward, one step back, Pao thought.

Finally, they set out for the river, the officers asking Pao and Dante questions about their normal route and if anyone else knew about their gatherings.

She and Dante answered as honestly as they could, but Pao didn't think they were telling the police anything very useful. Her restlessness was back, feeling like little robotic insects skittering up and down her bones.

No one was hurrying enough, and Pao couldn't reveal the reason for her urgency: The nebulous connection her nightmare had drawn between the figure they'd seen and the Mesa kidnapper.

"You okay?" Dante asked, snapping Pao out of dreamland.

"Yeah," she said. "Well, no. But yeah. You?"

"Same," Dante said. "Just . . ." He swiped a hand over his face. "What if we don't find her?"

"We will," Pao said with conviction, even though she had no facts to back it up. They needed to believe right now.

"This is it," Dante announced to the adults when they reached their usual spot. The water lapped gently against the bank, and not far in the distance loomed the cactus field—a place that kids always pretended was haunted.

They didn't have to conjure up any monsters today, though. They were in a real, living nightmare.

The officers asked for details: how far the trio normally strayed from this spot, what time they were supposed to meet, how long they waited, why they hadn't called Emma or her parents sooner.

"The Lockwoods mentioned you were supposed to meet them at the station," Officer Tyler remarked, looking at his notes. "Why didn't you come?"

"We did!" Pao said, instantly heated. "But that cop with the mustache threw us out! He said we were telling ghost stories."

Tyler's eyes widened, and he conferred with James in whispers.

"I'm sorry about that," Tyler finally said. "O'Brien can be a little . . . *overzealous.*"

Pao thought *racist pig* was probably a better way to describe him, but she had learned enough from her mom to keep that particular opinion to herself.

Tyler and James excused themselves to take photos of the scene. Trying to cool her temper, Pao took a few steps away, the memory of her dream taking hold as she moved closer to the water. She knew it was her imagination getting the better of her, but the riverbank felt sinister even in the light of morning. Pao could swear there was a remnant of a green glow. She imagined she could see the mysterious guy with the pixelated face, light spilling from his hands. . . .

Her mom peered at her sharply, and Pao shook herself. It was just water and sand and the overactive imagination of a girl who was raised on bedtime stories about drowned children.

In the sandy earth, Pao could see the imprint of the picnic blanket from last night and the footprints where she and Dante had paced their worries into the ground. Their trio had spent so many evenings here, Emma redoing Pao's messy braids with her patient hands, the three of them taking turns gazing through the telescope while Emma made up her own names for the constellations and Pao corrected her with the real ones.

Would they ever sit there again? Would Pao get to confide in her best girl friend about her changing feelings toward her mom?

Tears pricked her eyes, but Pao refused to let them fall. They *would* find Emma. They just had to.

"How often do you come here?" asked Officer James, finally pulling out a notepad and a pen.

Pao and Dante glanced at each other guiltily. "Once a week or so," Pao said. "We never go in the water, though!" she added hastily when her mom scowled.

"They're not allowed near the river," Pao's mom said to the officers. "I had no idea—"

"It's the best place to see the stars," Pao explained, trying her best not to sound whiny. "And it's so hot everywhere else. . . ."

"Has Emma ever expressed interest in swimming in the river?" Officer James asked, getting back to the subject at hand.

"No!" Pao said emphatically. "We all remember what happened to Marisa. We know it's too dangerous. Emma would never have gone in."

Pao's eyes drifted to the riverbank again. She'd seen the silhouette just over there. Had he—

"That's all we need for now," the officer said.

"Wait!" Pao said, feeling her anger reignite. "Don't you want to check out where the guy was?"

"What guy?" Tyler asked.

"Last night I told the cop—O'Brien—that we saw someone," Pao said. "Right over there." She pointed.

Tyler shifted toward his partner, flipping through his

notebook. "I don't have anything about that," he muttered to James, but Pao heard him anyway.

"Because he cut me off before I could finish," she said, her temper flaring again. The officers' expressions were neutral, so Pao couldn't tell if they believed her or not. "I *did* see a guy, I swear," she continued, wishing she were wearing something more grown-up than space pajamas. "In the reeds by the river." She gestured in the general direction, but neither officer even turned.

"Did he speak to you?" Tyler asked.

"Well, no," Pao said. "I don't think he saw us."

"And you didn't think to ask him if he'd seen your friend?"

"I'm sorry," Pao's mom interjected. "Did you just ask a twelve-year-old girl why she didn't approach a strange man at night? The answer is pretty obvious."

The look on the officer's face heated Pao's anger to red-hot. He was clearly trying to decide if her mom was stupid, or dangerous, or both. Even though Pao and her mom weren't exactly seeing eye to eye right now, she couldn't stand for that.

"Dante and I wanted to get home and call Emma," she said, drawing attention away from her mom, her heart fluttering like a hummingbird in her chest. "We still didn't know she was missing then. Just that she didn't show up."

"Can you describe the man in more detail?" James asked, though he wasn't taking any notes.

"He was short—about my mom's height—but I didn't see much else." The dream screamed from her subconscious, demanding that she make the connection. But she couldn't.

"Skin color? Hair color? Any identifying marks or tattoos?"

Pao tried to remember. "His hair was longish? He was in silhouette, so—"

Tyler cut her off. "We could try to find and question him," he said, "if you could remember what he looked like."

But Pao knew he was just being polite. He didn't believe the man had really been there.

"I saw him, too!" Dante said, tearing his haunted gaze away from the water and stepping up beside Pao, his fists clenched at his sides. "You have to believe us. Do you even *want* to find Emma?"

"I suppose you can't identify this mystery figure, either?" Tyler asked, narrowing his eyes when Dante didn't answer. "This isn't a cop show, kid. We need evidence. Facts. We can't just go knocking on doors asking if anyone with *longish* hair took a totally legal stroll by the river last night."

As infuriating as it was, Pao knew he was right. Dante remained silent. Without a description, their information was useless.

The restless buzzing she'd felt last night was back, the same sensation that had made her go all supernova and break her mom's velita. Without waiting for permission, or for anyone to follow, Pao stomped toward the reeds opposite the spot she'd seen the silhouette, feeling her mom's eyes on her like a tractor beam preventing her from going too far.

She ignored their pull. Maybe she'd find some footprints— something to prove she hadn't made it all up. Real evidence that the person she'd seen *wasn't* one of her mother's ghosts.

There was nothing.

Pao yanked on a piece of river grass in frustration, wincing when its razor-sharp edge sliced her hand. It stung, and suddenly Pao wanted to lie down on the sandy bank and cry herself to sleep like a child.

Blood trickled out of the cut, dotting her palm like a string of beads. Her bright red blood and dark brown skin blurred together as her eyes filled with tears. But when she blinked and refocused, she spotted something red by her feet, too.

Pao felt her heart kick into high gear.

It isn't blood, she thought, almost deliriously. Any drops would have soaked right into the ground. Pao bent down to investigate, and it was like the dream's current had caught her again. . . .

Because there, in the sand, lay Emma's ruby ring.

SIX

Stupid, Snarky Subconscious

The police got very tight-lipped after Pao turned over the
ring. She tried her million-questions routine, but it was clear
she and Dante had reached the limit of their usefulness as far as
the grown-ups were concerned. They didn't tell her a thing.

What does this mean? she asked herself. Had there been
something to her dream after all? Pao's subconscious making a
connection she couldn't prove with facts?

It happens, she told herself. *It's neuroscience, not magic.*

But dream science was still frustratingly nebulous, as Pao
had learned in her years of reading about nightmares. There was
nothing she could say about her dream that wouldn't make her
sound totally batty.

So she didn't mention it to anyone. Even though it continued
to nag at her.

The police left to go back to the station, where they said they
would get their resources together to begin an organized search.
They told her reassuring things they couldn't back up. Pao knew
the truth: The police didn't know any more than she did.

Pao's mom was due at the bar by noon, to work a double
shift. "Would you rather I stay home today?" she asked Pao. "I
could call in sick." But Pao saw the lines around her mother's eyes

grow more pronounced as she offered—probably at the thought of losing out on tips.

"I'll be fine, Mom."

"Pao can hang with me and my abuela until you're back," Dante chimed in as the polite tiptoeing between mother and daughter threatened to become awkward.

"Aren't you supposed to play soccer at the park?" Pao asked him, trying to keep the bitterness out of her tone.

Dante gave her a look that said *Don't be ridiculous*, and even in the midst of the world's worst circumstances, Pao felt a tiny ray of light break through the clouds.

"Oh, thank you," Pao's mom said, also reading Dante's expression. She hugged him impulsively. "And thank your grandma for me, too."

As glad as Pao was not to be alone, once they were back in Dante's room, she could barely breathe. The PlayStation stayed off, and the ceiling fan uselessly stirred the sultry afternoon air. The last thing Pao wanted to do was sit there doing nothing.

Ignoring the pile of as-yet-to-be-folded laundry on the floor and the milk crates of comics stacked everywhere, she paced the room as Dante threw a mini basketball against the wall again and again. The pounding was driving her crazy, but she didn't have the heart to tell him to stop—not after he'd given up his soccer game to stay with her.

Everything changed when I found the ring, she thought. Pao's discovery of hard evidence that Emma had been at the riverbank—a precious belonging she never would have left behind voluntarily—made her friend's disappearance real.

And serious. Pao was well acquainted with the looks adults

gave kids when they didn't think they could handle something, and today, after the ring, she'd seen it on three faces at once.

"I had a dream," Pao finally blurted out. Dante stopped throwing the ball and looked at her. She'd never told him about her nightmares before. But this felt too important to keep to herself, and who could she trust besides Dante?

"Okayyy . . ."

"Before Emma disappeared, I dreamed about a hand coming out of the river, and it had her ring on it," Pao said, the words bumping into one another as she spat them out too fast. "And then, last night, I dreamed that the guy we saw by the river was the same one from the news. You know . . . the Mesa kidnapper."

Dante's eyes were wide by the time she finished. He didn't say anything at first.

"It's probably a coincidence, right?" Pao asked. "I mean, dreams are just electrical impulses that take things from our memories. It's nonsense. I shouldn't have—"

"You gotta admit it's kind of weird, though," Dante cut in, looking even more worried now.

"Yeah," said Pao, biting her fingernails. "I guess."

Silence fell between them. Pao so intensely regretted bringing up her dreams, it was like a physical sensation. She might as well have quoted her mom: *Dreams are visions that have a purpose in our greater journey.* It was so unscientific. Dante probably thought she was an idiot.

When he mentioned lunch, Pao wasn't hungry at all, but she dragged her feet across the root-beer-brown carpet anyway just for something to do, dreading the pitying looks of another grown-up who wouldn't tell them anything important. Not to mention having to sit across from Dante while he regretted skipping soccer with his cool friends to hang out with the town weirdo.

But Dante's abuela wasn't in the kitchen. True to form, Señora Mata had left the TV blaring and food out on the "dining room" table. But when Dante called, "Abuela?" there was no answer from her bedroom.

He shrugged, but Pao could tell he was nervous. Everything felt off today. His abuela rarely left the apartment—only to go shopping at the grocery down the block and to play ¡Bingo en español! every Saturday at the community center.

They were picking at their reheated chicken enchiladas, when the local news jingle played from the television. Pao's heart raced. Would they report on Emma's disappearance? Pao snapped to attention, appreciating Dante's silence as the anchor began to speak.

"Silver Springs is reeling today over the disappearance of a twelve-year-old girl," came the first sentence, and the blood pounding in Pao's ears made the voice sound far away. Pao felt rather than saw Dante move his chair next to hers. His presence was comforting, despite her embarrassment over confessing her dreams.

"Emma Lockwood was last seen by her parents, Connor and Karen Lockwood, yesterday evening, when she left home to meet two school friends near the notoriously dangerous Gila River, the site of a drowning just last year."

The scene cut to a shot of the Gila, which looked more ominous than ever, dark and agitated in the late-afternoon light, while the anchor told of the many drownings that had taken place in town since its founding a hundred years ago.

Pao took another bite of her enchilada, but it felt like she was chewing cardboard.

"Police spent the morning investigating the possible site of Ms. Lockwood's disappearance, and a personal item of jewelry was discovered there. . . ."

"Yeah! By *me!*" Pao yelled at the TV, standing up too quickly, her knee colliding with the table. Dante grabbed her hand to pull her back down, and when she sat, he kept holding it. If her heart had been racing before, it now felt like it was trying to escape her rib cage.

But she didn't take her hand away. Even though his was kind of sweaty.

"Those of you following the recent disappearances in Mesa may recognize a pattern. Each of the five victims—all under the age of thirteen—was wearing expensive jewelry at the time of their abduction. There hasn't been any word yet from the Silver Springs police about a possible connection, but Maricopa County sheriffs plan to take over the local investigation starting tomorrow. . . ."

"Pao . . ." Dante said, pointedly not looking at their hands, which were still linked between their chairs. "Did you know that, about the victims and jewelry? Maybe that's why you saw the ring in your dream. . . ."

"Nah," Pao said quickly. "I just know Emma's ring really well, that's all. It's only—"

"Electrical impulses. Right." But Dante didn't sound fully convinced, and Pao didn't know if she was, either.

Before they could discuss it further, Señora Mata banged through the front door with a crocheted shopping bag swinging from one arm, her normally well-ordered hair wild and her face red, like she'd been running.

Dante dropped Pao's hand like it was a too-hot tortilla straight off the griddle, and even in the storm of other emotions coursing through her, Pao surprised herself by wishing he hadn't.

"¿Dónde estabas?" Dante asked.

His abuela's eyes flashed. "Oh, you're the jefe around here now? You make the curfew?"

Dante looked at his lap and mumbled, "No, señora."

"I needed a few things from the storage. Not that it's any of your business, hmm?"

He nodded, and Pao kept her eyes on her plate.

For the first time in living memory, Señora Mata strode over to the TV and turned it off, the bag still dangling from her elbow as she looked back at them, her gaze softer now. "Eat. Rest. You don't need to be watching this."

At any other time, Pao would have been thrilled to see her turn off the news, but today it made her heart sink.

"Eat," Dante's abuela said again. "Worrying is hard work."

But it was kind of hard for Pao to concentrate on eating when one of her two best friends had just held her hand and the other might have been the latest victim of a notorious kidnapper, and she couldn't form a sensible hypothesis about either occurrence.

That night, Dante's abuela made up the couch for Pao to sleep on. When they were younger, Pao and Dante had slept like sardines in his race-car bed, but Señora Mata had put a stop to that a few years ago for reasons she hadn't bothered to elaborate on.

Well, unless crossing herself and glaring at them counted as elaborating.

Pao was sure she wouldn't be able to fall asleep, but soon enough her thoughts grew fuzzy and disjointed. She was riding

Emma's purple bike, which turned into an eggplant that Pao's mom had once received as payment for a remedio. The eggplant became a jack-o'-lantern, opening its mouth wide to swallow Pao whole.

She wasn't surprised to eventually find herself back on the bank of the eerie river, its greenish glow still present, the strange shapes floating under the surface, beckoning. . . .

Pao felt a familiar restlessness build inside her—the same feeling she got when her mom lectured her for too long about candles or intentions or various creatures from folklore. Pao didn't have time for creepy dreams right then.

"It's not real," she said aloud, her voice sounding strange and muffled to her ears.

As if mocking her, the disembodied hand drifted toward her, Emma's purple-polished finger sporting its ruby ring.

"It's just a coincidence," Pao said, though goose bumps chased themselves up and down her arms as the hand came closer. "It's *just a coincidence*. Dreams are just dreams. And there's no such thing as—"

"Ghosts! We know! Don't you ever get tired of the sound of your own repetitive skepticism? I know *I* do."

Pao whirled around, her dream heart pounding, the hand now creeping clumsily toward her like a five-legged spider. "Who said that?"

"It's always the same inane questions," said the voice again, but there was no one around.

"I know this is a dream," Pao said, trying to sound brave even as she kept one eye on the approaching hand. "I'm not really here. I'm on the couch in my friend's living room. His grandma is snoring. I just have to wake up."

Beside her, where there had been nothing but strange, dream-dense air a second before, the shape of a bored-looking girl materialized with a *pop*.

If she hadn't been mentally reciting her *This is all a dream* mantra, Pao would have screamed, which would have been so undignified. As it was, all she did was jump back slightly, which, like, anyone would have.

Even if they were totally practical and levelheaded.

And not at all scared.

"Better?" the girl asked, tossing her nearly waist-length black curls behind her.

Pao gaped like a three-headed fish. The girl looked to be about her age. Her heart-shaped face was pale, and her wide, long-lashed eyes glowed eerily in the green light of the biolumi-nescent dream river. Her dress was black and old-fashioned, with a high collar and lace around the sleeves and hem. Her ankle boots, hovering strangely above the sand, had heels.

"My subconscious has a lot of explaining to do," Pao finally muttered.

"*Please,*" said the girl, rolling her eyes, a gesture she seemed to use her whole body to accomplish. "You think *you* have the imagination to create *me*? Tell me another one."

"Stupid, snarky subconscious," said Pao.

"My *name*," said the girl, "is Ondina. *Not* Subconscious."

"Please let me wake up now," Pao said, looking beseechingly at the utterly black sky of her dream world. "I promise I'll let my mom light candles for protection, or feed me weird tinctures for dreamless sleep, or do whatever else she wants to. Just let me wake up."

Nothing happened.

"How's that workin' for you?" asked Ondina, hand cupping her chin, long, thin fingers tapping impatiently on her elbow.

"Fine," Pao snapped, looking at her almost without meaning to, this stupid figment of her imagination that she'd probably (hopefully) forget about before breakfast. "If you're not a dream, what are you?"

"This is booooring," Ondina said, tossing her hair again. "It doesn't matter what I am. What matters is that your friend is missing, and you're obeying your bedtime just like the grown-ups told you to."

The hand was reaching for her again, the gem on its ring now glinting green just like Ondina's eyes. Pao's shoulders slumped. "There's nothing I can do."

"Do you really believe that?" Ondina asked, her gaze intense, all traces of boredom gone. "Or is that just what you've been told?"

"Now you're definitely starting to sound like my subconscious."

But before Ondina could retort, the hand finally reached Pao. It grabbed the toe of her shoe, and instinctively, she tried to shake it off.

"You can't run," Ondina said, but her voice sounded farther away now. "She needs you."

The hand clung tighter, its pale fingers twisting into her shoe-laces. Pao knew what would happen next.

"I can't!" Pao said, but the hand refused to let go, like it was really Emma and Pao was trying to abandon her. "I can't!"

"And when the time comes," Ondina said, watching indifferently as the hand started to drag Pao away once more, "don't hesitate. It won't save them."

"What do you mean?" Pao asked, fighting the pull, even though she knew how futile it was. "Save who?"

"You'll find oooout . . ." Ondina said in a singsong voice, and then she was gone.

The hand dragged Pao toward the river, and the green glow took over her vision as water soaked her clothes. She dug her nails into the rocky sand, trying to claw her way back out, knowing it was pointless but unwilling to go quietly.

It didn't help. Soon, the green blotted out everything.

Pao awoke to find a hand around her wrist. She thrashed her legs and pulled her arm away, a scream building in her throat.

But she wasn't at the river. There was no green glow. And the hand, she understood as real life came into focus in the dark living room, wasn't detached or ghostly pale. Above it was her mother's face, looking tired and worried.

"Sorry," Pao mumbled. "Time to go home?"

Her mom nodded. As Pao pushed herself up, she did her best to hide the fact she was shaking. She wondered if she'd been thrashing or moaning in her sleep. The feeling of Ondina's dark, accusing gaze lingered, as did the death grip of Emma's hand.

The clock on the wall read 3:30 a.m. Under normal circumstances, Mom would've let her sleep at Dante's until morning, but Pao figured she must have been thinking of the Lockwoods, whose daughter's bed was empty again tonight. Pao didn't mind the ridiculously early wake-up. It had rescued her from further terror, and even with the strangeness between the two of them, she felt better now that they were back together.

They tried to creep out as quietly as possible, but still Dante's abuela appeared in her bedroom doorway in a dressing gown, her eyes wide.

For a split second, Pao wanted to ask if she'd had a weird dream, too.

Instead, she raised a hand in farewell, and Pao's mom whispered her thanks. Pao could sense the señora staring at her until the door closed behind them.

"So, are you going to tell me what that was all about?" Pao's mom asked when they'd reached their own stuffy, candle-scented living room.

"What?" Pao asked unconvincingly.

"The nightmare."

"I wasn't having a nightmare. . . ."

"Paola Santiago, I know you stopped having those dreams years ago, but don't think I forgot what they look like."

But of course, Pao hadn't stopped having the dreams. She just hadn't told her mom that.

"Yeah, maybe everything with Emma is getting to me," Pao said, rubbing her eyes for effect. "It's been a long day."

"What did you see in your dream?" her mom asked, her eyes too sharp for someone just coming off a fifteen-hour shift.

Pao could have told her. Explained that she'd dreamed about Emma's hand and the ring before her friend was declared missing. Dreamed about the Mesa kidnapper before the police made the connection. Pao could have asked what it all meant and accepted the help she knew her mom was dying to give her.

But telling her would mean that Ondina had been right (and *real*)—that Pao's dreams had significance. It would mean admitting to herself that her best friend's crawling zombie hand and the weird snarky girl and the green-glowing river were something more than just Pao's subconscious reacting to a truly terrible day.

"I don't remember," she said, faking a yawn, even though she was anything but sleepy. "I'm sure it was just a one-time thing."

The look on her mom's face said she didn't believe that for a second, but after a very pregnant pause, she smoothed Pao's hair back off her forehead and let out a small, almost inaudible sigh.

"Get to bed, mijita," she said. "Tomorrow will be better."

Pao just nodded, but the space between them felt as big and empty as her dream's black sky.

Without overthinking it, Pao stepped forward and hugged her mom, hard. "I love you," she said.

Pao's mom hugged her back just as fiercely. "I love you, too, Paola," she said. "Por siempre. No matter what."

I hope you meant that, Pao thought when she was back in bed. Because her stupid, snarky subconscious had been right about one thing: She wasn't willing to let Emma go. She was going to do something about it.

And she wasn't sure her mom was going to like the way she planned to fight back.

In fact, Pao was absolutely positive she wouldn't.

SEVEN

Bad Plans and Big Surprises

Her mom was still fast asleep when Pao climbed up the fire escape to Dante's window a couple of hours later, at 5:30 a.m., lifted the screen to let herself in, and breathlessly explained her plan.

"Please tell me you've been body-snatched, and the real, slightly more rational Pao will be back soon," he said.

"Keep your voice down!" Pao whisper-scolded, flipping on the light and sitting on the corner of the bed as he continued to look at her in horror.

She couldn't exactly blame him. Going to the Gila had always been dangerous, but revisiting the scene of the crime with the hope that the deranged kidnapper would be there? Downright madness.

But if they didn't do something, they'd be doomed to inhabit the uninformed sidelines of Emma's investigation for as long as it lasted, and Pao wouldn't be able to stand that.

"If he comes back to look for Emma's ring," Pao explained, "we could be there waiting!"

"To do what, exactly?" Dante asked.

"Find out who he is! We'll see him, and then we can tell the police what he looks like, and they'll match him to the Mesa kidnapper and then catch him and find Emma!" It had sounded a lot less nonsensical in her head, she had to admit.

Dante looked at her with a pained expression for as long as he could, like he was hoping she'd poke holes in her own plan and save him from having to do it, but Pao did her best impression of a stubborn, chin-jutting statue, and eventually he relented.

"So you want to go skulk around the river—which is probably crawling with police and reporters, by the way—and just hope we spot a kidnapper?"

"Do you have a better idea, Dante?" She was beginning to regret not just going on her own.

"Yes!" he said, running a hand through his hair until it stood on end. "Stay home, sleep until a normal time, and let the adults do their jobs."

"On the news, they said the county sheriffs will be coming in today," Pao said. "We've got to get there now, before they do, and maybe just in time to catch the kidnapper while he's trying to remove evidence!"

Dante looked at her with big, pitying eyes, and the concern in them made Pao turn away. If she let that pity in, if she let herself feel sad, she might never recover.

"I'm leaving in three minutes," she said, her voice flat. "With or without you. If you'd rather save your energy for soccer or something—"

"God, I hate you sometimes," Dante interrupted, stalking to his dresser and pulling cargo shorts over the basketball ones he slept in. His hair was still sticking up funny. "I get why you want to do something—I'm worried about Emma, too," Dante said as he rummaged for something else. "But this seems . . . *extreme*."

For a minute, she pretended not to hear him. After all, she

couldn't admit that a girl named Ondina and Emma's disembodied hand were dragging her into it.

Dante found a baseball cap and jammed it over his unruly hair. He was still waiting for a response.

"You and I know Emma better than anyone," Pao said, kicking the leg of his bed as he adjusted his backpack straps. "Better than her parents, I bet. We're the ones who should be looking for her, even if they think we're too young." She thought of Ondina again. "We shouldn't let other people tell us whether or not we can help her."

Dante didn't answer immediately, and Pao found herself getting frustrated with him. With everything. Of course it wasn't a *great* plan! It wasn't like she had a lot to work with. But was that all that was bothering him? She'd only been trying to push his buttons before, with the soccer comment, but had she hit on the truth? Was this the new Dante? Too into hair flipping and sports to go on a mission to save his friend?

The sun was just starting to rise, and the desert outside Dante's window was washed in pinks and purples and sage greens. *Not a bad morning to risk your life for someone*, Pao told herself. *Even if you have to go alone.*

It would have been nice to have a dog, though. Pao had sung the praises of the Border collie for its search-and-rescue potential before, but she'd never thought she'd need one for an *actual* rescue mission.

"If you don't like it, you can stay home," she said, trying really hard to sound sincere. "I won't blame you."

"Well, *I* will," came a familiar voice, and Pao's heart sank. Señora Mata was standing in the doorway, the same crocheted shopping bag from yesterday dangling from her elbow. She looked more disheveled than Pao had ever seen her.

"Señora," Pao said, her mind going a mile a minute to come up with an explanation for why she was here and what they were doing. But then it came to a screeching halt. "Wait—did you say 'I will'?" Pao asked. "As in blame him? For not coming with me?"

A truly otherworldly smile lit up the old woman's face. "Of course I did," she said, her accent thick, the first rays of the sun bouncing off her glasses. "I didn't raise a coward, did I?"

Dante's mouth dropped open, and Pao barely kept hers from doing the same.

"But . . ."

"¡Dios mío! You need to hurry! Get in here before I change my mind about helping you."

"Helping . . . ?" Pao began, but she stopped when she saw the look Dante's abuela was giving her. "Yes, señora," she said instead, and followed her into the hallway.

The living room of Dante's apartment was being transformed.

Señora Mata had closed the blinds to the newly risen sun, plunging the space into darkness. Now she was rushing around lighting candles and muttering under her breath, which made Pao think guiltily of her mother, still asleep in the apartment downstairs.

Pao wanted to ask a million questions, but something in the señora's straight back and seriously weird expression made her swallow them. She had a feeling she was going to find out what was happening soon, whether she liked it or not.

Dante didn't hesitate, though. "¿Abuela, qué está pasando?"

he asked quietly, sounding more like a little boy than he had in a long time.

The señora didn't answer. She finally finished lighting the candles and stood beside her beloved recliner, rummaging through the crocheted bag.

"¡Abuela!" Dante said, a little sharper this time, and Pao wanted to shush him, but she found that, for once, she couldn't speak.

The room looked eerie in the candlelight, the icons and statues on the shelves seeming to come alive in the jumping, shivering shadows. Pao hugged herself to ward off a chill—something she'd never had to do before on a June morning in Silver Springs. But this chill had nothing to do with the temperature outside.

When Señora Mata finally looked up from her bag, there was something odd about her eyes, as if they were reflecting the river's green glow. "I wanted us to have more time," she said, her English slow and precise, as always. "But we'll just have to make do with what we have."

"What do you mean?" Dante asked, his voice higher than normal. "What is all this?"

"You have to go," his abuela said. "Now. Today. Before it's too late. The candles won't hold the boundaries of this space for long. And once they fail . . ." A dark look crossed her features. "You have to go."

"Go where?" Pao asked, finally finding her voice. "To the police? Do you know something?"

"Pah," Señora Mata said, waving a hand dismissively. "Maldito Policía. They wouldn't know what to do with what I know."

"What do you know, señora?" Pao asked. "Is it about Emma? Can you save her?"

"Quiet," she said. "There's no time. Just listen. The third quarter is almost here, and the boundary will be crossable again. The solstice approaches, and if she comes . . ."

"Who?" Dante and Pao asked together, but Señora Mata's eyes were unfocused. She didn't seem to hear them.

"Go toward the river," she said. "Take these." She shoved the lumpy crocheted bag into Pao's hands and snapped at her when she tried to open it. "There's no *time*. You only have five days to try to do the impossible. Go." She took off one old slipper and held it out to Dante, who flinched, though he had the good grace to look embarrassed afterward.

"What do I need your chancla for?" he asked, not reaching out for it, and Pao couldn't blame him. The thing looked about a thousand years old.

"¿Me estás escuchando?" she asked him, her voice rising, and she thwacked him on the arm with the house shoe before letting it fall to the ground at his feet. "There's no time! You have to go now!"

"Go where? Abuela, this is crazy. You can't just tell us to go to the river and not tell us why."

"Créeme, mijito, I would tell you more, but . . ." Señora Mata shuddered, her eyes closing, the room growing a little darker as she did. Pao watched as two of the candles behind the old woman went out.

The candles won't hold the boundaries of this space for long, she had said.

"What's happening, señora?" Pao asked, clutching at the bag, something icy cold settling in the pit of her stomach. Out of the corner of her eye, she saw Dante reach down to pick up the chancla. He yelped, and Pao whirled around to face him.

In his hands, the slipper was changing. The worn sole was stretching and widening, the once-pale-yellow terry cloth turning a deep blue, ridges forming in it like corduroy. Within a few seconds, the transformation was complete. Instead of an old lady's tiny and worn slipper/weapon, Dante held a brand-new blue house shoe that looked to be the perfect size for his foot.

Everything Pao had thought she knew about the fixed properties of material objects was slowly unraveling. She felt upended and dizzy, as though she had lost her gravitational connection to Earth.

But that was nothing compared to what was happening to Señora Mata.

Her mouth moved rapidly as she muttered under her breath, not seeming to hear Dante as he asked over and over what was going on. English, Spanish—nothing was getting through.

Was she praying? Pao wondered. "¿Señora?" she said again, glancing at Dante, who was backing away, finally going silent as three more candles extinguished themselves.

"She . . . seeks . . . the Dreamer . . ." Señora Mata said in a hollow voice. "She is coming. . . ."

"*Who's* coming?" Pao asked, and as if in answer, the light in the room changed. "No!" she exclaimed as the candlewicks caught fire again. This time, the flames burned bright green.

"Pao?" Dante asked, his back pressed against the wall.

"¡Señora!" Pao said, stepping forward. "What do we do?"

"She seeks the Dreamer," Señora Mata said again, coming back to herself a little. "You must bathe. And then go."

"Bathe?!" Pao asked, frustrated and afraid.

"The water . . ." she said, sagging as another candlewick caught green. "My water . . ."

"I don't understand!"

But Dante was coming up behind her, a large glass jar in his hands. "It's okay, Abuela," he said, unscrewing the lid. The smell hit Pao all at once—familiar, almost stinging her nostrils. Florida Water. Dante flicked some on his grandma, but she snapped at him, her eyes still closed.

"Not me!" she said. "*You!* Hurry!"

Pao didn't understand, but she dipped her fingers in the jar anyway and smeared the cologne across her forehead like her mom sometimes did. Dante did the same, but when their eyes met, they were wary. Almost all the candle flames were now green, and from what they could see through the cracks in the blinds, the sky outside was turning dark and ominous.

"Go," the old woman mumbled, still squeezing her eyes shut. "Go while she cannot see you. She seeks the Dreamer. The third quarter is almost here. Go."

"Abuela . . ."

"GO!" she yelled, and this time her eyes flew open, revealing two glowing green orbs that looked nothing like Señora Mata's kind (if slightly judgmental) brown eyes.

Pao nearly screamed, and beside her the jar of Florida Water slipped from Dante's fingers and shattered, soaking their shoes.

"¡Abuela!" he said, stepping forward, but she pushed him away with surprising strength.

"¡NO MIRES ATRÁS!" she shouted in a grating voice.

Pao's Spanish was basically nonexistent, but she knew this phrase: *Don't look back.*

"Dante," Pao said as the light from the candles and Señora Mata's eyes started to pull at her like Emma's hand in her dream. "Dante, we have to go."

"Are you crazy?" he shouted. "I'm not leaving her like this!"

But something was tugging at Pao. An instinct. A voice. A memory . . .

When the time comes, don't hesitate. It won't save them.

"We have to go," she said, the restless feeling building to a crescendo in her blood. "We have to go *now*."

Something was becoming horribly clear to Pao as the room was stained a venomous green and the walls between her dreams and reality came tumbling down. Whatever was happening couldn't be explained logically. All she knew, without hypothesizing or testing or gathering data, was that *she* was the Dreamer. And it was up to her to stop this before it got any worse.

Señora Mata slumped to the floor, green light spilling from her eyes. Dante went over to check her pulse, and she moaned softly at his touch. As tears streamed down his face, Dante lifted her gently onto the couch. He sat down next to her and started to sob.

Pao pulled at his arm. "Whatever's happening, it's about me," she told him. "If I go to the river, it'll stop."

"No!" Dante screamed. He wiped his runny nose on the sleeve of his T-shirt.

"I'm the Dreamer, Dante," she said. "I have to go, even if—"

"No! You're not going anywhere! We have to—"

But Pao was already leaving, the restlessness driving her down the hallway to Dante's bedroom. She was convinced that if she didn't, that green light would swallow Dante and his abuela,

Pao's mother, the entire Riverside Palace, and maybe even more.

This is insane, said a part of her brain. The same part that had won the sixth-grade science fair with solid research and testable hypotheses. The part that had executed countless eye rolls when her mother told stories about moments just like this.

When Pao reached Dante's room, she was knocked down by what felt like a wave. And yet, lying flat on her belly in the doorway, she found herself and the floor completely dry. From the living room came a hissing, raspy sound—an unfamiliar voice saying something in Spanish.

Don't hesitate, said Ondina in Pao's memory. *It won't save them.*

Pao managed to get up and make it to the window before a second wave hit, and this time she saw it coming—a green mist that rippled the shag carpet and pushed her against the screen with a force she couldn't hope to fight.

And it brought Dante with it, dumping him next to her before forming a translucent green barrier between them and the rest of the room.

This didn't make sense. Mist was just tiny droplets of water hanging in the air. Liquid, not solid. Even in its solid form, it would just be tiny ice crystals, not nearly dense enough to—

"No!" Dante screamed, cutting into Pao's attempt to reason as they struggled against the supernatural force. He still clutched the blue slipper. But even if both his hands were free, he wouldn't have been able to break through the mist. Whatever it was.

"See? Like your abuela said, we have to go. We have no choice now," Pao said, checking around her feet for the crocheted bag she'd never had a chance to look inside of. "Please, Dante."

"We . . . can't . . . just . . . leave her!" Dante said, struggling to breathe as he pushed against the barrier with every ounce of his strength. "We . . . don't . . . know . . . what's . . . It could—" His words cut off with a sob, and he slumped down to the floor.

"We will fix this," Pao said, putting a hand on his shoulder. "We will save her. But we have to go now if we want to have a chance."

She barely knew where these words or her certainty were coming from, but when she turned to the window, the force didn't stop her. The only way through this was forward. There was no going back.

The rasping Spanish in the other room had stopped, but the green light in the mist continued to intensify, and as it did, a keening sound began to build, raising the hairs on Pao's arms, grating against her eardrums.

"Pao?" Dante asked as the air pressure in the room increased.

"Dante!"

"PAO!"

The top part of the window shattered, and at first, Pao thought shards of glass were hitting her face. But then she realized the window had been blown *outward*. The stinging she felt, like a thousand biting ants, was coming from her forehead, where she had dabbed the Florida Water.

Forward, forward. There was no other way.

The green light was almost blinding. Unable to see Dante, Pao flung out her hand and called upon the weird boy-girl magnetism that had sprung up between them recently, causing them to keep bumping into each other with their shoulders, knees, or elbows.

Please . . . she asked the inconvenient phenomenon. *Just this once, let it happen when I* mean *it to. . . .*

Whether Dante could see better than she could, or her

wordless plea had actually worked, she didn't know. But his hand zapped to hers like a staticky sock to a sweater fresh out of the dryer. Before she could ask him one more time to come with her, the pressure sucked both of them out the open window.

They landed on their butts more gently than Pao would have hypothesized, given the speed of their ejection and the distance of their fall to the ground. Amazingly, their hands remained connected, the chancla in Dante's other fist, the shopping bag twisted around Pao's arm.

She spat out one of her braids. Her forehead and fingertips still stung, along with spots on her feet where spilled Florida Water had soaked through her sneakers. In Dante's apartment, green light glowed from every window. Seeing that, Pao was up in a second and, despite Ondina's dream warning, hurried back to the fire escape. Dante followed close behind.

But they'd only run a few feet when they hit another barrier, this one completely invisible. They bounced off the solid material, then explored it with their hands. It felt like Plexiglas and blocked their access to the apartment in every direction. As Dante pushed and pounded on it, tears streaming down his cheeks, Pao had the feeling that this part of their journey—the one that took place at Riverside Palace, where there were adults to tell them what to do—was over.

This time, she didn't ask Dante. She didn't beg or plead or explain. None of this made any sense, but it was happening, and they had to try to make things right again.

As Dante pummeled the barrier, Pao slid her arm under his and turned him around. When they were facing the same direction, she started to run, pulling him toward the river of her nightmares.

EIGHT

The Last Two People You'd Ever Expect to Meet in a Haunted Cactus Field

The river loomed in front of them, and Pao was surprised to see it looking perfectly ordinary. There was no bioluminescence, no hand breaking the surface, no unearthly wailing. Just an innocent dawn mist that hovered over the water and chilled the air.

Though Pao now had a new take on mist: It was a little more complicated than just water vapor.

So much of what had occurred this morning seemed to have come straight out of a dream, but being in their usual spot made Pao feel grounded in the real world. And yet she knew Señora Mata's world was here, too, lingering in the mist.

Dante hadn't spoken since they left the apartment complex, and she hadn't expected him to. His sobbing had stopped, but he still sniffled every now and then, and Pao couldn't help but feel guilty for literally dragging him along.

She seeks the Dreamer. Pao felt certain she herself was the Dreamer, but the rest was so unclear. Who was seeking her? And why? Was all this connected to Emma's disappearance?

Lost in thought, she didn't realize she'd walked all the way to the water's edge until Dante cleared his throat.

"So, where are we going?"

A hollowness in his voice made Pao look up. His eyes were narrowed and his jaw was clenched.

"Well?" he prompted when she didn't answer immediately. "Abuela said you would know where to go. So, where do we go? You said we'd fix everything. You *promised* me, and there's creepy stuff going on, and my abuela might be in danger, and you're just standing here, *so what's the plan, Pao?*"

"Why are you yelling at me?" Pao asked, hating how small her voice sounded.

"Because this was all your idea! You're the one who didn't want to trust any adults, you're the one who had this big plan to track down the kidnapper, and now apparently you know something about the totally messed-up thing that just happened to my grandma, even though all you've ever said is that you don't believe in ghosts. Or dreams. Or anything that can't be explained by your precious, perfect science. So I'm a little confused, Pao. And yeah, I'm mad! Tell me what the heck is going on!"

Pao felt like her limbs were filling with cement. She wanted to yell back at him, to say she hadn't asked for any of this. But was that true? Hadn't she resolved just last night to do whatever it took to find Emma?

"I don't . . . I don't know why your abuela said I would know where to go," Pao admitted, a humiliating tremble beginning in her lower lip. "I don't know. I *don't* believe in any of this, and I wanted to help, but I can't, and I just . . . wish I could go home."

The world seemed suddenly too big and too small all at once. They were just two kids with a shape-shifting house shoe and a useless crocheted shopping bag, and the world was full of kidnappers, and police who didn't believe you, and, apparently, sinister magical forces.

Everything Pao had thought she knew was dissolving in acid, or being burned away by the heat of an open flame, or exploding with such force that it shattered its test tube.

And right now, her brain felt a lot like the test tube.

"Look, it's okay," Dante said, moving closer to her. "I'm sorry. I'm just freaked out about Abuela . . . and I'm . . ."

"I know," Pao said. "This is all . . ."

The silence they lapsed into wasn't awkward—it just meant they had no strategies for talking about the situation. Pao scanned the river, thinking back on her dreams and everything that had come apart. She hadn't even been able to say good-bye to her mom.

Pao had yelled at her. Rejected her beliefs. Told her she was responsible for all the prejudice directed toward people like them.

The memory sat in her stomach like a cold cheese enchilada. What had she done?

Pao had always been hot-tempered. She wasn't the kind of girl anyone would hire as a babysitter; she'd never gotten one of those certificates teachers give out to reward helpfulness or a good attitude. She'd told herself it wasn't her fault—the world was full of things to be angry about. Pao had simply assumed she was more realistic than most people.

But what if her anger was part of something worse? She let herself wonder. The señora's ominous words rang in her ears.

Dante was looking at her like she should have answers, but all she had were dreams in which she drowned or got lost over and over again. . . .

Dreams that somehow showed her things before they happened.

Was there something wrong with her? What if all this was her fault?

"She called you the Dreamer," Dante said, breaking into her panicky thought spiral. "And you dreamed . . . about the kidnapper, and Emma's ring. . . ."

Pao nodded miserably.

"Did you dream about any . . . places?" Dante asked, rubbing the back of his neck. "Anywhere we could go? I know it sounds stupid, but—"

"It's not like we have much else to go on," Pao finished for him.

Dante nodded, looking at her intently.

She wished he would stop doing that.

But instead of saying so, she imagined the dream landscape: the glowing green river, the utterly black sky, the white sand. She shook her head, frustrated. Putting aside the weird colors, it looked like a stretch of the Gila. Any of the countless ones in this area.

"I just dream about the river," she said at last, feeling totally useless as she gestured at it. "And her hand . . . pulling me into it."

She shuddered, and Dante stepped closer again, but he didn't put his arm around her. Forced to admit she didn't know what to do, Pao felt her heart sinking like a stone into the murky water.

Before it could reach the bottom, an earsplitting scream echoed along the bank.

"Emma!" Pao said, and then she took off running.

"What the—" Dante began, but Pao barely heard him, because her pulse was pounding in her ears. He chased after her.

Can it really be this easy to find her? Pao wondered.

"Pao, stop!" Dante called.

The scream sounded again—all too familiar. She didn't stop, and to his credit, he didn't, either.

Pao didn't slow down until she had almost reached the edge of the cactus field. Dante was lagging behind, peppering her with reasons to be wary—"What if the kidnapper's there? Or the police? Or something even worse?"—but Pao was undeterred. If there was *any* chance it was Emma, it was worth the danger.

The cactus field was yet another place Pao's mom had told her to stay away from. Pao had never paid much attention to her warnings, or to kids' whispers about it being haunted, but after the morning she'd just had, she hesitated a little before passing between two massive cacti. (Cactuses? She could never remember which was right.)

After all, before today she hadn't believed in shape-shifting slippers or nightmares that decided to bleed into a random Friday morning, either.

"Look!" Pao said, pointing at the silhouettes of two figures in the distance. They were locked in some kind of wrestling match.

"You can't just go running over there!" Dante said when he'd caught up, not even remotely out of breath, while Pao felt like her lungs might burst from the exertion. "We have no idea what—"

"It could be her, Dante," Pao interrupted, knowing she must look a little unhinged, but not really caring at the moment. Anything was better than standing around feeling guilty for having no idea what to do.

If Dante replied, Pao didn't hear him—she was already charging toward the grappling twosome, passing cactus after cactus, the air growing thicker and hazier as she went deeper into the field.

This doesn't make sense, said what was left of Pao's practical, cause-and-effect–loving brain. Judging from the amount of distance she had to cover relative to her speed, she should have reached them by now. But they seemed just as far away as when she had started out.

And hadn't Dante been right beside her only a second ago?

Before Pao could get her bearings, the haze cleared. The air felt sharp and cool against her face, and her vision returned to normal. Pao could now tell the two figures were girls, not much bigger than she.

Emma, chanted a hopeful voice in her head. *Emma, Emma, Emma.*

When she was only a few yards away from them, Pao ducked behind a cactus to get the lay of the land.

"Stop!" shouted one of the girls, clearly losing the fight as the other took hold of her hair. "You don't understand!"

Her words turned into a screech as the other girl yanked her head back by her long black ponytail. "Do I look new to you? Spin your demon stories somewhere else. I have a job to do."

Pao's disappointment hit her faster than a rocket reentering the atmosphere, all her hope exploding like a volatile fuel tank. These two girls were around her age, but neither of them was Emma.

"You don't understand!" said the losing one again, her voice high and shrill as the other girl yanked even harder on her hair. "The third quarter is coming. . . . The solstice . . ."

Pao started when she heard the words *third quarter.* It was the same thing Dante's abuela had said. Emma wasn't here, but that phrase was the only clue Pao had, and if she wanted to find out what it meant, she was going to have to stop hiding behind this cactus.

At first, the girls were too consumed in their fight to notice her. So, despite her shaking knees and pounding heart, Pao stepped forward and said, "Hey!" Because what else was there to say?

When the girls turned to face her, though, she had a much bigger problem than what to say. Locked in suspended battle— one with an arm around the other's neck, one with a fistful of hair—were the last two people Pao had ever expected to see *alive*, let alone in a cactus field a couple of miles from her apartment:

Ondina, the snarky girl from her dream . . .

And Marisa Martínez, the girl who had allegedly drowned in the Gila River the year before.

Whether Marisa was a hallucination, a ghost, or a living girl who had returned from wherever it was she had disappeared to, Pao had no idea. But seeing her gave Pao hope.

She had imagined Emma in a car, with a stranger at the wheel, traveling hundreds of miles before nightfall. But with this other missing girl reappearing less than two miles from home, the terrifying radius began to shrink. What if Emma hadn't been taken away from Silver Springs?

What if she was right here in this cactus field just like Marisa?

"Finally!" said Ondina, her long hair tangled and frizzy with exertion, her black dress twisted, the lace torn. Her dainty boots hadn't served her well in the fight—one of them was lying on its side a few yards away.

But her eyes were fierce and intelligent, sparkling with intention as they fixed on Pao's.

"'Finally'?" Pao echoed, a little delirious.

"What?" Marisa asked Ondina with a sneer in Pao's direction. "You think some random tourist who can't even part her hair straight is going to save you? It's over for you, ahogada, and I intend to make sure of it."

Well, thought Pao, *alleged drowning hasn't made Marisa any nicer.*

Pao reached up to pat her own scalp self-consciously before dropping her hand, disgusted with herself. Sure, she couldn't quite part her hair perfectly yet, but this wasn't the school cafeteria. This was a haunted cactus field full of dream girls and ghosts. The rules of middle school survival didn't apply here.

Hopefully they didn't, anyway, because if popularity was part of this bizarre quest, Pao was royally screwed.

"I'm looking for a girl," Pao said, pleased that her voice only shook a little. "I mean, another girl. She's, like, this tall. . . ." She actually held a hand a little above her head, as if these dueling girls were paying attention. "Anyway, I really need to find her, and—"

"Go home," Marisa interrupted without even turning around, which was *so* typical, Pao thought.

Ondina, distracted by Pao's arrival, did something even most fifth graders in Silver Springs had known better than to do around Marisa Martínez. She let her guard down for a split second.

Wham!

Marisa didn't let the moment go to waste. She had Ondina on the ground in a flash, her long, pale limbs flailing everywhere as she struggled to right herself. But before she could, there was a long, deadly-looking knife at her throat. *Where did* that *come from?* Pao wondered.

Knowing it was stupid, reckless, and insane, Pao stepped forward before Marisa could use the blade. She got close enough to take it from her.

"If you touch me," Marisa growled without looking up, "you will regret it."

But Pao was delirious and hungry and really ticked off for about a hundred reasons, and watching Marisa bully someone *from beyond the supposed grave* was just too much to take.

"Leave her alone," Pao said.

"You don't know what you're doing, tourist," Marisa said. "Step back."

"No," Pao said, shaking her bangs out of her eyes. Her pulse was pounding, and an alarm bell was ringing in her head like, *Oh, no, you didn't just challenge the most vicious girl in school in a haunted cactus field. What in the formerly sane world is wrong with you?*

"Paola," said Ondina through gritted teeth, her face pressed against the ground as Marisa proceeded to ignore Pao's historic act of bravery. "There's not much time. . . ."

"Yeah, I've heard," Pao said. "What's the third quarter?" she asked, kicking dust into Marisa's face. A year ago, that would have been a declaration of war, but this Marisa didn't seem to mind dirt. "What does that mean?"

"The . . . moon . . ." Ondina forced out before Marisa viciously tightened her grasp and hissed again.

"Don't listen to her," Marisa said to Pao. "She's an ahogada. She's trying to lure you in while the barrier is still open."

Pao's mind got snagged on the word *ahogada*. It sounded familiar, but she was pretty sure it was from a radio commercial for a sandwich place downtown. *You know you really want-a/Torta ahogadaaaa. . . .* What did a sandwich have to do with this girl from her dream?

For the second time today, she wished she knew Spanish. Why hadn't her mom ever made her learn it?

As Pao was ruminating on sandwiches and languages, Marisa kicked Ondina in the ribs.

"Hey!" Pao shrieked. "I said, leave her alone! Or else I'll . . . I'll make you . . . *wish* you'd left her alone. . . ."

Okay, it wasn't her finest moment. But it wasn't like she'd had a lot of experience standing up to this girl.

Marisa looked Pao up and down, no spark of recognition in her strangely golden eyes. "I don't care whether you live or die, presently, but if you don't shut up, I may develop an interest. Now look away if you don't want to see a demon get vaporized."

Without another word, Marisa, the former queen of the Silver Springs Middle School cafeteria crowd, plunged a foot-long knife into a sentient creature's chest and smiled.

Ondina, for her part, didn't scream. She only winced slightly as the blade moved through her without resistance, causing her outline to shimmer and blur. "I'll be back," she said mildly, then closed her eyes and dissolved.

Pao did her best not to start crying, shaking, or puking, or any of the other things she felt like doing in that moment.

"What . . . ? She . . . and you . . ." She breathed in through her nose and out through her mouth, trying not to pass out, but knowing it was a real possibility.

Panic is just a series of chemicals, Pao told herself. She knew from science class that her brain, assessing danger, had told her glands to produce adrenaline, which in turn was increasing the flow of glucose to her muscles, providing her with the necessary fuel to deal with stress. Now her brain just had to decide the best course of action: fight or flight.

Pao was going to fight. Despite her best efforts, she swayed on her feet, and Marisa scoffed.

"Ugh, I do *not* have time to deal with you right now, whatever you are." Marisa took a step toward Pao, her long knife extended, a grim look on her annoyingly pretty face. "The good news is, if you're not a rift creature, this won't kill you."

"Won't . . . wh-what?" Pao stuttered. The reflection in the metal blade seemed to swirl like the river itself. It was almost mesmerizing in its beauty. "Oh, God. Um, okay. Please don't go all psycho mean girl on me," Pao said, backing up, her voice getting higher with each rambling word. "I know you don't like me or anything, but you can get in a lot of trouble for stabbing people, and I think you've probably pushed your luck in that department enough for one . . ." She trailed off as Marisa continued to advance.

It was time for flight. Definitely. Like, right now.

But because the fear center of her brain was overloaded, it was no longer sending signals to her nerves. She couldn't move her legs.

"That's right. Hold still," said Marisa. "You won't remember a thing either way. . . ."

Pao's legs figured out what they were supposed to do at last, but they were still shaky, and as she turned to escape, Marisa caught up to her easily.

When the knife went into Pao's back—right between two of her ribs—it didn't feel like metal.

It felt like water.

"I can't believe . . . you really"—Pao wheezed—"*stabbed* me! You're . . . crazy. . . ." She coughed and sputtered, and there was water in her nose, in her lungs. . . . She was drowning on dry land. Which was, of course, impossible.

Help . . . she tried to say, but instead of words, bubbles left her mouth.

And then she fell.

NINE

That Moment You Realize Your Mother Was Right All Along

"Pao! *Pao!*"

The words were coming from far away, and her ears felt pressurized, like she was at the bottom of the river.

"Mhhft," she managed, rolling onto one side. She'd had such a strange dream. The images swirled around behind her still-closed eyelids. The third-quarter moon. Ondina. And Marisa had freaking *stabbed* her?

"PAO!"

"Okay!" she said. "I'm up. . . ."

There was a noise like a sob-filled laugh, and beside her, something fell to the ground. The ground? Where *was* she?

She found it harder than usual to force her eyes open, and when she finally did, a cactus loomed in her vision.

The rest of the dream came rushing back, and on its heels the realization that it *hadn't* been a dream. There was a strange searing pain between her ribs, like Marisa's water blade was still in her. Marisa had said she wouldn't remember it. . . .

Dante had collapsed next to her in relief, but Pao's stomach was turning to lead. Despite compelling evidence to the contrary, the encounter had been real, and all her previous dreams were somehow connected to it. She wasn't dead, at least, but being alive wasn't much of a relief when she was even *less* sure of what to do than before.

"I thought you were . . ." Dante choked out. "I couldn't find you, and then I did, and then I thought . . ."

"Marisa . . ." Pao said, her voice sounding distant to her own ears. "Marisa Martínez stabbed me. . . ."

"Pao?" Dante said, his expression turning to one of alarm. "Marisa is—"

"Dead," Pao finished for him. "I know. But she was *here*, Dante. She vaporized some weird girl from my dreams right in front of me, and . . . and if *she* was here, then maybe Emma . . ." She struggled to sit up.

"Let me help you," Dante said, scrambling to his feet and hovering beside her.

"I'm okay," Pao said, even though nothing had ever been less true. She rose on her own, wincing at the pain between her ribs, feeling her back with trembling fingertips. But there was no wound. Pao pulled up her striped T-shirt without thinking, turning around to look at the spot she was *sure* a knife had gone into moments before.

"Whoa!" said Dante, whipping around and covering his eyes.

"Oh, calm down," Pao snapped. "I just got stabbed by a dead girl in a haunted cactus field. It's not like you accidentally walked into the girls' locker room before gym class."

He didn't turn back. "It's just . . . you're . . . and it's . . ."

"Yeah, yeah, me girl, you boy, I get it, but right now I need you to look and see if there's a paranormal stab wound in my back. So can you just press pause on it for a minute, please?"

It took him a few seconds to approach her, and Pao thought she could feel him steeling himself. She fought the urge to roll her eyes.

"Well?" she pressed, her arm cramping from holding up her shirt behind her.

"Nothing," he said, almost to himself. "There's nothing there. And can we go back to the ghost-vaporizing part? What is going on here? Are you sure this isn't all—"

"My imagination?" Pao challenged him. "Look, I know I'm supposed to be the Dreamer, but I was definitely awake when I saw Marisa." She hadn't been sure at the time, but she was now.

"Pao, you were pretty upset. . . . Are you sure it was her?"

She laughed then, even though it burned her throat. "Am I sure . . . ? I'm not sure of anything, Dante! Have you been here for a single second of what's happened today? Green light, and shape-shifting slippers, and weird mist, and now the ghost of a girl who tormented me in the lunchroom showing up to stab a girl from my dreams . . . It all sounds *ridiculous*—don't you think I know that?"

Dante's eyes went wide, and for a moment, Pao remembered the way he had let himself cry earlier. With a complete lack of shame. It had made her want to fix everything.

"Maybe all this *is* some bizarre nightmare, or I'm lying in a hospital bed in a coma right now, or we're all just zeroes and ones in some giant simulation of the human experience that's decided to malfunction at random."

Dante's face was frozen in a deer-in-the-headlights expression, like he was afraid to interrupt her tirade, and Pao took full advantage of the silence.

"This is what we have to work with right now, okay? Ghosts and impossible things. I don't like it any more than you do. But if Marisa could come back after disappearing, then maybe Emma will, too. Your grandma said we could still help her. . . ." She trailed off, hating how crazy she sounded, hating the hope that was welling up in her chest. "If there's any chance we can find Emma in here, don't you think we should take it?"

"I don't know," Dante said, his gaze finally falling to the ground at their feet. "Pao, maybe we can't do this. We're barely even old enough to babysit. You could have died. Maybe it's time to go back and tell someone what happened. The police or something . . ."

Pao laughed again, and this time it didn't hurt as badly—that was some progress, at least. "Dante, I told that cop we saw a suspicious figure by the river the night Emma disappeared. Remember what he said to me?"

"Yes," Dante muttered, still not meeting her eyes.

"If he thought I was a superstitious brown girl telling ghost stories *then*, what do you think he'd do if I reported an apartment full of green mist and a dead girl coming back to life to inflict an invisible stab wound?"

Dante didn't answer, and Pao could see him battling with the new weight that was settling on them. No one else could help them. Emma was in trouble, and it was up to Pao and Dante alone to save her before it was too late.

"Your grandma gave us this," Pao said, picking up the crocheted shopping bag. "And the chancla. I don't know what to do with any of it, but we have to try, because if we don't, who will?"

Pao turned over the bag and let its contents spill out. *These will convince Dante,* she thought. These magical tools, whatever they were, would energize him and lead them to Emma, and everything would be all right.

Unfortunately, Pao had overestimated Señora Mata's gifts.

On the ground between them lay a small bottle of Florida Water and a toy flashlight. Pao recognized the flashlight as the one she had carried around when she was seven. It was the only present her dad had ever sent her. The plastic case was covered in glow-in-the-dark star stickers, and when she turned it on, the beam projected an image of the full moon.

To her credit, Pao didn't even try to hide her embarrassment.

"*This* is what we have," Dante said, his voice quiet now. "This is *all* we have. Some stinky cologne, an old slipper, and a moon flashlight you stopped playing with in third grade. That's what's standing between me and dying, or me and watching you die." He seemed to steel himself. "I'm not doing this, Pao. I'm going back home. I'll tell the Lockwoods what happened, they'll tell the police, and then they'll have to help."

"Yeah, fine," Pao said, feeling an anger rise in her—an anger much older than this terrible week. "Go ahead—bail. That's what you're good at now, right? Hey, maybe if me and Emma both die, you'll finally be free to leave us behind! You can go be a cool kid without your dweeby elementary school friends holding you back."

Dante's jaw dropped, but he didn't deny it.

She didn't wait for him to come up with a response. "*I'm* going to find Emma," Pao said. "I *care* what happens to *my* friends."

It was hard to walk away, like moving through molasses instead of air, but she did it anyway, pointing herself toward the middle of the cactus field.

Dante would either go home or he would follow. He called out for her to stop once, twice, but she didn't. She couldn't. If she stopped, she might lose her nerve. She might go home, too, and Emma would never be found, and it would be all her fault.

She had to find Marisa Martínez and ask her why she wasn't at the bottom of the river. She had to find out what the third quarter was. She had to keep going.

The light was dim in the cactus field, and she couldn't tell what time of day it was. The sky was gray and sunless, and the plants cast no shadows. Pao walked straight ahead to keep herself from getting turned around. She hoped it would work.

Eventually, she told herself, she'd either find someone or reach the end of the field.

But the cacti just grew denser as she pushed on, blocking her view. Dante's calls had long since faded behind her.

Or maybe he'd just stopped calling.

Maybe he really had gone home.

The farther in Pao traveled, the faster her pulse began to pound. With her heart in her throat, she started to run, needing to feel like she was making progress, *any* progress, instead of just walking on a treadmill.

She'd felt so brave when she set out, but now she was alone, with no real plan, and she'd just yelled at her best friend, and it was so quiet in here. So hauntingly, horribly quiet.

Pao ran faster, tripping as the ground became uneven. She couldn't hear the river over the sound of her own accelerated heartbeat. Had she strayed too far from the Gila?

At last, the cacti started to thin out, and Pao's breath came easier despite her exertion. Maybe Marisa would be just around the next corner. Maybe Emma . . .

But when familiar terrain came into view, it wasn't the edge of the cactus field. It was a small clearing, and there was an impression in the sand where just a few minutes ago—or had it been hours?—she had lain unconscious on the ground.

Dante was on his knees, brushing sand off the bottle of Florida Water, and Pao felt the sobs in her throat before she heard herself make a sound.

"No!" she said. "No, no, no! I went straight. I was going straight the whole time."

"Pao?" Dante said, standing up and taking a step toward her. "Where are you going?" he asked, as if she'd never been gone at all.

"No," she said, holding out an arm. "No." She started off in the opposite direction, a terrible hypothesis forming in her head. She took care never to turn, to point her sneakers forward no matter what.

But this time, it took less than a minute before she was deposited back in front of Dante.

She tried again, despite his protestations, but no matter which way she set out, she always found herself right back where she started.

Pao's hands started to shake. Her breath came in gasps. There was no way out. She was stuck in this field, the cacti holding her hostage. Pao sank to the ground, wrapped her arms around her legs, and pressed her eyes into her kneecaps.

"It doesn't make any sense . . ." Pao whispered. "It doesn't make any sense. It doesn't make any sense."

"Pao, stop," Dante said, kneeling next to her.

But Pao couldn't contain it. Sobs came from somewhere deep

in her chest, her back heaving with the weight of them. "This . . . doesn't . . . make . . . sense. . . ."

Dante scooted closer and tried to put an arm around her, but Pao recoiled, jumping to her feet, feeling like every breath was being dragged from a throat full of broken glass.

"Emma is gone!" she said. "And I can't tell if I'm dreaming or awake!" Another sob broke free. Her hands were still trembling. "I can't fix this, Dante! I can't develop theories or test them! Everything I know is *useless* if nothing's going to make sense and this cactus field won't let us go. . . ." Another gasp. "What if none of this is real? What if I'm going crazy?"

Pao couldn't breathe. Her throat felt like it was getting smaller and smaller, the shards of glass overlapping until there was no space left for air. She clutched at her neck, thinking of all the things that had happened, of Emma, and of home—so close and so far away.

Whenever things got to be too much, Pao had always turned to science for reassurance. The science of the river. The science of the subconscious and dreams. The science of panic and adrenaline. Up until now, there hadn't been anything she couldn't explain or justify.

But here, her best tools were useless. Here, there was no logic for her to rely on.

Mom would know what to do, Pao thought, possibly for the first time in all her twelve years. Her mother would have known how to solve the riddle of the cactus field. She would have understood what Ondina was and why Marisa didn't seem to be dead and what the third quarter was and why no one would shut up about it.

And if only Pao had listened to her, had just believed that the world might be bigger and stranger than she thought, maybe she wouldn't be stuck here with all her useless science knowledge and no way out.

Dante tried to meet her eyes, no doubt on the verge of attempting to comfort her again, but she turned away, stumbling to the nearest cactus and kicking something hard that went spinning off into the strange early dusk. She doubled over, trying to draw in a breath that would satisfy her, and failing. Always failing.

If this wasn't a dream . . . if she couldn't wake up . . .

"Mama," she heard herself say, the tears spilling over. "Help me. . . ."

"Pao," said Dante, and something in his voice made her look at him. Had she managed to summon her mother here? Stranger things had happened today. . . .

But when she straightened up, they were still alone, and Dante was staring at the ground with an expression that told Pao this was all about to get even weirder.

If that were at all possible.

Pao walked toward him, still hiccupping around her sobs, not entirely sure she wasn't going to start yelling again.

"What is it?" she asked, her voice wobbling in a totally undignified way.

"Look," he said, pointing down. "The flashlight."

It was up against the base of a particularly ancient, half-petrified saguaro. Pao had kicked it when she stumbled away to cry, and the impact had caused it to switch on.

But that wasn't the strange part.

The strange part was that the flashlight was pointed at Pao, but its beam was shining to her left. Bending in the air like there weren't laws of nature that *definitely* prevented that kind of thing.

Dante nudged the flashlight with his toe, turning it toward himself, and as Pao watched in disbelief, the light bent at an even more extreme angle, continuing to point to what Pao thought might have been east, if directions even mattered in here.

No matter where Dante aimed the case, the beam stubbornly shone in an easterly direction.

Maybe it was the sheer absurdity of what was happening, or maybe she was just tired of crying, or maybe her mind had really and truly snapped. Whatever the reason, Pao felt a giggle bubbling in her throat like sparkling cider, and before she knew it, she was doubled over, laughing so hard her stomach hurt, until tears leaked out of her eyes.

Dante looked at her in alarm.

"I'm sorry," Pao said, still howling. "But *come on*! Even *physics*?! Like, PHYSICS isn't real? It's just . . ." And then she was lost to the laughter again, and this time Dante was guffawing along with her.

"This shoe!" he said, shaking the chancla at her. "This shoe can change into other shoes!"

Pao slapped her knee—literally slapped it. She'd never known that was a thing people actually did.

"We can't get out of here!" she shrieked, causing them to laugh even harder.

"My grandma is, like, some kind of witch?" Dante offered, sinking to the ground, clutching his knees, his eyes streaming now, too.

"MY MOM WAS RIGHT!" Pao said, lowering herself down beside him, banging the ground with her open palm.

It took a while for the hilarity to fully subside, and when it did, it left a numb feeling in its wake, like the novocaine the dentist used so the drilling didn't hurt.

"I care, you know," Dante said when they were finally quiet. "I care a lot, okay? You're still my best friends. Both of you."

Pao nodded, taking it in, not sure if she wanted to laugh again or cry.

"I don't know what to do next," she admitted, and there was something freeing about it. She was a girl who always knew. She knew which bill was due next, and to put it at the top of the pile so her mom wouldn't forget. She knew as much math and science as some high school kids. She knew how things worked, and how to fix them if they stopped working. Admitting she didn't know wasn't just difficult for Pao—it was unprecedented.

"Come on," Dante said. "I bet you're dying to check out that flashlight."

Pao had to admit she was. Even if the laws of physics were useless in the cactus field, there had to be a reason the light was behaving like that, sticking to its current track like it was glued there. Not that light particles could be glued . . . but anyway . . .

"It *is* kind of interesting," Pao said, trying to be nonchalant. "None of the normal rules seem to apply, but that doesn't mean there aren't rules. . . . It's just that we don't know what they are yet."

Dante smiled.

Pao tried to scowl, but excitement was starting to crackle to life in her veins.

"I'm not promising anything," she said.

"I believe in you," said Dante. He picked up the flashlight

and handed it to her, the beam still bending unnaturally, like Matthew Promise's broken arm when he'd fallen off the jungle gym in third grade.

Pao wanted to be skeptical. She wanted to cling to the disbelief she had worn like armor against her mother for as long as she could remember. But this wasn't just a story. This was a new discovery.

"Okay," Pao said to the flashlight. "Let's see what you can do."

TEN

Does Doing the Right Thing Always Involve
So Many Demon Lizard-Dogs?

It turned out the flashlight didn't do much—if you didn't
count that whole defying-the-laws-of-physics thing.

While Pao flicked it on and off, Dante held the chancla, turning it over and over in his hands, narrowing his eyes at it like it
was failing some kind of test.

"If I at least had my stupid Boy Scouts compass, we could use
it to get out of here," he grumbled, chucking the slipper to the
ground, where it kicked up a little cloud of desert sand.

"Yeah . . ." Pao said, but her brain was already taking his
words and running with them. *A compass.* That's what the flashlight was acting like!

Pao thought fast. A compass was a magnet that interacted
with the earth's own magnetic field. But there was nothing magnetic about a flashlight, was there? How could the beam of light
be reacting to the earth?

"I think we have to follow it," Pao said, knowing how crazy
she sounded. She couldn't explain why the flashlight was acting
like a compass, but she'd never been so in need of a true north.

"Huh?"

"The light . . . it's holding its direction, like some kind of
freaky compass. Maybe if we follow it . . ."

"It'll lead us out!" Dante said, cramming the slipper into his back pocket again and coming to stand shoulder to shoulder with Pao.

Even though she normally despised being interrupted—especially when she was on the verge of a scientific breakthrough—Pao let him have this one. It was the first thing that had felt like progress in a long time. In . . . wait, how long had they been in here, anyway? The sky hadn't changed at all. It was still a uniform gray, even though it had to be approaching dusk, and they had left the apartment complex at dawn.

You have five days, Señora Mata had said. Five days until what?

A chill crept up Pao's spine, and she flicked the flashlight on again, the beam faint but definitely visible. They needed to get out of here, and soon. And if this flashlight could help them, Pao decided she wouldn't hold its fundamental disagreement with the laws of science against it.

"Let's go," she said, keeping her new sense of urgency to herself.

Dante nodded, and together they rotated until the beam of light was pointing straight ahead. Pao drew an *X* in the dirt with her sneaker toe to mark their starting place.

"So we'll know if we're backtracking," she explained, and Dante nodded again, his face anxious and a little pale in the strange light.

They had only been following the beam for a half a minute or so when it abruptly changed direction. The hair on Pao's arms stood up.

"Whoa," Dante said under his breath.

"It's sending us back the way we came," Pao said, feeling defeated. "We can't go that way. Let's just keep going straight for a little longer."

"But I thought the whole point was to . . ." Dante began, then trailed off when he saw Pao's expression. "This way it is," he said, holding up his hands in surrender.

Pao turned off the flashlight and focused on a cactus a few yards ahead that she was sure had been in the path of the beam before. She kept her eyes locked on it as they walked, but like the flashlight beam, the daylight itself seemed to bend and shimmer, and in less time than it had taken them to get this far, they were back at the X again.

"This doesn't make sense," Pao said again, but with notably less hysteria. She remembered a Thomas Edison quote from a poster in the science room at school: "I have not failed. I have just found ten thousand ways that will not work." She glanced at Dante, who was pinching his lips closed. "Don't gloat," she said.

"I didn't say a word."

This time, they left the flashlight on. When it changed direction, so did they. Relinquishing control was not Pao's favorite thing to do, but she tried not to keep track of where they'd been, or think about which way they were headed. She just followed it, and Dante followed her, and after thirty minutes or so of zigzagging and backtracking and what felt like walking in circles, they still hadn't returned to the X on the ground.

Pao didn't understand. But so what? Whatever was happening, it was working. They'd be out of here before they knew it.

When the terrain changed, Pao could have cried from relief— if she hadn't already done too much crying for one day. The gray of the sky began to deepen and change, taking on the purples and reds of an Arizona sunset. Had they really been out here for twelve hours?

The cacti grew thicker—saguaros giving way to shorter, scrubbier versions Pao didn't recognize, even after her many units on the local flora and fauna in school. The plants were round and pale, and they almost glowed. Pao thought they looked a little like jellyfish.

"Any minute now," she said, her throat parched from a long day without water, her empty belly grumbling. Any minute now, they'd emerge from the field, and then they could figure out where they were and what to do next.

Right?

"PAO, LOOK OUT!"

She reacted instinctively, before she even knew what she was supposed to be looking out for. Grasping the flashlight tightly, she spun out of the way as a dark shape came running straight toward her.

"What the—" she began, but there was no time to finish the thought. There was another shape, moving too fast to make out, and another. Pao's heart was in her throat as she ran in the opposite direction, the crocheted bag flopping against her stinging back wound, her hand clammy around the flashlight's case.

"Dante!" she called out behind her, but there was no answer. "DANTE!"

Out of breath, she stopped for just a minute, clutching at a stitch in her side, her eyes wide open in case there were more of . . . whatever those were. That's when she saw it, a few yards away, standing perfectly still. She froze, too, afraid that if she moved, it would set the thing off.

The scientist in Pao couldn't help but try to categorize it, even as the rest of her was panicking and seeking escape.

It wasn't a dog—it was way too big and terrifying for that. Plus, between clumps of matted fur, it had scaly patches that looked like lizard skin covering at least half of its body. Its eyes glowed the same green as her dream river, the same green that Señora Mata's candle flames had turned before she and Dante were forcibly ejected from the apartment.

But the really bizarre part was the spines running from the top of its head to the tip of its tail. Long green things that almost looked like tentacles, waving in a nonexistent breeze.

There were large, fearsome dogs. Pao had always avoided those breeds during her research, but she conjured up images of them now: the Doberman pinscher, the rottweiler, the German shepherd. . . . This was nothing like any of those.

The thing snarled, one scaly lizard lip curling up to reveal a crowded row of what appeared to be *very* sharp teeth. *Fangs, really,* thought the awestruck part of Pao's brain as the rest of it tensed her muscles to flee. Or fight. To do anything but stand here like bait.

Only she never got the chance.

Before Pao could move an inch, before the beast could release its coiled stance and launch for her throat, something collided with it at an alarming speed.

So much for not standing here like bait, she thought, paralyzed with horror and fascination as a human-shaped blur with dark skin and silver-white curls battled with the monster.

There were grunts, and thuds, and the occasional doglike whimper, but mostly there was the pounding of blood in Pao's ears. What could she do? All she had were a shopping bag, a flashlight, and . . .

The Florida Water.

Pao's mind raced back to the Riverside Palace as she dug down into the bag for its last remaining item. She and Dante had smeared the smelly stuff on themselves before the green light and the mist and that horrible screaming. Had it helped them get out of the apartment unscathed?

And if so, could it help here, too?

About twenty yards to her left, her silver-haired savior seemed to be running out of steam. There was nothing to do but try.

With a war cry she'd be totally embarrassed about later, Pao charged toward the fight, the shopping bag swinging wildly from her flashlight hand, the cologne bottle at the ready. Her pulse was racing, thanks to the person—girl?—who was about to become dog food in front of her.

It was definitely a girl, Pao decided when she got there. Her hair was silver gray like the old ladies at Señora Mata's bingo nights, but her skin, darker even than Pao's, was youthful. The girl was on her back on the ground, scrabbling for a weapon just out of reach, while a hundred-plus pounds of slavering paranormal demon beast stood on top of her, pressing her into the grit.

Pao took a deep breath, then clenched her teeth and pushed herself to sprint across the last few yards between them.

"Oh *no*," groaned the girl when Pao came into view. "Not now!"

But Pao was undeterred. She uncapped the bottle, full of premature righteous triumph, and poured it with the utmost confidence on the beast's head. "Take *that*!" she screamed, causing the horrifying creature to look up at her in confusion.

A second passed, and then another, and nothing happened.

The demon lizard-dog didn't disintegrate, or start to smoke, or howl in pain, or do any of the dying-creature things Pao had hoped for. It just stared at her with those fathomless glowing eyes—eyes that promised the underworld full of monsters her mom had always said were real.

"Oh no," Pao said, steeling herself for certain death as the beast exhaled hot, putrid breath in her face. But the fight wasn't over. The not-dog's moment of distraction had given the silver-haired girl a much-needed advantage. She found a reserve of strength and heaved its massive body off her much smaller one, leaping to her feet and kicking out hard with a worn black combat boot.

The beast rolled over and whimpered, and Pao joined in with the kicking enthusiastically, her sneakers making less of an impact than the girl's boots, but the dog creature didn't get up.

"Here!" shouted the girl, tossing Pao a length of silvery rope. "Tie her back legs!"

Her? Pao wondered, almost deliriously, but she did as she was told, taking advantage of the animal's position—on its back, all four appendages waving in the air—to grasp the back legs in an awkward hug before wrapping the rope around them.

The cord was slippery and hard to tie, like moonlight turned into rope, but once she got it secured with one of Dante's Boy Scout knots, the legs went still.

The girl had managed to tie up the front legs, too, and now the only movement the dog-that-was-not-a-dog seemed capable of was thrashing its head back and forth, its green eyes rolling madly, a black tongue hanging from its mouth.

"Wow," Pao managed weakly, embarrassed when her knees turned to Jell-O as all the adrenaline left her. "I . . . Wow." She sank ungracefully to the ground, her head spinning like the washing machines at the laundromat.

Once Silver Hair had tied up the beast's snout, subduing the creature completely, she walked over and looked down at Pao disdainfully, like she was some stupid kid, even though this girl couldn't have been much older than Pao.

Without a word, she pulled a knife from her belt—not as ornate as the weapon Marisa Martínez had used to stab Pao, but reminiscent of it all the same—and with a fluid, practiced gesture, slid it between the beast's ribs.

Pao watched in fascination and horror as its body quivered, as the atoms it was made of seemed to let go of each other one by one until it was gone.

"What were you thinking?" Silver Hair asked, picking up Pao's bottle of Florida Water with two fingers, like it might bite. "You wanted her to smell *worse* before she tore you into little tourist shreds?"

It turned out Pao wasn't too freaked out to be mad, which was a good sign, she thought.

"I was *thinking* that you probably saved my life, and that letting that thing, like, literally eat you in front of me wouldn't be a very polite way to repay you. Plus, I mean, it worked, didn't it?"

The girl scoffed. "Your perfume didn't do anything—she was just confused that a human *snack* was running up to her instead of running away in fear. You're lucky she didn't rip your head off."

"Oh, yeah," Pao said, getting back to her feet, pleased that her irritation seemed to have steadied her knees. "Maybe you can show me that move you were doing—the one where you lie on the ground while a monster gets ready to rip out your throat."

"Pao!" A voice rang out from behind them, but Pao didn't turn, afraid to lower her guard around the now-murderous-looking silver-haired girl. Just because they had teamed up against the demon not-dog didn't mean they were on the same side.

"I'm here!" Pao called, not breaking eye contact.

"Are you okay? I couldn't find—" Dante stopped short just inside Pao's field of vision. "Who's your friend?"

"Oh, lovely," said the girl. "*Two* tourists. Just what I need. Why don't you both just go back to where you came from?"

Pao thought about that suggestion as she sized up the girl. She wasn't even an inch taller than Pao, and her scraggly clothes looked like they'd weathered more than one night in the desert without being washed or mended. Her hair caught what little light was in the sky and glowed like the rope they'd used to tie up the beast. She oozed confidence and was battle-worn and tough, but her face was still round, her cheeks soft, her eyes large and dark, like a doll's.

She's a kid, too, Pao thought. *Maybe an eighth grader—definitely not in high school.*

"We can't go home," Pao said, deciding to tell the truth. "There's something freaky going on there. And we're stuck in here *and* our friend is missing. We think she might be here somewhere, because . . ." She trailed off, not sure how much she should share about Marisa Martínez rising from a watery grave.

"There're no other tourists here besides you two," said the girl, unconcerned with whatever facts Pao might be leaving out. "And that's two too many. Now get lost."

She turned to leave, and Pao felt panic rise in her throat.

"Wait," said Dante, and Silver Hair stopped. "We're tired,

okay? Hungry. We've been out here I don't even know how long. Can we at least trade you for something to eat?"

The girl sized him up, and Pao did, too, trying to imagine see-ing him for the first time. His cheek was cut and bleeding, his hair full of sand. *He looks tough, like Silver Hair,* Pao thought. He might be someone she'd listen to. Someone who wouldn't do something foolish like dump smelly water on a demon dog.

But the girl didn't seem interested in Dante's appearance, or his wound. Her eyes, Pao could see even from here, were zeroed in on the slipper still dangling from his left hand.

Great, Pao thought. *If she didn't think we were crazy before . . .*

"Where did you get that?" Silver Hair asked, gesturing at it.

"What, this?" Dante asked, lifting the chancla, which now looked even more worse for wear.

Silver Hair flinched when he held it up, which confused Pao more than ever. Sure, chanclas were scary enough, but this girl had just taken on a monster single-handedly. Was she really afraid of a grandma's slipper?

"Do you know what that is?" Pao asked her, and the girl rolled her eyes.

"Of course I do. I know an Arma del Alma when I see one." She paused. "Oh, God. Do you *not* know what it is?"

Pao wondered again how much to tell her, about Emma, about Señora Mata, about the green light and the kidnapper and the weird mist around the Riverside Palace. About the dreams, and Ondina, and Marisa. About Pao's fear that this was her fault. That being the Dreamer (whatever that was) had brought this on all of them.

In the end, she just shook her head. "It's a slipper," she said.

"His grandma calls it the chancla. It . . . changed . . . when she gave it to us. It turned blue."

The girl looked sideways at Pao. "I guess you'd better come with me after all," she said. "Carrying that thing around without knowing how to use it makes you a danger to yourselves and everyone else."

It wasn't much of an invitation. Silver Hair turned and walked off, not even looking back to make sure they were following. Pao thought she was going the wrong way, but if she'd learned anything about this place today, it was that directions, and memories, and basically reality in general, could be misleading.

Dante looked at Pao and shrugged.

She shrugged back.

What else was there to do but follow?

The glint of the nameless girl's hair led them into the strange, misty dusk, and Pao couldn't shake the feeling that no matter which route they were taking, home—even the idea of it—was getting farther and farther away.

ELEVEN

One Free Night at the Camp Between Worlds

With Silver Hair leading the way, they didn't need the flashlight.

Pao and Dante followed her until the sunset began to fade, the sky darkening toward night. *Was it really only this morning that I climbed through Dante's window?* Pao wondered. But no matter how long this day seemed, if Señora Mata and Ondina were to be believed, Pao and Dante couldn't afford to waste any time. They had to keep moving.

As they made their way across the field in silence, Pao thought of Emma. If she were here, she'd be doing goofy things to make them laugh. Holding her arms at weird angles to mimic the cacti, or reciting ominous heading-into-battle speeches from their favorite movies in a theatrical, over-the-top voice.

Silver Hair was a poor substitute, Pao thought, with her long, purposeful strides and her perpetual scowl.

"A day may come when the courage of men fails," Dante whispered, doing his best Aragorn impression, like he'd read her mind. Or maybe he was just thinking of Emma, too. *"When we forsake our friends and break all bonds of fellowship."*

Despite the weight of the situation, Pao giggled. *"But it is not this day,"* she whispered back.

When their eyes met, there was a spark. Something with potential. But the absence of Emma was still there, too, like a black hole.

Sure, Pao and Dante had known each other for forever, but Emma was the reactant that had rearranged their molecules and turned the three of them into something special.

They had to find her.

"Are we getting close to wherever you're taking us?" Pao asked Silver Hair, her restlessness back, driving her forward even though she was hungry and tired and sick of walking. What did any of that matter when Emma's life was in danger?

Silver Hair didn't answer, even though she was definitely within hearing range.

Pao felt her irritation bubbling like a science fair volcano, but this time, Dante beat her to eruption.

"Excuse me?" he said, jogging up to Silver Hair. She stopped, and he stood in front of her with his legs apart and his hands on his hips in what Pao had come to think of as his soccer team stance. "She asked you a question. Our friend is missing, and people are in danger, and we're following you because you said you had answers. So *answer!*"

Pao joined Dante and saw in Silver Hair's eyes that he had crossed a line. Pao wasn't sure how much good he would be if it came to a fight. Hopefully his soccer friends had taught him more than how to overuse hair gel and strut around hallways.

Their staring contest went on until the tension coiled in Pao's stomach like a snake. Just when it felt like the snake was ready to strike, Silver Hair jerked her head forward.

"We're almost there," she said. "Don't say anything until I give you the go-ahead, and *please* try not to embarrass me."

Pao wanted to make a rude comment, but the snake in her stomach seemed to have relocated to her throat, so she settled for a loaded glance at Dante.

"Where's *there*?" he asked Silver Hair, turning around in a circle. "Looks like the same old cactuses to me."

With a truly withering glare, Silver Hair returned to her purposeful strides. All they could do was follow.

Wherever they were, Pao thought, they were getting closer to finding Emma. She had to believe that.

Within two minutes, the air in front of them started to shimmer like heat waves, though the temperature was cooling. Pao blinked once, hard, aware of Dante stopping beside her and also trying to make sense of what they were seeing.

But before they could, the shimmer parted like a curtain to reveal a scene that had certainly not been there a moment before.

"What the—" Dante began as they took it in.

It was some kind of . . . campground. At its center was a massive firepit lined with a chest-high circle of white stones. They sparkled like quartz even in the waning light, and within the circle the flames easily reached ten feet into the sky, licking at the gathering dusk like fiery horses tossing their manes.

Arranged around the firepit, spread out for about a half mile, were black canvas tents of various shapes and sizes, their sides painted with a bright yellow sun. A few tents had their flaps open to the cooling air, and Pao could see people sitting inside. Other campers were walking around—talking, laughing, and calling to each other—or hanging out near a smaller cooking fire in front of what appeared to be a kitchen tent.

None of them looked old enough to be in high school. Some were even younger than Pao. But, judging from the state of their clothes, and their grubby skin and messy hair, it seemed they'd been here quite a while.

Pao wanted to charge in through the scrub brush, the towering cacti, the salvaged furniture, and demand to know what this place was. How it had been here, just a few miles from her front door, without anyone knowing?

Dante was frozen beside her, absorbing it all, as Silver Hair checked the knife at her belt. Her posture was more relaxed, like she'd finally arrived somewhere familiar and safe, but Pao didn't feel safe at all. She felt even more exhausted, like this was just one more mystery she had to solve before she could move on to the next. When would it end?

When would they find Emma? Was she here somewhere?

"What is this place?" Dante finally asked, after almost a full minute had passed.

Silver Hair sighed. "Welcome to the campamento of Los Niños de la Luz," she said.

Before Pao could ask what that was, Silver Hair went on.

"Remember what I said about embarrassing me," she said with a scowl at Pao and her shopping bag. But a glance at Dante's shape-shifting chancla seemed to strengthen her resolve, because she steeled her shoulders and walked toward the kitchen tent without looking back.

Kids stared as they passed, whispering among themselves, eyes bright with curiosity. Silver Hair wasn't the only one dressed in patched-up black clothes. She also wasn't the only one with silver hair, Pao realized, so it was probably time to find out her real name. She couldn't very well call them all the same thing.

Over the cooking fire in front of the kitchen tent, some kind of food was steaming in a pot hanging from a metal rod. Off to the side, two boys wrestled in the dust. One of them had hair as black as Dante's, but the other's was shot through with white like Mr. Sharpe's, Pao's language arts teacher.

Only, Mr. Sharpe was fifty. This boy barely looked nine.

An older strawberry-blond girl sat in front of the cooking fire in a chair made of what looked like milk cartons and cinder blocks and old couch cushions. As she stirred the pot, steam rose out of it, obscuring her face.

One of the younger girls, maybe four or five years old, spotted Silver Hair and jumped to her feet. "Naomi!" she called. Her hair was brown, brittle, and wispy, and there were dark circles under her eyes. She threw herself at Naomi, who caught her and swung her around, smiling for the first time Pao had seen.

The girl at the cooking pot raised her head at the commotion. She tapped a wooden spoon against the side of the pot and then set it down. The steam cleared, and the fire lit her features. There was a jolt in Pao's stomach when she realized who it was. Beside her, Pao heard Dante suck in a sharp breath.

"I told you," Pao muttered.

Dante stomped on her toes.

"Well, well," Marisa said, getting to her feet slowly, gracefully. "I didn't expect to see you again."

Pao hadn't had a chance to examine Marisa carefully earlier (because, stabbing), but she did now as the girl picked her way around the firepit and came toward them.

She appeared older by more than just the year that had passed since they'd last seen each other across the lunchroom. Marisa hadn't grown much taller, if at all, but her hair—which had once downright sparkled under the school's fluorescent lights—was now dull with dust and grit, and had been braided severely in two long plaits. Then there was her expression. It wasn't the same pampered, condescending face of a bully who enjoyed harassing younger kids in the halls.

Before, Marisa had been scary because she'd always had something to prove, and she usually used Pao as the lowest rung of the ladder she wanted to climb. Pao hadn't been mature enough to recognize it at the time, but the former version of Marisa had been more insecure, desperate, and afraid than anyone had realized.

She was none of those things now.

But as interesting as these changes were, they didn't answer any of Pao's questions. They just raised more. Marisa had drowned—everyone had said so—yet here she was in a haunted cactus field, walking and talking and bossing people around. During the fight with Ondina, she'd insinuated that the other girl was some kind of ghost, so what did that make Marisa?

And what did the answers to these questions mean for Emma? Was their friend here, in one of these tents?

Marisa was sure to know. There was no doubt in Pao's mind that Marisa was in charge—it was painted on the faces of all the kids around them. Pao saw it in the way they looked adoringly up at her, or gave her a wide berth, or oriented themselves to her as she passed.

Why were they following her? Pao wondered. Were they all the same kind of cactus-field ghosts?

Pao hated to admit it, but Marisa was a little bit magnificent as she stood before her and Dante in her patchwork regalia, with her long braids and freckled, no-nonsense face. The look was a far cry from the short dresses, hair extensions, and makeup she'd worn in Silver Springs Middle School.

But Pao had more important things to do than admire her old rival.

"What is this place?" she asked Marisa. "What are you? I need to know how it is you're here when you're supposed to be at the bottom of the Gila."

Marisa arched an eyebrow at Naomi like Pao was speaking a foreign language.

"I told you not to talk until I gave you permission!" Naomi hissed, but Pao ignored her, looking at Dante for support. His nod gave her the jolt of courage she needed.

"It's not about you, or you stabbing me, or anything like that," Pao said, fighting the urge to look down at Marisa's shoes when she spoke to her, like she'd done throughout fifth grade. "It's about my friend. She disappeared near the river, too. And if you're a ghost—if you're all ghosts—that means . . ."

"I'm not a ghost," Marisa said, her voice aloof and impatient, like she had much more important things to do. "I'm as alive as you are. We all are."

"You mean this place isn't haunted?" Dante asked, some color returning to his cheeks, which had gone pale when he saw Marisa.

She made a sharp, impatient noise. "Not that it matters, but I didn't drown. I was . . . taken, and I escaped. It was a long time ago."

"Escaped from who?" Pao asked urgently. "A kidnapper?" She looked around the camp. "Were all these kids—"

"If you escaped," Dante interrupted, "maybe our friend did,

too. Is she here? Emma Lockwood, she's about as tall as me, blondish-brown hair—"

"Stop."

Pao had the distinct impression that she and Dante weren't the first people to fall silent in the face of Marisa's authority.

"Your friend isn't here," said Marisa. "We haven't taken in any newcomers lately."

"If anyone could get away, it's Emma," Dante said, as if he hadn't heard her. "She's alive—I know it!"

"You couldn't fill a *teaspoon* with what you know," Naomi snarled. "You've been here for what, all of three minutes?"

"Then *help* us," Pao pleaded. "If Emma isn't here, where could she be? Where do we start looking?"

"I don't know," Marisa said, shaking her head slightly to silence Naomi. "Not everyone who disappears from Silver Springs is lucky enough to end up here. And if she's not here . . ." Marisa and Naomi exchanged a dark look. "Let's just say there's no place as friendly as this camp for kids who have been taken."

"Which brings me back to my original question," Pao said, trying not to let their pessimism crush her. "Taken by *who*?"

For an endless minute, no one spoke. Pao's restlessness and frustration built to a fever pitch. Beside her, Dante clenched his hands into fists.

"You can't expect to just walk in here and ask any question you want," Naomi said, glancing at Marisa for confirmation. The other girl didn't disagree. "We don't know you. We have no reason to trust you. That takes time."

But time, Pao thought desperately, was something they didn't have.

"What brings these tourists here, anyway?" Marisa asked Naomi, as if Pao and Dante weren't perfectly capable of answering for themselves.

Naomi jerked her chin toward Pao. "She was about to get her face ripped off by a chupacabra, and her friend showed up later, after I'd taken care of it."

Chupacabra? Pao mouthed to Dante, who had gone a little pale again.

Pao's mom had raised her on stories of the red-eyed creatures that prowled the desert, draining the lifeblood from goats through vampiric incisions in their throats. More lizard than dog, more demon than creature of God.

Pao had always considered them the stuff of legend, of course. It was yet another thing Pao had been wrong about. She felt vaguely ill.

"Another chupacabra?" Marisa asked, a very adult wrinkle appearing between her eyebrows. "That's the fourth one this week."

"I know," Naomi said, shaking her head. "Third-quarter problems. We just have to get through tomorrow."

"First of all, we fought it together," Pao said, more irritated than she wanted to be about the older girls ignoring her. She hadn't come all this way and been basically traumatized by weird monsters, ghosts, and disappearing girls just to be treated like a middle school outcast. "The . . . chupacabra—if that's even a real thing—I helped her defeat it. And second of all, what's the third quarter? We need to know. To help us find our friend."

Naomi's glare was almost as sharp as the knife Marisa had stuck between Pao's ribs, but Pao gave her a pretty good glare of her own.

"A tourist fighting a chupacabra without a weapon?" asked Marisa, interrupting their eyeball showdown. "I'm almost sorry I tried to banish you earlier."

"Don't be," said Naomi through gritted teeth. "All she did was pour some smelly perfume stuff on it, which didn't even work, and then *I*—"

"What perfume?" Marisa asked, finally looking directly at Pao.

Pao didn't want to show it to her, but what choice did she have? She pulled the half-empty bottle from her bag and handed it to Marisa, who glanced at the label before unscrewing the top and sniffing the contents.

"Florida Water?" she asked, handing it back to Pao. "That's old-school. I mean, that's not what it's for, and it never would have worked, but still. Where'd you learn about old energy wards?"

"It's . . . a long story," Pao said, her knees feeling weak again, her head pounding from hunger and exhaustion. It seemed like a week had passed since she'd woken up with the half-baked plan to grab Dante and find the kidnapper.

And how did that jewelry-stealing creep fit into all this, anyway?

"That's not all," Naomi said to Marisa, turning her back on Pao and Dante. "They have an Arma del Alma."

Marisa raised an eyebrow. "Are you sure?"

"Show her," Naomi snapped at Dante.

Dante glowered. "Why should I trust you if you don't trust us?" he asked. "I don't know what this thing does, but you guys obviously think it's pretty powerful, and you want me to just hand it over?"

Marisa met Naomi's eyes, and some kind of wordless

communication passed between them before the leader turned to Dante. "We don't know who's been taking the kids," she said with irritation in her voice, though for once it didn't seem directed at them. "We know *how* it's happening, and *where*, but we don't know who's giving the orders."

"How is it happening?" Pao cut in before Marisa changed the subject.

"The ahogados drag them into the river," Marisa said, her voice haunted.

"Ahogados?" Pao asked, remembering the sandwich jingle again. "Like Ondina?"

"There are too many to remember them by name," Marisa said tiredly. "They come; they take. We banish as many of them as we can."

"But you think someone else is behind the drownings?" Dante asked.

"Most of the ahogados are barely sentient," Naomi said disdainfully. "They don't know how to plan anything. Someone is sending them."

"So they're . . . ghosts?" Pao asked.

"What's your obsession with ghosts?" Naomi asked.

Pao wanted to laugh at the sheer irony. Until yesterday, she would have been the last person on *Earth* ever to be asked that question.

"The ahogados have a physical form," said Marisa, "but they are . . . drained. Husks of the children they once were. And they're not the only monsters in the area."

As if she knew Pao was about to pounce on this newly opened line of questioning, Marisa turned her sharp eyes on Dante.

"We've given you information about our enemies in good faith," she said. "Will you insult us by refusing to return the confidence?"

Dante looked like he wanted to argue, and Pao couldn't blame him. After all, the girls had barely told them anything, and certainly nothing useful.

But if they returned the gesture, Pao figured, they might learn something they needed to know to save Emma.

When Dante glanced at her for approval, Pao nodded once.

He pulled the chancla out of his back pocket. His jaw was clenched, and his knuckles were pale against the blue corduroy when he handed it over.

"So, what's an . . . Arma de Alma or whatever?" Pao asked, trying to lighten the mood.

Marisa's mouth twisted slightly.

"I mean, besides a slipper that can change into other slippers," said Pao.

"You mean . . . you've never used it?" Marisa asked Dante.

"We haven't had a chance to," he said defensively. "My . . ." He swallowed hard, a little of the fight leaving his face. "My abuela gave it to me before . . ."

"Before what?" Marisa asked, her eyes sharp.

This time when Dante looked at Pao, she shook her head infinitesimally. She had a strong feeling it wouldn't be wise to show their whole hand to Marisa.

"Before we left to find our friend," Pao cut in before Dante's emotions could get the best of him. She had always been the better liar. Whenever they got caught doing something his abuela had forbidden, he always counted on her to spin a story that would keep them out of trouble.

His frustration was always so close to the surface, Pao thought, tied to his every worry and fear. It had gotten him in trouble before, and today the stakes were too high to gamble.

"The point is," Pao said, "she gave Dante her slipper, and it changed into this as soon as he touched it, but . . ."

"But its weapon form hasn't been revealed yet . . ." Marisa said, examining the deceptively ordinary-looking blue slipper in her hand. "Interesting."

"Well, can you show us?" Pao asked. "Its . . . other form?" As open-minded as she had vowed to be, Pao still found this almost too absurd to take seriously. Here they were, four middle school–aged kids gathered around an old slipper, discussing its potential properties as a magical weapon.

"It will only reveal itself when he is in need," she said, looking Dante up and down. "The Arma del Alma is tied to the soul of the wielder. To their life force. It is a rare and potent thing, usually handed down through bloodlines."

"So basically what you're saying is my abuela's been walking around with a powerful ancient weapon on her buniony foot for my whole life?" Dante asked in what Pao knew was a heroic attempt at lightheartedness.

"No wonder you were always so scared of the chancla . . ." Pao said under her breath, and he shot her a dirty look.

Marisa didn't seem to notice. "Strange that she didn't explain its purpose to you . . ." she mused, but her eyes were narrowed, suspicious. "It seems a little odd to give you something so valuable without even a word of instruction."

Pao shifted under her scrutiny, and Dante's temper flared again.

"You said you wanted to see the chancla, and I showed it to you. There's no need to criticize my family."

Pao saw Marisa and Naomi exchange a glance.

"You're here because we're allowing you to be here," Naomi said, her temper rising to meet Dante's. "I'd watch your tone if I were you."

"Well, you're not me," Dante said, stepping forward. "And I'll use any tone I like."

"There's no need for posturing," Marisa said, waving a hand in a casual way that made Naomi step back. Dante's shoulders relaxed just a fraction. Pao, on the other hand, was on guard. Marisa Martínez as a peacekeeper?

Pao had a lifetime of memories of this girl. Marisa in second grade, stealing a kindergarten boy's cookie right out of his lunch box. Marisa in fourth grade, telling one of her own best friends that if she didn't stop wearing scrunchies she'd have to sit at a different lunch table.

Marisa had been the kind of person more likely to start fights than put a stop to them, but the girl didn't seem to remember fighting with Pao. In fact, she didn't seem to remember her at all. Had living in the cactus field done that to her? And if so, what else had she forgotten? Momentarily panicked, Pao searched her brain, making sure she could recall her mom's face, the green candles on Señora Mata's living room shelves, Emma and the Lockwoods, and even Mr. Spitz, the science teacher.

Pao's memories were all still there. So what was going on with Marisa?

"How long have you been here?" Pao asked, mostly to break the awkward silence caused by Dante's outburst.

It was a simple question, but Marisa's expression clouded over. "The Niños de la Luz have been here for more than a century," she said.

"The what?"

"The Children of the Light," Dante translated.

"Yes," Marisa said, her eyes faraway. "As long as there have been shadows, there has been light. We keep the darkness at bay."

"How did you, um . . . become one?" Pao asked.

Marisa regarded her with a searching expression, but after a second, she closed herself off. "That's a story for another time," she said, though her tone implied that she doubted they'd be around long enough to hear it.

"You may take sanctuary here for the night. Tomorrow, we'll decide what to do with you. In the meantime, eat, sleep, make yourselves at home."

She turned away from them, but Dante cleared his throat.

"Um, my shoe?"

Was it Pao's imagination, or did Marisa's eyes flash? An uneasy feeling took hold of Pao, but after no more than a moment's pause, the older girl handed back the chancla.

"Of course," she said. "My mistake."

Still, as she walked away, Pao's apprehension lingered. She might not have understood the Arma del Alma, or the rules of this strange place, but she knew one thing for certain: There was much more to this new Marisa Martínez than met the eye.

And if she and Dante were smart, they wouldn't trust her as far as they could throw her.

TWELVE

The Boy from Apartment B

As she sat near the camp's central bonfire, Pao ate bean stew with the kind of gusto she usually reserved for Señora Mata's arroz con pollo.

She'd never been this hungry in her life, not even on the nights when her mom forgot to make dinner. Every spoonful felt like it was restoring feeling to her limbs, sharpness to her thoughts.

Beside her, Dante listlessly stirred his bowl, his eyes troubled as he stared into the flames. He still buzzed with the frustration that had flashed in their conversation with Marisa and Naomi, and despite her mind's renewed clarity, Pao didn't know what to say to make him feel better.

So she puzzled over something else instead: the chupacabras.

Pao had researched the monsters once, in fourth grade. She'd never had the heart to tell her mom what she'd found out on the internet. The so-called paranormal creatures that had decimated herds of goats back in the nineties were actually just coyotes with a severe case of mange, making them too weak to catch wild predators and forcing them to go after the easier prey of livestock instead. The mange had caused their fur to fall off, leaving dry, scaly patches on their skin, and turning their eyes bloodshot and weary.

Pao had been so sure back then that what her mom called a chupacabra was simply the result of a species falling prey to disease. But today she had seen the Great Dane–size creatures for herself, up close. The murderous, dilated eyes, the scales glinting in the muted light, the tentacle-like spines as green as the river in Pao's dream . . .

Pao had stuffed all her mother's tales into a mental box and fastened it with a lock of her own irritation. She'd always thought being a scientist meant having to dismiss things that couldn't be tested or proven.

But Pao realized now, not without some guilt and shame, that she'd been too close-minded. Scientists had to be open to all kinds of possibilities. Who would have thought, for example, that algae could be a source of fuel? In fact, what major scientific breakthrough *hadn't* involved a little faith in something previously believed to be impossible?

Around Pao and Dante, the campers sat in pairs or threes, talking animatedly or half snoozing over their stew. Pao saw Naomi's silver head resting in the lap of a long-legged girl across the fire, a content smile on her face as the other girl braided and unbraided her hair. A few yards away, three boys who couldn't be more than eight years old flung spoonfuls of stew at each other, speaking in rapid Spanish.

With a stomach-dropping feeling, Pao recognized one of the them: the boy from apartment B. The one who, she thought, had been taken away with his parents.

Pao hadn't seen that little boy around the apartment complex since the day ICE came, and he always came to mind whenever she saw stories about tent cities on the news, showing women who looked like her mom crying over lost children who looked like Pao. Eventually those stories went away as it became clear that viewers preferred to pretend that brown-skinned kids weren't disappearing, being put into cages or taken to places they'd never known.

And now, six months later, the boy was here, his cheeks still round, his hair long and curling around his ears. He roughhoused with other boys as if he'd never had parents. As if he'd always lived in a world where a lost fourteen-year-old was in charge and the first rule was *Stay vigilant in case of fairy-tale beasts.*

Pao was about to point him out to Dante, but then she saw that her friend's chin was on his chest as he snored lightly, his stew bowl still in his lap. The anger was gone from his face, and he looked as carefree as the little boys playing across the fire. She envied him a little. For her, sleep was never so restful.

The boys whooped in their game, drawing Pao's attention again. *Sal,* she remembered when he pulled ahead of the others, laughing, taunting them. She wondered how he had gotten separated from his parents.

Had anyone ever even noticed he was missing?

Dante snorted in his sleep, and Pao took the bowl from his lap, setting it carefully on the ground while her eyes scanned the rest of the kids sitting nearby.

Most looked content, though tired and bedraggled. Almost all of them wore small knives on their hips, and patched-together clothes, and if they hadn't been so young, Pao would have called them an army.

But since when did she live in a world with enough lost, neglected children to make up an army? How many of these kids had families somewhere waiting for them, people desperately trying to find them?

Pao would do anything to find Emma. Ondina might have disappeared, along with the knowledge they were seeking, but there was no reason Pao couldn't get information elsewhere. She knew there was plenty Marisa wasn't telling them. And, tired as she was, Pao didn't intend to rest until she found out what it was.

She had a feeling mining the Niños for intel would be frowned upon, but Marisa couldn't get mad if she didn't know Pao was doing it, right?

Besides, Pao had a theory to test.

Sal's friends had run off, chasing each other through the cacti with real knives the way ordinary little boys played with sticks or toy swords. Instead of joining them, Sal stayed behind and settled close to the fire, staring into its depths.

"Be right back," Pao whispered to Dante, who was still asleep. She felt a little strange walking away and leaving him vulnerable, but he needed his rest, and she wasn't planning to let him out of her sight.

Pao approached Sal with as little fanfare as possible. "Hi," she said when she was standing beside him. "Mind if I sit?"

There was no question about it—Sal's eyes widened when he saw her. He recognized her.

He gestured to the open spot next to him, but his expression wasn't welcoming.

"It's Sal, right?" Pao asked. "Do you remember me?"

Sal shook his head and closed his mouth in a tight line, as if worried that a sound might escape.

"What about the Riverside Palace?" Pao probed further. "Do you remember it there?"

Another head shake.

"I live in apartment C, and you lived next door. With your parents. Do you remember them?"

This time, he didn't shake his head. He froze, his eyes still fixed on the fire.

"I was there that day," Pao said gently, looking straight ahead, too, remembering the sinking dread she'd felt. "What those men did was wrong, taking you all away like that. I'm really sorry that happened."

Sal sniffed, and out of the corner of her eye, Pao saw him nod slightly.

"I bet you really miss them," she said, turning to face him, her heart squeezing in her chest. She missed her mom, and they'd only been apart for a few hours.

"I do," he whispered, his chin quivering.

"So you do remember?" Pao asked as softly as she could.

"We're not supposed to talk about it," he whispered, his big dark eyes darting around the camp. "About home or our families or anything."

"Why not?" Pao asked.

"She says home is gone. That we're better off here. That, if we go back, the monsters will get them all."

"What monsters?" Pao asked, too quick, too eager.

Sal shrank into himself a little, and Pao cursed herself for the mistake.

"It's okay," she said, smiling. "We don't have to talk about that. It's just that I'm new here. I don't know much, and I was hoping someone could fill me in. . . ."

Sal shrugged, but his eyes darted between her and the fire again and again.

"How did you get here?" Pao asked. "Can you tell me about that?"

"After we were taken, and my parents . . ." He swallowed in a way that reminded her of Dante when he was trying not to cry. "I ran away. But I got lost. Marisa found me and said I could stay at the camp if I learned how to fight."

"Did these other kids get lost, too?"

No response.

"Sal, do you know what the third quarter is?" Pao asked, undeterred.

He nodded.

"Can you tell me?"

Sal thought for a minute, and Pao waited, not wanting to scare him back into his shell.

"The third-quarter moon," Sal said at last. "Naomi says that's when the veil gets thin. It's when the monsters can get through."

Monsters again, Pao thought.

"You mean the chupacabras?"

A pause, and then a nod.

"But there are others, too?"

Sal didn't answer.

"What's past the veil?" Pao asked, her curiosity sizzling again. "Where do the monsters come from?"

But this time she had pushed too far. Either that, or Sal just had the typical short attention span of an eight-year-old boy. He got to his feet. Interview over.

"I remember you," he said, and then he scampered away to join his friends in their chase.

Pao walked back to Dante, who was rubbing the sleep from his eyes.

"What was that about?" he asked when she reached him. "Wasn't that the kid from apartment B?"

"Yeah," Pao said. "He ran away, and Marisa brought him here to fight. And there's more—"

But before she could tell him about the monsters, a horn blew, shattering the cozy quiet of the night. Around them, chaos erupted.

THIRTEEN
Out of Hand

"To your stations!" Marisa shouted, leaping to her feet.

Her face was all lines and angles, her braids whipping to and fro as she drew her knife and began rounding up stragglers.

"What's happening?" Pao asked, dread spreading like molasses through her veins.

"I don't know," Dante said. "Maybe we should—"

"Get outta the way!" Naomi said, approaching from behind them. "That's the *only* thing you'll be doing."

"Naomi, what's going on?" Pao asked as the older girl seized her elbow and began dragging her away from the fireside. "Is it the chupacabras again?"

"These things make the chupes look like lazy, snoring porch dogs," Naomi said, reaching a tent on the outskirts and shoving the two of them inside. "Trust me. Stay out of the way. We'll come for you when it's safe. And before you even say it," she said, noting Pao's mouth falling open in protest, "no smelly water is gonna help you now."

Before they could ask any more questions, Naomi left Pao and Dante alone in a musty tent full of holes patched with duct tape. It looked like a storage place for extra cots and bedrolls.

The moment Naomi was gone, Dante turned to Pao, his eyes blazing. "We're not staying in here."

Pao had been thinking the same thing, but when Dante said it, the frustration back in his tone, the idea sounded more reckless than it had in her head.

He sensed her hesitation. "Oh, now you *want* to stay out of it?" he asked. "I don't get you, Pao."

"Because I'm not charging out there to fight something I have no knowledge of just to prove my worth to complete strangers?" she said, her anger rising to meet his. "Not everyone does whatever their temper tells them to do, Dante. Or didn't they teach you that at soccer practice?"

"It's always gonna come back to that, isn't it?" he said. "Like, I dare to make a friend who isn't you, and suddenly I'm your enemy. I like soccer, Pao! It's not a crime!"

"It's not about soccer," Pao said. "And if you don't get that, you're an idiot."

Pao stormed out of the tent, her blood boiling. How dare he? She didn't resent his new friends, and if he believed that—

A shriek interrupted her train of thought, and despite her protest just a few seconds ago, she couldn't stop herself. She ran toward the sound. She had helped Naomi with the chupacabra, why couldn't she help now? The shopping bag was back in the tent, but Pao pulled the flashlight from her pocket, not stopping to wonder how it might be useful.

The sky had turned a reddish color, casting an ominous glow over everything. The single shriek had quickly become a cacophony of battle sounds, and Pao followed them back toward the center of camp.

Just before she reached the bonfire, Dante jogged up beside her, determinedly looking anywhere but her face.

"I don't need your help!" she said, jogging faster out of spite.

"Don't be ridiculous!" He kept pace. It infuriated her. Almost as much as the fact that he kept patting the chancla in his back pocket, like he was afraid to draw it but still wanted to know it was there.

"Watch out!" he cried for the second time that day, and Pao jumped aside, narrowly avoiding a dark shape coming toward her on the ground, hating him for seeing it first.

It was like a massive, hairy spider, and she almost screamed, but upon closer examination, the reality was much more chilling.

Scuttling toward her was what looked like a human hand, covered in dark brown hair as thick as fur, its exposed fingertips wrinkled like it had been in the bath too long. It stopped in front of her, and Pao kept a wary eye on it, backing away.

"It's La Mano Pachona!" Dante shrieked, his voice going up to an octave he hadn't used since before his eleventh birthday. "You have *got* to be kidding me!"

Pao couldn't help it—she softened toward him. Something about his squeaky voice combined with the prospect of imminent doom . . .

"What are you talking about?" she asked in a fearful whisper as she continued to back up. The hand dug its fingertips into the sand like a crab's legs, and she saw a bone protruding from the place where the wrist should have been.

"¡La Mano Pachona!" Dante said again. "The demon hand! Don't tell me your mom never—ahh!" The hand pulled free of the grit and lunged at his foot. He darted away to avoid it, and it landed on the ground behind him, tapping its fingers impatiently.

Though it was hard to think clearly in this surreal moment, Pao racked her brain. Her mom had never mentioned a demon hand, but it did sound like something she would believe in. The only disembodied hand Pao knew was the one from her dreams, wearing Emma's ring. . . .

"Abuela told me the story," said Dante. "There was this rich merchant guy—he was greedy and gave out loans at really high interest and destroyed a bunch of people's lives." His words overlapped as he stood back-to-back with Pao, both of them doing a jig to avoid the hand's attempts to reach them. "The villagers focused all their, like, bad thoughts or whatever on his hands, because he wore these huge, gaudy rings, and finally he died. But his big hairy demon hand came out of his grave and, I don't know, terrorized them?"

As if to illustrate his point, the Mano Pachona swiped at Pao's ankle. She kicked it away, hearing a satisfying crunch, but it didn't seem any worse for wear.

"So how do you *kill* it?" Pao screeched.

"She . . . never told me that part!"

"Typical! Just don't get too close to it, okay? I'll figure out something."

"Not a problem!" Dante said, but before he could make good on his promise, it leaped for him again, and this time its aim was true. It fastened itself around his ankle just like Emma's hand had grabbed Pao at the dream river, and it didn't look like it was planning to let go anytime soon.

"No!" Pao shrieked. She clutched Dante's wrist. "Get off him!"

"I don't think it can *hear you, Pao!*" Dante bellowed as the hand began, somehow, to drag him backward by one leg, as if the strength of its former body was behind it, allowing it to get leverage and pull and do plenty of other things a disembodied hand shouldn't have been able to do.

"Right, right," Pao muttered, yanking hard against it as Dante fought to keep both feet on the ground.

The Florida Water was back at the tent, and the flashlight couldn't do anything except . . . what? Show her how hairy the hand was? Useless.

Think, Pao! she commanded herself as the hand continued to pull, its knuckles popping. "What does the hand do in the story?" she asked, her voice higher and more frantic than she would have liked.

"It *drags you into hell*, Pao! So get it off me!"

"I'm trying!" Pao said. Of course it had to be hell. Why was it *always* hell?

The Mano Pachona was stronger than Pao and Dante combined, and despite their best efforts, they were being pulled inexorably away from the campfire's light and into the shadows, where God only knew what else could be waiting for them.

Dante tried kicking at the hand, but all he did was lose his balance, and when he fell, he took Pao—who wouldn't let go of him—down, too.

Pao spat out a mouthful of sand, but Dante's arm was still in her grip.

Dante began sliding on his stomach as the hand pulled him even faster. "Pao!" he said, his voice hoarse, his eyes wide with pain and fear. "It's going to break my ankle! I can't get it off me!"

"I know, I'm trying! I'm trying!" Unable to rise to her feet, she reached for Dante's arm with her other hand, trying to get a two-handed grip.

And then Pao saw it, in Dante's back pocket:

The blue corduroy of the slipper.

"Dante!" she shrieked, cursing herself for not thinking of it sooner. "The Arma . . . Alma . . . whatever!"

He didn't seem to hear her. His face was twisted in pain.

"THE CHANCLA!"

Nothing. He was wincing, and Pao could see the fingers of the hand digging in deep, blood beginning to stain the cuff of his jeans.

There was nothing else for it. She was going to have to let go of Dante, try to get the chancla herself, and pray that the slipper would do something cooler than change color this time.

"Don't!" Dante said when he felt her grip loosen. His face was a grim mask, his eyes bloodshot, his cheeks turning gray under their normal coppery brown.

"You have to trust me," she said, and she let go of him.

Pao was on her feet in an instant, chasing Dante, who was being dragged much faster now that her weight wasn't slowing down the Mano. For a minute, she thought she wouldn't be able to catch up. The hand seemed to be getting stronger the farther it pulled him. Dante had stopped struggling and was moaning in pain.

But the slipper was there, folded in half in his back pocket. All she had to do was get to it. . . .

The second she was close enough, she dove, landing on Dante's back with her head near his knees, driving the air out of him with a slightly alarming *oof* sound.

"Sorry about this," she said, reaching for his back pocket

with one hand, well aware that her weight was compounding his suffering.

When she finally extracted the chancla, it was unnaturally warm against her palm—almost hot, like it knew its time had arrived.

But Pao had no idea what to do next. Just hold it?

She pointed it toward the demon hand and waited for something to happen, recalling the awe with which Naomi had looked at the slipper. And the reverence with which Señora Mata had presented it to her grandson.

Any second now, Pao thought as the Mano recovered from the addition of her body and pulled faster. The darkness was closing in. She looked over her shoulder to see that the campfire was too far away to spot behind them. Even the circle of light cast by the torches surrounding camp was barely visible.

The inky blackness made the air thicker somehow, and Pao coughed, trying to rid her lungs of its clamminess while staring in desperation at the slipper. Their last hope.

Nothing happened.

Pao yelled a curse word her mom would have flicked her in the nose for using. But these were extreme circumstances, anyone would have to agree.

"Pao . . ." Dante's voice was tight with pain as he said, "Give it here. . . ." He offered his hand.

Of course, Pao thought. It wasn't her weapon—it was his. It had changed for him once; maybe it would do it again.

She shoved the chancla into his grasp, closing her eyes with hope, as well as against the fear and knowledge that if this didn't work, they were done for.

But the reaction was immediate. The shoe began to glow with

golden light and emit a faint hum. The Mano Pachona sensed it, Pao knew, because it slowed down, its fingers trembling as it fought to keep pulling.

The glow was making Dante stronger, too. Pao could feel him resisting the Mano's pull once again. She clutched his thighs for dear life as the ridges of corduroy on the slipper began to smooth out, the blue turned to black, and the toe lengthened.

"Hurry up!" Pao yelled at it, but Dante lifted his head farther off the ground and she could see that the corner of his mouth was up in an almost smile.

Then the shoe exploded like a beaker when you heat it too high.

Pao screamed, but the sound was lost in the sonic wave that accompanied the explosion. The hand stopped dragging them, though it didn't relinquish its grip on Dante's ankle.

Pao rolled off Dante's back and he stood up easily, looking straight-backed and strong, while the Mano seemed dazed (as much as a severed body part *could* seem dazed) as it clung to his bloodstained pant leg.

But the most amazing thing about the scene in front of her wasn't the supernatural hand, or her revived friend. It was the weapon he held—a three-foot-long club, narrow at the handle but swelling into a solid mass of formidable, bone-crushing awesome.

Arma del Alma. Even though the phrase wasn't familiar, the name seemed perfect. Like it couldn't possibly be called anything else.

The club's surface was dark and swirling, like glass, but shot through with lines of pearlescence that shone white. It was beautiful, and Dante looked completely natural with it in his hand.

"Whoa," he said, reaching down to help her up. The Mano was mostly limp, like a dead spider clinging to a dusty curtain. Dante kicked it off him and it skittered across the dust, curling into a fist. He advanced on it, limping just a little on the ankle it had been fastened to.

Dante turned to ask Pao, "Do I . . . kill it?"

Pao smiled. Here he was, an almost man-size boy with a giant weapon, looking bloody and battle-hardened and, for lack of a better word, *cool*. Yet he was asking her what to do.

"I don't know if you *can* kill a sentient severed hand," Pao said practically. "But, I mean, crush the heck out of it, yeah."

Dante hoisted the club over his shoulder like a baseball bat. Then he hesitated. "Do you want to do it?" he asked her. "Using it was your idea."

From a distance, Pao could hear battle sounds back at camp. She and Dante would have to hurry if they wanted to go to the Niños' aid.

"Nah," she said, even though the club was awesome and, if she was being totally honest, she *did* kind of want to be the one to wield it. "It's your smelly old shoe—you do it."

He grinned at her, and her stupid stomach swooped. It *had* been her idea, but it wouldn't kill her to let him have a moment of triumph.

This time, when he pulled it back, he swung without hesitating and landed a heavy blow.

The Mano let out a strange, high-pitched shriek, almost like a boiling teakettle. Then it exploded into a disgusting puddle of lime-green goop.

"Cool . . ." Dante said, even though a lot of it had landed on his shoes. "Abuela never mentioned the gross green stuff."

"Oh, now you *like* gross green stuff?" Pao asked, thinking of algae. But she smiled to let him know she was joking.

"Maybe it's growing on me," he said, looking at Pao. He was smiling, too.

Another clang interrupted the moment. "We should probably . . ." said Dante.

"Yeah," Pao said. "Let's go."

They ran back toward the camp, the torchlight growing brighter as they got nearer. Pao shuddered when she thought about the darkness they were leaving behind, and how that heavy, inky blackness had felt in her throat. They'd come so close to losing light altogether.

When they reached camp, there was no time to dwell on what they'd just gone through. The Niños de la Luz, for all their bravado and battle stations, were in way over their heads.

More hairy hands skittered across the ground—at least ten of them.

"Guess there was more than one mean rich guy in Silver Springs back in the day!" Pao shouted to Dante, who was already charging forward.

He stopped short at the only thing more terrifying than a demon hand: Naomi.

"I thought I told you two—" she began, but Pao stepped out of the way so Dante's club could be seen in the full light of the bonfire.

Naomi stopped in her tracks, her mouth hanging slightly open.

"You were saying?" Pao asked.

"Swing that thing at any hand that isn't attached to a body, and do it *now.*"

"That's what I thought."

Naomi ran off, but Dante turned to Pao, holding out the club.

"Ready for a turn?" he asked, his smile confident, and Pao couldn't help it—she reached out for the weapon.

"Maybe just one." Then she hesitated. "But it's your club. . . . Do you think it'll work for me?"

"Only one way to find out."

A few yards off, Pao saw Sal climbing the stone barrier around the bonfire as he tried to escape a Mano. His expression was frozen in terror.

The club was warm and heavy in her hand, and Pao felt heat spread through her muscles. She ran faster than ever before, her strides longer, her braids trailing behind her.

She reached Sal in seconds, and as the Mano gained the top of the first tier of stones, Pao thought, randomly, of playing T-ball at the YMCA in kindergarten. Her team had always won.

She pulled the club back and, with a strength she didn't know she had, smashed the Mano to bits just inches from the ragged hem of Sal's black jeans. Some green goo got into the fire and exploded, scorching the pristine white stone.

"Thanks!" Sal said. He stared at her with big, round eyes, and Pao saw herself and the Arma del Alma reflected in them.

"No problem," she said, feeling like a superhero in a movie. "Now get somewhere safe, away from the hands and the goo."

"Pao! Over here!"

Three of the monsters were swarming Dante, and Pao ran again. When she was ten feet away, she tossed him the club. Marisa, who had been busy slashing away with her knife, stopped to watch as the weapon soared straight to Dante, end over end, like it was attracted to his hand. He caught it and took out all three Manos with one swipe.

Pao stayed close to Dante as he made his way around the fire's perimeter, smashing interlopers into that same disgusting goo. She would never have admitted it aloud, but she felt a little empty without the club now, like a light in her chest had dimmed.

Luckily, she didn't have much time to think about the scary flash she'd seen in Marisa's eyes when she'd thrown the Arma del Alma. Unluckily, it was because Naomi was on fire.

Silver Hair rolled on the ground, extinguishing the flames on her back, but they had spread to a nearby couch, and Pao raced over to put them out. She picked up a dirty rag and bent over the cushions while she beat them with it. That was a mistake.

A single hairy knuckle between the pillows was all Pao saw before a Mano sprang up and locked with surprising strength around her throat.

Her first reaction was shock. She couldn't breathe. And the fighting around her was so intense, no one even noticed her plight. Dante was a few yards away, defending Sal and some of the other younger boys.

Pao scrabbled at the hand on her neck, trying to dig her fingernails into its hairy flesh, to fasten her own annoyingly small hands around it and pull it off as her lungs screamed for air.

But she couldn't. It wasn't going to budge.

Dante, she thought desperately, though she realized he wouldn't be able to help. What was he going to do, swing the club at her throat? Probably not a good idea. And even if he did manage to hit it with something, the goo would burn right through her skin.

Pao pried and pulled, and tried not to panic, but it had been thirty seconds by now, if not more, and she thought she remembered that forty-five was the longest she'd ever held her breath during swimming lessons at the Silver Springs community pool.

Think, she told herself for the second time that night. But there was no magical shape-shifting weapon to help her now, and she couldn't scream, and her arms and legs were getting tingly and numb.

Since she'd always paid such close attention in class, she knew that her brain wasn't getting enough oxygen, and soon it would shut down to conserve function. She would pass out, and the only person here who knew her name was also the only one with a monster-busting weapon that everyone wanted on their side, and no one would even notice she was gone until it was way too late.

How long can a person last without air? she wondered almost sleepily as her arms fell to her sides like they'd decided on their own to stop fighting. The body's shutdown, she remembered, would happen in stages.

After a minute, brain cells would start to die. That was probably now-ish.

After three minutes, there would be serious brain damage. Or was it five? Why couldn't she remember? There was a huge difference between two more minutes and four more minutes.

She felt her legs give out next, and she fell facedown onto the couch cushions. They smelled like smoke. She couldn't move her arms, and everything was so, so fuzzy.

Really? Pao thought, her snarky inner monologue reminding her absurdly of Ondina. *After everything I've been through today, this is how it ends?*

On a smelly couch, being suffocated by a disembodied, hairy hand?

It was barely even a good story.

Okay, it was a *pretty* good story.

But just as the black spots were starting to take over her vision, the most ridiculous thing happened. Pao heard a voice. Ondina's, she was almost certain.

Not her, it said.

The Mano's fingers gripped her throat even tighter.

NOT HER! came the command, louder, and this time the Mano Pachona, fearsome folktale monster, obeyed.

It released her.

Without the pressure on her trachea, the peaceful feeling created by the lack of oxygen dissipated immediately. Pao gasped, all the sounds and smells and pains of the battle rushing back like a tidal wave to the ramshackle coastal town of her senses.

She reached for her throat and took long, gasping breaths, heaving and sobbing as snot and tears ran freely down her face.

"Pao?"

It was Dante, but she couldn't answer. She was on her back, half on the smoldering couch, half off it, still clutching at her tender throat, every breath like swallowing hot metal.

"Are you okay? What happened?"

His voice was coming from too far away, as if there were cotton in her ears, but everything else was so loud. Her heart had never beat this fast.

Finally, the metal in her throat cooled and became liquid, and each breath came easier and easier.

The moment feeling returned to her limbs, she dug savagely

through the ruined couch until she found the Mano, lifeless now, because it had been deactivated. But by whom? A ghost girl Marisa claimed to have dispatched? Pao looked around, but there was no sign of Ondina or anyone else who could have intervened.

It made no sense.

But right then, it didn't matter. With a disgusted snarl, Pao flung the vile thing into the fire, wanting to see it turn to ashes.

Instead, it exploded, singeing her eyebrows and causing several people nearby to scream and beat out embers that fell on their clothes.

Typical, thought Pao, and then she puked onto the toes of her shoes.

FOURTEEN

Meatheads and Monsters

The battle didn't last much longer. Between Dante's club and the newly discovered knowledge that the hands would explode in the campfire, the fighters made quick work of the rest of the Manos.

Pao told Dante more than once that she was fine, but he didn't seem to believe her. He hovered every second his club wasn't necessary until they had rounded up the last Mano and scoured the camp three times over for any more hidden predators.

When Marisa and Naomi declared the area clear, everyone in the vicinity seemed to collapse right where they were—Pao and Dante included.

As the adrenaline ebbed (her glands were getting a heck of a workout today), every part of Pao ached. Her throat and neck were by far the worst. But her arms and legs were sore, too, and her nose was full of the rank odors of singed flesh, green goo, and the former contents of her stomach.

She had never been so exhausted in all her life, but her mind was still going a million miles a minute. *Who made the Mano release me?* she wondered as she was surrounded by the sounds of weary Niños recapping the battle.

Had that voice been real, or just part of her delirium?

When she could, Pao sat up, finding Dante close beside her. It was both a comfort and an annoyance. She felt like a hairball coughed up by the neighborhood cat. Dante, on the other hand, looked like a hero.

"You okay?" he asked, getting to his feet and pulling her up after him.

"Stop asking me that!" Pao snapped, her impatience surprising her.

"Sorry."

Pao saw him deflate a little—his heroic glow seemed to dim. She didn't want to be happy about that. She wasn't a monster.

Was she?

"It's okay. . . . It's just . . ." To make up for her crappy thoughts, she was going to tell him about her near-death experience and the weird voice. She really was. But just then, Naomi walked up, looking almost sheepish.

This ought to be good, Pao thought. Contrite wasn't a side of Naomi they'd seen before, and Pao didn't want to miss it.

"So, Marisa is asking everyone to meet in the mess tent to plan the cleanup."

"Did you want to drag us off to a dark corner first so we don't get in the way?" Pao asked. Siphoning off her confusion and frustration on Naomi was much more satisfying than doing it to Dante. Naomi didn't wilt in response. She bristled.

But whatever Naomi initially wanted to say, she swallowed it. "Look, you guys saved us out there. The club, the thing with the fire . . . We'd never thought to burn the hands before—that was really good. I'm . . . I'm . . ."

Pao was a chronic finisher-of-other-people's-sentences. It wasn't her best quality. But this time, she let Naomi wrestle with the words until they finally bent her to their will. That was satisfying, too.

"I'm sorry," Naomi said finally, like she was spitting out a porcupine. "I shouldn't have tried to get you out of the way. I shouldn't have left you alone unprotected. It was foolish, and it won't happen again."

Pao wanted to say something snarky, but Dante stepped forward before she could. "People make mistakes," he said, sticking out his hand for Naomi to shake. "They don't define us."

It was a totally hero-y thing to say, Pao thought, and she hated it. She also hated how Naomi took his hand and looked up at him, her smile dazzling against the dark brown of her skin. She shook his hand for a beat too long, and the way Dante tossed the hair out of his eyes and grinned back was utterly nauseating.

Where was the petulant kid who had yelled at her in the tent before the fight?

Where was the boy who had cried over his grandma?

Why did he always insist on changing just when Pao was starting to get the hang of knowing him again?

"So, cleaning!" Pao said too loudly. They both looked at her in surprise, like they hadn't realized she was still standing there.

As if she had anywhere else to be.

"We're cleaning, right?" she said to cover her urge to slink off and sulk. "Monster parts and goo and probably blood all over the camp? Sounds like a blast."

"You should get your neck looked at," Naomi said, finally turning away from Dante. "It's starting to bruise." She stepped closer to Pao, examining the exposed skin of her throat.

Pao resisted the urge—just barely—to growl at her like a dog.

"I've never seen anyone get away from a Mano once it's locked on like that," Naomi said, shaking her head. "How did you do it?"

"I'm just that good, I guess," Pao said, pulling up the collar of her T-shirt.

Naomi rolled her eyes, but it was almost affectionate this time. "Mess tent, five minutes," she said. "There will be medics there."

"How *did* you do it?" Dante asked quietly when Naomi had jogged off to round up the stragglers.

Now is the time, Pao thought, her inner voice stern. She had to come clean, tell Dante about the voice that had saved her. Tell him that, for some reason, she had been given a pass.

But his face was so earnest, and he looked so impressed, and all Pao could think about was the way he had smiled at Naomi, and how beautiful she'd looked next to him.

"My mom's always telling me to cut my fingernails," she said, holding up the too-long, slightly ragged things for him to see. "Good thing I don't listen. I just dug them into the hand and pulled until it let go."

"Cool," he said, and there it was. The same grin he'd given Naomi. Maybe even a better one. "We did okay, right?"

"We did great," Pao said, high-fiving him.

The Arma del Alma was still hanging from his left hand, but as Pao watched, it started to change. For one absurd moment, it looked like a plush version of a club, like a toy weapon you'd buy at Target. But in another moment it split open down a seam and got smaller and smaller until it was just a boy's slipper again.

"Whoa," Dante said, and Pao nodded her agreement.

"You think your abuela ever made it turn into a weapon,

just for fun?" Pao asked, an undignified giggle escaping her sore throat. She winced.

"I can just picture her," Dante said, smiling and shaking his head. "Walking back from bingo, stopping in a dark alley, swinging it around a little to see how it feels."

"I wish she'd had time to tell us where she got it and stuff," Pao said, as Dante lovingly folded it in half and stuck it in his back pocket.

"Me too," he said, his smile fading. "I hope she's—"

"She's fine," Pao said, before he could finish. "She will be. We'll make sure."

"We were pretty awesome tonight," Dante said, holding out his arm for hers as they set off for the mess tent.

Pao took it instead of answering, another pebble of guilt dropping onto the pile already sitting in her stomach. What would happen if they had to fight hand monsters again? Or even worse ones? Would everyone expect Pao and her *fingernails* to be able to hold their own?

Fingernails, she chastised herself as they passed the firepit. *Of all the stupid things . . .*

In the sky above the tent Naomi had pointed them toward, a single star was visible. Pao felt her shoulders relax just a little under the weight of the secrets she was carrying. It felt like a good sign. Tomorrow they would find Emma.

"Every one of you fought bravely," Marisa was saying to the crowd when Pao and Dante walked in.

There were no tables or chairs, just old wool blankets and crudely stitched cushions on the floor. They found a place to stand in the back, and Pao was surprised by how many Niños were stretched out in front of them—at least thirty. She'd never seen them all gathered in one spot before. They seemed to range in age from four to fourteen.

Now that the danger had passed, Pao felt restless, thoughts of Emma surging in. Surely if all these missing kids had survived, Emma would have, too. But if she wasn't here, where was she? Was she was out in the choking darkness alone, facing Manos and chupacabras without protection?

And what if she wasn't alone? What if whoever was sending the monsters had taken her?

Pao couldn't get comfortable, not when she didn't know whether Emma was safe. She would hear out Marisa, and then she would get her questions answered.

Naomi sat beside Marisa, her back straight, her chin jutting proudly. But the rest of the kids were exhausted, Pao could see. They limped around, their shoulders slumped, or lay on the blankets, propping their heads on one another's laps and poking at wounds.

"Tonight, we will rest," Marisa said, a ring of authority in her voice. "Tomorrow, we will get the camp in order and prepare to fight again. The third quarter ends tomorrow at midnight, just as the summer solstice begins. They haven't overlapped this way in twenty-eight years. The barrier will be weaker than ever for a time." She tossed a half-unraveled braid over her shoulder.

"The rift creatures will be back," she continued, her eyes seeming to pierce all of them at once. "And they will be desperate. But *we* will be ready. I promise you that."

Marisa made what looked like a hashtag symbol with two

fingers from each hand over her chest. It must have meant something to the assembled Niños, because most of them—the ones
without obvious wounds to their hands or arms—imitated the
gesture.

"Have your injuries checked out," she said, her tone a little
gentler. "Get some rest. I'll see you all at sunrise."

Pao looked at Dante. "I'm not going anywhere until she tells
us who—" she began, but Marisa's voice carried across the tent,
interrupting.

"Except you two," Marisa said, her eyes lasering in on them.
"I want a word."

Pao bristled. She'd imagined striding up to Marisa, demanding answers and not taking no for an answer, but instead, she was
being summoned to the front of the classroom. Dante, however,
stood up a little straighter, adjusting the chancla so it was visible
above his pocket.

They crossed the tent together.

"I want to apologize for being short with you earlier," Marisa
said when they reached her. She gestured for them to sit down
and Dante lowered himself to the ground immediately.

Pao looked at Marisa for a moment before complying. She
didn't like taking orders from the older girl, but if she wanted
answers, she'd have to pick her battles. Her throat was raw, and
the bruises ached terribly, but she held her head high. She had to
look strong. For Emma.

Naomi, who had gotten up to usher out the other kids, joined
them once the tent was empty, sitting closer to Dante than Pao
would have liked.

"As you probably gathered from my speech, you couldn't have

come at a more appropriate time," Marisa said. "The Niños de la Luz guard the liminal spaces in the world. This area is under our protection, and—"

"Sorry," Pao interrupted, "but what's a 'liminal space'?"

"I apologize," said Marisa, backtracking without condescension. This definitely wasn't the same girl she knew from the lunchroom. "A liminal space, in this context, means a place between the world we know and the magical world. The one populated with supernatural beings—spirits, monsters, that sort of thing."

"So the cactus field is one?" Pao asked. "But there are others?"

"Countless others," Naomi said. "Each protected by their own soldiers."

"But this is a critical border," added Marisa. "The Gila River is the source of a concentrated amount of magical energy. We're not sure why, but that energy seems to be mostly malevolent."

Pao gave her a look.

"Er, bad. It's mostly bad. 'Dark magic' would probably be the way you've heard it phrased." She waited until Pao nodded, then continued. "This cactus field is near a rift—an opening between the two worlds. The Niños de la Luz are tasked with protecting the border when it grows weak. This area is most vulnerable during the moon's third quarter—a time of letting go and forgiveness on this side, and a time when the beings on the other side seem bent on anger and vengeance. The tension between the opposing forces causes the barrier to deteriorate."

"So you're saying there will be more monsters," Dante said, setting his jaw like he was the hero destined to protect them from all things evil. Even though Pao was the one who had saved his butt by remembering the chancla. She wanted to shake him.

Naomi and Marisa exchanged a glance.

"Yes," Marisa confirmed. "And we are here to stop them during the periods when this world is vulnerable. The rest of the month, the barrier stays closed."

"But there's something different about the summer solstice, right?" Pao asked, her voice sounding more accusatory than she'd intended. "Something worse?"

Another shared glance. Another long pause.

"Yes," Marisa said again. "This time, our job will be much harder."

Pao opened her mouth to ask another question, but Marisa anticipated it.

"And no, we don't know what will happen," she said, her voice taking on a hint of impatience. "Not with any certainty, anyway. But it will be easier for the rift creatures to cross over. We have to be ready for whatever comes, including the ahogados. If they get out into the human realm . . ."

"What's with those ahogados, anyway?" Pao asked. "Are they angry?"

"They no longer have human feelings," said Marisa. "And they're fed by an evil so deep, they have no mercy." Her eyes were fixed unflinchingly on Pao's. "If they come in numbers, I fear we won't be able to stop them."

"What will happen then?" Dante asked.

"They'll start with the town outside the cactus field," said Marisa.

"And . . . ?" prompted Pao.

"We believe they'll kill the humans," said Naomi. "All of them."

Pao's sore throat closed up as if the Mano were still gripping it. Dante clenched his jaw tighter, his only reaction, but Pao knew he was thinking about his abuela, just like she was thinking of her mom.

"You're tourists here," Marisa said after a moment of stunned silence. "You're under no obligation to help us. The Niños have battled their way through third quarters for a hundred years. But what we're seeing now, leading up to the solstice, is like nothing we've experienced before."

She paused long enough to let this sink in, looking between them, her face somber and serious in the torchlight. Pao couldn't help but admire her, just a little.

"The way you two fought today," Marisa said, shaking her head in appreciation, "we could use your help. We'd be honored to have you join the Niños de la Luz."

Another beat of silence followed. Marisa and Naomi had their eyes on Pao, but she looked at Dante. He had leaned forward at the invitation, and she knew he was about to open a rift of his own between them.

She could easily read his thoughts on his face. He wanted to say yes. To swing his shiny club and vanquish monsters and have girls feed him stew at the end of a long day of heroic deeds. He wanted it in the same way he wanted to score the winning goal in soccer games and go to parties with cheerleaders in attendance.

In that moment, Pao realized he'd been right about her. It was always going to come back to this: her wanting things to stay the same, and him always wanting to leave her behind.

She turned back to Marisa and Naomi. "We're not committing to anything right now except rescuing our friend," Pao said, speaking for Dante, too, and knowing he would hate it. "We asked for information, and you barely gave us the time of day. If you won't help us save her, we'll find someone else who will."

"Pao . . ." Dante said under his breath, as if they weren't all sitting right next to one another, "we can't save Emma if we're all dead."

"Of course," said Marisa, pretending she hadn't heard Dante. Was that respect Pao now saw in her eyes? "What would you like to know?"

Pao was surprised, but Dante looked at her smugly, even though he had rankled under Marisa's thumb just a few hours ago.

Pao would deal with him later.

"The kids who disappear from our world . . ." she said. "The ones you said weren't lucky enough to end up in the cactus field . . . Is that where they end up? In the rift?"

Marisa sighed. "We don't know." She held up her hands. "And that's the honest truth. We don't know where the children get taken."

"Well, has anyone *checked the evil magic rift?*"

"It's not that simple," Naomi said, her eyes narrowing despite Marisa's chastising nudge. "And it's not safe. The Niños protect against the rift—we don't go gallivanting around inside it, getting ourselves killed."

But, judging from Naomi's prickliness, coupled with the look on Marisa's face, Pao knew they weren't telling the whole story. Something in that rift was stealing kids, and Pao wasn't planning to rest until she found out what it was.

"Our friend disappeared two nights ago," Pao said, looking directly at Marisa. "If you had to guess where she is—if the safety of all your Niños depended on it—what would you say?"

Marisa held Pao's gaze for a beat before answering.

"I'd say she's beyond your help," she replied unflinchingly, "and you should fight for the living."

Pao and Dante both gasped.

But Pao wasn't willing to accept it as fact. Not without further exploration and evidence.

"We'll have to think about it," she said, getting to her feet.

Pao was halfway to the tent flap before she realized Dante wasn't behind her. "You coming?" she asked without turning around, trying to sound like she didn't care one way or the other.

"I'll be right back," she heard him say to the older girls, and she couldn't tamp down the anger that flared in her chest.

"So kind of you to spare a moment of your time," she snarled when he caught up. "I know you're in high demand after your little display earlier."

Sometimes, when Pao got snappy with him, Dante looked like a wounded puppy. It always ended their arguments way sooner. But tonight he wasn't rolling over.

"Don't," he said. "I'm not trying to pick a fight. I just want to know what you're thinking. Didn't you hear them? If we don't help the Niños get through the solstice, everyone in Silver Springs will be in danger."

"My *ears* are working just fine!" Pao said, eyes flashing. "It's my spontaneous cult-joining organ that seems to be malfunctioning."

"*Cult?*" Dante echoed, his eyes going wide and incredulous. "They're heroes, Pao! They're trying to save our families, our entire town! Maybe even the world!"

"And what about Emma, huh?" Pao asked. "Who's going to save her?"

Dante looked a little chastised. "We don't even know where

she is," he said, but the tops of his ears were purple again, and Pao knew she'd hit a nerve. "And you heard what Marisa said— we have to fight for the living. We have to survive if we want to find her."

"Staying here and playing whack-a-monster with these kids isn't going to help her!" Pao said. "And if you'd paid attention to how *weird* they were when I asked about that rift, you'd know exactly where the answers are."

Dante opened his mouth to argue, but Pao wasn't done.

"In case you forgot, *that's* the reason we're in here! Not to impress a bunch of *girls* with our shiny new weapons, but to find our best friend, who needs our help."

Angry Dante returned in a flash. "You know what I think, Pao?" he asked, though he didn't wait for an answer. "I think you're just *jealous*."

"Of some meathead wannabe jock with a glorified baseball bat?" Pao said, knowing it was cruel, and wanting it to be. "In your dreams."

When she stormed off, he didn't follow. And that was fine with Pao.

Just *fine*.

FIFTEEN

A Dream Within a Dream Within a Dream

Pao was finally alone. As she meandered in the blissfully quiet cactus field, everyone else asleep in the tents far behind her, she wondered what time it was. She couldn't tell by the position of the moon, because it was obscured by something—stratus clouds, she assumed.

Things in outer space had always mattered more to her than things down on Earth. It was amazing how much her life had changed in the span of a day.

She stalked past cactus after cactus, not at all sure where she was going.

Oh well. If I stray too far, the stupid cactus field will just spit me out right back where I started, she thought bitterly. *Probably right in front of stupid heroic Dante flexing his muscles for stupid Naomi.*

Pao was exhausted, but her mind still raced. As much as she wanted to kick him in the shins right now, she had to admit that Dante fit in well with the Niños. He was brave and a little foolish. He looked cool with a weapon, and he had that floppy-hair thing going on. Plus, he smiled a lot. Way more than Pao did.

If this were a book, he would definitely be the hero. She would be the grumpy sidekick whose one shockingly convenient skill helped him save the day.

That thought made her even grumpier.

Dante had the club, the grandma to avenge, and the most intimidating girl in camp hanging on his every word. And what did Pao have? The crocheted shopping bag clunked against her sore rib as if to prove a point. She almost laughed at the reminder, shoving her arm inside it up to the elbow and closing her hand around the flashlight.

It looked so juvenile in her palm, with its peeling glow-in-the-dark stickers and its worn brand name on the case: LITTLE TYKES LUNAR LIGHT.

Slowing to a stop, Pao recalled the moment she had first seen it. Her mom had somehow managed to pull off Christmas that year. There had been a little tree with presents under it, and the house had smelled like fresh-baked cinnamon rolls and hot chocolate.

After breakfast, Mom had pulled out a package with a weird stamp and no return address on it, getting quiet before saying it was from Pao's dad. Pao was so young at the time, she didn't yet know she should be angry at him for not being there to give it to her in person. She only knew, from what her mom said, that it could be hard for two grown-ups to live together and sometimes it didn't work, no matter how much you tried or wanted it to.

Pao remembered her dad as someone who read thick books too heavy for her to lift, wrote obsessively in tiny notebooks she wasn't allowed to touch, and took long walks in the desert after her bedtime.

Sometimes she would watch him from her window as he paced, just a silhouette beneath the starry sky, gesturing like he was talking to the moon.

For a while, that's where Pao pretended he had gone: to live on the moon, where he would watch her get tucked into bed every night through a long white telescope.

She'd grown out of the daydream but never her obsession with the moon.

That Christmas morning, when Pao had first opened the flashlight and realized it projected an image of the moon, she had made her mom turn off all the lights so she could use the toy right away. The impression of the full moon hadn't been very bright—the blinds let in some light even when they were all the way closed—but Pao hadn't cared. The beam had been strong enough to show the craters.

Now, in the cactus field, Pao recognized that the flashlight had seen better days. It was embarrassing and ridiculous compared to Dante's hero club. She wanted to throw it far away, to hear it crunch satisfyingly against one of the billion-year-old cacti here, to show Señora Mata and her dad and whoever else was watching what she thought of the dumb thing.

Instead, she clicked it on, remembering the way the beam had bent before. This time, it pointed straight ahead, just like it had on the morning she'd first unwrapped it and put in those two shiny new D batteries.

She didn't think of her dad much anymore, but she felt a strange kinship with him tonight as she paced around the desert alone, working out something in her own convoluted way.

Pao turned 180 degrees, just to see what would happen. The beam of light, faint even in the darkness, bent around her body and pointed back the way she'd come.

I was going the right way. Even though it was nonsensical, the thought comforted her. She turned again so the beam was pointing straight ahead.

Was it her imagination, or did it look a little brighter now?

When she'd first started to understand how the magic flashlight worked, Pao had thought it was like a compass—the beam pointed in a fixed direction even when the "liminal vibes" of the wonky cactus field warped the way forward. Before, it had led her and Dante toward the camp. Now it was pointing away.

To where? Pao wondered, taking a few steps forward.

"Paola!" came a voice from behind her. She hastily shoved the flashlight back into her bag. Dante might like showing off his flashy weapon, but pathetic as the thing was, Pao thought she'd keep the Lunar Light to herself for now.

When she turned, she saw it was Sal who had tracked her down. Pao did her best to hide her storm cloud of a mood as she met his eager gaze.

"You're going to stay with us, right?" he asked, his voice high and breathless.

Pao sighed, the momentary distraction of the flashlight gone. It had been easier to put off Marisa and Naomi. But Sal? With his big *I miss my parents* eyes and his almost-quivering lip?

"I don't know," Pao said. "It's complicated. I'm looking for someone."

Sal nodded bravely. "I understand."

"I'll do what I can for you, okay?" she said, hoping she could keep her promise.

He nodded again, looking at her bag, then back at her face. "It's dangerous to go too far from the fire," he said, and even though Pao's Spanish was worse than her mom's cooking, his accent still tugged at her heartstrings. It sounded like home.

"I guess I just got turned around."

"Camp is this way," he said, pointing behind them. Away from wherever the flashlight had been leading her.

"Good thing you came along, then," she said, smiling, and Sal tentatively smiled back.

They had returned to the bonfire before Pao realized how exhausted she really was. She was sure she wouldn't be able to sleep—not with all the questions spiraling around in her head—but she could lie down for a little while, right?

In the tents all around her, the Niños were curled up on their cots. Some preferred to sleep out in the open, in bedrolls, or sprawled out on blankets. There were even a few hammocks suspended between particularly sturdy cacti. Pao took a sleeping bag from the pile nearby and went as far from the others as she could while still remaining in the protective circle of firelight.

The Niños were a family, she thought as she unrolled the bag. Even Dante seemed to be part of this group now—or on his way. Pao tried not to think about him, or where he might be, but his absence was a physical thing that ached in her chest.

She didn't belong here. She hadn't earned her place the hard way. A rift monster had spared her, and Pao still felt guilty for it. Also a little afraid.

Pao had always been angry. She had a quick temper and she distrusted people. She'd thought these were just hallmarks of a great scientist growing up in an increasingly scary world. But if Marisa was right, Pao had grown up two miles from a source of *malevolent* magic.

What if Pao wasn't just a little too realistic for her age?

What if her anger was being piped into her by an external source?

Pao felt the worry settle on her chest like a rock as she lay back on her bedroll. Finding Emma was her first priority, of course, but that wasn't the only reason Pao had put off Marisa. This deep-seated fear had been plaguing her ever since Marisa had mentioned the rift.

Pao had been haunted by nightmares for most of her life. And in her dreams, she saw things she had always assumed were just part of her repressed imagination. But now they'd all come to pass.

The glowing green light that had filled the apartment.

Ondina, whom Marisa had banished for being a monster.

Even a disembodied hand dragging her away.

When Pao dreamed, she walked with ahogados and ghost girls and monsters. Was that what being the Dreamer meant, that Pao was a monster, too?

The questions and suspicions continued to loop until Pao could imagine herself with glowing green eyes and white hair, patrolling the riverbank, attacking the Niños. Her thoughts turned to visions before she could tell waking from sleep, and her mouth tasted metallic as she chased a boy who ran from her in terror.

Though she was familiar enough with nightmares, this one was the most visceral Pao had ever experienced. She could feel the air whipping back her white hair, and she could hear the boy's panicked heartbeat. But there was something else beneath her senses: an otherworldly pull, like there was a fishing hook in her chest, the line growing more tight and painful as she ran.

Pao caught up to the boy easily. He was unarmed, and when she tackled him to the ground, he screamed.

His voice was familiar.

Too familiar.

Turning him over, the pulling sensation in her chest worse than ever, Pao realized it was Dante.

Unable to stop herself, as if some dream puppeteer were holding the strings, she grabbed him, ignoring his cries, and started to drag his body toward the river. The closer to the water she got, the more the tugging on her eased. She moved faster, oblivious to his kicking and shouting, her name leaving his lips again and again as the glowing green current came into view. . . .

The scene dissolved then, Dante fading away, a victim of the corruption she didn't know how to eradicate from her bones.

When the vision was gone, Pao was alone, back in her usual body, dark-haired, and moving at human speed. But the dream wasn't over. The sky was the same ominous, empty black it had been in her previous nightmares. Pao wanted to scream and run, but she knew that wouldn't do her any good.

She would see what she was supposed to see. Resistance was futile.

The landscape looked the same as always, the glowing green water and bone-white sand beneath the oppressive sky. Pao walked along the riverbank, taking some comfort from the fact that she was back to being herself. That the taste of blood, and the boy she'd taken it from, were gone.

Like an old-timey movie reel, the bonfire from the Niños camp flickered to life in front of her, where before there had been only sand. Beside it was an altar made of stacked milk crates, topped with bunches of marigolds and bowls of fruit arranged around a newspaper obituary with a photo of a smiling, dark-haired teen.

Pao's stomach lurched. Somehow, she was sure the young

man in the photo was the pixelated face she'd seen on the news. The same boy who had wielded green light and laughed in her dream the night Emma had disappeared.

The kidnapper.

And in script below his photo was a name:

Franco

Before she could find out more, another figure stepped up to the altar.

It was Marisa, her strawberry-blond hair wavy and loose, freed from the severe braids Pao had almost gotten used to. Her face looked younger, too, and somehow Pao understood that this was the Marisa she had known in school. The clever, cruel girl she hadn't been able to find in the face of the Niños' leader.

Marisa covered her mouth with her hand, choking back a sob. "Oh, Franco," she said, her voice low. "I'm so sorry."

Franco couldn't answer, of course, but as Pao observed Marisa mourn the person who was almost certainly responsible for Emma's disappearance, Pao felt an icy hatred forming in her chest.

She should have known she couldn't trust Marisa. Not for a second.

The bonfire was just as Pao had seen it when she was awake, with the white stones surrounding it, at least ten feet in diameter. But before, the flames had been reaching for the sky, and now it was burning low.

When it was down to a single glowing ember, Marisa climbed up the white rocks, tears streaming down her face. "I'm so sorry," she said again.

But she dropped his picture in the fire, and then there was no one left to apologize to.

Pao watched as Marisa stepped, barefoot, into the ashes, and dug into them for the last cinder. "Don't!" Pao shouted instinctively when Marisa lifted it with her bare hands.

But Marisa didn't flinch, not from the heat, and not from Pao's warning.

It was like Pao wasn't there at all.

Pao moved closer, secure in her invisibility, and gasped as the crying girl put the glowing coal to her lips.

"Mi corazón es la llama," Marisa whispered, kissing it. "La llama es mi corazón."

The ember had left white marks on Marisa's mouth, burns that had to be agonizing. But the girl seemed immune to any pain.

"Mi corazón es la llama; la llama es mi corazón," she said, a little louder now as her eyes blazed with determination. *"Mi corazón es la llama; la llama es mi corazón."* This one was the loudest yet, and the sound rang eerily against the empty sky of the dream river.

The moment the words left her, Marisa closed her eyes, opened her mouth, and put the ember on her tongue. Pao's stomach turned. She imagined she could hear Marisa's tongue sizzling behind her closed lips.

Once the deed was done, Marisa stepped out of the firepit and sank to her knees, her hands clamped over her mouth, every muscle in her body convulsing, trying to reject the pain even as she forced herself to accept it. Even as she swallowed it whole.

It took a long time, but Marisa finally screamed. Over and over, the sound high and keening and desperate, like a dying animal. The screams gave way to sobs, racking and terrible, and then, at last, Marisa lay down with her eyes closed and was still.

In the dream, Pao lowered herself to the ground on shaky legs, running the Spanish words over and over in her mind. If only Pao had tried harder to learn the language when she'd had the chance. She'd always thought there would be time enough later on, and besides, Spanish seemed tied to her mom and the spiritual stuff Pao hated. But in this moment, she had never wished so much that she'd studied it.

If I ever get out of this vision, she vowed, *I will.*

She sat like that, with unconscious Marisa nearby, until the white sky went dark.

When Pao opened her eyes for the third time, she was back on her bedroll by the fire. The relief came so fast and hard, she almost cried. The nightmare had finally ended.

But where was everyone? Where were the other Niños? And the fire . . .

The flames were green.

So the bad dream *wasn't* over after all.

"I wanted you to see for yourself," said a voice, and a pale figure came into view, washed in the green firelight. She wore the same black dress, its lace back to its pristine condition after her tumble with Marisa. Her curls were glossy. "She calls us ahogados, and monsters, but what is she? She should be dead, too, Paola. She's no better. You don't belong with her."

Ondina stood beside the sleeping bag, her ankle boots planted firmly on the ground this time, her wide eyes glowing eerily, curls tossing in a wind Pao couldn't feel.

"What do you want from me?" Pao asked, trying to keep the tremble out of her voice, but in a blink, Ondina had disappeared.

Pao got to her feet, her knees still shaking, still seeing bloodless Dante and hearing Marisa's shrieks of pain. "What do you want from me?" Pao screamed at the sky, which was now glaringly bright.

"It's a *touch* melodramatic, don't you think? The whole screaming-at-the-sky thing?"

Ondina was back, on the other side of the fire this time, her long eyelashes casting spidery shadows on her face.

"Do you do that *just* to creep me out?" Pao asked, her nerves jangling, her temper flaring in her chest. "Can I request a new dream ghost or whatever?"

Ondina affected a little shudder. "Trust me, if you knew your options, you'd be happy to see me. I mean, unless you *like* putrid pig demons or talking birds of prey with intestines hanging from their beaks."

"Marisa says she banished you," Pao said, ignoring the grotesque images. The glow from the river and the intensity of the sky forced her to squint down at the white sand. Her feet were bare in this dream world. She didn't remember being barefoot before. "Is that why you're here instead of in the cactus field?"

"The Banisher lies," Ondina hissed. "That's what I'm trying to show you! You can't trust her. You can't trust any of them. Promise me, Paola."

"Oh, but I can trust *you*?"

"Well, for one thing, I know my way around a bathtub," Ondina said, turning up her nose. "Have you *smelled* those miscreants? They have *untrustworthy* written all over them. In grime."

"Can you be serious for three seconds? Do you even know what you just put me through?"

Ondina yawned exaggeratedly, lifting a pale hand to her

mouth. "I get one mortal to talk to in . . . well, in a long time . . . and she has to be literal and boring. Just my luck."

"Are you really what she said you are?" Pao asked. "An ahogada or whatever? She said you would try to lure me into the water. And when the Manos had me by the throat, I thought I heard you—"

"We don't have time for this," Ondina said, waving a hand impatiently. "It doesn't matter. The solstice approaches, the third quarter has almost passed—"

"I know, I know," Pao said, like this spooky, mystical moon stuff was old news. "They told us that after the Mano attack."

"Oh, really?" Ondina asked, arching a perfect eyebrow, her expression saying she knew it was flawless. "Did she try to recruit you to fight an endless horde of monsters? Or did she tell you that the solstice is your only chance to get through the rift?"

As if on cue, a shape began to move toward them through the water. Pao didn't have to look to know what it was: Emma's hand, wearing the ruby ring.

"They said it's too dangerous to go into the rift," Pao said, turning to face Ondina, who was examining her nail polish, looking bored.

"But they also didn't bother to mention they were mourning thieves and murderers. Am I right?"

Pao hated how right she was, how her own diamond-hard anger got sharper whenever Ondina spoke.

"You don't belong with them," Ondina said. "You're meant for so much more."

"Then *tell me what it is*!" Pao shouted.

"Do you think we're here for my health, Paola?" Ondina

asked, rolling her eyes with the precision of an expensive scientific instrument. "Do you think I *like* this toxic beach and the severed hand with its tacky jewelry? I'm *obviously* trying to show you something! You need to *pay attention!*"

"Why does everyone talk in riddles?!" Pao asked, throwing her hands up in exasperation. "Can't you just tell me what to do?"

Ondina smiled, revealing strangely pointed incisors. "Well, that wouldn't be any fun for *me*, now, would it?"

Pao wanted to strangle her, or at least pull one of those annoyingly bouncy curls, but before she could so much as take a step in Ondina's direction, the ahogada was gone.

Emma's hand had almost reached Pao by now, crawling toward her on the sand, the severed bone protruding from the wrist, the ring sitting too heavy on her fourth finger.

"Where are you, Emma?" Pao whispered to the hand, but it didn't answer. It just latched onto her ankle, and for the third time, tried to drag her into the glowing green water.

For a change, Pao didn't bother to struggle.

But just then, when the darkness was closing in, at the point she usually woke up swallowing a scream, Pao saw her. Hair floating around her like a cloud of gold, blue eyes open, lips faintly smiling.

Emma.

"I'm here, Pao," she said, reaching out, moving toward the surface as Pao was dragged into the fathomless depths. "Don't give up on me."

SIXTEEN

Truce with a Side of Abject Humiliation

Pao awoke gasping in her bedroll with no idea of how long she'd been asleep.

"Emma!" she cried, reaching out before she realized the river was gone and the dream had ended at last.

Dawn was breaking in the cactus field, leaving the horrors of the night in the past.

Pao rolled over, stretching her stiff muscles, getting ready to wince her way to her feet. Then she froze. Sometime while she'd been dreaming about killing him, Dante had placed his sleeping bag right next to hers.

He could be infuriating. He cared too much about what other people thought. He valued things that Pao couldn't even understand. But he was also trusting. Loyal. Not afraid to be exactly who he was. Dante loved with his whole self, and he protected what he loved, and Pao wouldn't let anyone put him in danger for it. She knew what she had to do.

"Who's Franco?"

Marisa hadn't been hard to find. She was on her "throne" in front of the mess tent, just staring into the cooking fire like she was remembering something that had happened a million years ago.

Spread out on the ground in front of her was a handkerchief, and whatever was on top of it sparkled in the dancing flames.

"Excuse me?" Marisa asked.

"Franco," Pao repeated, letting her anger infuse every word. "Do your little lackeys know about him? Do they know he's a kidnapper and a thief? That he *stole kids from their families* and they were never seen again?"

For the first time since they'd come face-to-face—or knife-to-ribs, anyway—Marisa looked almost afraid. "How on earth . . . ?"

"It doesn't matter how I know," Pao said, trying to sound spooky and ominous. "But I do. And I want you to give me one good reason why I should trust you, because . . ."

Pao trailed off. She had just gotten close enough to see what was laid out on the handkerchief. One half of a friendship locket. A bracelet with a star charm. A ring like Emma's, with a sapphire star instead of a ruby heart.

"You were working with him," Pao said, her body cold despite the warmth of the fire. "You knew what he was doing, and you helped him."

Marisa pinched the bridge of her nose like Pao had seen her mom do a million times. It was typically when Pao was asking a lot of impossible questions, come to think of it. Pao's usual instinct was to fill the silence, but in this instance she waited. It was Marisa's call which way this was going to go.

"Sit down," Marisa said at last.

"Why would I sit down with a kidnapper?"

Marisa actually chuckled. "Because I'm not one. And neither was Franco. Let me explain."

Pao didn't intend to believe a word she said, but she obeyed her order and sat. Marisa just had that effect on people.

"Franco was the leader of Los Niños," she said when Pao was settled. "He was . . . my friend. He recruited me when I was wandering lost in the cactus field. He gave me a new home."

Pao waited, even though she had a thousand more questions.

"We grew close quickly, and then Naomi came, and the three of us were inseparable. Franco had been here for generations, fighting the ahogados, protecting the town. But he thought there was more to the job than that. . . ."

"Wait," Pao said. "Generations?" The boy in the video footage hadn't looked any older than eighteen.

"Our leaders become immortal when they take the flame," Marisa said, like it was a throwaway fact.

"You mean *eat* the flame, right?"

Again, Marisa looked shocked at how much Pao knew.

Pao motioned for her to keep going.

"Uh, right," said Marisa. "It's how we remember."

"But you don't remember your family?" Pao asked. "Is that the price? Forgetting them?"

Marisa smiled wanly, shaking her head. "I haven't forgotten my family, as much as I would like to. But when I took the flame, I inherited the memories of every leader before me. And since the fire was lit a hundred years ago, it makes the mind a little crowded. Some things naturally fall by the wayside."

For a minute, Pao forgot the reason she was there. "So . . . you remember me?"

"Remember what?" Marisa looked genuinely curious, and Pao wondered how much to tell her, whether it would change things.

"I . . . knew you," she said. "In Silver Springs. We went to the same school. Paola Santiago?" She waved.

Marisa's eyes widened for a fraction of a second, and then they returned to their timeless stare.

"You . . . We didn't like each other very much," said Pao.

Marisa laughed a little at that. "I'm sorry," she said. "From what I remember, I wasn't always pleasant. But I had my reasons. I had . . ." She paused, her face twisting in pain. "It's over now. This is my home."

"So why are you stealing kids and keeping them here? You and Franco . . ."

"Franco risked his life," Marisa said, an edge to her voice. "He never harmed anyone. He was searching for an important artifact, one that would give him access to the rift. He believed we could stop the monster attacks if we could get inside, but . . ."

"But what?" Pao asked when Marisa was quiet for too long.

"He died trying. He never found the key. He saved us, but he didn't . . . He couldn't . . ."

Pao waited as Marisa pulled herself together.

"Franco knew of another opening between worlds, some-where up north, where the magic wasn't mala. He believed that our rift had somehow gotten corrupted."

"By what?" Pao asked, immediately on edge.

"We never got far enough to find out." Marisa's gaze grew even more distant for a moment, and then she shook her head. "He asked Naomi and me to go with him to the spot where the field meets the Gila. The most dangerous part of this area. We agreed, of course—we wouldn't have denied him anything."

Pao thought Marisa's eyes sparkled a little when she talked

about him. Pao didn't know much about love (except that what most people called love was actually just an overproduction of the oxytocin hormone in the brain), but she *did* know a lot about crushes, and it looked like Marisa had had a *big* one on Franco.

"The only thing we had to go on was a line from an ancient poem he found while he was researching rifts. Franco said the key would 'reflect the light of the wearer's soul.' He was convinced that meant the key was a jewel. But . . ." Marisa gestured to the jewelry on the handkerchief.

"Wait a minute," Pao said. "The 'wearer' . . . Those were innocent people, right? *That's* why you were stealing jewelry from them?"

"We told them what was at stake," Marisa tried to explain. "Of course, most of them didn't believe us. . . ."

"And you just expected them to hand over their prized possessions?" Pao asked incredulously, thinking about how much Emma's ring had meant to her.

"We didn't have much time for discussion," Marisa protested. "We had to protect them from the ahogados. Those infernal spirits were always right behind us."

"And did you?" Pao pressed. "Did you save any of the 'wearers'?"

Marisa shook her head.

In the silence that fell between them, Pao pictured it—Franco, Marisa, and Naomi thinking they were heroes, preparing to vanquish evil. Instead, they were no better than common thieves, and they'd led the ahogados right to their victims. Pao struggled to remain calm. She needed to hear more about what had happened to Emma.

"Finally, the time came," Marisa went on. "The river was getting low—Franco said going into the rift when the barrier was weak would be our only chance, and we would have to enter without the key. I tried to talk him out of it, but he believed we could make it through, and we believed in him."

No doubt about it, Pao thought. *MEGA crush on Franco.*

"We spent hours searching for the place where we thought the rift would appear. We believed it would open during the third quarter. And we were right. Once we found it, we intended to return to camp and wait for the solstice, when the veil would be thinnest, but they descended on us before we could get away. Hordes of them. We never stood a chance."

"Ahogados?" Pao asked, not sure she wanted to know.

Marisa nodded. "There were hundreds of them, maybe thousands. The rift opened and they poured out like smoke. We fought, but they never stopped coming. There was no way to escape."

Pao waited as Marisa regained control of her emotions, pressing her hands against her knees.

"Franco had an Arma del Alma, so he was better off than we were," the older girl continued at last. "He told us to leave him, but we didn't want to. Finally, he managed to convince us. We ran, but as soon as we felt it was safe, we hid and looked back. We watched as the ahogados drained his life force. We watched as he . . ."

Marisa couldn't go on. She wasn't crying, exactly, but she covered her mouth with one hand and curled her shoulders inward. Pao almost felt bad for asking her to drag it all up, but she was too busy wondering. Hypothesizing.

"After the ahogados took him, Naomi recovered his things. The ahogados had no use for them." Marisa waved a hand over the bits of jewelry. "They're all we have left of him now."

Naomi's silver hair, Pao thought. *Is that what happens when you fight an ahogada? Your life force is partially drained? And what happened to Franco's Arma del Alma? If it was such a powerful weapon, why hadn't it been enough to save him?*

But Pao didn't articulate any of those questions. Instead, she asked, "And then you ate fire? To be the leader?"

"It's what you do," Marisa said, before Pao could describe what she'd seen in her dream. "It's how you tie yourself to the luz—to the cause. He chose me before we left him. My life is connected to the magic of the rift now, no matter where I go. We're all protected from aging inside the boundaries of camp, but as leader, I'll be immortal as long as I serve the light."

"Unless the ahogados get you like they got him."

Marisa nodded soberly. "He's only been gone three days," she whispered. "Sometimes I think he's going to walk out from behind a cactus and take back his rightful place. . . ."

Pao felt guilty again. She had accused Marisa of succumbing to evil, but hadn't she saved Pao from Ondina? Despite her shady methods of trying to find the key, Marisa was a well-intentioned, grieving girl who had been forced to assume leadership under the most difficult of circumstances.

And what was Pao? Pushy, angry, stubborn—

"You were wise to ask me about Franco," Marisa said when Pao didn't reply. "Trusting the wrong people in this world can be the end of you. Your friend is eager, wide-eyed. But you're discerning, capable. You'd make a fine leader."

"Thanks," Pao said, surprised at Marisa's appraisal, so different from her own. "Just don't ask me to eat any burning coals, okay?"

Marisa smiled, and in the light of the fire, Pao could see scarring on her lips from the ember.

"Too soon?"

Marisa shook her head. "Franco was just as irreverent as you are."

The silence that followed was comfortable for a change, but it couldn't last. There was still so much to be done.

"If Franco wasn't the one stealing the kids," Pao asked, "who is?"

Marisa hesitated. "Franco had theories about it. That the rift feeds on children. That their life forces fuel the corrupted Source of magic. I have his memories, but his conclusions weren't complete. He believed that the ahogados and the Manos and everything else are just soldiers for the 'general' inside the void, but he never found out who or what it was. And now—"

"Oh, God," Pao said, interrupting Marisa, who stopped, looking concerned by the terror on Pao's face. "Oh, God . . ."

"What is it?"

"Missing children . . ." Pao said, and her voice sounded far away to her own ears. "The monsters, the general . . ."

"Santiago, spit it out!"

Pao gathered her thoughts, the lifetime of tales, the strange things she'd seen today alone. A week ago—even a *day* ago—she would never have thought she'd be offering this as a viable solution.

"My mom's stories have all turned out to be true," Pao said, looking Marisa dead in the eye. "And her scariest one was about a woman who stole children by the river. . . ."

The older girl watched her intently.

"Marisa, I think I know who the general is."

If they were in a movie, this would've been the moment when the soundtrack swelled just before the big reveal.

"I'm listening," Marisa said.

"I think it's . . . La Llorona."

Instead of climactic movie music, Marisa's reaction was the sound of a record scratch. Pao had been expecting a dropped jaw, a hand clapped to the forehead, something—*anything*—to indicate amazement. Instead, Marisa held a hand to her mouth, eyes sparkling, clearly trying not to laugh.

Pao's cheeks heated up, irritation flaring as the horror of her realization waned. "Oh, so *chupacabras* and some minor folktale about hairy hands are real, but La freaking Llorona makes you giggle?" She knew how childish and defensive she sounded, but she couldn't help it. "Sorry if my *Who's Who in Fairy Tales That Come to Life* manual is outdated."

She folded her arms, and Marisa lowered her hand.

"I'm sorry," the older girl said, amusement still playing around the corners of her mouth. "You're not off track about La Llorona. Most of the local folktales were inspired by creatures from the rift."

"So she's real?" Pao asked.

"She *was*," Marisa said. "But come on, a sad woman who lost her mind and drowned her kids only to regret it? A ghost who can't stop crying isn't exactly a threat. Franco said he dispatched her in his first week as leader. She was nothing more than a nuisance."

Pao thought this wasn't a very feminist assessment, but she

was too busy being annoyed about every riverside birthday party she'd missed for no reason to say anything.

"Don't be embarrassed," Marisa said. "It's an understandable theory for someone who's been here less than two days. It's just . . . the general we're looking for will have a lot more in his arsenal than the ability to wail really loud at night."

"Noted," Pao mumbled, wondering when her cheeks would cool—or if they ever would. She was a *scientist.* Even if ghosts and monsters *were* real, Pao had jumped to a premature conclusion, which was so unlike her. *This place must be getting to me,* she thought.

"So, you were going to ask about your friend . . ." Marisa prompted when Pao's humiliated silence had stretched on long enough.

"My friend . . ." Pao said. "Emma. Right." She shook her head, vowing to leave this uncharacteristically gullible moment in the past. "Franco tried to take her ring, and you said the ahogados were usually right behind you guys. So does that mean they got her? Is she in the void now?"

"I don't know," Marisa said. "If I did, I would tell you. It's not a bad theory, but there's no way to find out for sure."

"No way besides going into the rift ourselves."

Marisa's silence was answer enough. She was obviously still haunted by the memory of a boy who had tried to do just that. But Pao couldn't be bound by Franco's failures. If there was any chance Emma was still alive, and her *Don't give up on me* message in the dream was real, Pao had to know.

"We'll fight with you," Pao said decisively as she got to her feet. "If you'll still have us."

"Gladly," Marisa said, rising also. "And thank you."

"There's one condition," Pao said, matching the leader's determined gaze. "We'll fight with you until the solstice, but we won't be joining Los Niños de la Luz. We fight as ourselves—as 'tourists.' And in exchange, you tell me everything you know about the rift and the key. My main goal is still to rescue my friend. If I can find a way into the void, I'll have to take it."

Marisa nodded. "I understand. A good leader doesn't leave her people behind." Her face crumpled when she added, "I shouldn't have left Franco." She took a shuddering breath and then said, "You have my support."

When Marisa extended a hand for her to shake, Pao accepted it.

Finally, she was moving forward.

Pao shook Dante awake. He snorted as he emerged from sleep, and she laughed.

"Shut up," he said. "What do you want?"

"I want you to take out that fancy club of yours, hero boy. I just told Marisa we'd fight with the Niños de la Luz." She said the name of the group with as much fake, goofy gravitas as she could.

"For real?" Dante asked, sitting up, his hair flat on one side and sticking out like crazy on the other. This time, Pao smoothed it down for him, smiling when his cheeks flushed.

"For real. But there's more. I think I know where Emma is. So we fight until we can figure out how to get there, and then we go. Deal?"

"Of course deal!" He got to his feet, and Pao straightened up. They shifted awkwardly for a moment before Dante stepped forward and hugged her tight. "Sorry I said you were jealous."

"Sorry I called you a meathead."

When they finally let go, it felt like all was right with the world.

Which was how they should have known something awful was going to happen soon.

SEVENTEEN
Stupid Savior Complex

As the rest of the Niños woke around them, Pao filled in
Dante about most of what Marisa had told her: Franco, the jewelry,
and the rift. The way Franco had been drained by the ahogados
and Marisa had become the immortal leader of the Niños. She left
out the part about La Llorona—she'd dealt with enough embarrassment for one day.

"So you know where Emma is?" Dante asked when she'd finished, and Pao could feel him itching to draw the chancla. "What
are we waiting for?"

"Calm down, Superman," Pao said. "It's *possible* to get into
the rift on the summer solstice, but it's still not easy. Franco died
when he tried to go in without the key, so—"

"Where do we find this key?" Dante interrupted, and this
time he really did pull the slipper out of his pocket, thwacking it
against his palm until sparks flew into the sand and he dropped
it in surprise.

Pao raised an eyebrow but didn't say a word as he slid it back
into his pocket sheepishly.

"I don't know yet," she said, trying to keep the frustration out
of her voice. "Marisa has Franco's memories now, but it will take

her a while to sift through them, because he lived for so long. She said she'll tell me if she finds anything useful."

"Whoa," Dante said, running his hand over his shaggy head. "The guy you have a crush on dies and you have to eat fire and live forever with his memories? And here I thought *we* were having a bad week."

"It's a sacrifice," Pao said, and they were quiet for a long minute, not quite meeting each other's eyes. Pao wondered if he was thinking about crushes, too, then mentally berated herself for being so shallow at a time like this.

And when she wasn't thinking about Dante and crushes, she was remembering all the things she wasn't telling him, and that was so much worse.

The secrets between them were growing, multiplying like her mom always said they do. As the hopeful feeling of making progress toward Emma waned, Pao's worst fear took its place. And she was alone with it.

How could Pao tell Dante she might have corrupted magic in her? Some monster part that was making her constantly angry and sad and giving her these terrible dreams. She couldn't reveal that all this trouble might be her fault.

Maybe before, she could have. The old friend duo of Dante and Pao had been more resilient. But the new Dante and Pao had weird boy-girl spiderweb cracks in their windshield, caused by magical clubs and Naomis and secrets and loss.

Pao couldn't risk losing him, too. Especially now, when Emma needed them both.

"You're still here!" Sal came bounding toward them, tousle-haired and smiling.

Pao was grateful for the interruption.

"Does that mean you're staying?" he asked.

"For now," Pao said, smiling. "We heard you guys might need some help fighting monsters."

Sal surprised Pao by leaping forward and throwing his arms around her. She laughed, squeezing him back. "Thank you!" he said, and Pao had never felt less like a monster herself.

"As cheerful as this little scene is," Naomi drawled, walking up on the other side, "we haven't done anything worthy of celebration yet. Sal, cleanup duty." She jerked her thumb over her shoulder to where ten or more Niños were already gathering by the fire.

Pao and Dante started to join them, but Naomi shook her head. "Not you guys. Marisa wants you in the pit."

"The pit?" Pao asked, not missing the way Dante squared his shoulders and checked obviously for his chancla.

"It's where we train to fight monsters," Naomi said, looking Pao up and down. "It should be . . . fun."

"Fun for who?" Pao muttered as they followed her to the other side of the mess tent.

"Be nice," Dante said. But he checked for the chancla again.

"It's in your back pocket," Pao stage-whispered. "Right where you put it after you *dropped* it."

"Shut up," he retorted, blushing. But he didn't reach for it again.

The pit was exactly what it sounded like—a hole in the ground about six feet deep and the width of a boxing ring. Marisa was standing inside, up against the farthest wall. Pao imagined it must have taken weeks to dig this out, but with the desert dirt packed down so hard, it seemed like it had been here forever.

"Welcome," said Marisa, somehow looking rested even though Pao guessed the girl hadn't slept since before the Mano fight. Did eating burning coals make you immortal *and* immune to the need for basic things? She made a mental note to ask later.

Assuming they survived the day.

"Paola, why don't you choose a weapon?" Marisa offered, motioning behind her to a blanket on which several were laid out. "Dante, I doubt you'll find anything better than the one you're carrying, so you can practice with the Arma del Alma."

In honor of her recent truce with Dante, Pao decided not to make any more snarky comments.

But it wasn't easy.

The weapons looked like they'd seen better days: a rusty sword, a warped wooden staff, and a pair of pitted daggers. In all the novels Pao had read, the weapon a character chose somehow reflected their personality. But she didn't feel particularly drawn to any of these.

Everyone was staring at her, though, so Pao knelt down and tried to pick one, despite the disappointment that was settling in her stomach. Dante got to fight with this fancy legendary club that basically painted the word *hero* across his back, and Pao was going to be beside him with what, a long stick and a shopping bag?

"Pao?" Naomi said. "We're kind of burning daylight here."

"Yeah," Pao said, picking up the sword, whose tip snagged the corner of the blanket and pulled it back. "Wait, what's this?"

Under the blanket was a short, fat knife with black duct tape wrapped around its handle. It looked even more worn than the rest of the weapons, but for some reason, Pao could picture herself using it, twisting through a crowd of monsters, stabbing them until green goo covered everything.

"I want this one," she said, dropping the sword with a clang.

"Really?" Dante asked, wrinkling his nose.

"Really."

"It looks a little . . . dull. We can get that sharpened up for you after practice," Marisa said, her own long, graceful knife hanging at her hip, its surface swirling like an oil slick on the river. "Honestly, I'm not even sure where it came from. . . ."

She fell silent at a fierce look from Pao, who felt weirdly protective of the ugly little dagger.

"But I'm sure it'll be great!" Marisa added hastily. "Come on in, please, both of you."

Pao held her chin high, leaving Señora Mata's crocheted bag behind as she hopped into the pit. Dante dropped down beside her.

"Now, hold your weapons out in front of you."

Pao turned her attention to the knife, which fit perfectly in her grip. The tape was a little warm, like someone had just set it down. It was comforting in an odd, potentially germy kind of way.

Dante pulled out the chancla. The slipper was still folded from being in his pocket all night, and Pao tried not to laugh at its less-than-impressive appearance as he stood there in front of the three armed girls.

"Go ahead," said Naomi, watching him with shrewd eyes.

"Go ahead and what?" he asked, though it was pretty obvious what she wanted.

"Transform it."

"Right," Dante said, shifting a little back and forth, which Pao knew was a sign of nervousness. Her mean-spirited inner monologue went silent at once.

First he tightened his grip on it.

Then he took a deep breath, and kind of . . . squinted at it.

Nothing happened.

"It's okay," Pao said under her breath. "Just try to remember what it felt like before."

"I *know*," he snapped without looking at her, and Pao bristled. She was only trying to help. Boys were so sensitive.

Every muscle in Dante's body was tense. He was focusing so hard, he was starting to sweat at his hairline. But the slipper didn't grow fuzzy bunny ears, much less transform into a fearsome soul weapon.

"It's a state of mind," Marisa said, stepping closer, drawing her own knife in one fluid motion, like she'd done it a thousand times. Pao hadn't noticed before, but it had the same shimmer as Dante's club.

"Is that . . . ?" Pao asked before she could stop herself.

"It was Franco's," Marisa said simply.

His Arma del Alma. Pao had about three thousand questions for her. (Did it have a common form? How many of them were in the world? How had she gotten it from Franco? Was it as powerful as Dante's, or were they all different?) But Marisa's eyes were a little sad, so with considerable effort, Pao kept her queries to herself.

For now.

"What was happening when it changed before?" Naomi was asking Dante, joining Marisa at his side.

"That stupid Mano was about to kill us," Dante said, his face flushed now. "It just . . . happened."

After I came up with the idea to use it, Pao thought. Her snark was alive and well, but she didn't let it escape through her mouth.

"You were in danger," Marisa said, walking around him like a jungle cat stalking its prey. "You wanted to protect yourself, and your friend—"

At the last second, just when it seemed like she would lunge for Dante, Marisa changed direction and leaped toward Pao instead, her knife extended.

Pao's reflexes weren't bad—she'd always done okay in gym class and stuff—but nothing had prepared her for a sneak knife attack. She didn't even have time to step out of the way, let alone lift her dagger to ward off Marisa's blade.

As it turned out, she didn't have to. A wave of energy from behind her caught Marisa midstride, causing her to stumble and overcorrect, then sent her straight past Pao and into a neighboring cactus.

With her out of the way, Pao had a clear view of Dante, who was looking triumphantly at the fully transformed, shining club in his hand.

"I figured as much," said Marisa, picking a cactus spine out of her palm. "You savior types are all alike. It's never about self-preservation."

Dante suddenly seemed very interested in the toe of his left shoe—or basically anything that wasn't Pao's face.

Inside her, a storm of conflicting feelings swirled around—which was one of her least favorite things in the world. On the one hand, she was a little offended that Dante thought she needed to be protected. On the other, it was kind of nice that he had wanted to . . . wasn't it? Was she a bad feminist for thinking that?

Being best friends with a boy was so confusing sometimes.

Especially when the boy had nice hair and a magical weapon and kept holding your hand at key moments.

"We're not going to be able to threaten her life every time you need to draw your weapon," Marisa said, breaking the awkward silence between them. "So I suggest you figure out how to do it on your own."

"Got it," Dante said. He still wouldn't look at Pao.

"Okay, moving on," said Naomi, stepping forward. "You got lucky with that club during the fight against the Mano Pachona, but it won't help you with some of the other things the rift spits out. You'll need combat skills."

Pao tried to listen, but it was hard when she was too busy wondering what Naomi meant by "other things" . . . and whether Ondina's voice would save Pao from those, too. And if anyone would notice. And—

"The most important thing is to protect your face," Naomi said, interrupting Pao's thoughts. "Their number one priority will be to pull you toward the rift, but if they can't, they will go for your soul-stuff. Your life force. They attack the mouth, the eyes, the ears. So that's where you need to focus."

Dante raised his club higher, obscuring his face completely.

Naomi jabbed him in the stomach with the butt of her spear.

He doubled over, wheezing, and Pao didn't know if she wanted to laugh or punch Naomi. She settled on neither.

"That doesn't mean you can neglect the rest of your body,"

Naomi said, as if nothing had happened. Dante straightened up, wincing. "These things are monstrous, but they're not dumb. If they can't get to your face, they'll do whatever they can to bring you to the ground."

Pao remembered how helpless she'd felt when Dante was being dragged away, and her sense of panic when that hairy demon hand was choking the life out of her. The worst part of it was thinking that she had failed Emma. . . .

While she was recalling all this, Pao held her dagger loosely at her side. Naomi took advantage of her distraction and lunged at her without warning. But somehow, Pao was ready.

The fat little knife deflected Naomi's spear before it could reach Pao's face.

"Good," Naomi said, a little begrudgingly.

For the next half hour, Pao and Dante practiced repelling attacks—usually to the face and neck, but sometimes Naomi and Marisa switched tactics and went for the ankles, too. Pao tried to let go of her anticipation and keep all possibilities open.

She stopped more attacks than Dante did by a pretty wide margin, and soon Pao started to see telltale signs that it was bothering him. It was like they were back in his room playing a video game instead of training for combat in a mystical cactus field. His actions became erratic, and he paid more attention to her movements than his own.

Pao deflected another blow.

Dante took a second hit to the ribs.

We don't let people win out of pity, she reminded herself, and the next time Naomi left an opening, Pao charged into it, taking the older girl by surprise.

"Nice work!" she said once she had Pao on her heels again. "That's a good segue into offense. Let's huddle up."

Pao waited for Dante, who was engaged with Marisa on the other side of the pit. When they were done, he walked past her without a word.

Pao rolled her eyes. He didn't see, but Marisa did, and she raised an amused eyebrow.

"Okay," said Naomi, clearly in her element now, a few white curls straying from the knot on top of her head, her eyes blazing. "During the third quarter, offense is tough, because you never know what the rift is gonna spit out. Obviously you guys have seen the chupacabras and the Manos Pachonas, but that's not everything you'll have to face by a long shot."

In her mind's eye, Pao saw a parade of red-eyed rift creatures swarming them, wings and scales and talons and manes. She looked at the little knife and fought the urge to scream or run away.

"Now that we're so close to the solstice, things are getting dire. Whoever's in charge in there always sends the worst at us just before the rift closes, and since the solstice makes the veil even thinner, it means they can send the worst of the worst."

Marisa and Naomi exchanged a glance, and Pao wondered if they were thinking of Franco. Of the night the rift monsters had drained him of his life force and dragged him inside to die.

"What are they?" Dante said. "Giant lizards? Massive birds or something?" He choked up on his club, as if to prove he was ready.

Marisa shook her head. "The ahogados will be next," she said.

"What exactly—" Dante began.

Naomi, her eyes full of hate, didn't let him finish. "They're the corrupted souls of the kids who were taken. The ones who couldn't escape. And if you think you're ready for them, you're sadly mistaken."

Pao felt her stomach turn over. She pictured the kids from her English class, only venom-eyed and soulless. How was she supposed to kill them? They were just kids. . . .

For a moment, she was back on the black riverbank of her dream, her white hair hanging around her face, her own glowing green eyes searching for targets. But then, worse even than that, she saw Emma, her skin pale and translucent, her sparkly purple nails reaching for Pao's throat.

No. She's not dead. She hasn't been corrupted, Pao told herself. In her dream, Emma had still been corporeal, her voice still human. *She's alive, and I'm going to save her.*

But as Naomi got them into fighting formation, Ondina's taunting words came back to her unbidden. *Did she tell you that the solstice is your only chance to get through the rift?*

Suddenly, Pao was distracted, antsy. Her bargain to help the Niños seemed reckless when she was faced with the prospect of Emma's blue eyes turning green forever. She couldn't stand the idea of Emma's love for comics and Kit Kat bars and those springy shoelaces you don't have to tie being replaced by a horrible mindless hunger. . . .

But Pao couldn't get into the rift alone. This was still the best way forward.

Wasn't it?

Marisa got into a defensive stance, her water blade extended. Pao tried to listen to her instructions: Stay out of range so their arms can't get around you. Attack the mouths and hands before you're sucked dry or dragged off.

But her heart wasn't in it anymore. All she could think about was Emma, and Ondina's words. Pao was afraid she wouldn't be able to get inside the rift. Or worse, that there was something corrupted within her. That somehow the rift would find a way to use it to hurt her friends.

Dante was better on offense than he was on defense—he and Naomi were locked in battle a few yards away. Pao could tell Marisa was about to give her a talking-to about her lack of enthusiasm, but the sound of a horn echoing in the distance stopped them all.

"What does that mean?" Pao asked, alarmed by the way Naomi gave up the fight against Dante and headed straight for Marisa. It had to be something bad if Naomi was walking away from probable victory.

"It means we're under attack," she said when she reached them, taking her place at Marisa's right side.

"In the middle of the day?" Dante asked. "I thought you said they only came at night!"

"The first rule of monster-fighting is that there are no rules," Marisa said. "Especially not on the solstice." She looked at Naomi. "Sounds like the east quadrant."

"Do we all go?"

Marisa shook her head. "We'd be leaving the camp unprotected."

Naomi nodded, her eyes dark and serious, her white hair proof of all her previous battles. Of everything she had lost. "I'll get a team together and go," she said. "You stay here."

"I'm coming with you," Dante said, and Naomi nodded.

Pao wanted to strangle him for his stupid machismo. Instead, she said, "If he's going, I'm going."

But Naomi shook her head. "You stay here," she said, already turning away.

Pao saw red. "Excuse me," she said, "but I don't take orders from you. If he's going, I'm going." She felt her eyes narrow, her features twisting into what her mom called her *This means trouble* expression.

Naomi's face softened, and she stepped closer to Pao. "We need his club," she said. "But if you're there, he'll be distracted. It could be dangerous for both of you."

Pao had never felt more useless. "I'll keep out of his sight line," she said. "I'll . . ."

But there was no leniency in Naomi's eyes. "Stay with Marisa," she said. "Protect the camp. I'll make sure he comes back in one piece."

It took everything in Pao not to go on a rant about how girls shouldn't have to be responsible for boys' inability to control their stupid savior complexes. But this was life and death, and she had more to worry about than Dante's scattered focus.

White-haired, green-eyed, rage-filled Pao stared back at her from the dream world.

"Okay," Pao said quietly, before stomping across the ring to where Dante was practice-swinging his club. "If you get hurt, I will *kill* you." She shoved him squarely in the chest.

He stumbled a few steps, then crossed the distance back to her in one.

Instead of shoving her like she expected him to, he looked

at her uncertainly and then swooped in and kissed her on the cheek.

For possibly the first time in her life, Pao was stunned into silence.

"I'll be back soon," he said. "Stay safe."

He followed Naomi out of the ring before Pao could do more than gape like one of the Gila River's three-headed fish.

EIGHTEEN
How to Get That Supernatural Glow

After Dante and Naomi left, things happened quickly.

Marisa told Pao to keep close, then proceeded to move at lightning speed through the camp, providing instructions to those staying and words of encouragement to those in the group heading to the east quadrant.

Weapons were drawn and cleaned, and the bonfire was stoked until the flames seemed to lick the sky.

"If we're lucky, the ahogados won't make it this far," Marisa said, probably in reaction to the panic on Pao's face. "And your friend will be fine." She put a hand on Pao's shoulder.

Pao didn't shrug it off, but she took little comfort from it. Having to fight wasn't what she was worried about. She knew Dante. He wanted to be a hero, and now that he had found a purpose in this bizarre setting, he wouldn't quit in the face of danger. No matter what it meant for his own safety, he would fight to protect them all.

What he didn't seem to care about was that Pao would never be the same if something happened to him.

The horn blew again—two short blasts this time. Pao looked to Marisa, whose mouth was set in a grim line. "What does that mean?"

"It means they're heading for the boundary."

Pao's stomach sank even further. The ahogados weren't coming for them—they were going toward Silver Springs instead. Toward Dante's abuela, and Pao's mom, and every other unsuspecting person taking a walk, or reading a newspaper, or commuting to work.

"There's nothing we can do for now," said Marisa. "We just have to wait and hope that Naomi and the rest of them can defeat the forces or redirect them here. Our job is to protect the camp. If it falls . . ."

But she didn't have to finish. Pao understood. The camp was the last defense against the corrupted rift. If the Niños were scattered, or worse, there would be nothing to protect Silver Springs, or anything beyond it.

"Do you think they'll be okay?" Pao asked, trying not to let her voice waver.

"Naomi is the best fighter I've ever seen," Marisa said, not really answering the question.

The last of the Niños who were headed to the battlefront left a few minutes later. Marisa nodded at each of them in turn, touching their hands or shoulders, imparting strength. Pao stood beside her like a statue, trying not to think of Ondina's voice, or Dante out there, risking his life without protection, or that *kiss*. . . .

She tried, but she didn't succeed.

There were only five of them left at camp—Marisa, Pao, Sal, and two other kids she didn't know. Twins, a boy and a girl, probably eleven or so. It wasn't a very impressive line of defense if the worst happened and the camp was overrun by ahogados. Still, Pao thought it would be better if the enemy came to them.

At least the Niños knew what to expect. The residents of Silver Springs would be helpless.

Time dragged like at the end of a math test when you're done and everyone else is still working. Only this was much worse, because people were in danger. People like *Dante*. No one seemed to have anything to say. They all stood with their backs to the fire, facing east, squinting into the distance in case figures appeared in the haze.

Pao tried to recall all the drowning victims she had heard of over the years. Relatives and friends had mourned them, of course, but the Gila River was known to be dangerous, and people had come to accept the tragic accidents as part of living alongside it.

But would the casualties of its icy depths appear here today? White-haired and green-eyed and ready to drag other kids to their watery fates?

Would Emma be among them?

Who was responsible for setting all this in motion? Pao was used to having Franco's pixelated face on her mental dartboard, but now the target just had a big question mark in the middle. It couldn't be an ahogado—they were supposed to be terrifying but not intelligent. And obviously a severed hand wasn't leading the charge, nor was a slavering demon dog.

She thought of Franco's metaphor about the soldiers and the general.

If Pao's mom had gotten it wrong, and La Llorona wasn't the scariest thing this area had to offer, what was? Who was the rift's commander? And what did he want with all these kids?

Try as she might to keep the thought out of her head, Pao

couldn't help but see herself as one of the ahogados, as she'd been in her dream. Her own eyes glowing green, her white hair proof that everything human had been drained from her. She'd had one single thing on her mind: to grab hold of Dante and drag him into the water.

If only the dream had revealed whose orders she'd felt so compelled to carry out.

Beside her, Marisa appeared relaxed, her shoulders straight, weapon in hand. Her eyes—unlike everyone else's—were closed, as if she didn't need vision to know the spirits were coming. Pao remembered watching Marisa put the burning ember into her mouth. Marisa had said she was tying herself to the light, taking in the memories of past leaders, but what if she'd done more than make herself immortal that night? What if she'd inherited some superpowers, and she really *didn't* need her eyes to know what was happening to her Niños?

Pao wanted to ask about it, of course, but on the other hand, she didn't want to disturb what might be the last moments of peace Marisa got before the battle. The last moments any of them got.

The horn blew again, and Pao nearly jumped out of her skin. It was just one blast this time, long and mournful. Pao looked at Marisa, though a sinking feeling in her stomach told her that this sound didn't mean anything good.

"Someone's been taken," Marisa said without opening her eyes. "One of ours."

Dante's not one of yours, Pao thought, tears already stinging the backs of her eyes. *He's mine. And he's coming back. He promised.*

But she knew that was just wishful thinking. Dante was as much a Niño as Pao wasn't. They would blow the horn for him. And he would deserve the honor.

If time had been slow before, it seemed to have stopped now. Pao couldn't feel the campfire burning at her back anymore. Everything inside her was frozen. She tightened her grip on her knife. If one of those soulless things had taken Dante, she wouldn't rest until she had killed them all.

When three short, sharp blasts sounded, Pao didn't have to ask what they meant. It was evident in the shifting stances of the Niños around her. In the way Marisa opened her eyes at last, scanning the field in front of them like a well-trained warrior.

"They're coming," Pao said.

It wasn't a question.

No one corrected her.

She tried to remember everything she had learned in the pit that morning. Offense and defense, and weak points, and all the rest of it. But the only things in her head were the sound of that long, funereal horn blast and the vision of herself as a monster, dragging Dante toward the water.

Would the ahogados take her, too? Or would she be spared again?

And which was worse? If Dante *had* been taken, did she want to be spared?

"Up ahead!" shouted Marisa, and Pao snapped back to the present, shifting her gaze to where the leader was pointing. Through the mist—which had only grown thicker over the past hour—several silhouettes could be seen moving quickly toward them.

Were they ahogados? Or was it Dante and Naomi's group fleeing back to safety?

Marisa gave her the answer. "Defend the fire," she said in a low voice. "They will try to douse it."

Pao met her eyes and nodded once. The Manos had exploded when they met the flames. The creatures of the watery rift obviously couldn't withstand the heat. It was an advantage, and they had few enough of those.

There was no space in the air between Pao and Marisa for words of comfort. The horn was blowing frantically, the code long forgotten. These sounds meant panic and danger, and Pao was afraid, but the reason for her fear wasn't the same as everyone else's.

Her fear was that she was safe, and everyone else around her was in danger, and it was too late for her to tell them.

She had never felt so alone.

"They're almost here," Marisa said, and Pao could see the ahogados now. Their eyes and the auras around them glowed green through the haze. Green like the mist that had chased her out of Dante's apartment. Green like Pao's nightmares.

She scanned the shapes coming closer, hoping to recognize Dante's form among them, but so far it was only ghosts. Middle school–size kids with green eyes and white hair moving with the feral grace of animals. Of predators.

Marisa charged forward, her water knife cutting through them and taking chunks of their bodies with it. Like frozen smoke, their parts shattered in the air. Yet the ahogados fought on, limbless, half-headless, and still terrifying.

Pale lips curled back over teeth that were gapped, or crooked, or covered by metal braces. Pao didn't recognize any of the kids' faces, yet they were still familiar. They were children, like her, but with a horrible toxic glow where the light in their eyes should have been.

How many generations of drowned children were here today? Pao wondered as they swarmed. There were twenty of them—fifty, maybe more. With all the swirling and the shattering, Pao couldn't keep track long enough to count them.

Instead she looked for Dante, for the firelight glinting off his club, or for Emma, her Arizona tan gone pale, her glittering purple nails reaching for ankles or wrists or throats.

She didn't see either of them, and terror started to choke her. She stood paralyzed in the middle of the chaos, everyone around her screaming and fighting as Naomi's group caught up and the combat around the fire began in earnest.

Where is Dante? Pao's thoughts screamed. Her whole body screamed it. *Where is Dante?*

A ghost girl got too close, and Pao reacted instinctively, stabbing with her knife, watching the shock and anger on the monster's face as her wrist shattered, her pale hand left dangling by only a thin strip of skin.

Is it skin? Pao wondered almost hysterically, but this was no time to question the biological makeup of ghosts. Another one was coming at her—a boy, taller than Pao and broader in the shoulders.

This time, her knife was too slow. He got ahold of her arm, and the shock of his touch caused her to drop the dagger. She pulled with all her strength, twisting and writhing in his grip, an unnatural cold burning into her skin until she couldn't tell heat from ice and she felt dizzy.

"Help me!" she tried to scream, but her vocal cords were frozen, too.

The boy started to drag her away from the fire, and though she fought as hard as she could, Pao was no match for his supernatural strength.

Just give in, said a voice in her head. Was it her subconscious? *Let them take you. There's a place for you here. . . . The Source takes care of its own. . . .*

"No," Pao managed to squeak. Her voice was weak and feeble, and she was oh so tired.

Just when the phantom was about to pull Pao outside the protective circle of firelight, Naomi slammed into him, her staff glinting in the haze as she took chunks off his body. At last, he collapsed in a heap.

"You okay?" she asked Pao.

"Dante . . ." Pao said through frozen lips. "Is Dante . . . ?"

The defeated look on Naomi's face was all the answer Pao needed.

Behind them, someone screamed, and Naomi was already moving toward the commotion. She paused to put a hand on Pao's shoulder. "Get back to the fire, and don't stand still," Naomi said, and then she was gone.

Pao tried to stay focused and alert, but all she could think of was Dante. Dante being dragged away, the horn blowing long and low for him. Dante taken to wherever Emma had gone.

Gone. Gone. Gone.

That's when the second ghost grabbed her. A girl this time, and she was faster than the last. Her arms locked around Pao's middle as she dragged her away from the warmth of the flames.

Any minute now, Pao thought. Any minute the voice would

come to her rescue, tell the ahogada to let her go. But instead, another specter joined in, clutching Pao's legs and pulling her hard to the ground, knocking the breath from her lungs.

A third one came then, sneering and slit-eyed, putting his clammy hands around Pao's throat. Where was that stupid voice? Where was Ondina? Wasn't Pao monster enough to be spared?

Like the faint smell of smoke, doubt wafted into her head. What if she was wrong? What if no one was going to save her this time?

Her knife was long gone, but the shopping bag was still on Pao's shoulder. It was all she had.

Around her, everyone was engaged in battle. Out of the corner of her eye, she could see Marisa swinging her water knife with abandon, and Naomi was letting loose a war cry somewhere nearby. There was no one to save her on either side. She was alone, and losing ground.

With her one free hand, Pao dug into the bag and pulled out the flashlight. She wasn't even sure what she planned to do with it—she just felt better holding it than being unarmed. Perhaps she could hit one of the ahogados in the head with it. Or shine the light in their eyes. Maybe, if she was lucky, they would be stunned enough to let her go.

But when she clicked the on button, something else happened:

Warmth returned to her body, too fast, like she had put cold hands under scalding water coming from the faucet. She almost lost her grip on the plastic handle, but she had learned her lesson from losing the knife, and she held on to it for dear life.

As the warmth spread through her arms and legs, the ahogados dragging her seemed to slow. Or was that just her imagination? Against the green mist swirling around her, Pao's skin began to glow golden.

The ghost boy let go of her legs with a furious hiss, like he'd been burned. But there were still two ahogados left.

The warmth continued to travel, spreading to her torso and pooling in her stomach. The girl hugging her middle let go as well. As Pao glowed, she felt the sharp pulling sensation from her dream deep in her chest. It hurt, and pain worsened as the beam got brighter.

But Pao knew she shouldn't let go of the flashlight. Not even if it turned into a supernova.

Confused, looking to his mates for cues, the third ahogado loosened his grip around her neck, and Pao lay on the ground limp with relief, the toy hot in her hand like it had just been taken out of the oven.

Her body continued to blaze until it couldn't hold the light inside anymore. The heat in her veins dissipated as a glow radiated out from her center. Soon she was surrounded by a translucent golden sphere that repelled the ahogados, leaving only the Niños within its brilliant bubble.

Pao sat up, her vision swimming, her extremities growing cold as the sphere continued to grow, robbing vital energy from her as it did so. But it was working. Outside the circle of its glow, she could see the ahogados fleeing. Their wails and screams pierced the night, and the sound was familiar to Pao, though she couldn't quite remember where she'd heard it before. . . .

In a matter of minutes, the battle was over, and all Pao could hear was the crackling of the fire. Using the last of her strength, she clicked off the flashlight, and the glow disappeared, taking the warmth with it.

Her whole body trembled as she pushed herself to stand. Around her, every last one of the Niños was looking at her, thunderstruck.

"Dante . . ." Pao said, feeling her knees buckle just before everything went black.

NINETEEN

La Hija de Lágrimas

When Pao came to, she was lying on glittering black sand, her mouth and throat full of water.

She rolled over and retched, the weedy taste of the river washing over her tongue as she gasped for air. Her clothes and hair were soaking wet, like she'd nearly drowned, and her veins looked greenish under her washed-out skin.

The bloodred sun was setting over the river.

Pao felt a wave of dread wash over her.

She was having another dream, and somewhere, in "real life," the Niños were in trouble. Dante was gone. And he and Emma were running out of time.

"Just haaaad to play the hero, didn't you."

Great, Pao thought, struggling to sit up. She coughed, each spasm making her chest ache. "Not . . . you . . ." she said, the words burning her throat on their way out.

"Always so gracious," said Ondina from her seated position near Pao's feet. Her hair seemed to drift eerily around her shoulders, and her eyes were somehow more absorbing than usual, like the girl was becoming less human every time Pao saw her. "It's no wonder your friends keep disappearing. Who'd want to hang around with someone who has such a bad attitude?"

"My friends are disappearing because *your friends are taking them*," Pao said, her anger burning through, pushing her to her feet. "Where is Dante?" she asked, getting closer to Ondina than she'd ever been, almost nose-to-nose.

She smelled like the river—fishy and metallic and cold.

"Where's Dante?" Ondina parroted, her voice high and reedy. *"Where's Emma?"*

"Shut up," Pao growled.

"Who am I going to sit with at lunch now? Oh, woe is me!"

"I said, shut *up!*" Pao shoved Ondina in the chest with both palms.

She shouldn't have been surprised to find Ondina solid, especially after Pao's very physical tangle with the ahogados, but the black-clad girl was so different from them, part of Pao had expected her hands to pass right through.

But they didn't, and Ondina stumbled back, stabilizing herself just before she fell, adjusting the high collar of her dress with a snooty expression and extracting several strands of black hair from her pouty little mouth. "Pushing me isn't going to solve your problems."

"Then what is?" Pao asked, at the end of her rope. "I fought with the Niños today because they *trusted* me, they told me things—they didn't just show up in my dreams and speak in riddles!" She took a deep breath. "You know where Emma and Dante are, I know you do. So tell me. Just *tell me!* Or maybe I'll let one of those monsters drag me to wherever they're always trying to take me and find out for myself."

"No!" Ondina shouted, with a ferocity that flashed like lightning, surprising them both. "If you do that . . . You can't do that, do you understand me? There's no getting in that way. Not for you."

"How *do* I get in, then?"

"It's so obvious," Ondina said, rolling her too-large eyes, her thick eyebrows adding extra disapproval to the expression. "You have all the information at your fingertips—just *use your brain*."

"You *can't* tell me, can you?" Pao asked, one corner of the puzzle starting to come together. "You act like you're this big badass, but you're really just a scared little girl with puppet strings still attached."

She could tell she'd hit a nerve when Ondina didn't even attempt a snarky comeback.

"Is it the ahogados?" Pao asked. "Er, the other ones, anyway? Do they control you?"

Ondina scoffed, flipping back her curls with a pale hand. "Please. Those brainless things? All they can do is follow orders. And for the last time, I'm not one of them."

"Then what *are* you?" Pao asked, knowing she was close to figuring it out from the electricity that sparked between her synapses. It was the feeling she always got when she was about to make a big breakthrough, her favorite feeling in the world.

Ondina's eyes flashed, and in them Pao could see something more than just a petulant dream girl who showed up at the worst times. Something timeless and hungry and terrifying. "La Hija de Lágrimas," Ondina said, her voice flat and expressionless. "That's what they call me."

Once again, Pao's faulty Spanish was going to be the end of her. *Hija* was *daughter*, but *lágrimas*? Pao didn't think she'd ever heard that word before.

"Whose orders?" she asked, seeing Ondina in a new light. Was *she* the general? "Who do the ahogados follow?"

For the first time, Pao detected fear in Ondina's expression. It was fleeting, but it was there.

Ondina wasn't the general, but she knew who was.

"Who is it?" Pao asked, stepping closer to her again. "They know where Emma and Dante are. They're responsible for all of this, so *who is it?*"

"You're running out of time," Ondina snapped. "That isn't important. Don't ask yourself who . . . ask yourself *how. . . .*"

Her voice was fainter now, and she began to shimmer in the air.

"Don't you dare!" Pao said, grabbing her by the shoulders, their faces closer than they'd ever been. Ondina's skin was shockingly cold through the fabric of her dress. "Don't you dare disappear before you tell me what's happening. Not this time."

"Silly girl," Ondina said, her gaze far away now. "Silly, stupid girl."

She was gone before the last word was even all the way out, and Pao's hands clutched at nothing while the landscape in front of her evaporated again.

Something jerked Pao to the side and she landed on her back again—this time on sand as white as bone. Around her, black moss hung in curtains from cacti ten feet tall. The river was green again, but in front of her, yawning, gaping, terrifying, was a giant mouth.

Pao screamed like she hadn't in a dream since elementary school. She screamed in a way that told her she was screaming in real life, too.

The mouth opened wider, and she could see down its long black throat. That fishing-hook feeling was back, tugging at her chest, pulling and pulling until Pao's shoes were pressed against a massive tongue and the teeth were surrounding her and its hot breathing was threatening to suck her in.

But just before the mouth swallowed her whole, everything went still.

And, as if her body were being controlled by puppet strings, Pao got to her feet and walked calmly into the darkness.

This time when Pao woke up, she knew she was really back.

Back in her body, back at the Niños' camp. Her eyesight was blurry at first, but it didn't take long for faces to start coming into focus.

She was on the ground, she knew that much. Marisa's braids were the first thing she identified, followed by Naomi's wide brown eyes and tangle of white curls. Pao coughed, then pushed herself up to sitting even though every muscle in her body screamed at her to stop.

"Are you okay?" Marisa asked, but there was a strange edge to her voice.

Pao's memory came back in snippets. The ghost kids hanging on to her . . . the flashlight turning on . . .

That's when Pao realized—her hands were empty.

"Where's my flashlight?" she asked, her voice hoarse, every word scraping her throat like sandpaper.

No one answered.

"Where is it?" she asked again, finally upright. She didn't like the way they were looking at her. "I need it back."

"The key, you mean," Naomi said, and Marisa elbowed her to shut her up.

"What?" Pao asked, but Naomi's words, combined with what had just happened with the flashlight and what she knew of Franco's theories, finally brought it all together. "The key . . ."

"You had it the whole time," Marisa said quietly. "Why didn't you tell us?"

Suddenly, Pao was very uncomfortable on the ground with the two of them standing over her. She pushed herself to standing instead, not quite as tall as them, but meeting them as equals at least.

"I didn't know," Pao said honestly. "Not until . . ."

Marisa nodded, but Naomi looked skeptical. "You didn't *know*?" she asked. "When you followed it here? When you used it against the ahogados? What were you doing, then?"

"Honestly?" Pao said, her head pounding. "I was kind of just making things up as I went along." That much, at least, was true. "All I've ever wanted to do is find my friend."

Naomi scoffed. Marisa's expression didn't change.

"Tell me what happened," Pao said, before they could ask her any more questions about the flashlight.

"They retreated," Marisa said, her voice faraway sounding. "The light made them let go of you and anyone else they were holding, and they ran off. The scouts are sweeping the area now, but they're gone."

"And Dante?" Pao asked, barely getting his name out.

Naomi's sneer softened, if only just a little. "He fought bravely," she said, shaking her head. "We weren't prepared. We didn't know. . . ."

"Was he killed, or taken?" Pao asked, not needing to know how Naomi felt or what she'd failed to account for.

The silence went on for a heartbeat longer than Pao could stand.

"Naomi! Was he killed or taken?"

Naomi looked at Marisa, who nodded slightly.

"Taken," Naomi said. "I'm so sorry, P—"

"I want my flashlight," Pao said, cutting her off. "Now."

"We can't let you—" Marisa began, but Pao didn't let her finish, either.

"You don't have the authority to stop me," Pao said. "We had a deal, remember?"

"The deal has changed," Marisa said, the lines of her face hard. She was a leader now, not a friend. She wasn't going to negotiate. "We can't let the key go now. Not when it can protect us through the solstice."

"You promised!" Pao shouted, trying to stay standing, even though her head was spinning from exhaustion and grief. "You told me you would help me. . . ." She wanted to believe Marisa was no longer the evil girl who had tormented her in school, but all she could hear were Ondina's words, cautioning her not to trust Marisa, telling her the solstice was her only chance to get Emma back.

And now Marisa was trying to keep her from doing just that.

You don't belong with them, Ondina had said. And maybe she'd been right. Because Pao was pretty sure that the giant, yawning black mouth had been the rift. And she was all the way sure she knew how to get into it.

"I know what you're thinking, Pao," said Marisa. "But it won't work. You can't get through. And even if you could, you don't know what you'd be up against in there. None of us do."

"It doesn't matter," Pao said. "I can't just sit here and let the window close. Not while my friends need me."

"*We* need you!" Naomi said, the words exploding like a ball of flame. "You saw what that light can do! You could protect the whole camp with it! Keep the monsters at bay!"

But Pao was already shaking her head. "And then what?" she asked. "We drive them back, we lose some friends, and then it all happens again next month? Next year? It's time to deal with the rift once and for all. To put an end to this. Because one day, you won't be able to stop the monsters. It may not be today, or tomorrow, or even for another hundred years, but eventually they'll get through. And then Silver Springs will be gone. The whole *world* will be gone."

No one said a word.

"Give me my flashlight, please."

Neither girl moved.

"The key takes something from you," Marisa said. "All magic has a price. You can't use it again so soon or you could—"

"I don't have a choice!" Pao exploded. "The solstice starts in a few hours! I don't know how long it'll take me to find the rift, or how hard it'll be to get in. I don't have time to waste."

"Would you just *look* at yourself?" Naomi said, pulling a compact mirror out of her back pocket and holding it up to Pao. "You're not invincible. And you won't be of any use to anyone once you turn into one of them."

Pao took the mirror, her hands strangely steady. Her face was the same—same round cheeks, same long nose. Same heavy eyebrows, threatening to meet in the middle.

Only now, the left brow was pure white.

She pulled the mirror a little farther away from her face and surveyed the full picture calmly. It wasn't just her eyebrow. One of her braids, from the part to the tip, was white, too. Like she was a little brown Cruella de Vil minus the puppy-skin coat.

"Oh," said Pao, her voice sounding very far away. She remembered the pulling feeling in her chest, the way the heat had spread through her, the way she'd held on to the flashlight despite the pain. Was this the result?

And whatever it was, hadn't it been worth it? She'd saved the camp, saved herself. . . .

"The key," Marisa said again. "It draws energy from you to power it. Franco said—"

"I get it," Pao replied, not wanting to talk about Franco or what had happened to him. Not when she needed to be able to do what he did and survive. "It drains you, just like the ahogados do."

Pao's brain was just as tired as her body, but even so, something was sparking there. If the flashlight drew from her life force to repel the ahogados, were the ahogados powering themselves by drawing energy from the living?

From Emma, said a voice in her head. *From Dante.*

"Whatever you decide, you have to rest first," said Naomi, her voice pitched too high, trying to sound concerned and sweet.

It was unnatural, and Pao didn't trust it. But she would have to play along for now. She was outnumbered and weak, and she was running out of time.

"You're right," she said, in just as saccharine a tone. "I'll rest awhile, if that's okay."

"Of course," said Marisa, too quickly. "Here, lie down in one of the tents. We'll keep watch in case the ahogados come back."

Pao nodded, allowing herself to be led to the tent full of cots—the one Naomi had banished them to before the Manos Pachonas attacked. Dante had been with her then. Pao had argued with him about *soccer*, of all things. And now—

"Here," said Naomi, gesturing to a cot near the back. "We'll wake you in an hour, and then we'll decide what to do."

Pao nodded again, even though she knew there was nothing to be decided. She would lull them into a false sense of security, and then she would find her flashlight and get out of here. She would do what she had to do.

She would pretend to sleep.

She only had to stay awake a little longer.

Just a little . . .

It was dark when Pao opened her eyes again. She had slept without dreaming. Had the flashlight stolen her dreams? Or had she just seen enough for one day?

Her eye itched, and she reached up to scratch it.

At least, she tried to.

Pao's wrist was tied to the side of the bed, as was her other one, and both her ankles.

"Let me go!" she shouted. But her voice was all but gone, too.

Her heart was racing, her thoughts struggling to catch up with her reality. They had made her their prisoner. But why?

Had they started to suspect her connection with the corrupted magic? Had they restrained her for their own safety?

If they did, you can hardly blame them, said her critical inner voice, but something was telling Pao that wasn't the reason.

She pulled again at the ropes, but they didn't give, even a

little. Her heart wouldn't slow down, and her thoughts were racing, too.

Was it dark only inside the tent, or had night really fallen? If it had, she had a lot less time than she'd planned on. The solstice could be over by now, for all she knew. She was alone, weaponless, and powerless. . . .

Someone sniffed in the darkness, and Pao's pulse reacted, pounding faster still.

She wasn't alone after all.

"Who's there?" she whispered, and the cot beside her creaked. A shape moved in the darkness. "Who is it?" She was trapped. If the person wanted to hurt her, there was nothing she could do to stop them.

Pao closed her eyes, then opened them again, hoping to catch even the faintest light from outside to see who was approaching with shuffling footsteps.

"I may not be armed, but I can still scream," Pao said, hoping it was true, that her ravaged throat would obey.

"Please don't scream."

The voice was quiet, timid, the accent familiar as home. Every muscle in Pao's body relaxed.

"Sal?" she asked, her voice finally catching, giving her a little more volume than a whisper.

"Shhh," he said, stepping close enough that she could see the lines of his face. "They don't know I'm here. . . . And if they found out, they'd . . ." He trailed off, his eyes darting every which way in the darkness.

"What's happening, Sal?" Pao asked, her whisper as quiet as she could make it. "Why am I in here?"

"They said . . ." Sal began, then took a shaky breath. "They said you'd leave with the key. That it was our only hope. They said you were . . . un poco loca from being sad and you were going to put yourself—and all of us—in . . . danger."

Pao was suddenly so mad there could have been steam coming from her ears. "So I'm crazy, huh? And they're keeping me and my flashlight hostage so I don't endanger us all. That's just great. Totally true and not at all self-serving and just totally, *totally great."*

"Paola?" Sal asked, his voice tiny.

"Yeah?"

"I didn't believe them." He held out her flashlight.

Before she could process what was happening, Sal was untying her left wrist.

"Sal, what are you doing?" Pao asked. "You can't!"

"I'm doing what is right," he said, focused on undoing the knots. "You are not loca. You are brave, and your friends need you. It's not right for Marisa to take your things. To take you . . ." He choked up then, his hands going still on the rope until he could breathe again. "People shouldn't be taken," he said firmly, and then her arm was free.

As he worked on her other wrist, Pao struggled not to tear up. This boy had been through so much. They'd all been through so much—the invisible kids. The stuck-in-between kids.

Maybe she didn't agree with the way they'd gone about it, but could Pao really blame Naomi and Marisa for wanting to protect the Niños? For not wanting their best chance of survival to disappear on what they assumed to be a suicide mission?

"I'll come back," Pao said to Sal as he finally freed her other hand. "I'll find my friends, and we'll return before the rift closes."

It was a big promise, she knew. Even if she made it to the rift by midnight, got inside, figured out what was causing all the supernatural strife, and found Dante and Emma . . . there was no guarantee she'd make it back out before the solstice was over. Before they were all trapped in the rift, and the key was trapped with them.

"I believe you," Sal said, and together they worked to untie her legs.

Within a minute, Pao was on her feet, her head swimming from exhaustion, hunger, and the key's drain on her. She would have to be careful. If her hair color was any indication, she would only be able to use it once more—and even then there was every chance it would drain her completely. There was no time to test the way it worked, no time for hypotheses or trial runs.

Would she turn into an ahogada? Or was this different? Maybe she would just die. Was that what had happened to Franco?

Somehow, Pao felt like she was still missing part of that story.

But she had the key, and he hadn't, so maybe . . . just maybe . . .

Pao took a step and immediately tripped over something bunched up at her feet. She stood again, irritated . . . until she realized what it was—her shopping bag. The one Señora Mata had given to her like a million years ago. The bottle of Florida Water was still inside, and Sal was handing her the flashlight.

"You have to go now," he said. "Before they come back. You have to go."

"Thank you," Pao said, taking the flashlight—the *key*—from him and examining it closely. It had a long crack down one side that hadn't been there before, but otherwise it was intact. Pao flicked it on and off experimentally, wondering if she'd feel it, the pull on her life force.

All she felt was her stomach growling.

But at least the light still worked.

"Here," said Sal, pulling a small backpack off his shoulders and offering it to her. "Food, water, supplies. You will need these. Marisa says it's a long way."

"Sal . . . I wouldn't have been able to do any of this without you," Pao said, touched by his kindness. "How can I ever thank you?"

"Do a good job, Paola Santiago," he said in a tone way too solemn for an eight-year-old. "Then come back and help us kill the monsters."

"If I do a good job, Sal, there won't be any more monsters to kill."

He nodded only slightly, like he didn't really believe her, and then hugged her unexpectedly. When he let go, she heard voices and footsteps outside the tent. Pao's pulse sped up.

"Go!" Sal said, smiling once more as he scampered outside.

There was no time to wonder what Marisa would do to him when she found out he'd let her go. But Sal wasn't the same boy who'd had his parents taken away six months before. He was strong now, and she would have to be, too.

She clicked the flashlight on again and the beam was clear and strong, pointing just a little to her left. Turning her sneakers to follow, Pao let the light lead her, away from the fire and the camp, away from the people who were trying to protect her world.

TWENTY

Someone Get This Paranormal Beast a Breath Mint

Pao followed the beam for what felt like an hour without stopping, wanting to make sure she left the firelight of camp far behind before she rested.

Fear and doubt were creeping into her mind like a fog, stealing the spring from her steps, urging her to turn back, but she kept going.

Finally, when she was sure she was alone in the field, she sank to the ground on her trembling legs and put her head in her hands.

What had she done, leaving the protection of the camp behind? Taking the key, leaving the Niños defenseless. Pao's breath came in shorter and shorter gasps, and she struggled to regain control. This far away from Marisa's capable attitude and Naomi's attack power, Pao felt impossibly small and defenseless.

The sky seemed to agree with her, opening up completely for the first time, revealing its distant, indifferent stars in glimmering clusters you could almost never see from Silver Springs.

Pao tried to feel comforted by the constellations, as she had so often before. But her problems were no longer those of an almost seventh grader stuck in a tiny apartment with her superstitious mom. Before, her world had been too small. The stars had encouraged her with the promise of more.

Now her world was too big, too full of impossible problems that rested on only her shoulders. Now, though she was reluctant to admit it, she wanted nothing more than to return to her old life.

But there was no going back, and the clock didn't wait for uncertainty. The solstice began tonight, and from the moment midnight hit, she'd have twenty-four hours to get into the rift, rescue her friends, save the world, and get back out.

The moon was sinking. Midnight was coming too fast. And Pao still didn't know any more than she had when she'd left camp.

It doesn't matter, she told herself, rubbing her tired eyes and getting back to her feet. Adventures, she was learning, weren't really about what you knew. They were about what you were willing to do.

In the shopping bag on her shoulder, the Florida Water bottle lay on the bottom, the sole item remaining. Pao reached in and pulled it out. The cologne hadn't worked on the monsters, but Pao remembered Dante splashing it on them before they left the apartment. It had made her skin burn when the apartment filled with green light.

She'd never liked its scent, but she sprinkled it on herself anyway, surprised to find she didn't mind it as much as she used to. It smelled like Señora Mata . . . her mom's cards . . . Dante's room. It smelled like home.

The reminder of it made her feel stronger.

Maybe home wasn't an apartment with burn marks in the shag carpeting and a fridge full of condiments and tinctures. Maybe it wasn't candles and rosaries and depictions of saints.

Maybe home was something you carried with you. Something you could call on, even if you couldn't go back to it.

It was with that comforting thought, the smell of the Florida Water in her nose, and the flashlight warm in her hand, that Pao forged ahead, toward whatever was next.

The key's beam changed directions seemingly at random, but Pao had learned her lesson about underestimating it, so she followed, even when it made no sense.

She walked in circles. She doubled back. She went left for what felt like hours only to take three right turns in a row. But the landscape kept changing, even when the path seemed the same, and soon the cacti were growing taller and more spindly, their silhouettes looking skeletal and creepy against the starless night sky.

How long had it been since she and Dante had first wandered into the cactus field? Pao wondered. How long since the Mano Pachona had let her go? How long since she'd yelled at her best friend for wanting to be a hero?

How long since he'd kissed her and she'd lost him?

Pao didn't have the answers, so she walked. She followed the flashlight when it bent around her body, urging her back the way she'd just come. She walked because she didn't know where Dante was, or Emma, or if they were still alive.

She walked because there was, even now, something angry and sharp inside her. Something that had been born with the first dream she'd ever had about the riverbank. Something that might have been responsible for Emma's disappearance and all that had come crashing into their lives after that.

She walked until the sky started to lighten and the flashlight's beam began to fade. Her legs were just starting to burn with the strain when she heard it, somewhere up ahead—a low growl. Low enough for Pao to imagine it was coming from a very large animal.

Her heart sped up, beating so hard she was afraid the beast would be able to hear it. If this key was really on her side, shouldn't it have steered her away from danger?

When she used the flashlight as a compass, it didn't seem to drain her, but as a weapon, it definitely would. If Marisa's story was any indication, she could only risk using it once more, and she'd need one heck of a light blast from it to get past the ahogados and into the rift.

So whatever monster was here, she would have to face it with just her knife and what little combat training she'd picked up.

As if on cue, the creature growled again, and Pao heard a scratching sound, too. She stopped walking and drew her dagger, pointing the flashlight at the ground and turning in slow circles so she wouldn't be surprised when the beast came close enough for her to see.

In that moment, for the first time since she was a little girl, Pao almost wished she'd had a father. Someone to teach her where the thumb goes when you throw a punch (inside or outside, she wasn't sure which) or what to do if a bear attacks you in the woods.

But today it was just Pao, who had been trained by her mom in ghostly drowning and dismemberment when she was too young to understand what they were.

Get it together, she told herself. *This is hardly the time to be waxing nostalgic about childhood.*

Up ahead, there was a fallen cactus, so ancient that its husk looked as hard as rock. *Do cacti petrify?* Pao wondered, but she reined herself in again. Biological queries about the flora and fauna of the area weren't top priority right at this moment, either.

The growl sounded again, and now that she was closer, Pao could hear an echoey quality to it. Either that, or there was more than one of whatever it was.

She tightened her grip on the knife, remembering the way the ahogado had shattered when she'd stabbed it. If she was lucky, it would be just as effective on the monster lurking here. For a second, Pao thought of the way Marisa must have looked standing in front of the rift with Franco, holding her knife futilely when her world was about to come crashing down.

You'll be way better than that, Pao told herself. But the idea was too hollow to be much of a comfort.

The growling intensified, reacting to her footsteps, though she'd tried to keep them as quiet as she could. Maybe this creature had exceptional hearing, like some kind of mutant bird, or rodent. . . .

Pao shuddered, but she didn't stop walking forward. This was what she had signed up for. She would just have to hope she was equal to it.

The cactus husk was near enough to kick, and there was no doubt about it—the growling was coming from inside. But now that she was practically on top of it, the sound had changed. It was more of a yelp than a growl. Maybe the creature was in trouble. Regardless, she didn't let her guard down. There were plenty of terrifying things that yelped . . . weren't there?

The yelping turned into whimpering. Pao walked around the

fallen cactus until she reached its bottom. The thing had to be ten feet long. Did the weird magic energy in the field make them grow abnormally tall?

She was two yards from the cactus. Then one. Then just a couple of feet. Pao's pulse was kicking like a bass drum across the entire surface of her skin. Was this it? Was she about to die, right now, before she ever reached the rift?

Before she ever found out if she was possessed by some kind of terrible magic?

When she was three steps away, the creature fell silent. Whatever it was, it knew Pao was there.

Two steps. The darkness inside the hollow cactus husk was absolute. Pao couldn't see a thing.

One step. Wait . . . was something glimmering in there? It looked like an emerald. . . .

Pao knelt down at the opening just before the yawning tunnel's entrance exploded in a whirl of fur and teeth and glowing green eyes.

She screamed, falling onto her butt with an undignified thump, swinging fists and shopping bag and knife and flashlight indiscriminately as the thing finally made contact.

But it didn't sink its terrifying fangs into her flesh, or peck at her with some mutated beak, or hiss at her before it wrapped its body around her torso. . . .

In fact, when Pao calmed down enough to realize she *wasn't* being devoured, she realized that the thing—which was barely bigger than the neighborhood cat back home—seemed to be . . . *licking* her.

"Ewww, get off!" she shrieked, scrabbling back across the dirt in a sort of panicked crab walk as the thing bounded after her, its black tongue hanging out of its mouth in a goofy way totally unbefitting a terrifying paranormal beast.

With a foot or two of space between them—space the creature was trying its hardest to close as Pao held it off with her foot—she could see it more clearly. Its fur was midnight black, and glossy—though it was dirty and ragged in places—and it seemed to have several cactus spines poking out of its body.

Its eyes were green and glowing like the other rift monsters—but these were round and curious, almost playful. Along its back were two ridges of tentacle-like protrusions barely the length of Pao's pinkie finger.

Though it bore little resemblance to the one that had almost taken off her face the day before, there was no doubt about it—this was a chupacabra.

Correction, Pao thought as the creature finally overcame her sneaker to barrel back into her lap, a chupacabra *puppy*.

"Get off me!" she screeched again, as the pup resumed its enthusiastic—and incredibly smelly—licking of every inch of her exposed skin. But her heart wasn't really in the scolding. In fact, with its big feet and playful yelps and still-floppy ears, the thing was actually sort of cute.

"Okay, okay," she said, scratching behind its ears, avoiding a particularly scaly spot in favor of the familiar dog-like fur. It was definitely a he, she decided. Not nearly enough survival instinct to be a female. "It's okay, little guy. What are you doing out here all alone?"

As if in response, the chupacabra puppy howled a sad little howl.

Pao's heart leaped into her throat. "No, no," she said, having a sudden vision of a pack of bloodthirsty void beasts bearing down on her, thinking she'd stolen their baby. "Shh, it's okay."

She gathered the floppy thing in her arms and held him close to her chest, making shushing, soothing sounds as he wriggled himself into a more comfortable position.

Before two minutes had passed, he was fast asleep.

Pao leaned back against the petrified cactus, which, thankfully, had lost most of its spines, and let the puppy sleep. He was hideous, she thought. Dangerous. A monster. But he trusted her, and right now that was enough to make up for the rest.

Isn't that what everyone wants? Pao asked herself. *To be loved even though they're kind of a monster?*

The thought should have made her scoff. Instead, it almost made her cry.

"Who cares?" she said out loud. "There's no one here."

In her arms, the chupacabra puppy snorted in his sleep.

"Well, except for you . . ." Pao had come up with a list of puppy names a mile long when she was trying to convince her mom to get her a dog, but right now she couldn't remember a single one of them. And plus, those names had been for cute yellow or brown puppies from the pound. Not a demon hell beast from a malevolent magic void.

As she racked her brain, all she could think of was the only dog that had ever lived in the Riverside Palace apartments. He'd been a massive rottweiler named Spooky, and when he barked at all hours of the night, Dante's abuela used to scream down at him, "Callate, Bruto!"

Pao had always giggled at how out of sorts it made Señora

Mata, that barking dog. He hadn't been so bad, really. But Pao had always secretly thought Spooky was a terrible name for him. He was fearsome, and Spooky was not a fearsome name.

"Bruto . . ." Pao said thoughtfully, stroking the little spot on his head where fur grew over the weird scales. "Is that your name? Bruto?"

He cracked open one eye, which glowed green, and then every muscle in him tensed joyfully as he resumed his enthusiastic licking.

"Okay, okay!" Pao said, standing up, laughing for the first time since Dante had disappeared. "Bruto it is. Now come on, make yourself useful."

Pao took out the flashlight and clicked it on. But Bruto was not a fan. He ran in circles around her, yipping and yapping at the thing, growling at it like it was another animal and not just an inanimate object.

"What's the matter?" she asked, shining the light at him. But, of course, the beam continued to point to her left, even as his yapping became a more determined bark. "You don't like it?" Pao got down on her knees and offered the flashlight for Bruto to sniff. "It's okay!"

But the creature refused to get near it. In fact, he backed away, his hackles rising, the tentacle-like things on his back waving like he was floating instead of standing on solid ground. Pao supposed it made sense. Bruto was from the void, and the flashlight was a magical key made to destroy the creatures from there.

"Fine!" she said, standing back up. "You don't have to like it. But we do have to use it. Come on."

She oriented herself until the beam of light and her sneakers were pointing in the same direction. She was feeling almost rested, and more hopeful. Maybe she could pull this off after all.

Bruto lingered a few feet away, his green spines still waving as his eyes stayed narrowed in suspicion. For a moment, Pao wondered if he would follow her. Was the flashlight offensive enough to send him scurrying back into the cactus husk for good?

The prospect seemed almost unbearable, squeezing Pao's chest. Before, she had thought she could do this by herself, but now there was no denying that it was nice not to be alone.

"I won't make you come with me," she said, her voice a little wobbly. "But I . . . would really like it if you did. Okay?"

He cocked his head to one side, looking more like a real puppy than ever.

"Okay. Here goes."

Pao took a step. Behind her, Bruto whined. She took another step, and then another, her heart sinking more with each second she didn't hear his little monster claws following.

She was twenty-five paces (not that she was counting) away from him, her heart somewhere near her left sneaker, when his constant whine became a high-pitched bark, and in a tiny cloud of dust, Bruto barreled into her ankles, panting and looking very pleased with himself.

"Good boy," Pao said, her big, genuine smile so out of practice it started to hurt her cheeks after a minute. "Good boy, Bruto."

With the puppy at her heels, Pao double-checked the flashlight and, still smiling, continued on.

TWENTY-ONE

This Mouth Is No Metaphor

In its winding, twisty way, the flashlight kept them going, its path never making any more sense than it had before.

The solstice day was dawning. They had until midnight tonight to get in and out of the rift or else . . .

Well, Pao was trying really hard not to think about what happened if she failed.

She dug into Sal's food pack when her hunger got unbearable. There was tough skillet bread, dried meat and fruit, three bottles of water, and, at the bottom, a sleeve of Starbursts. Pao let out a whoop of joy that echoed strangely in the mist.

Bruto startled, bounding away and then creeping back.

"What, no Starbursts in the heart of darkness or wherever you came from?" Pao asked, taking the pink square at the top as a good omen. She popped it in her mouth, and Bruto whined.

"You want one, too?" Pao asked him, and his ears perked up.

She pulled out a yellow and unwrapped it. There was no way she was gonna eat that one, anyway, even if it was the last source of calories on earth. When she tossed it to Bruto, he just watched it fall, then gobbled it up off the ground afterward, dirt and all.

If they'd just been able to walk in a straight line, they could have traveled so much faster, she thought. But they never passed the same landmark twice, and for about the hundredth time since entering the cactus field—geez, had it only been two days ago?—Pao gave in to the nonsense. Wherever the light led her, she followed, and wherever she went, Bruto came, too.

Along the way, she started to teach Bruto tricks, just to pass the time. There were five yellow Starbursts in the pack, and Pao pulled pieces off them as they went, trying *sit*, *stay*, and *come* commands whenever they paused for rest.

Bruto was fine with trotting alongside her (or up ahead), but he was utterly hopeless at following orders. Even if Pao told him to do things he was already doing, he would immediately stop and do the opposite.

Training a puppy is hard work, Paola, said her mom's voice in her head, but Pao waved it off. This wasn't just any puppy! It was a creature of the void! Shouldn't it have powers and stuff?

Pao told the creature of the void to come.

He ran away.

She told him to sit.

He jumped.

"Useless!" she shouted, and he ran right up and jumped on her. "Down," she said.

He turned in a circle and jumped on her again.

"Forget it!" Pao told him, putting away half of a yellow Starburst. After that, there was only one whole one left. "Stay here for all I care."

When she walked away, Bruto followed obediently.

Another hour passed, and still there was nothing interesting in the landscape. Just the same spindly cactuses and bone-like rocks littering the never-ending dust. They had walked miles, Pao thought as they sat down to rest, though she wasn't sure how many. The first of the three water bottles Sal had given her was almost empty, and Bruto had eaten half the dried meat.

"I'm going to starve because of you," she told him, but she dribbled water into his mouth and rolled her eyes affectionately. "And my mom said I couldn't take care of a puppy. Just look at me now."

Bruto was appropriately impressed, and Pao was thankful she had someone to talk to besides herself. Even if it was a demon lizard-beast.

"Roll over!" Pao said, holding up the yellow Starburst half.

Bruto sat.

She gave it to him anyway. "Terrible," she said in a cooing, affectionate voice. "You're a terrible, disobedient wretch."

He licked her face and rubbed against her ankles like a cat.

"You know," she said in a conversational tone as they walked, "if I die out here, you'll probably eat me, won't you?"

The puppy whined, and Pao chose to take it as a promise that he wouldn't instead of a complaint that the Starburst was sticking his jaws together.

"If we run into any of your big brothers, maybe we can use the candy to incapacitate them."

It was a ridiculous thought, and Bruto didn't even dignify it with a response. But Pao stashed the last yellow square in the pocket of her jeans, just in case.

"Come on, boy," she said. "We're almost there."

He cocked his head to the side.

"You're right," Pao admitted. "I'm full of it. I have no idea where we're going, let alone how long it'll take to get there. Come on!"

Bruto took three steps toward her. Was he finally learning a command? Pao's heart was in her throat.

Not even half of the way to her, he sat down.

"Ugh!" Pao threw up her hands and walked away. Ten seconds later, he darted past her and lifted his leg on a scrubby bush.

They continued on. What else could they do? Pao tried not to think about the fact that the flashlight couldn't take them back to camp. This was a one-way trip.

"It better be worth it," she grumbled.

As if someone had heard her, the landscape started to change.

Under their feet, the sand grew lighter, going from black to gray to bone-white while the skeletal rocks sprang up bigger, like mushrooms.

The cacti widened, arms spreading out like they could hold up the moon—which was visible for the first time, low and almost orange along the horizon line. Black mosslike stuff started appearing in little clumps on the cacti, and as they walked on, it grew longer and dripped from the arms until Pao was pushing aside curtains of the stuff.

This was what the landscape had looked like in her dream: the white sand and black moss of the place where the giant mouth had opened in the sky. They were getting close.

Bruto didn't seem at all alarmed, Pao noted. But why would he? He was a monster and this was his home.

It terrified Pao, though. Did that mean she wasn't a monster after all?

I guess that's what I'm here to find out, she told herself, straightening her shoulders and taking comfort from the presence of the little beast beside her.

The sky was hazy now, the sun casting a strange bloodred light over everything. Pao thought the air felt different, too—more humid, like they had walked from the desert straight into a swamp.

For the first time since she'd first turned it on by accident, the flashlight's beam wasn't bending at weird angles—it stayed straight. The target had to be nearby, didn't it?

Pao's legs cramped, and her eyes burned from the effort of holding them open. She wanted to rest, to lie down in her bed under her star comforter and sleep for a whole day. Maybe two.

But this wasn't her room.

It might as well have been an unexplored planet, and there was no guarantee the next alien creature she encountered would be as friendly as Bruto. The thought of outer space gave Pao the strength to go on, as she pretended this was her first mission to another world and the fate of the universe depended on her.

Just like in the games she and Dante had played on the shag carpet, with one spaceship and one astronaut between them.

But Dante wasn't here now. And that was why she was doing this—to find him and Emma.

For a long stretch, Bruto's bouncing energy kept her going. She'd given up on the training, thankful that for now he was staying close, urging her on when she lagged behind.

Just a little farther, she told herself when she was so tired that it felt like her very soul was being sucked from the soles of her shoes. *Just a little farther.*

Miles shrank to yards, yards shrank to feet, feet shrank to single footsteps. One after the other. Pao stopped noticing the landscape, just looked down at her shoes against the pale sand as she dragged one foot past the other one more time.

One more time.

One more time . . .

It was when she didn't think she could go another step that she saw it—a black hole the size of a golf ball, just floating in the air. But what was it?

She kept her distance from the spot, examining it as best she could from where she stood, but the discoverer in her wanted nothing more than to measure it. To touch it. To find out what was glinting like metal at its edges.

That's another world, Pao thought, and goose bumps broke out on her arms. Imagining the opening had been one thing, dreaming it another, but this was the real deal, right in front of her, and Pao felt the gravity of the moment settle over her, making her stand up straighter.

Bruto ran around her ankles, yipping and snuffling happily. Pao understood. He was a monster and this was where he was supposed to be. Deep down inside, she shared his joy, which came from more than just her satisfaction at accomplishing a goal.

The entrance was a bit like the Florida Water—it felt like home. Not as much as her apartment, but enough to make her wonder.

As if it were reacting to their presence, the hole began to grow, like a cosmic finger was wiggling into the knitted sweater of the universe. Its outer ring gyrated, and the blackness in the center was so absolute Pao wasn't sure she should look at it. Like the sun during an eclipse.

The glinting edges elongated into fangs, and the darkness took shape until Pao—for the millionth time since she'd left the Riverside Palace—could hardly tell dream from reality.

She'd figured, from her nightmares, that the mouth was some kind of metaphor. But now, watching the opening widen, she realized she should have known better. There were no lips, just spreading edges of darkness, teeth at the top and bottom, and a tongue extending back like some kind of horrible carpet.

The emptiness spread across the sky, as though the whole landscape were just a photograph and someone had spilled a bottle of ink on its surface. It didn't bend or reshape itself to accommodate the surroundings. It didn't care if it was obliterating sand or cactus or sky. It just opened wider and wider until Pao could walk through it.

What she didn't expect was something inside her to urge her to do just that. She would have obeyed, wouldn't have been able to help it, but then she got a better look at what was waiting inside.

Hundreds of eyes, green and glowing, slitted with malevolence. This was another thing her dream hadn't depicted accurately. The ahogados were waiting in that gloom, and they were hungry.

But Pao had been waiting, too.

She stuck the flashlight in her belt, knowing she could only use it once. If she turned it on too early, all this would end before it even began.

Pao pulled out her knife—the one Marisa had disdained—and peered into the obstacle that, just a few short days ago, had defeated the centuries-old, immortal leader of Los Niños de la Luz.

But she wasn't Marisa, and she wasn't Franco. She was Paola Santiago, not a Niña de la Luz coming to snuff out darkness.

She had darkness within her, and that part of her was coming home. She was certain of it now.

Bruto stood completely still at her feet, the protrusions on his back dancing as the rift yawned wider and wider, the air blowing out of it moldy and damp, every bit as spooky as a malevolent magical realm's breath should be. The opening was twice her height now, and the eyes inside it seemed to be multiplying, if that were even possible.

She thought of the Niños, waiting at camp for a deluge of monsters. If she did what she'd come here to do, they'd never have to face them again. Pao pictured Sal and smiled.

Pao knew the ahogados were ready to swarm her, to feed on all the shining confidence she hadn't known was lurking just under her skin.

"Bring it on," she whispered into the toothy chasm, and the ghosts obeyed.

TWENTY-TWO

How to Banish Demons in Ten Easy Steps

The first thing Pao felt was the drop in temperature.

As a child of Arizona, she wasn't used to being cold, and this was far worse than the winter mornings when she could see her breath on her way to school. This chill was almost sentient.

It did battle with her skin and clothes. It crept inside and nestled until she was foggy and slow with it. But she drew her knife anyway, waiting for the worst.

She didn't have to wait long.

The first wave of ahogados came like the hounds of hell let loose at last. They slashed at her with ragged, sharp nails, and they grabbed at her with long, wasted arms. The places where she'd doused herself with Florida Water burned, like they had when the green mist pushed her out of the Riverside Palace.

She could only hope it would somehow protect her now, because it was already clear this fight would be nothing like the one at camp a few hours earlier.

Those monsters had just wanted to drag her off. These were protecting the entrance to their world. They wouldn't stop until she was dead or fully one of them—she could feel it in the desperation of their movements.

But they weren't the only ones who were desperate.

Her knife seemed to spread warmth into her arm as she wielded it, trying to remember what Naomi and Marisa had taught her about timing and defense. She quickly realized, sizing up the approaching mass of enemies, that their lessons in the pit would be useless against this many foes. So she just made sure the pointy end of her knife was facing the right direction and swung wildly, connecting with the nearest ahogada in the nick of time.

Its body wasn't entirely solid, but it wasn't entirely phantasmal, either. She had seen the way they shattered against the weapons of more experienced fighters, and she'd even delivered a blow to the wrist of one she had fought at the fireside.

None of that had prepared her for landing a killing blow.

The knife resisted as it went through the ghostly chest, but only for a moment before there was a cold crunch, like ice being crushed between back molars. A wet sort of shattering. Too close to hers, the face of the ahogada twisted in pain and fury, and Pao took advantage of her surprise to strike again.

When the specter was on the ground, oozing green from her various wounds, Pao turned to confront the next, and then the next. From somewhere nearby, Bruto yelped in confusion, but his loyalty was stronger than Pao had thought, and soon he was snarling and tearing at the legs and feet of any ahogado that came too close.

He's taking them by surprise, she noted proudly as her knife connected with the neck of a boy a foot taller than her. The spirits didn't see the puppy as a threat until it was too late.

But even with Bruto's help, Pao's arm grew sore, her muscles screaming and her heart pounding as she danced to avoid attacks from all directions. She was fighting with everything she had, and the throat of the rift yawned beyond, waiting to disgorge as many of its monsters as was necessary to make sure Pao never reached its heart.

Bruto yelped again, this time a sound of pain, and Pao cast around anxiously until she saw him limping away from a snarling ahogada who looked a lot like the girl who'd put gum in Pao's hair last year in gym class.

"Back off!" Pao screamed, lunging at her, careful not to step on Bruto.

But they were losing ground, she and her brave puppy being pushed farther and farther back toward the cactus field, and Pao knew there was only one thing left to do.

"I really hope this doesn't kill me," she said, scooping up Bruto with one arm and pulling the flashlight out of her belt with the other hand. "Choke on this, you weird zombie ghosts!"

Pao closed her eyes and clicked the flashlight on. She was afraid to look, worried that it would be like Naomi and the chupacabra all over again, and nothing would happen. Had she been an idiot to assume this key story was even true? Franco could have lied to Marisa, or simply been wrong. . . .

But she had felt it at the fireside, the light building up inside her. It had chased the monsters away. Could she count on that happening again? It was too late to hope for anything else.

Pao hugged Bruto tightly to her chest, her eyes still closed as she envisioned everyone she was doing this for. Dante and Emma, who would never be rescued if she didn't find them. Sal. Naomi. Marisa. Señora Mata.

Her mom.

Pao thought her heart would burst when she saw the familiar face in her mind.

Her mom, with her perpetually flyaway hair, and one eyebrow slightly higher than the other. Her mom, with her smile that lit up the room, even if she was talking about something boring like juniper tincture.

Her mom, who had done nothing but love her.

Her mom, who had been right all along.

A tear slid down her cheek as Bruto snapped at an ahogado from her arms. This had to work. It just had to . . .

That's when it happened.

The flashlight began to vibrate in Pao's hand, and she opened her eyes. The beam was glowing brighter than she'd ever seen it before.

Pao held on as the vibration intensified, the handle trying its best to leap out of her hands. Bruto barked as light spilled from the crack in its plastic case.

But the ahogados didn't scatter like they had at camp. They kept pressing in, smelling of rot and cold, like something that had gone bad in the refrigerator. Pao hissed in pain when one of them swiped at her exposed forearm with its jagged nails.

Still she held on to the flashlight.

The heat built until Pao was sure she couldn't take it anymore, until she was sure it was melting her flesh and taking none of the bad guys with it.

But then she felt a change deep inside.

She sensed the light within her *joining* with the key, as if her life force was powering the beam. And the energy was much more potent than it had been by the campfire. So much so, in fact, that her instinct was to turn off the flashlight, throw it down, and run away. But her hand was stuck to the key, which was unlocking something buried deep in her chest, acting as a conduit for the light and heat and vibration.

This is it, Pao thought. *This is it.*

The key was going to drain the last of the life force from her, she thought clinically. The rest of her hair would go white, and she would become an ahogada. The key would be lost. The solstice would end with Emma and Dante doomed to be part of the void forever.

Her legs went weak and wobbly, and Pao sank to the ground, light still unspooling like ribbons from the crack in the flashlight's plastic case. "Bruto," she said, tears streaming down her face. He licked them up as they fell, and once again she was grateful for him.

Grateful she didn't have to be alone at the end.

The vibration built to fever pitch, and Pao wondered if she would come apart before she was drained, if the thing would turn her to dust right here at the doorway between worlds.

Instead, the key exploded.

A ball of light engulfed her like combusting hydrogen. The ahogados flew back as though a tornado were twisting through them, leaving Pao all alone in the center with the trembling puppy in her arms.

Once she had recovered her sight, she stood up on unsure legs. She was still encircled by light, but the flashlight's plastic case was in pieces at her feet, the bulb blackened and shattered.

The darkness of the rift was inhaling the ahogados, but Pao

could no longer hear its rattling breath. Inside her ball of light, everything was safe and quiet and peaceful.

She set Bruto on his feet, and together they walked deeper into the void. Her brave demon puppy still limped a little, but there was no visible wound.

The rift trembled around them, and Pao could sense its weakness.

The third quarter is a time of letting go and forgiveness, Marisa had said, and now Pao realized why that had sounded familiar. Her mom used to tell her the same thing. She saw her mother again, this time as a younger woman, sketching the moon phases for little Pao, who had to stand on tiptoes to reach the table.

Letting go, Pao remembered. *Forgiveness.*

As Pao walked, she forgave Dante for loving his Arma del Alma and wanting to be a hero and thinking she needed saving all the time. She forgave Emma for having a shiny cell phone and a perfect family. She forgave Naomi for being such a know-it-all.

The sphere glowed brighter around her, and the rift seemed to shrink back a little, forming a tunnel into which Pao walked without fear.

Just like in her dream.

Pao forgave Marisa for the way she'd treated her at school, and for tying her up and stealing her flashlight.

Pao closed her eyes, putting one foot in front of the other. She forgave her mom for all the stale pizza and tarot cards, the candles that couldn't pay the bills. She even forgave her dad for leaving.

But when she thought of her dad, a familiar worry surfaced. Why had he left, anyway? Had it been because of her?

She opened her eyes to see that the rift was closing around them. The ball was growing smaller, the light dimmer. Pao could feel the darkness pressing on the bubble like it was her own skin. It was fighting against the intrusion. Trying to cough up Pao and launch her back into the haunted cactus field.

She tried to run, Bruto whimpering as he looked behind him.

I wasn't good enough, Pao thought. *I was a bad daughter and a bad friend. I was jealous of Emma, and of Dante and his weapon, and I didn't listen to my mom when she tried to warn me. . . .*

"I'm sorry," she choked out, still running, even though the light around her was barely a second skin at this point. She was cold again, and the long dark throat of the rift seemed to extend for a thousand miles.

She couldn't go forward. She couldn't go back. It hadn't been enough. All this effort, and it hadn't been enough.

Pao tripped and went down hard, the ground wet and gritty beneath her, sharp rocks—were they rocks?—stinging her knees and palms. The light of the key, flickering and dying, played across her skin as she shivered and sat up.

"I'm sorry," she whispered, the cold wet creeping into her throat like another tongue, choking her, ready to take her at last.

Bruto bounded over and she brought him into her lap. He licked her face and hands, his green eyes shining up at her.

"I'm sorry. . . ."

He whined, licking her again, his black tongue warm as he tried to keep her from fading away.

He's forgiving me, Pao thought as the darkness threatened to obscure her thoughts, her memories. . . .

"Thank you," she whispered, stroking him. If these were her last moments, there was only one person left for her to forgive.

Pao had made mistakes. She had lied, lost her temper, been impatient. She had underestimated her mom and led her friends into danger. She had definitely turned in a lot of homework assignments late. Once, she had thought really hard about cheating off Simone W.'s math test when she didn't know the answer. She hadn't actually done it, but she'd thought about it.

Pao recounted all the things she'd failed at, the things she'd screwed up. She remembered the people she'd let down.

But hadn't she also been brave? Hadn't she risked everything to stand up for her friends, to save them? Hadn't she taken a chance on a monster in the wasteland and named him and shared her food to keep him strong?

He had forgiven her, in that boundless, love-filled way that only dogs really could.

Maybe it was time for Pao to forgive herself, too. To remember that she was only twelve, and under normal circumstances she would still have time to grow. To change. To figure out what kind of person she wanted to be.

"I did okay, right?" she asked, and her voice hitched, sobs threatening to escape. "I did my best."

Around her, the white light gradually began to inflate again, like a beach ball. Pao got to her feet, no longer shivering, and ran ahead as fast as she could, Bruto right behind her. The light moved along with her, expanding with a faint humming noise. As the brightness grew in intensity, the hum got louder, until it sounded like the whistle of a massive teakettle. Bruto shook his head and whined.

And then the bubble burst into a shower of golden confetti.

When all the glitter settled, the long, dark throat of the rift was gone, and Pao and Bruto found themselves standing in a huge domed space. It looked like a graveyard—an expanse of barren ground about the size of a soccer field, interrupted by protruding stones and a few spindly, leafless trees. In the distance there was some kind of tall, multitiered, spired structure that Pao couldn't quite identify in the gloom, but it made the hair on her arms stand up nonetheless.

"Whoa," she said to Bruto. "I should probably have forgiven myself for the whole Simone thing a long time ago, huh?"

Bruto just panted, but his mouth was stretched into a pretty good approximation of a smile. Despite the dire circumstances, Pao wondered if any other chupacabra had ever smiled before.

The pressure the dark tunnel had exerted on her could be felt here, too, as Pao walked to the edge of the dome, which crackled occasionally with what looked like toxic green lightning bolts. On the other side of the dome, a black river eel swam past, its eyes glinting with each flash.

"We're underwater?" Pao asked, though it was pretty obvious.

Bruto cocked his head to the side, his tongue lolling out absurdly.

"You could *try* to be a little more fearsome," she said, but he only stretched up and licked her hand.

Turning away from the water outside the dome, Pao surveyed the inside more closely. It wasn't a graveyard after all—it looked more like a ruin. Stone pillars leaned on their sides—were they the remains of some kind of castle? The faraway structure— glowing faintly green, she realized—was a glass palace, twisted in elegant lines toward the very top of the bubble, ribbons of lightning shooting from its spire. The air here was so thick with magic, you could taste it.

Pao turned in a circle, testing a hypothesis.

Sure enough, there was no sign of the entrance they had just come through. She couldn't see any exit tunnel, either. And her key had exploded.

"How are we supposed to get out of here?" Pao asked, picking up a stone from the ground at her feet and chucking it almost absentmindedly at the dome.

The green lightning gathered, zapping the rock until it was nothing more than dust motes floating through the air.

"Not that way, I guess," she muttered, but her last word was swallowed by an earsplitting siren. At the glowing palace, spotlights kicked to life, sweeping the wasted courtyard. "Run!" Pao shouted when one of them illuminated her shoe.

Luckily, Bruto's survival instinct made up for his obedience issues, and he was pretty fast, even with a bum leg.

Dodging the next beam of light, Pao checked for her knife and sprinted toward one of the broken pillars dotting the landscape. She didn't know what the green lights were for, but she'd read enough graphic novels to know she wasn't going to like what happened if she got caught by one.

She wedged herself into a little corner created by two overlapping pillars and waited, every muscle tensed, to see if she'd been exposed. Bruto stayed close, whimpering, with his tail between his legs.

Pao wondered what he had to be afraid of in here. Wasn't he home? But while she was looking out at the strange world they'd found themselves in, heart hammering, Bruto only had eyes for Pao.

"You're not afraid of this place," she said to him quietly, scratching his ears. "You're afraid for *me*."

In response, Bruto whined again, pressing himself into Pao's calf.

"So much for my fearsome void beast," Pao she said, but tears prickled her eyes, and she patted his head as he licked her shoe.

Thirty seconds passed, then a minute. Pao peered over the rough stone to see the searchlights making another sweep. The ruins looked eerie in silhouette, but Pao's heart sank when she realized that a bunch of rocks wasn't the only thing between her and the glass palace.

There were ears, and tails, and hundreds of waving tentacle-like protrusions. There were long fingers on spiderlike hands. There were snakes standing upright on their tails, heads swiveling like they were just looking for something to latch onto with their fangs.

In the air, bats with green glowing eyes swooped in and out of the beams.

Pao had fought her way through the rift only to be deposited in the world's most dangerous underworld safari. And unfortunately, she was short a vehicle and a guide.

"What is this place?" Pao muttered, not expecting an answer from Bruto, but glad to have someone to talk to all the same. A few days ago, she would have thought this was some strange experiment being housed at the bottom of the river, some kind of energy plant the government didn't want people finding out about or something.

But now, armed with her new knowledge of the paranormal, Pao wondered if they were even still on earth. Was this hell? Some kind of purgatory? Was she even alive?

Her skin felt clammy, her head woozy.

What had she done when she walked through that mouth?

Bruto nipped her fingertips, bringing her back to reality.

"Right," she said, shaking the haziness from her head. There would be time to ponder the nature of existence *after* they got out of here. "The good news is," she told him, "it can't get any worse."

He whined, and Pao had the sudden urge to knock on wood. She settled for his head, which made a satisfying *thunk* sound, though he looked mildly offended.

As if some angry ghost gods had heard her ridiculous, clichéd sentiment, the searchlights suddenly went out, reducing everything to shades of gray.

There were hundreds of bloodthirsty void creatures between Pao and that citadel, she knew now, and unfortunately, her magic flashlight was in pieces on the ground somewhere behind them, in a place they could no longer access.

Pao looked at Bruto, then nodded once, decisively. "I have to say, these aren't even the worst odds we've faced."

She could have sworn he nodded in agreement.

TWENTY-THREE

Even Bigger Dragon-Lizard-Dogs

They made slow progress across the field to the palace, doing their best to move in absolute silence.

Well, Pao did her best. Bruto, on the other hand, seemed determined to whimper and whine and bark at everything that moved. Eventually, she stopped trying to keep him quiet. He was a void beast, after all. Hopefully the others wouldn't consider his presence out of the ordinary.

Pao kept her knife at the ready and the shopping bag with the tiny bit of remaining Florida Water under her arm even though she was sure the latter wouldn't be of much use to them here. The bag reminded her of Señora Mata, and to distract herself from the terrifying task she was trying to accomplish, Pao thought back to that fateful morning a few days ago when she'd tried to convince Dante to come with her to go looking for a kidnapper.

If only she'd known then that the "kidnapper" in question was an immortal Niño de la Luz in search of the very key she'd just used to cross the barrier into a magical world.

She would have laughed if even the slightest sound wouldn't have brought a horde of angry fantasy creatures down on her.

That almost made her laugh, too.

Pao had been a scientist. A girl who believed in equations and hypotheses and the accepted rules and physical limitations of the universe. A girl who'd rolled her eyes at her mom when she told stories of wizards taking third daughters for wives and dog-lizards that prowled the desert and wailing women who searched for their drowned children night after night.

What were the odds that *Pao*, of all people, would end up in some twisted version of one of those stories?

If Dante were here, he'd understand, she thought. But Dante was gone, and so was Emma. Pao was on her own.

She suddenly didn't feel much like laughing anymore.

The palace still seemed so far off. They'd barely moved a fraction of the way across the dark minefield of murderous creatures, and even over that little distance, it was a miracle they hadn't been attacked yet.

What would the creatures do to them in here? Were the rules different now that they were through the rift? Would Bruto be safe, since he was one of them? Or would they consider him a traitor for helping her?

"I hope they don't smell the Starbursts on your breath," she mumbled to him as they moved from a fallen pillar to a pile of loose bricks. As the terrain stretched on, there were fewer things to hide behind. They'd have to be even more careful.

Miraculously, through a combination of very quiet footsteps and little breathing, they made it to the halfway point. There were as many monsters behind as in front of them, Pao thought, though she wasn't sure if that was comforting or not.

They wedged themselves behind yet another stone something

or other—this one might have been the ruins of a wall—and Pao wondered what had stood there before. What this sinister glass structure had replaced.

Pao could see things more clearly from here, in the palace's weird green glow. Unfortunately, up ahead, the courtyard was wide open—the ruins had been removed closer to the center—and she spotted more monsters than ever.

Even worse, there appeared to be some kind of moat surrounding the palace, and from what Pao could tell, it was spanned only by a single bridge—guarded by two giant horned beasts she'd never seen before, not even in the most comprehensive of her mom's bestiary books.

"How are we gonna get across that . . . ?" Pao whispered, and Bruto sniffed sympathetically. A few feet to the left of their hiding place, a chupacabra the size of a small horse snorted and licked his lips as if to prove that it would be impossible.

A dozen twisted trees dotted the landscape between them and the moat. Pao didn't think they were large enough to hide even Bruto, but they were the best hope of cover they had for now.

Their only hope.

Between the giant chupacabra to their left and a horrible swarm of Manos Pachonas Pao spotted to the right, there was one very straight, very narrow path to a place where three trees sort of clumped together. They'd make for that, Pao decided, trying hard not to feel like she was on a playground slide hurtling toward a landing pad that was on fire.

She took a deep breath, getting ready to run more silently than ever, when green lightning struck the ground between the trees and the bridge. A black hole appeared in the dome's ceiling, just big enough for three living people and four ahogados to drop through.

Pao's heart leaped into her throat. The void had opened again, and there were real, actual, breathing people inside. She wasn't alone anymore.

If she could get to them, free them from their captors . . . maybe as a group they'd have a better chance of getting inside the palace. Of getting Emma back. Of finding—

"Let them go!" The voice was loud—too loud—and its familiarity punched Pao in the gut. In the palace's glow, Pao saw a boy-shaped shadow sprinting across the courtyard toward the new arrivals. "Let them go or I swear to God I'll vaporize every last one of you!"

"No!" Pao said, forgetting to be quiet, Bruto nipping her ankle as a reminder. But it didn't matter. Every creature in the vicinity—maybe in the whole field—was looking at the tall, broad-shouldered boy who had decided to make a spectacle of himself in order to save others, even though he was hopelessly outnumbered by enemies.

Only one boy in the world—any world—would be that stupid.

Pao felt tears stinging her eyes as a club came into view, green light reflecting off the streaks of pearl as the boy swung it, shattering three ahogado heads in one swipe before turning to face the fourth.

From the palace, the siren wailed again, and now that she was closer, Pao could see the source of the searchlight. At the top, a bulb of poisonous green light was now scanning the ground for the source of the commotion.

Time slowed, the danger receding as all the memories came

flooding back. All the thoughts Pao had repressed just to enable herself to keep putting one foot in front of the other. All the things she'd thought she'd lost forever.

Dante telling her he liked her algae when they were saying good night. Dante losing at video games and trying to be a good sport.

He'd taken her hand when the world was ending. He had brought his Arma del Alma to life by trying to protect her.

He'd kissed her on the cheek.

And he was alive. Alive and fighting.

The ribbons of green light were still sweeping the field, searching for him as growls and hisses and screeches kicked up like wind around them. The monsters were reacting to the presence of the shouting boy as he splintered the last ahogado and turned to face the next foe.

Maybe it was the fact that she had almost lost him and she couldn't lose him again. Maybe it was his bravery-to-the-point-of-stupidity pheromones changing the chemistry of the air in the bubble. Maybe Pao was just tired of tiptoeing around.

Whatever it was, she didn't hesitate. She didn't overthink. She just used the commotion and the distraction he was causing, and she ran toward him, leaving the shopping bag behind.

No longer worried about moving quietly, Pao found the magic-dense atmosphere surprisingly satisfying to sprint through. It snapped and sizzled around her. She flew through the air, and it seemed to take her only seconds to reach the clump of twisted trees.

Only one more dash like that and she'd reach the palace.

Bruto caught up to her just as she was squeezing between

the trees. She knew she should stop and make herself at home in the cozy little space while she planned her next move. But she didn't. Instead, she drew her knife and did the exact thing she had wanted to throttle Dante for more than once since this whole mess had started.

She acted brave to the point of stupidity.

"Over here, you ugly dog!" Pao shouted at a medium-size chupacabra approaching Dante too fast from behind. The three children who had come through were helpless, huddled together at the foot of a pillar as Dante fought to save them.

Unfortunately for him, the searchlights found them all at just that moment. Bathed in almost blinding green light, Pao didn't panic. Instead, she remembered Naomi's technique and baseball-slid into the monster's back legs, taking it out with her dusty sneakers before slitting its throat with her knife.

She hoped Bruto hadn't seen that.

"Pao?" came Dante's voice, disbelieving, full of hope and fear and a thousand other emotions.

"Didn't think I was gonna let you get all the glory again, did you?" she asked, throwing off her fallen assailant as a cloud of green-eyed bats dive-bombed her. She ducked, rolled, and came up right beside him, her heart full even as it pounded in border-line terror.

"How did you . . . ? You were supposed to stay at camp! And what happened to your hair?"

Pao could see the end of her one white braid out of the corner of her eye as she pivoted to avoid a Mano Pachona skittering toward her ankles. "It's a long story! How did *you* get here? And why aren't you—"

"Pao, watch out!" Dante yelled, charging toward her with his club outstretched. She didn't see the danger, but she understood just in time as Bruto approached.

"No!" she shouted, swinging around to protect the confused pup.

"I know he's little, but he's still one of them," Dante said, a grim look on his face.

"He's a long story, too," Pao said, scooping him up and letting him lick her face. "But keep your fancy weapon away from him, hero boy."

Dante looked like he wanted to argue, but then Bruto's black tongue flopped out of his mouth in a smiley way. Dante rolled his eyes, flexing his shoulders as he turned to face whatever was coming next.

"I know you're desperate for a puppy, but geez, Pao, isn't this—"

But what Dante thought it was, she never found out. Another ahogado had been lurking nearby, and it chose that moment to strike. Dante swung his club, and Pao jumped out of the way as it connected. Unfortunately, she landed facing the bridge, and what she saw there froze her in her tracks.

"Oh no . . ." Pao said. It wasn't just the ahogado she hadn't seen coming.

Heading across the bridge in a slow, almost processional march were the two horned beasts. At first they seemed ram-like, but as they got closer, Pao saw that they were chupacabras, too. Massive, ancient ones whose scales had overtaken most of their bodies. The green protrusions along their backs had grown long, wrapped around their ears, and calcified so they looked like horns.

Their eyes were green, Pao noticed as they drew closer, but

not the same bright, toxic shade as the other creatures. This was the milky green of a jade, like the stones her mom put on altars for luck and friendship.

Around them, all the void beasts, including Bruto, went still. Even they seemed cowed in the presence of these chupacabra elders, which, Pao realized, were about the size of those big horses with the furry legs. She could never remember the name of that breed. . . .

Dante came over to Pao and stood so close their shoulders almost touched. The way the chupacabras walked was peaceful—regal, even. Pao knew Dante was thinking the same thing she was: Attacking these creatures would be wrong, unless they attacked first.

Together, they hoped for the best, even as they expected the worst.

"Sorry I couldn't—" Pao said at the same time Dante said, "Sorry I didn't—"

They laughed together, a strange sound in this desolate landscape.

Pao bumped Dante's shoulder with her own, feeling curiously light considering what was approaching. They were together again, she thought, and so far, they had made it through everything else this crazy week had thrown at them. Why not this?

"It's okay," she said as a chill settled around them, shadows trailing the massive, ancient creatures like cloaks. "I'm all about forgiveness these days."

"You?" Dante asked, raising one eyebrow, not daring to look away from the chupacabras.

Pao shrugged, but her light feeling evaporated quickly as she craned her neck to meet the eyes of the fantastic creatures. They stopped before Pao and Dante, surveying them impassively.

"What do we—" Dante whispered, but Pao elbowed him with the arm that was not holding an immobile Bruto. She didn't know why, but she felt it would be best for them to stay as quiet and still as possible, too.

The chupacabras in the field had been more dog than lizard, but these two were almost dragon-like. Their scales glimmered a pale green, and their few remaining patches of coarse hair were pure white. Their faces were scaly, too, with reptilian noses, and the calcified protrusions were even more majestic up close. Like crowns.

"Put the club away," she whispered to Dante. The part of her that had felt welcomed by the rift was telling her that showing any kind of aggression toward these creatures was a line they shouldn't cross.

She had an almost reverent feeling, like she wanted to kneel or make an offering, as ridiculous as she knew that was. But before she had a chance to freak out Dante even more, something detached from the top of one of the beasts and slid neatly to the ground.

"Well, well, well," said Ondina, straightening her dress and approaching Pao. "Took you long enough."

TWENTY-FOUR
The Bloodthirsty Stairs

"You?"

"Like you're surprised? You basically came here on my orders." Ondina rolled her eyes and casually flipped her hair, like they were at a sleepover disagreeing over which movie to watch.

Ondina looked both more solid and more surreal here. Her skin glowed faintly, her eyes still poison green. Her hair and dress were somehow darker and drew Pao's eyes hypnotically.

How had Pao ever thought this was just a girl?

"Sorry, who are you?" Dante asked.

"Long story," Pao and Ondina said together.

"I've been hearing that a lot lately," Dante said under his breath.

Pao ignored him and glared at Ondina, who was as unfazed as ever. "Look," Pao told her, "I don't know how you got in here, too, but you were right. Dante and I need to find our friend and figure out how to get out of here before the barrier closes."

Dante stepped forward. "Yeah, or before one of these psycho ghosts tries to strangle me. Again."

"Oh, they won't do that," Ondina said, glancing back at the

bridge, where another hundred ahogados had begun to gather.

"Are you kidding me?" Dante asked. "That's, like, what they do. It's the *only* thing they do."

"They do what they're told," Ondina replied, beckoning over her shoulder with her little finger. The mass of green-eyed ghosts began to move forward.

"What are you doing?" Pao asked, a chill settling in her stomach.

Ondina held up a hand. The procession stopped. All but three, who beelined for the kids huddled against the pillar.

"What are you *doing*?" Pao repeated, every cell in her body ready to run, to save them. But her limbs were heavy and slow. She couldn't take a step.

Ondina didn't answer.

Even Dante watched, his eyes strangely unfocused, as the ahogados led the kids into yet another black hole.

"What's going to happen to them?" Pao asked, her words as slow as her limbs.

"We're taking them to Hogwarts," Ondina said snottily.

"You said-d-d . . ." Pao stuttered, Bruto barely stirring in her arms. "You said you weren't one of them. You said you wanted to help me."

"I'm *not* one of them," Ondina said with disdain. "As for the other thing . . . well, it shouldn't come as a *huge* shock to you that it was *me* I was really trying to help. But don't worry—it won't be too bad for you." She grinned, and on another face, in another setting, it might have been one of those too-cute beauty-pageant smiles.

Here, it was downright terrifying.

"How exactly do you two know each other?" Dante asked, and Pao felt guilty. For a moment, she'd almost forgotten he was there.

She looked at him, feeling her eyes do that *I'm sorry* thing before she even spoke. How could she tell Dante *now* about a lifetime of dark, twisted dreams? Dreams that connected her to this girl and this place and all the evil they had been fighting since this started.

How could she tell him it might be all her fault?

"As fun as it would be to watch you try to wriggle out of this one, Paola," said Ondina, "we have an appointment. Let's go."

"A what? What are you talking about?" Pao shook her head a little, trying to focus. Why was she so tired all of a sudden? "I told you . . . we have to find Emma, and . . ." She actually yawned. "We have to find Emma and—"

"The only thing you're doing," Ondina interrupted, "is exactly what I say. Just like every other living creature in this bubble."

Ondina clapped twice, and something flickered in the eyes of the closest ancient chupacabra. He lowered his head.

"Climb on," she said to Pao and Dante. "Or I'll have to force you to do it at knifepoint, and that's just so *boring*, don't you think?"

"Knife . . . what?" Pao knew there was something wrong, but she was so, so tired all of a sudden, and Dante was already hoisting himself up. Stiff-limbed, like he was sleepwalking.

The sight of him turned robotic made Pao feel sharper, just for a moment. "What's wrong with him?" she asked. "What's going on?"

"Oh boy, back to the *what* questions," Ondina said, faking a yawn of her own. "And here I thought our relationship had grown."

Pao could only stand there. Nothing in her brain seemed to be working.

"I could knock you out first," Ondina said, "but I'd be doing you a disservice. The view of the palace on the way in is really *breathtaking* this time of year. Now, please, *get on.*"

She said this last part with such authority it seemed to ring in the air. Like a general, Pao thought. Or a lieutenant at least . . .

Her eyes were so green. . . .

It would be so easy to just do what she said. . . .

"No," Pao said, still trying to fight, to hold on.

But to what? She couldn't remember.

Pao climbed up the ancient chupacabra's scaly side one-handed, Bruto's head hanging strangely over her arm. Already on the back of the twin chupacabra next to her, Dante didn't look over. He was still staring at Ondina.

"Very good," she said, vaulting onto the beast effortlessly to take a seat in front of Pao. She turned with a smirk. "I have a feeling your friend's the obedient one. You, I need to keep a closer eye on. Now, let's get on with it, shall we?"

She clapped again, and the beasts began to move.

Ondina was right about one thing, Pao thought, her mind sluggish. *The view crossing the bridge really is beautiful.*

The palace doors opened with a wave of Ondina's hand. Inside the green light wasn't as harsh, though everything glowed with it.

In Pao's arms, Bruto slept with his tongue lolling out, and the warm weight of him made Pao even sleepier. *Would it be so bad to nod off for just a little while?* she wondered. She looked at the mount beside her to see that Dante's eyelids were closed.

See? said a calming voice in her head. *He's perfectly safe. . . .*

The front hall was magnificent, with glass walls, green veins running through them like circuitry. It made Pao think of the robotics kit she'd been trying to get her mom to spring for and giggled. A robot castle. How ridiculous.

Almost as ridiculous as riding through a robot castle on the back of a chupacabra-dragon. A few days ago, Pao was pretty sure she'd been a girl who didn't believe in folktales or ghosts.

She giggled again, feeling loopy and disoriented.

The chupacabras halted at a sweeping glass staircase that disappeared up into the second level. Pao smiled when she pictured the creatures trying to go up the stairs, but she managed to keep her amusement to herself this time. Bruto snorted in her arms, opening his left eye just a crack.

Beside her, Dante did the same.

"Time to disembark," Ondina said, returning to the ground soundlessly once again. She waited as Pao maneuvered her clumsy, heavy legs over to one side of the chupacabra and slid down beside her. With Bruto in her arms, she landed awkwardly, and he spilled onto the ground, yelping indignantly at the rude awakening.

"Sorry," Pao said, the words thick in her mouth like oatmeal that had been cooked too long.

"Leave it to you to bond with one of these things," Ondina said. "You think you're so *good* and *pure.*"

"I don't," Pao said, recalling her dreams and the way the opening void of the rift had felt like home. Ondina didn't question her statement, and Pao didn't elaborate. The thoughts drifted away, replaced by relief when Dante joined them on the ground.

She didn't know why, but Pao felt stronger when the two of

them were together, and she leaned into his shoulder heavily, forgetting to be embarrassed.

He leaned into her, too.

"Adorable as you two lovebirds are, we have places to be," Ondina snapped, and Pao—despite her exhaustion—couldn't help but notice that the girl seemed different than she'd been outside. More nervous, like a kid during a test when the teacher stopped to look over their shoulder.

When Ondina began climbing the stairs, Pao's confusion took a back seat to dread. Her legs were heavy as stone, and she could barely keep her eyes open. There were at least a hundred stairs— more, if they continued past the point she could see.

Which, with her luck, they probably did.

"Emma . . ." Pao said, a cold feeling starting to creep into her sleepy haze. "I have to get to Emma."

"Sure," Ondina said, her voice razor-edged. "Now get moving."

If Pao had thought she was tired before, it was nothing compared to how she felt when they reached the halfway point of the staircase. Bruto—whose energy didn't seem affected by their surroundings ever since he woke up—nudged worriedly at Pao's ankles when she slowed, but he couldn't help her.

The places on her body that had burned before, when the key had drained her, now ached, making her want to curl up on the floor right then and there.

She stumbled, almost losing her footing.

Bruto licked her hand.

"I know," she mumbled, feeling worse than she ever had when her mom woke her for school. "Keep going."

She kept climbing.

Another flight. Then another. Eventually, at the edges of her fuzzy vision, Pao noticed that the weight of her foot caused each step to glow brighter as she trod on it.

Or was that just delirium setting in?

It hadn't been that long since she'd slept, had it? Sure, she'd done some fighting. And there'd been that whole traveling-through-a-dark-portal-between-worlds thing. And the key-turning-her-hair-white thing. Twice. But still, her exhaustion couldn't be explained, even by everything she'd gone through in the past twenty-four hours.

She felt like her bones were being leached of their nutrients, making them brittle and achy. Like her brain's synapses were growing dimmer until it was a struggle to remember who she was, or why she was climbing.

Bruto nipped at her sneaker heel.

She climbed anyway.

Fifty steps, a hundred. There was no doubt about it now—her swimming eyes caught the change in the light when her feet hit the stairs. But what did it mean? What was happening?

Pao knew, as if it were a distant, historical fact, that she was an inquisitive person. Clever, even. And this was certainly a mystery. But she couldn't make her brain puzzle it out. Right now, the only thing she cared to know was when she'd be allowed to lie down.

Dante groaned beside her, his eyes half-closed. She wanted to say something to him, but she forgot what it was before she started to speak. There was nothing but the next step. And the next.

"Not much farther now," Ondina said, not seeming tired in the least.

Emma, Pao thought, and she said it aloud unconsciously. "Emma . . ."

"Ugh, has anyone ever told you a one-track mind doesn't make you a very pleasant traveling companion?"

The question didn't seem to require an answer, but Pao, even surrounded by glowing green, barely able to drag one foot past the other, felt like she had indeed been told that many times in her life.

She just couldn't remember why. Or by whom.

The second floor's main feature was a massive chandelier, hanging in the very center of a large circular landing.

Seventeen more stairs to go, Pao guessed, closing one eye to see through the haze of exhaustion. Sixteen. Fifteen.

But she stopped counting at that point, because waiting for them at the top of the stairs were three tall skeletal figures with massive black-feathered wings sprouting out of their backs, and faces twisted in expressions of perpetual pain.

"What's this?" Pao asked. "I thought . . . Emma . . ."

Apparently, talking and walking at once was too much for her overtaxed coordination, because Pao slipped on step fourteen (or was it thirteen?) and caught herself with both palms on the sharp edge of a glass stair.

She could feel the warmth of blood on her hands, and she looked down to find deep cuts in her skin. But there was no red stain on the stair. The creatures at the top screeched hungrily, but Ondina silenced them with a wave of her hand, waiting for Pao to stand.

A drop of her blood fell, and she watched it as if in slow motion. The tiny bead splashed up at the sides when it landed. But it disappeared before it could pool.

The glass had absorbed it.

It's draining you, said a part of her subconscious that was apparently still thinking clearly. *Just like the ahogados. Just like the key. . . .*

But why?

More of her blood dripped to the floor. The light under the stair went off like fireworks, nearly blinding Pao. Her eyes filled with tears. She didn't understand . . . and she *always* understood.

Dante will catch me, she thought as she swayed on her feet.

But he didn't. When she fell, there was no cushion, only hard glass. She felt it.

She heard Bruto yelp.

And then there was nothing at all.

TWENTY-FIVE

Never Cage a Lechuza

Pao awoke feeling like her skull had been split in two. She couldn't open her eyes. They were too heavy.

"Dante?" she called out before she thought better of it. No one replied. "Bruto?" Her voice came back to her like she was in a small space. Muffled, almost. She forced her eyes open then, and her stomach dropped as she took in her surroundings. She was in a glass cell.

Dante was gone. So was Ondina. And Bruto was nowhere to be seen.

"Hello?" she called, sitting up on the smooth glass floor.

She looked for a door.

There wasn't one.

Pao's heart rate sped up, like she'd just woken from a nightmare. It was a familiar feeling, but this time sleep had been the escape. Her real life was the bad dream.

She walked to the wall. She could cross the space in four steps. "Help me!" she shouted, pounding on the glass, which swallowed the sound just like it had swallowed her blood.

Frantic, Pao felt along every smooth, slick wall for a seam. Some kind of hidden panel that could slide open and get her out of here. But there was nothing. She might as well have been inside a snow globe.

Her heart hammered against her ribs, her breath coming shorter and sharper as she wondered about the amount of air in the space. Would she suffocate soon? They'd learned in science how much oxygen a human being used per minute, but she couldn't remember now.

"Help me!" she screamed, louder this time, banging on the seamless wall with both fists.

Beneath her hands, the wall lit up with the pressure.

"No," Pao said, remembering her blood drop on the stair. The wall was feeding off her life force. And if her hypothesis was correct, the more worked up she got, the quicker it would drain her.

She slid down to the floor and pulled her knees into her chest, trying to make herself smaller, and to slow her pulse and her breathing. But tears slid silently down her cheeks, and where they hit the glass beneath her, it glowed greedily.

Pao didn't know how much time she spent sitting there. The light didn't change in her cell. It could have been an hour, a day, a week. The solstice had probably already ended. The Niños could all be gone by now, victims of the monsters from this place.

Maybe she would never get out. And neither would Dante. Perhaps Pao's dreams about her friend's hand in the river had only been a fantasy, and Emma wasn't here after all.

She had seemed so real, though, with her sandy hair and her purple nails.

Don't give up on me, Emma had said, and Pao had promised she never would. . . .

Pao's desperate memories were interrupted by a red arch

appearing in the wall in front of her. It disappeared almost as quickly as it had formed, leaving Ondina inside in the cell, the wall as impenetrable as ever.

The possibility of a way out acted like a stimulant on Pao, and she felt her brain kick into gear, forming a plan almost without her permission.

And it wasn't half-bad, either, if she did say so herself.

First, Pao whimpered, like someone had kicked her. Then she curled up tighter to appear weak and scared. Her eyes were open only slits, and she hoped they looked closed.

"Get up," Ondina barked. "It's time. She's waiting."

Who's waiting? The effort of holding back the question almost ruptured something inside Pao. But there would be an opportunity to get answers later, if she did this right.

She whimpered again.

Ondina approached her, shoving her with a neat black boot. "I said, get up!"

There was no power in the kick, Pao noted. Did that mean Ondina didn't really want to hurt her?

"I . . . can't . . ." Pao answered, wheezing and coughing.

"This is just pathetic," Ondina said. "And we don't have *time* for pathetic."

Pao went still, though every muscle in her body screamed at her to get up and run. *Wait,* she told them, relaxing them one by one. *Just a little longer.*

Ondina called her more names, but in the end she had no choice. She bent down and took Pao by the armpits, hauling her to her feet with surprising strength given that they were almost the same height.

"If I ruin my hair hauling you around this place, you'll pay for it," Ondina muttered, but she slung an arm under Pao's and shouldered most of her weight, walking her toward the spot in the wall where the door had appeared.

This time, Pao knew what to do. She had to be faster than the light.

She closed her eyes. A dangerous move for a scientist, but Pao had learned a few things about faith since leaving home. She could feel it in the air when Ondina decided to open the wall, and with the last bit of strength she had, Pao stood on her own two feet, shoved the other girl behind her into the cell, and threw herself through the doorway.

Passing through the opening chilled her to the bone, and for a moment, Pao worried that she'd miscalculated and the wall would claim her. Suck her dry until she was nothing more than a monster minion.

At least when I'm an ahogada, I can kill Ondina without feeling bad about it, she thought.

But then, miraculously, she had made it, and she was still Pao, standing on the circular landing of the second floor.

There were only two ways to go—upstairs, deeper into the palace and the unknown, or downstairs, toward the exit. Pao knew she had only seconds before Ondina righted herself and made another door, so she did what any stupid, brave hero would do. She forsook the passage back to the courtyard and took the stairs up, where she hoped she would find Dante.

"PAOLA!" The shriek was so loud, the glass chandelier rattled above her. But Pao didn't stop. She didn't answer, either. She just kept running. Two steps at a time, then three, and whether it was her speed or her victorious feeling from tricking Ondina, the stairs didn't seem to want any of the energy she was putting out.

"PAOLA!" Ondina was at the bottom of the stairs now, but Pao had almost reached the top. "You have no idea what you're messing with," Ondina said, her footsteps too loud behind Pao.

How can I find Dante? Pao wondered. *I don't even know where he is.* She pushed herself harder, but fear was creeping in, and the walls started to pulse with their hunger for it.

At the top of the stairs was a long, high-ceilinged hallway full of cells with slotted glass doors, all glowing green. Pao barreled toward the first one, and it zapped her with an electric shock when she got too close.

How had they managed to get glass to conduct electricity? Pao wondered briefly. But that was a mystery she'd have to solve later . . . if she got out of here in one piece.

She jumped back just in time to see Ondina coming up behind her, her normally pale cheeks flushed, her dark eyebrows drawn in an angry expression Pao had seen more than once in her own reflection.

"Give it up, Santiago," said Ondina, her voice disturbingly low and calm. "You did your best. But your best isn't as good as mine, and it never, ever will be."

Behind the glass that had almost electrocuted Pao, something hissed. All around her, void creatures were coming up to the slats in their cell doors, sniffing, beginning to growl and screech as they smelled a living human in their midst.

Ondina walked slowly toward Pao, her hands extended like she had won a contest and was approaching to accept her prize. "It's time to come with me now," Ondina said in an eerie, flat voice.

That's when Pao realized what was going on. Ondina was trying not to upset her. She had certainly never cared about upsetting Pao before—in fact, she'd seemed to relish it. So what was different?

Pao looked at the ground below her feet as Ondina advanced with careful steps. Of course, Pao thought. They'd never been in a life-force-draining palace before. Pao's eyes snapped to Ondina's, which were wide and cautious. The other girl didn't want the glass to bleed Pao dry.

But why?

Right now, that didn't matter. Ondina couldn't risk moving quickly. She couldn't anger Pao too much. And that gave Pao just the advantage she needed.

She reversed directions abruptly and charged full tilt at Ondina. The girl threw up her hands in surprise as Pao crashed into her, gripping her cold shoulders and pushing her back, back, back.

The monsters went wild, the corridor filling with the sounds of their frenzy.

In the commotion, Pao heard a whine that stopped her in her tracks. Sure enough, in the cage just behind Ondina was a familiar little face, his green eyes round as coins instead of narrowed in anger and fear. When he saw Pao, he yelped with joy.

"Bruto!" Pao cried, and her own joy gave her the strength to counteract Ondina's lunge.

Pao pushed Ondina's back right up to the door, then rammed her into it as hard as she could.

But Ondina apparently wasn't susceptible to shocks. Instead, her body killed the current, and the door opened wide as Pao—armed with the surprising results of her most recent experiment—changed her strategy.

Bruto rushed out and tried to jump on Pao, but he only succeeded in scratching Ondina's legs. The other girl's hands were still locked on Pao's shoulders, pushing back with all her strength, but her collision with the door seemed to have weakened her.

"Good boy!" Pao said, steering Ondina toward the next cell.

"I'm not a hotel key card!" Ondina growled, resisting harder, digging with her fingernails in a way Pao was sure would leave marks.

Just when it seemed like Ondina would finally gain control, the two of them connected with the next slotted door. The three skeletal bird-people from the stairs stepped out as it opened, stretching their necks and wings.

Up close, without the drain of the stairs making her hazy, Pao could see that the bird-people were female. Their leathery skin was gray and sagging, their faces cruel with razor-sharp beaks.

Lechuzas—shape-shifting witches. The drawings Pao had seen in her mom's books hadn't done them a bit of justice. They were terrifying—much more so than the chupacabras or Manos Pachonas. Maybe even more than the ahogados.

One of them let out an earsplitting screech, summoning from the cell a cloud of bats that attacked the girls with abandon, not caring who they scratched or bit or beat with their wings. Pao screamed and let go of Ondina to cover her head with her hands.

"Stop this at once!" Ondina shouted, waving her hands at the bird-women as though she could open a door in the air and send them through it. But whatever authority she'd once had over the creatures seemed to have evaporated after their who-knows-how-long stay in the electric cells. One took flight and circled overhead in the cavernous space while the other two just stood there, watching and cackling, waiting for their turn to strike.

Pao pressed herself against the wall opposite the cells as Bruto leaped into the air, biting at the bats whenever they got too close. Pao knew she had to get out of here while Ondina was distracted, take the stairs, find Dante. But she couldn't leave without her demon puppy, not when they'd only just been reunited.

"Bruto!" Pao called, remembering with dread their training work and his limited talent for it. This time, he looked up at the sound of his name, cocking his head, and she could have sworn his big green eyes darted to the pocket where she kept her Starbursts.

Ondina was still warding off about ten murderous bats with her arms, squealing as they twisted her hair into a tangle on top of her head. But Pao knew she wouldn't be waylaid for long.

Time slowed as Pao locked eyes with her puppy. "Bruto, come!" she said firmly, loud enough that he could hear her over all the squeaking, shrieking commotion.

His head tilted again, and a wayward bat talon caught his ear.

"Come!" Pao said in the same tone, though she wanted to scream it in panic. Another bat dive-bombed her, and she barely missed being cuffed with a wing that looked big enough to break her neck.

But then a miracle happened. A real, honest-to-God, clouds-parting, rainbows-arcing miracle.

Bruto came.

He trotted across the glass, his nails tapping on the surface as if it were a rich lady's parquet floor.

She wanted to shout *Good boy* until she was blue in the face, but all the reputable dog-training sites said to wait until they'd actually accomplished the task. Even if there were a swarm of bloodthirsty bats and three bird-women ready to strip the meat from your bones.

Well, she assumed they *would* have said that, anyway.

She waited, and her proud little puppy broke into a run, not stopping despite a billion distractions until he was right in front of her.

With a smile that looked much too smirk-like to be on the face of a dog, he plopped down on his haunches right at her feet.

"GOOD BOY!" Pao shouted at the top of her lungs, startling several of the bats. She gave herself a moment of peace as she patted his head with one hand and dug around in her pocket with the other for the very last yellow Starburst in the magical underworld.

She tossed it to him, testing her luck, and because this was still a miracle, he caught it neatly in his mouth.

"Now let's go!" she said, running toward the stairs.

Bruto followed behind, barking and snapping at the bats that chased them. Ondina was still preoccupied with the bird-women by the deactivated cell door. The fourth floor was so close. . . .

"No!" Ondina shrieked from behind them. "You idiots! They're getting away!" And then: "Not the hair!"

Pao laughed, and Bruto let out a happy puppy yip like she was throwing a Frisbee for him at the park.

"When we get out of here, buddy," she said as he took the stairs two at a time beside her, "I'm definitely gonna show you a park. And a Frisbee. And all kinds of other awesome dog stuff."

If she made it back from this alive, her mom could hardly

refuse her the void beast that had gotten her through the rift, could she?

The fourth floor came into view, the glass walls darker up there, like the tinted windows of the cars that drove through Pao's neighborhood at night. The temperature was lower, and Pao felt the drain pulling at her again—harder than ever before, like her energy was a milkshake someone was trying to get the last slurp of.

"We need to find Dante," Pao said, the words visible as puffs of air in the cold. But it couldn't have been clearer—Dante wasn't on this floor. No one was. The glass was dark and ominous, and the hair on the back of Pao's neck tingled.

Bruto whined, and for the first time since they'd entered the palace, he sounded afraid.

"It's okay," she tried to say. "We'll go back. . . . This was the wrong way. . . ."

But when she looked behind her, the floor was uninterrupted dark glass. The stairs were gone.

That's when the screaming started.

It was soft at first, but it built on itself, echoing around the now-sealed chamber like a hurricane wind picking up.

As the sound slid up the octaves into a desperate wail, Bruto yelped and pawed at his ears. Pao covered her own with her hands, but it did little to muffle the screeching, which continued to increase in volume until Pao was sure she'd lose her mind.

But then, just as abruptly as it had started, it stopped, and the momentary silence was somehow worse.

Don't think this has anything to do with your resourcefulness, said a woman's voice, as layered and echoing and terrible as the wailing had been, though Pao saw no one else in the room. *It's all because of* her *failure.* A dark diamond rose from the floor, Ondina writhing in its center. The crystal turned to liquid that splashed across the floor, disgorging Ondina and soaking Pao's sneakers.

"I'm sorry." Ondina was on her hands and knees, sobbing and coughing.

Sorry won't save you. The voice echoed in Pao's skull. *Only I can do that. I'll be back for you. For both of you.*

After that, the voice stopped, the silence left behind broken only by Ondina's sniffling. Meanwhile, Pao's whole body had gone cold. If the owner of the voice could reduce Ondina to *this*, what chance did Pao have of getting out of here? Much less of finding Dante and Emma.

Franco had been right. There *was* a Source in the rift— someone who could intimidate and control the void's most fearsome creatures. But who *was* it?

It had seemed so hypothetical before, an interesting puzzle. But now Pao had the horrible feeling she'd just been trapped in a glass cage by the very general the Niños had been looking for.

And she didn't have the first idea how to get out.

TWENTY-SIX

And They Say Relentlessness Is a Bad Thing

"Can't you just open a door in the wall?" Pao asked when she'd gotten sick of Ondina's whimpering and her own spiraling, hopeless thoughts. "You were walking around like you owned this place like an hour ago. Or was that all just an attempt to impress me?"

"You're an idiot," Ondina said, but the insult carried less weight in her *I've been crying* voice, and she seemed to know it. "I can't open a room she's sealed. . . . Not without sending us somewhere even worse."

"So . . . you're *not* the mighty overlord of this creepy palace?"

Ondina just glared.

"I just want to hear you say it *once*: *I'm not in control.*"

"If you don't shut up, I'll punch you."

"Are you sure you have the *authority* to do that?"

Bruto licked Pao's hand, which she figured was his version of giving her a high five, but before Pao could scratch his ears, Ondina lunged at her, tackling her to the ground.

"This is *all. Your. Fault.*" she said as they rolled over and over on the slick glass floor, slapping and elbowing and pummeling each other in a good old-fashioned playground brawl. Bruto circled and barked in a vain attempt to get them to stop fighting.

Ondina grabbed one of Pao's braids, but Pao got a fistful of Ondina's long curls, right at the nape of her neck.

"Ow!"

"Serves you right, coward!" Pao screeched, unwilling to admit Ondina's grip on her braid hurt even though her eyes were watering.

"Oh, *I'm* the coward?"

Pao rolled over again, pulling Ondina with her until she finally let go of the braid.

Both girls sat up, panting and disheveled, Pao's face flushed. Ondina's remained pale.

"Yes," Ondina said. "You're the coward."

"I'm not seeing your logic," Pao said between winces as she blotted at her bloody lip with the collar of her T-shirt. "You're the one taking orders from some disembodied voice. Do you even *want* to be a junior overlord? Why don't you just leave?"

Ondina shot her a withering glare. "You have no idea what you're talking about."

"Well, *tell* me, then!" Pao said, a plan starting to form like crystals in the bottom of a beaker, absorbing all her fear for the moment.

"I can't," Ondina said, but she was staring off into space like something horrible was barreling toward her. Pao knew that feeling. She could work with it.

"Why not?" she asked, trying to sound casual. "I mean, if you and disembodied boss lady have your way, I'll be dead soon anyway. Or some horrible soulless ghoul. Might as well get it off your chest."

"I don't need to *confess* to you," Ondina snapped. "I'm not *troubled*. I'm just . . . acclimating."

"To what?"

"You're relentless—has anyone ever told you that?"

"Has anyone ever told *you* that?"

Pao was just firing back, bantering, hoping to get the girl's guard down. But the words seemed to have more of an effect on Ondina than she'd expected. The other girl deflated, her eyes dropping to her shoes.

"What?" Pao asked. "Being relentless isn't so bad."

"It's not that," Ondina said, and then her eyes snapped to Pao's. "Stop trying to get me to talk to you. We're stuck in this room together—that doesn't mean we have to braid each other's hair."

"Fine," Pao said. "I suck at braiding anyway. My mom always does mine. And for what it's worth? Whatever your boss has on you isn't worth all this. You don't seem like *that* evil a person—a little annoying, and definitely completely narcissistic, but not *evil*."

Ondina narrowed her eyes, but the expression was halfhearted.

"You could just get out of here . . . and help me in the process," Pao said, knowing she was overplaying her hand, but she was running out of time. She could feel it. The glass all around them was getting darker, and the blood from Pao's lip sat on top of the floor. It wasn't draining her anymore. Instead, it was saving her for later, like leftover pizza. But for what?

Or worse, *whom*?

"I can't 'get out of here,'" Ondina said. "There is no me out of here. At least . . . not yet."

"So that's what she promised you?" Pao asked. "To turn you from a . . . whatever you are . . . into a real girl?" Pao still hadn't figured out what Ondina was exactly. All she knew was that she packed a mean punch. "How do you even know she can do what she says?"

"Because she's done it before," Ondina said, her mouth set, her eyes still fixed on the shiny patent leather of her shoes.

"So . . . do *I* have something to do with this magical girl-making ritual?" Pao asked, cold dread creeping in around her plan like a fog.

Ondina's stony silence said it all.

"And you think, once she does whatever thing she's gonna do, she'll let you walk out of here and live your life?" Pao asked. "No more lecturing you about failure, or dragging you through the walls, or locking you in rooms you can't get out of?"

"You don't know her," Ondina said, but suddenly she didn't look so sure.

"I don't," Pao admitted. "But I've been wandering around this weird place long enough to get the gist. Do what you want with me and my friends—I can't stop you. But don't be disappointed when things don't change. I've read enough books to know that evil overlords don't just give up their minions."

"I'm not her *minion*."

"Oh, definitely not," Pao said. "Running weird dream errands to lure people into her lair. Shuttling said people around the palace. Checking on her demon pets. Doesn't sound like minion behavior at all."

"It's not *minion* behavior; it's—"

"Wait, let me guess. She's a *benevolent* overlord and you're doing all this because you *love* her . . . but totally not in a clichéd, brainwashed kind of way."

Ondina was getting angry—Pao could tell by the way her fingernails pressed into her palms. And anger could be useful, as Pao knew better than anyone. She kept going. "Just so you know, that's what every single overlord says to their min—"

"She's my *mother*, you half-wit!" Ondina said, the words exploding out of her. "She's my mother, okay? I'm not her minion—I'm her *daughter*."

Pao whistled long and low. "Ghost princess of the spooky underwater palace? No wonder you're such a brat."

"I'm not . . . You know what? Think what you want about me. My mother made a promise to me, and I made one to her. We've been waiting a long time for this moment, and I'm not going to let you or your incessant questions mess it up for me."

But Pao barely heard her, because the mush at the bottom of her beaker was crystallizing again.

Marisa had dismissed Pao's theory about who the general was. Of course starry-eyed Marisa would take Franco's word over a tourist's.

And Pao, limited by her own closed-mindedness and embarrassment, hadn't pushed it.

But she should have.

Because there is no one stronger, or more resourceful, or more *ruthless* than a mother who believes her children are in danger.

No matter who she is or what she herself has done . . .

Franco had underestimated the thin, ragged, wailing spirit who'd held the world in thrall for generations. He'd believed himself stronger, thought he could dispatch the ghost of a mother and laugh about her afterward.

Pao knew that mothers don't go down easy. They wait, build up their strength. They *never* give up.

"Franco, you foolish, arrogant boy . . ." Pao said, not realizing she'd spoken aloud until Ondina's gaze snapped to her face.

"What did you say?"

"Nothing . . ."

"Whatever you're thinking, just spit it out, okay?" Ondina snapped, her smooth, sarcastic exterior gone, her nerves exposed. "The mumbling mad-scientist routine is getting old."

Pao looked at Ondina, who met her gaze, unflinching.

"La Llorona." Pao tried to keep her voice even, and watched Ondina's face for a reaction. For proof that she wasn't wrong. "That's who stuck us in here. Your mother is La Llorona."

Ondina didn't deny it, and in Pao's bloodstream, dread battled with the thrill of discovery.

"But that means . . ." Pao said, peering closer at Ondina, at her old-fashioned clothes, at the wariness around her eyes. "That means she's not just trying to bring you back to life. It means . . . It means . . ."

"It means she killed me," Ondina said, her voice as dry as a cactus spine. "Yes. She killed us all."

TWENTY-SEVEN

There's No Halfway When You Have to Fight a Villain

"We have to get out of here," Pao said, getting to her feet. Sure, Ondina wasn't exactly alive, but Pao had seen her in the cactus field in the full light of day. They'd find a way. They had to.

But Ondina didn't move.

"Ondina, she's dangerous. How can you possibly believe anything she says? We have to go! You can come with me!"

The not-quite-ghost girl sat eerily still, but when her gaze turned on Pao, it was obvious: Pao's pushing and prodding had backfired. Ondina's confession had only made her extra determined. *Less* human, not more.

"There's no way out," Ondina replied as she stood up. Her voice was calm, all traces of her hiccupping sobs gone. "Not for you, anyway. We've been looking for you for such a long time, Paola."

"What do you mean?" Pao asked, backing away slightly. "Why me?"

"You said it yourself earlier." The green glow in Ondina's eyes was manic as she surveyed Pao. "We're relentless, you and I. Mother and I needed a match. Someone whose energy would be at home in my resurrected body."

Pao continued to walk backward, even though she knew there

was no exit door. No window. No secret escape hatch. Ondina was wavering between the almost-human girl Pao had only seen glimpses of and the dead-eyed heir to the glass palace.

"The boy was immortal and timeless—clever, too—but he was too much a part of that wretched campfire brigade. His heart wasn't his own."

"Franco?" Pao asked. "You took Franco? Where is he now?"

"And the girl was smart, cunning. She had style. But she was too naive. She hadn't seen enough of the world. . . ."

"Emma," Pao choked out, her heart sinking. "What did you do with her? With Franco? Where are they?"

"The other boy was never a match, but he charged in here looking for you, and Mother knew—*we* knew—we could use him. That you'd do anything to save him. Even walk right into the last place you should have."

Dante. They had taken Dante to lure her in. And it had worked.

Pao would have laughed if fear weren't choking her. She had accused *him* of being the dumb hero, but look who had stormed the haunted palace looking for the dude in distress in the end.

"But you . . ." Ondina approached Pao like she was a dress in a shopwindow. "You were different. I could tell from the first time I visited you. You had something the others didn't. . . ."

Pao watched Ondina, transfixed by the longing in her eyes. Hundreds of years of waiting, gathered right there on the surface.

"You weren't just smart, and cunning, and a little rebellious. You were *wicked*. There was something in you that you tried to repress. A secret rage smoldering away. *That* was the final ingredient."

And now, at last, Pao understood. All this *was* her fault. Her anger was the perfect breeding ground for this supernatural bacteria.

"She's going to use me to bring you back to life," Pao said, her voice hollow.

"It's an amazing technique," Ondina confirmed. "Although she was always a gifted healer, even in life. For centuries, she has been draining the life force from people, hoping that the combination of their souls and the void's power would enable her to bring her children back." Ondina shook her head, like it was a silly thing to believe. "She's given me a physical form, allowed me to retain my mind and my memories, made me stronger than any other fantasma—"

"That's for sure," Pao muttered, rubbing the bruises their fight had left on her arms.

"But I'm still tied to this place until we find the right soul to make me fully human again," Ondina continued.

"And I'm the lucky winner," Pao said, trying to remain deadpan despite the terror freezing her throat and chest.

Ondina's eyes flickered between those of a human and those of a monster. She didn't reply.

"Because you feel like you've earned it, the right to take someone's life. The right to take *all* these people's lives." Pao was getting mad now, the kind of mad that made her want to cry. "You want to walk free knowing that someone's daughter had to die, someone's friend, so you could flounce around showing off your hair?"

Ondina looked at her, humanity winning out for a moment. "It's not personal. I just—"

"You're just doing what Mommy tells you to," Pao cut in. "Have you even asked yourself if you want it?"

The other girl's eyes went dark, and Pao knew she'd hit a nerve.

"It doesn't matter what I want."

"But if it did . . ." Pao said, and a ray of sunlight burst into the cold night of her fear. A path through the darkness.

She'd been so focused on the ways she was like Ondina, but if that were true, didn't it mean Ondina was like *her*, too? That there was something brave and righteous in her like the feeling that was burning in Pao's chest?

"If it mattered," Pao began, ready to roll the dice, "what would you want?"

"To be free," Ondina answered without hesitation. Then she looked startled, like she hadn't meant to say that.

Pao held her gaze, vindicated. "And you think you'll be free once she does it? That you can just go and live your life? Do you want an eternity of facing her disappointment, Ondina? Because it doesn't seem to be making you very happy now."

"Stop it," Ondina said, trying to hitch her unfeeling persona back into place. But there were gaps in it, Pao knew, and she went for them. Relentlessly.

"You deserve to be free," Pao said, keeping her voice soft. This time she was the one walking forward while Ondina backed up. "You deserve to know you were good, because you were—I can see it. And all the people who will die if you do this—the Niños, Dante, Emma, Franco, me—we don't deserve it, Ondina. Just like you didn't."

"It was my fault," Ondina said, looking away from Pao. "I

deserve to be punished. It was my fault she did it. I started to cry, and—"

"That's not true," Pao said, and she thought of everything she'd forgiven herself for as the rift closed in on her. All the times she'd distanced herself from her mom, rejected her, betrayed her beliefs. "Your mom is supposed to love you, no matter what." Her heart was in her throat now. "She's not supposed to hurt you. It's not your fault."

Ondina's mouth was open, but no sound came out. Tears, black this time, coursed down her ghostly face. "Stop it," she sniffled. "It's too late. There's no way out."

"We can find one," Pao said, her own eyes watering. "Together. I'll help you."

"Why would you want to help me?"

"Because I want to do what's right," Pao said. "And I think you do, too."

She was close enough now to reach out and take Ondina's hand, and she extended hers, waiting as the ghostly girl battled internally with something Pao could tell was much older than this moment. Something she'd buried that was now being dragged up.

"I can't," Ondina said, taking a tentative step back. "I don't have a choice."

"There's always a choice," Pao said, catching her eyes again and holding them. "I'm going to try, with or without you, but I think we both know I don't have a chance on my own."

"You don't," she said. The hint of a smirk even under her sniffling made Pao bolder.

"But together . . . together we could do this. We could save them. We could get you your freedom, Ondina. I can help you. Will you help me?"

The battle raged, the human girl still inside Ondina at odds with the monster the void wanted her to become. Pao left her hand extended, waiting, willing her to cross the boundary, believing she could, because here was Pao, despite her anger, wanting to do what was right.

Ondina folded her arms. "Even if we wanted to, it's not like we could just waltz out of here."

"So we take it one step at a time," Pao said. "What's first?"

Ondina hesitated. "I could . . . make a door," she said. "But it won't go straight to her. There's only one way to get through if you're not escorted, and it's not a picnic."

"And everything we've done so far has been such a picnic."

"Shut up. I'm trying to tell you I'll make the door, but I'm not going through it with you. You'll be on your own after that."

"She'll know you helped me. There's no halfway when you fight a villain. Haven't you ever read a book?"

"Do you want the door or not?"

"Will you meet me on the other side?"

"If you even *get* to the other side," Ondina muttered, a wrinkle between her eyebrows. "This is what I can do for now," she said at last, decisively. "Don't count on me being there."

"You'll be there," Pao said, smiling at her. "And thank you in advance."

"Ugh, this would be so much less distasteful if you were . . . literally anyone else."

"You know that saying *You only dislike about others what you dislike about yourself* or whatever?"

"Stop."

"It's *especially* true in this case."

"Okay, now I'm just making the door to get rid of you. I hope whatever's in there eats you."

"You don't *know* what's in there?" Pao asked, alarm bells ringing in her head.

"Do I look like the kind of person who goes the long way?" Ondina replied, her nose in the air.

"Stupid princess."

"Stupid hero complex."

Pao smiled. There was that word again. *Hero.* She didn't hate it as much as she used to.

"My friends . . ." Pao said. "They're still alive?"

Ondina nodded. "They're . . . needed. For the ritual. They'll be with her."

The smile was gone as quickly as it had come.

"What if I can't . . . ?"

"I don't have time to babysit you right now, Paola. Do you want to try to save them or not?"

Pao gritted her teeth. "I take it back. I dislike you, and it has nothing to do with disliking myself."

Ondina didn't answer, just rolled her eyes once more for good measure before laying both hands on the wall and closing her lids.

For a moment, nothing happened, and Pao's stomach twisted with fear. But of what, exactly? That it wouldn't work? Or that Ondina had betrayed her, and this performance of hers was just a distraction?

Pao was about to say something when, at last, there was movement.

It was almost too subtle to notice at first—a section of glass, warping and swirling until it looked like a face. And then, beside it, another visage formed, and another, until there were more faces than blank wall.

They were grotesque, their features becoming more animated the longer Ondina pressed her hands against the glass, their many eyes forming and opening wide, their mouths gaping in terror.

Pao shuddered and took a step back, but it was too late to abandon the plan now.

Beneath Ondina's hands, one of the mouths yawned wider than the others. Wide enough to walk through.

This time, even Bruto looked afraid.

"Come on, boy," Pao said, but he whined and sat down. "Bruto, come on!"

"He won't go," Ondina said quietly. "He was made here—he knows it's not safe."

"He'll come," Pao said, but suddenly she wasn't so sure.

"He's a monster, Paola," said Ondina, looking at him sadly. "You can't trust them."

She was saying more than that, Pao knew. She was saying Pao couldn't trust *her*, either. And she was right. But Pao didn't have any other choice.

The way ahead was as dark as the rift had been, and Pao glanced at Bruto once more, then at Ondina, verifying that it was time.

"Take care of him for me," Pao said, and she stepped into the darkness without waiting for a response.

TWENTY-EIGHT

Rising Water, Rising Panic

All the false bravado that had propelled Pao into the mouth in the wall was torn away as she walked through it.

The people behind the grotesque faces she'd seen in the glass clogged the passageway ahead. Long, spindly fingers clawed at her, leaving cold, clammy trails where they touched her skin. Pao tried to keep moving forward, but she spun around every time a new horror appeared, and fear choked her when she realized specters were surrounding her.

Ondina had acted like this was a punishment. But for whom?

A man with a backpack and blank staring eyes grew from the dust at her feet, and Pao screamed. The hallway seemed to catch the sound and bounce it from surface to surface until it turned into a wild, awful wailing that had Pao clamping her hands over her ears.

"Mis hijos . . ." A voice cut through Pao's own echoing moans. "Where are my children?"

The dust became water, lapping at her sneakers, soaking them.

Then the faces disappeared. And the walls. Everything was gone except the dark water and a pinprick of light ahead, which expanded to illuminate the ghostly form of a dark-haired woman in a long white dress.

"Mis hijos . . . ¿Dónde están?"

The dread in the pit of Pao's stomach was cold and sharp. It screamed at her to run, but she knew there was nowhere to go.

Up ahead, the woman clutched at her face, her long, matted hair trailing behind as she cried again and again, "My children are gone. . . ."

The punishing cold of her fear made Pao feel five years old again, listening to her mother's stories at bedtime and pretending not to be afraid. Afterward, she would stay up for hours with the lights on, jumping at any small noise.

The spectral woman, closer to Pao now, looked at her own hands. They were stained up to the elbows with blood. The ghost screamed in horror, and try as she might to stay quiet, Pao screamed, too.

The water grew more turbulent, rising to Pao's knees.

That's when La Llorona lifted her eyes.

"Te llevaste a mis hijos," she said, her voice a low growl. The green of her eyes turned electric.

"No!" Pao said. She didn't understand all the words, but there was no mistaking the look in those eyes. Pao backed away, the water getting deeper.

"You were bad," La Llorona said in a singsong voice. "You were bad, and you took my hijos y vas a pagar por eso."

Her bloodstained hands reached for Pao's face, and suddenly the air was crowded with three ghostly children—two boys and a girl—all wailing, their eyes black as ink.

"No!" Pao shouted. "I didn't take your children! It was you! They're gone because of *you*!"

"I would never hurt my children." The words were a snarl,

and Pao took another step back, only to find herself in water up to her waist.

"You *did*," Pao said, the story springing to mind effortlessly, despite the many years she'd spent trying to ignore its existence. "You did hurt them."

There were many versions of the tale, but Pao knew only one by heart. She stopped backing away. She looked at La Llorona, past her glowing eyes, and saw a mother.

"Their father left," Pao said as gently as she could. "He said the children were a sin. A crime."

La Llorona screamed again, a terrifying sound like a thousand saws going through metal, but Pao could hear the sadness beneath it now. She stood her ground and waited for quiet to return.

"They weren't a sin," Pao said. "It was just what he believed."

The silence stretched on, and the monstrous face of the ghost woman eased a little, pink appearing high in her cheeks, her hair smoothing out, then knotting, then smoothing again, like she couldn't decide if she was a monster or a mother.

Maybe she was always both, Pao thought, waiting.

"We weren't married," came a whisper into the space between them. La Llorona's blazing eyes dimmed just a little, going almost hazel before glowing their too-bright green once more. "Pero quería casarme."

"Yes, you did want that, but he left," Pao said, stepping closer. "You couldn't have made him stay." There was sadness in her own voice now as she remembered her mom out on the patio, crying when she thought Pao was asleep.

It wasn't my fault, or Mom's, that Dad left. She understood it now, in a way she never had before.

"You were grieving for him," Pao said, not bothering to wipe her wet cheeks. "You were alone, with no one to help you. You were doing your best."

Tears poured out of La Llorona's eyes like a faucet had been turned on, and they were black, like Ondina's. *Hija de Lágrimas* . . . Pao figured it out at last: *the daughter of tears.*

Pao and Ondina had more in common than the princess even knew.

"But Ondina . . ." Pao said, her fear thawing. "Ondina needs you. She needs you to let go."

"No," sobbed the woman, the water rising to their chests now. "¡No puedo!"

"She needs to be set free," Pao said. "You killed them, and you're sorry, but killing more children isn't going to save them."

"It will. . . . It *will!*"

The light in La Llorona's eyes was dazzling again, and the black water turned red.

"No, don't!" Pao said, her panic back in full force. The water was climbing to her neck, and she knew what was coming next.

"Lo siento," said the woman, the black tears still falling, dropping like ink into the red water around them. "No puedo seguir sola. I can't. . . ."

Pao was out of options. She didn't know if this was real or a dream or some illusion in the wall, but when La Llorona took Pao's head in her hands, her grip was terrible and sure.

She tried to think of her own mother . . . of Emma, Dante, all the people she had ever loved. . . .

But when the water took Pao, it took them, too.

TWENTY-NINE
The Source Unmasked

Pao woke, as she had so often before, coughing and sputtering, drowning on dry land.

Only this time, she was on the stone floor of what appeared to be a cave, and everything around her was bathed in green light. It reflected off the wet rocks, turning her skin a sickly color, her white hair into a witch's wig.

Pao had drowned in blood. And La Llorona . . . she had won. What did that mean? Had it even been real?

"Oh, please. You didn't think that was it, did you?"

Pao used what little strength she had to turn her head toward the voice, immediately recognizable even without the ghostly echo that had carried it through the palace's glass walls.

"That was just a memory." The voice was coming from a shadowy corner of the cave. Pao squinted, but she couldn't see anyone there. "Just a story. I was so weak back then, prowling the riverbanks, unable to see what was right in front of me—bound to a single frail phantom body."

She was describing the pathetic ghost Franco had discounted a century ago, Pao thought as she struggled to sit up. A wraith who had not yet become shrouded in legend.

"When that upstart boy attacked me," she continued, as if she could read Pao's thoughts, "I was still half-broken, mourning the loss of an unworthy man, bound to my earthly concerns. The boy thought he'd won when his banishing knife sent me here, but it was the best thing that ever happened to me."

"Why?" Pao asked, wanting to buy herself time, but also shamefully fascinated by La Llorona's transformation. From a wailing pauper barely worthy of local gossip to the scourge of the rift and beyond. . . .

"This is where I found my true calling," La Llorona said, her disembodied voice still floating to Pao through the darkness. "Where I discovered that a true warrior can never be destroyed. Not when there's power to be had. Not when her desire is strong enough to survive anything."

As she spoke, Pao pushed herself up to standing, her legs shaky underneath her. She cast around for a sharp rock, a shell, anything that could be used as a weapon. But there was nothing.

"We're always underestimated, aren't we?" The voice turned seductive, and Pao wished she could cover her ears. "But is there anything more determined than a mother parted from her children?"

The words were eerily similar to the ones Pao had thought when she'd realized who the general was, and what part Ondina had played in this sad, horrible story. Pao didn't want to hear any more, didn't want to know what other ideas she shared with the monster who had ruined so many lives.

"Where's Emma?" Pao asked, steadier on her feet now, squinting into the darkness. "Dante. Where are my friends?"

From reminiscing and boastful, La Llorona's tone turned

speculative. "Your stubborn little loyal streak," said the voice, footsteps accompanying it now. "It could have been the end of us all."

The voice was like a snake, or a leech. As it slithered and probed, it felt like something crawling over Pao's skin.

"My little girl—she's brilliant, beautiful, and cunning. She's relentless. But she's a survivor. She won't be held back by ties to others." The voice was coming closer, and Pao strained even harder to peer into the darkness. "We'll have to break you of that before the end, Paola Santiago."

As she said Pao's name, La Llorona stepped out from the cloak of shadow.

It was true—there was no comparing this woman to the white-dressed ghost sobbing on the riverbank. Her body was now corporeal, though her skin was pale and waxy. She was easily six feet tall, draped in a gown of kelp and river stones, her long black hair lustrous, shining in the green light. She was magnificent. Strong. The void's magic had turned her grief into something shimmering and deadly.

Her face, though, was truly horrifying. Her mouth was stretched open in a perpetual scream, her eye sockets wide and empty. She moved like a living person, but her voice was projected from inside her somewhere, her features frozen in eternal grief.

"My daughter," said the unearthly woman, "wants to survive. And by the time I'm through with you, that's all you'll want, too."

"You underestimate her," Pao said loudly, despite the way her knees trembled and every cell in her body quavered in fear. "Ondina is loyal, too. And what she wants is to be free."

It would be really cool, Pao thought, if Ondina showed up

right now. Like a punctuation mark to Pao's defiance. It would give Pao the incentive to keep fighting when her fear was rapidly overtaking her bravery.

But Ondina was nowhere to be seen.

Probably off teaching Bruto to bark sarcastically, Pao thought bitterly.

"She *will* be free," said La Llorona as she came closer to Pao, trailing the smell of mildew and rot. "Free to leave this place and return to it as she pleases. Free to spread what we've created here beyond this sad corner of the world. Thanks to you."

La Llorona reached out and, before Pao could stop it, took her by the throat with one hand. The phantom lifted her to eye level, Pao's feet dangling three feet off the ground as she choked and scrabbled at the monstrous woman's pasty skin with her fingernails.

"We've waited a long time," the ghost breathed, and from her tortured mask came the faint screams of hundreds of children, dragged from their homes and playgrounds to feed this woman's guilt. Her vengeance.

As she held the struggling Pao in one hand, she waved the other through the air, and a circle in the floor began to rise in the center of the cave. Behind La Llorona, four glass prisms descended from the ceiling. She waited until all was still to let go of Pao, who fell into a twisted heap on the stone.

Immediately, Pao pushed herself up, ignoring the way her knees stung from the impact and her palms were bleeding freely again. The stone didn't take her blood—it displayed it like a warning.

"This is the last phase, Paola. Consider yourself lucky to be witnessing it. You are by nature a curious girl, are you not? Like me, unwilling to merely accept without question—"

"I'm nothing like you," Pao interrupted, and she would have said more, but when she looked closer at the changes to the cave's landscape, all other thoughts fled her mind.

In three of the four glass enclosures now standing at the room's west end, a person was suspended in water but somehow still breathing, eyes closed as if asleep.

Two of the faces were familiar; the third Pao could identify without recognizing it.

In the first prism was a tall boy, sixteen or so, dark hair waving around his face.

Franco, Pao thought, remembering the way Marisa had mourned him.

Beside him, her dirty blond pigtails floating on either side of her pale cheeks, was Emma, looking too small, too helpless. Pao choked back a sob.

In the third, Dante had his chin on his chest, his arms crossed in front of him like a shield. If she didn't know any better, Pao would have said he was snoring.

Hopelessness dragged at her like cement, threatening to pull her under.

They're alive, she reminded herself, ordering her legs not to collapse, her tears not to fall. *They're alive. It's not too late.*

The fourth prism stood empty, and Pao knew instinctively that it was waiting for her. She too would be placed in suspended animation as the final step in restoring Ondina's wasted life.

"She doesn't want this," Pao said, not taking her eyes off Dante and Emma. "Ondina doesn't want it. Giving her back her life won't fix what you did."

"She's a child," said La Llorona, walking close to Franco, tracing a line in the glass in front of his face. "It's up to me to know what's best for her, not cater to her silly whims."

"It's not a silly whim to want to prevent suffering," Pao said. "It's heroic. If you were ever a true healer, you would know that."

"Heroic." La Llorona laughed, examining the other prisms before turning to Pao, who didn't back down. "We aren't heroes here," she continued. "We're survivors. We make the best of what we're given."

"So what was killing your children, then?" Pao asked, trying not to flinch as she stared into the woman's ghastly face. "Was that you doing your best?"

La Llorona snarled, "You pathetic little girl. You know nothing about what I've sacrificed, nothing about how people treated me in that terrible place. You have no idea what those children's lives would have been like with an unmarried mother." She seemed to pull herself together before saying, "You may think me a monster, but I did them a kindness. And now I can do Ondina an even greater one."

"Only Ondina?" Pao asked, remembering the three pitiful ghosts she had seen in the passageway. "What about your two boys? What happened to them?" She was grasping at straws, already feeling suffocated by the prospect of La Llorona forcing her into a water coffin of her own.

It was impossible to read emotion on a face frozen by centuries of grief, but Pao thought something in La Llorona's manner stiffened.

"My sons were not as strong as my daughter," she said, her tone flat within her twisted mask. "One I lost in my first attempt at restoration. The other . . ."

Pao waited, her breath trapped in her throat.

"Men are ungrateful fools." La Llorona grunted with a sound like a door slamming shut. "My daughter will be my masterpiece. She will never leave me."

"Daughters leave all the time," Pao said, thinking of her own grandmother, who had crossed the border alone at twelve years old to live with relatives she'd never met. And herself, leaving home to enter another world entirely. If her mom wasn't in grave danger herself, she'd be worried sick by now. . . .

"Enough!" La Llorona cried, and she turned to the dais in the middle of the room.

Pao had almost forgotten the platform in the shock of seeing her friends again, but it was hard to ignore it now, with La Llorona's pale form sweeping toward it, trailing strings of rocks and what looked like eel skins behind her.

The ghost woman peeled off its black surface like a magician pulling a tablecloth, and suddenly the green light bathing the room intensified a hundred times. Pao threw up an arm to shield her face.

When her eyes had adjusted, Pao squinted at La Llorona, who was standing in front of a glowing green globe. The illumination threw her face into harsh relief, making it look triumphant even though its expression remained fixed in screaming terror.

The sight chilled Pao to the bone.

"It's time . . ." La Llorona said, more to the glowing sphere than to Pao. "The solstice has weakened the barrier." She drew a small glass container from her cloak and shook a ring of white crystals around the base of the pedestal. Salt, Pao knew from her mother's rituals.

As La Llorona prepared the space, Pao examined the globe at

its center. It wasn't simply a ball of green light as she'd originally thought. The sphere was surrounded by separate particles, like the bodies of a hundred illuminated snakes twisting in a cluster. Pao could see through the cracks between them to the pure light underneath.

Pao thought back to what Marisa had said—Franco's theory about the rift itself being neutral, and something corrupting its magic.

What if it was this globe, and not La Llorona, that was the source of the void's power? What if the green coursing like venom through the palace—absorbing the negative emotions of anyone who walked its halls, lighting up the eyes of the beasts and the ahogados—was the corruption?

La Llorona, now muttering with her eyes closed, didn't notice when Pao crept over to the glass prisms and pressed her palms to the ones that held Dante and Emma. They didn't react—not that she'd expected them to. When she was doubly sure they were still breathing, Pao's eyes darted to the fourth enclosure—the one waiting for her—and her mouth went dry.

She felt the urgency of the moment, as if it were up to her to prevent a nuclear core meltdown before it exploded and took everything with it. Her life. The lives of her friends. Ondina's freedom. The Niños' safety . . .

Pao took advantage of La Llorona's distraction to think harder than she ever had in her life.

The power source was obviously part of the ritual. In her vision in the passageway, Pao had seen La Llorona from the days before she had absorbed strength from the void: a ghost woman doomed to wander the riverbank wailing for her lost children. She'd been haunting—scary, even. But Franco had been right on one count: That pitiful specter could never have been the general.

With the power of the void in her hands, however, she was deadly. Unstoppable.

Turning her back on Dante and Emma wasn't easy, but Pao found herself walking toward the orb before she could decide against it, transfixed by the color of the pulsing light, the way the cords of energy seemed alive as they moved.

She would have to destroy it, Pao knew, but that seemed impossible. How did one obliterate pure energy? You could divert it, maybe. Use it up. But could you just . . . stop it?

Pao had always been told she was smart for her age. But now she was up against the vengefulness of a ghost turned god, who'd had hundreds of years to plan and experiment. How could she overcome that?

The horrible truth dawned on her as she stared into the light.

She couldn't.

Not alone.

The cave began to vibrate, small rocks dislodging from the walls and ceiling and clattering to the ground. Beneath the orb, another platform was rising, lifting the power source higher, where Pao couldn't have reached it even if she'd known what to do.

"Wait!" Pao blurted out.

La Llorona laughed. "It's too late," she said. "It's beginning."

And she was right. The orb was inaccessible, La Llorona was moving toward her, and the empty glass prism was yawning, waiting to take everything inside Pao and turn it into green light.

Waiting to bring Ondina back to life.

La Llorona raised a hand, and a tiny cord of the orb's power wrapped around her wrist like a vine. She grabbed it and flicked it at Pao. A line extended like rope and lassoed Pao around the waist.

Pao began to slide inexorably toward the prism. Toward the end.

"No!" she screamed, struggling against the cord, but La Llorona just stared at her with those empty eyes, reeling her in until Pao could feel the glass coffin pulling at her.

Cold air wormed its way under her skin, freezing the blood in her veins and the thoughts in her brain.

And then, inexplicably, the pressure ceased, the rope of energy falling from her waist. Pao looked up slowly as her body and mind gradually thawed.

"Get off me, you beast!" La Llorona was shouting, and there, ripping the ends of her trailing river robe, was Bruto.

How did he get in here? Pao wondered. She looked around for Ondina, but there was no sign of her. Pao and Bruto were on their own. It would have to be enough for now.

Now that she was free from the unbearable pressure and La Llorona was distracted by the puppy, Pao did the only thing she could. Even though the cave was barely the size of the middle school gym, and there were no doors, windows, or other escape routes, she ran.

There was a yelp and a crunch, and then La Llorona laughed, a horrible, grating sound like nails on a chalkboard.

Please let him be okay, Pao prayed. *Please let him be okay.*

"Tricks won't protect you," La Llorona said, stalking Pao, snapping three more cords of energy into her own hands. "This time, I'll put you in there myself."

Pao dodged one cord, and then another. The third caught her around the ankle, but she stepped out of it before it could tighten. She kept moving, remembering the time in sixth-grade gym when Mrs. Roberts had told her she had "good footwork" during a basketball unit.

La Llorona didn't seem as impressed. As Pao darted in and out of the shadows, the specter screamed in frustration, summoning four more cords, her eyes pulsing with power.

But she didn't send the cords after Pao. She stood stock-still in the center of the room as they suctioned themselves to her bone-white arms, glowing green as they pumped her full of the void's power as though she were taking steroids.

Before Pao's eyes, La Llorona grew taller and more fearsome than ever. The cords fell away and she lunged for Pao, her reach much longer now.

Pao baseball-slid to get away, like she'd learned from Naomi back what seemed like a hundred years ago. Then she scrambled to her feet.

"You can't escape me," the woman screeched as Pao evaded her grip by a hair. The ugly sound echoed off the walls as the orb rose higher and higher, taking with it Pao's last hope of ending all this misery.

Pao's world shrank to the muscles in her legs, the pounding in her chest, and the sound of La Llorona behind her. Sure, the wailing woman had gotten bigger, but that just made it more difficult for her to move in the small space, and by dodging, zigzagging, and sticking to the shadows, Pao managed to avoid capture.

But to what end? she wondered, panting as the exertion of the day, the *week*, began to catch up with her at last. La Llorona's swipes were getting closer and closer. They had covered every inch of the cave's floor twice at least.

Pao was only stalling now, delaying the inevitable.

"Bruto!" Pao called, but nothing stirred in the cave. She was alone. And the prism's terrible cold was reaching for her. . . .

The next time the woman grabbed for her, Pao seized her

hand and wrenched it backward. Her pursuer stopped short, screaming in shock and pain. Pao hadn't been sure La Llorona was human enough to feel pain. She filed away the results of that experiment for later use.

Unfortunately, the injury had only created a little distance between them, and it was quickly closed by La Llorona.

Pao was tired. Spent. She slipped once, her knee hitting the rock floor with a crunch. She landed a hard kick at La Llorona's ankle but stumbled afterward, twisting her own.

There was nowhere left to go. The specter was close, and she was furious, green light pulsing in the hollows where her eyes should be. Pao had backed herself into a wall, her knee throbbed, and her ankle was protesting any weight on it.

It was the end of the line.

Tears sprang to her eyes when she realized what would happen. Not just to her, but also to Dante and Emma. To Franco and the Niños. To her mom and Señora Mata.

"Now you'll see what your little tricks are worth in the face of *absolute power*," La Llorona said, reaching toward Pao, who pressed herself futilely against the rock wall, closing her eyes, praying to every ancestor her mom had ever called on and every white protection candle she'd ever lit for Pao's safety.

The scent of Florida Water wafted by, overcoming La Llorona's river mildew-and-death stench for just long enough to make Pao feel warm inside. But when she opened her eyes, it wasn't a long-lost ancestor she saw behind the ghost woman.

It was Ondina.

"Enough, Mother," came her voice, a little shaky, but resolute. "Let her go."

THIRTY

Down the Mythological Drain

La Llorona's huge hand was only a few inches from Pao's throat when the sound of her daughter's voice stopped her cold.

"You're not supposed to be here yet," La Llorona said crossly. "I didn't send for you."

"I found my own way," Ondina said, her chin in the air.

Pao's heart beat wildly. She hadn't dared to hope.

Something rustled behind Ondina, and out from the shadows came Bruto, limping slightly, but his tail wagging.

"This is none of your concern," La Llorona snarled, half her attention on Pao, half on Ondina. "I made the preparations—everything is set. There's no turning back."

"It *is* my concern," said Ondina, stepping forward. "It's my life. And I don't want to live it this way. If I say we turn back, we turn back."

La Llorona whirled to face her defiant daughter, and Pao sagged against the wall, boneless with relief. In seconds, Bruto was by Pao's side, jumping on her, licking every part of her he could reach.

"Good boy," Pao murmured, but her eyes were on the scene unfolding in front of her.

"Let them go," Ondina said, sweeping her arm imperiously at Franco, Emma, and Dante. "Let them all go."

"You think this is just about you? You selfish brat. This is what we've been working toward for decades. This is what your brother *died* for."

"Luis died for your mistake," Ondina said, her voice every bit as cool as her mother's. "Twice. And Beto—"

"Don't say his name to me," La Llorona snarled. "That ungrateful—"

"He wasn't ungrateful, Mamá," Ondina said, her face softening just a fraction. "He was good. He didn't want to live if someone else had to die for it, and neither do I. Haven't we done enough?"

"It will never be enough," La Llorona said, growing taller and more terrifying in her anger. "Not until I've recovered everything I lost."

"Everything you *threw away*," Ondina spat, looking more like her mother than Pao had ever seen. "How long are we supposed to keep pretending you didn't do this to us? To yourself? How long is the world going to keep paying for your terrible choices?"

"The world owes us this!" she shouted, advancing on her daughter. "The world wouldn't let me have a family. I was branded a sinner for loving. For daring to have joy without penitence and fear. And your father—"

"My father was a closed-minded fool who couldn't handle small-town gossip," Ondina said, sadness tingeing her every word. "He walked away. You're the one who turned it into a tragedy. I'm the last Hija de Lágrimas, Mother, and I'm telling you, it ends here."

For a moment, Pao thought that *would* be the end of it. La

Llorona's silence stretched on and on as Pao held Bruto against her shins and waited.

But she should have known better.

"It's too late," the ghoul said, straightening up, her voice as cold and impenetrable as frost-covered glass. "I'm your mother, and you are my child, and I will take whatever I need from the world to right this wrong." And La Llorona reached out for her daughter's throat.

She had momentarily forgotten about Pao.

Before the demoness could get ahold of Ondina, Pao did the only thing she could think of. She ran up and shoved La Llorona from behind, feeling like she was taking down the schoolyard bully for stealing lunch money.

The horrible, twisted woman stumbled forward, giving Ondina just enough time to dart out from under her arms.

"No need to thank me," Pao said, smirking at Ondina, who rolled her eyes and tossed something to her without warning.

Luckily, Pao caught it by the handle. It was her knife; she must have lost it in the field outside the palace.

"A heads-up would have been nice!" Pao shouted as Ondina raced across the cave.

"I was hoping it would cut off your hand!"

Pao shook her head, but she laughed. She hadn't been wrong about Ondina. Yes, they shared some darkness, but they also shared some light, and Pao was no longer alone in this battle.

"We're almost out of time!" Ondina said from the base of the pillar.

"Yes, you are."

La Llorona had righted herself, and Pao knew her knife wouldn't be of much use against this monster who was more magic than flesh. Even so, Pao felt better with it in her hand.

The ghost woman stalked toward Pao, who ducked her first swing and ran in the opposite direction. Pao's knee and ankle still hurt, but she was reenergized by her assailant's scattered focus, one eye always on her rebellious daughter, who was edging along the cave wall.

Pao caught Ondina's attention after a quick double-back to dodge another swipe of those giant hands. Ondina tipped her head toward the towering column that held the orb.

Nodding in acknowledgment, Pao assessed the layout of the cave. Ondina was going to climb the pillar to the orb. If it was really the power source, she would know what to do when she got there. Ondina could end all this, as long as Pao could keep La Llorona busy in the meantime.

The chase became a dance, Pao drawing the woman to corners of the cave where Ondina and the orb would be out of her line of sight. And it worked.

Until it didn't.

"No!" La Llorona shrieked when she looked over her shoulder and caught sight of Ondina. By then the girl was almost to the top of the pedestal, clawing her way up. La Llorona forgot Pao instantly. Her mutinous daughter was the much greater threat.

Pao placed herself between the desperate mother and the column, knowing it wouldn't mean much, hoping a few seconds of distraction would be enough to suit Ondina's purpose.

La Llorona swiped at Pao as she passed, much stronger since absorbing the extra energy from the orb. Pao flew into the cave wall like she'd been lifted up and tossed, her shoulder crunching against the stone, the pain making her dizzy.

She hadn't even bought Ondina those few seconds. Pao was

nothing next to the might of this legendary ghost woman on her chosen path.

La Llorona was too fast, and Pao watched, pain warping her vision, as mother and daughter reached the top of the pillar at the same time and squared off on the small platform, the glowing orb between them. In the face of her mother's shining, unnatural strength, Ondina looked small and pale, a waif clinging to the boundary between life and death, threatening to let go.

But there was something in Ondina's eyes, Pao thought, pushing herself up to sit against the wall, her shoulder screaming. Something that made Pao certain this would be a tougher fight than La Llorona was expecting.

"Are you going to push me off, Mother?" Ondina asked, steel in her spine, ice in her tone. "It wouldn't be the first time you killed me to get what you wanted. Just remember, this body is barely hanging on. I don't think it would survive the fall."

"Don't be melodramatic, Ondina," said La Llorona, inching closer. "I only want to help you. To give you the life you've always deserved."

"The life you took from me, you mean," Ondina said, more resigned than angry. "Some things can't be undone."

A moment of silence stretched between them, hundreds of years of history crackling like static electricity in the air before a storm. Pao finally made her painful way to standing, feeling helpless from so far away. All she could do was watch as both women held their ground, the orb throbbing between them with its poison power, waiting. . . .

And then it happened.

They both lunged at the same moment, their movements

eerily similar despite the unnatural size and pallor of La Llorona's form. But Ondina was more nimble, and Pao gasped as her hands closed around the orb with a sound like lightning splitting a tree.

The cave went dark, like a flame had been doused. Only Ondina and her mother were visible, lit by the green glow of the orb, La Llorona's concentrated fury a contrast to the mania that had overtaken her daughter's features.

Her eyes were unnaturally wide as the power of the orb danced in them, the crackling green cords snaking their way around her fingers, moving too fast.

"Ondina!" Pao shouted instinctively, and Bruto barked once, short and sharp.

Whether it was her voice or the puppy's yip that snapped her out of it, Pao would never know, but Ondina's eyes went dark again, and her expression changed to one of pain as the cords stopped climbing her wrists.

As if she sensed her daughter's indecision, La Llorona leaned over and reached for the orb, a terrible hunger in her eyes.

"No!" Pao screamed, and Ondina's eyes snapped to hers. An understanding passed between them like an electric current.

Despite the fire in her shoulder, Pao pushed off the cave wall and sprinted with the last of her strength as Ondina raised her arms and tossed the coveted prize over the platform's edge.

Pao watched it fall as if in slow motion, sure she wouldn't be able to get into position in time, and all would be lost. But the moment she was in range, it was like she became a magnet. The orb zapped into her hands as if it had been made to fit them, and the green energy snakes wrapped around her wrists and hands, holding them in place.

Pao braced herself for a shock. For pain. She wasn't the least bit ready for what happened instead.

The cave walls around her disappeared, replaced by a web of glittering white light strands. She felt a pulsing from the orb, which Pao could now see was a massive ancient freshwater pearl. The vibration passed through her skin and into her bloodstream, filling her veins with something fizzy—like the rose lemonade her mom made with soda water.

Pao's mind was sharper than it had ever been, suddenly able to stretch in any direction, to sense and hear and feel *everything*. There inside the web she could see La Llorona's life force—a deformed thing bound up with the green snakes of energy, trying to feed off the pearl. Ondina's was there, too—a lighter green, flickering and fading.

Pao could even sense her own, as well as the moment it disappeared into the white-hot power of the pearl, fusing with it until she couldn't tell them apart anymore.

A heat spread from her palms to her forearms, the fizzing intensifying as it did. Around her, she could feel the river and the glowing nodes of every life-form that was supported by it.

Time slowed, running like warm honey. Pao saw how her lifetime had barely been a blink in the endless timeline that stretched behind her, and ahead of her. She was everything and nothing. She was pure power, pure light.

When she looked down at her hands and arms, she noticed as if from a distance that the green snakes had wound up to her elbows.

Moving effortlessly through the web of glittering strands, Pao's mind focused on La Llorona, on the history that had twisted to become her tragic legend. The lover who had suddenly turned on her, shaming her for the children she'd borne him. The stares and jeers and insults of their neighbors. Despite it all, her passion for him, the ferocity of it.

And then his abandonment, and her inconsolable grief, pushing her to the edge of madness. Beneath it all, the fear for her children, brown-skinned, born out of wedlock, and now fatherless, too. She had worried endlessly over them, loved them with all her heart.

Until, eventually, the intensity of her love twined so closely with her fear that it drove her to commit an unspeakable act. One that broke her mind and body. It sent her wailing along the riverbanks in search of a way to get back the lives she'd taken.

Pao saw Franco through La Llorona's eyes on a summer solstice a hundred years ago. The way she'd clutched at him with filthy, desperate hands, and he'd stabbed her with the very knife Marisa had used on Pao in the cactus field.

Pao, a living human, had only lost consciousness. The knife was meant to be used against phantoms, and La Llorona had felt it when it tore into her, banishing her to the rift, where she should have let go of her form and become part of the magical fabric of the void.

But the ghost woman had been more than her form. She had stubbornly clung to all the love and madness that had driven her to take the lives of her children. And then, nearly spent, she had encountered the pearl. . . .

Franco assumed he had rid the world of her, but instead, he had sent her to the fire to be forged. La Llorona had entered the void a wasted, defeated phantasm and used its power to become a formidable demon.

The rest was only flashes. The resurrection of the ruined

palace. The experiment that had cost her her youngest boy for a second time. A flash of another boy—older, nearly a man.

His face . . . Pao thought, before he turned his back on his mother, leaving her wailing in this very cave. It was so familiar. . . . But how could that be?

Once La Llorona's story was complete, any sense of the woman's future grew cloudy. Pao began to see her own instead. La Llorona had used the void's magic for selfish gain, corrupting it in the process. But Pao was different. She could do so much good with the power that was now radiating in her elbows, crawling up her biceps, reaching for her shoulders. She could create alternate fuel sources, restore ecosystems. Bring peace and prosperity to the residents of Silver Springs and beyond.

She saw herself in a white lab coat, a flight suit, her intellect boundless, her life never ending. She saw adoring crowds cheering for her, books and papers with her name on them.

Paola Santiago . . .

Pao knew it then, that she could own this power. She could control the void. It was offering itself to her here and now, the green winding up her neck and across her chest.

Once it reached her heart, her brilliant new senses told her, there would be no turning back. If there was a choice to be made, it was now. And how could she refuse it? All this . . . it was everything she had ever wanted.

Her greedy heart showed her a porthole and the epic vastness of space beyond it.

Everything she had ever dreamed of . . .

But underneath the shining good deeds, the rewards, and the dreams, Pao saw the human imperfections in herself. Her self-doubts and petty jealousies, the quick temper that had bonded her to Ondina and set this whole thing in motion. Those flaws would feed on the power and pervert it, she knew.

She envisioned herself as the girl from her dream again, white-haired and green-eyed. Terrible, beautiful, all-powerful.

"Pao!" A voice penetrated the glowing cage. "Pao!"

The sound came from far away, bringing with it the scents of Florida Water and too many burning candles, the taste of Coke and orange Popsicles, the feeling of home. . . .

It took everything in Pao to reject those images of her super-bright future, the power she craved but couldn't trust herself to wield. But she did. She focused all her energy into repelling the green snakes, and she felt them resist, twisting around her arms and holding on for dear life.

She blasted the pearl with thoughts of home. Of Emma and her comics and her purple nails. Of Dante and the way he'd kissed her cheek.

Of her mom, and cold pizza, and tarot cards, and more love than Pao could possibly receive.

The kind of power that didn't hurt. Didn't destroy.

The memories gave Pao the strength she needed to say good-bye to the void's promises. She shut her mind against the pearl and immediately saw the energy snakes shrivel and draw back.

When the last of the warmth that wasn't her own left her body, Pao found herself back in the cave. It was like no time had passed, even though she'd seen hundreds of years, lived and lost a lifetime.

"Pao!" That voice again. Fingers squeezing her arms. Fingers with sparkly purple nails.

"Emma . . ." Her own voice seemed to be coming from a long tunnel, but it worked, and Emma smiled. "You're . . . Are you . . ."

"Pao, for now I really just need you to let go of that thing. . . ."

The scene around them snapped into focus. Emma standing in front of her, as vital as ever. Franco on his hands and knees, coughing, and Dante, his club shining as he faced down a growling La Llorona, who was trying desperately to get to Pao. Ondina, teetering on top of the pedestal, looking weaker than ever now that the pearl had been unplugged from the palace.

"Ondina!" Pao shouted, and with the remnants of the void's power left in her, she projected a thought to her. Her solution to the puzzle. The way to finally end this.

She knew it had reached Ondina's mind when, from the top of the pedestal, the ghost girl smiled serenely. She nodded once.

Pao felt a tug in her chest, but Franco was struggling to stand, and Dante was barely holding off La Llorona. It was time.

"Stay with me?" Pao asked Emma, and her friend squeezed her arm again.

With the last bit of the strength the pearl had left behind, Pao raised her hands high. La Llorona saw her and, swiping Dante to the side, lunged across the space between them.

But she was too late. Pao threw the pearl as hard as she could at the stone floor. It flew at a hundred times the speed it should have, shattering right at the warped woman's feet like the devotional candle Pao had smashed in her kitchen.

"No!" La Llorona gasped, and the cave—so full of frantic activity only moments earlier—suddenly went eerily still. The phantasm grabbed at her own throat, the green light in her eyes extinguishing in a way that seemed final.

Pao, however, only had eyes for her friends.

"Quick!" she shouted, linking her arm with Emma's, ignoring the terrible cold that had begun to spread through her the moment the pearl left her hands. "We have to stay together!"

Dante found his way to Pao and took her other arm. Franco stumbled over, bleeding from a cut on his forehead.

"You too," Pao said as Ondina's feet touched the ground. "You're a hero. You're one of us now."

"Ew," Ondina said, but she stepped closer anyway.

"Bruto!" Pao called, suddenly panicked, but the little chupacabra limped over from a pile of fallen rocks. They were all together. Together and safe.

Just as Pao thought the words, the ground began to shake.

"The palace is going to fall," Ondina said, her voice faint.

"I know," said Pao, and somehow she did. Was it the power of the pearl? "And when it does, there will be a way out of here."

What she couldn't see was whether the palace's collapse would kill them all first. She would just have to hope this wasn't going to be the end of her future. The version she'd chosen.

La Llorona had crumpled to the ground, her hands gripping the stone floor like she was holding on for dear life.

"The power won't let go until she does," Ondina said with a note of wonder in her voice. "She's been its master for too long."

"Isn't there something you can do?" Dante asked.

Ondina left Pao's side and walked toward her mother as the others clung to one another in shock and confusion.

They watched as Ondina knelt down beside the woman who had held her as a baby. She stroked her mother's grotesque face tenderly. "It's okay, Mamá," she said. "We can go home now."

"No . . ." sobbed La Llorona, but even as she did, her appearance began to change. Her masklike features relaxed as her massive, terrible form shrank. Soon her visage had transformed back into her human one. "I wanted to save you. . . ."

"*This* is how you save me," Ondina said, her face radiant. Pao could swear the ghost girl was beginning to glow from inside—but not green. Not this time. "Forgive me, Mamá. I forgive you. Set us free."

"My daughter," La Llorona moaned, taking Ondina in her arms. "Lo siento, mi hija. Fue solo porque te amo. . . ."

"What did she say?" Pao hissed to Dante, but it was Franco who answered.

"It was only because I love you."

Pao knew that would stay with her for the rest of her life, this last image of the two of them. Mother and daughter. Shining. Peaceful.

Free.

And when they had faded completely, the walls came tumbling down.

THIRTY-ONE
Lonely in a Crowd

Pao, Dante, Emma, and Franco stayed in the center of the cave as the rock walls disintegrated and water began to pour in from all sides.

"Trust me," said Pao. "This is how we get out."

If I'm wrong and this is the end, Pao thought, taking a deep breath just before the water closed over her head, *at least we did what we came to do.*

The surge of water carried them upward, and Pao did her best to keep her eyes open so she could watch what happened to the void. The dome was gone. She saw green light flicker and die across the ruined landscape below. Faint white clouds drifted alongside them like jellyfish.

Those were the ahogados, Pao realized, their peaceful faces turned toward the light that was just becoming visible above. And not only them. Pao also saw chupacabras, Lechuzas, even Manos Pachonas floating up, their spirits freed from the malevolence that had been holding them prisoner for so long.

Pao gripped Emma's arm, and Dante's, and at last, she closed her eyes, focusing on holding her breath for one more second. Just one more . . .

When their heads finally broke the surface of the Gila, they swam for the nearest bank, and Pao didn't think about ankle-snagging branches or cold pockets or the dangers of invisible currents. She only thought of home.

Emma was struggling, and Pao tried to pull her along, but in the end, it was Franco who heaved her onto the riverbank, while Dante—already standing in the shallows—took Pao's arm as they sank into the gritty sand, coughing and sputtering. Alive.

There was a screeching sound, and then a clunk, like a heavy steel door slamming shut. Pao peered into the river just in time to see a massive dark mouth close just beneath the water's surface.

The solstice was over. The pearl had been destroyed. The rift was sealed.

Pao felt a tug in her chest, a phantom of the pain she'd experienced when the key had drained her. But when the portal could no longer be seen, she felt a weightlessness, too. A sense of relief.

Sitting up, Pao looked at her exhausted friends spread out along the bank, its familiar white sand and dripping black moss seeming positively ordinary compared to the horrors they'd seen. She felt close to her comrades, but also separate somehow.

When she'd held the pearl, she'd seen the potential of what she could be, and she'd given it up. She was in mourning, while everyone else was waking from a nightmare.

Pao felt a little lonely as her eyes roved over them, but she tried to shake it off. To find joy in the sensation of solid ground beneath her. To remember why she belonged with them.

That was when she realized Bruto was nowhere to be seen.

"Where are we?" Emma asked.

Pao blinked back the tears in her eyes. There was no way to

explain Bruto to her, any more than she could explain her sense of loss at the closing of the void.

"The rift opening wasn't too far from the Niños' camp," Pao said, though her journey between the two had seemed endless. "I think this is the same place I went in."

Franco nodded, getting to his feet.

"Wait, the what now?" Emma asked, looking a little dazed, and Pao suddenly felt overwhelmed by how long they'd been apart. How much had happened to both of them in the interim.

"It's a long story," Pao said, trying to smile.

"I have a couple of those myself," Emma replied.

"But you're okay?" Pao asked. "Everyone's okay?"

Dante stepped up between them and put an arm around each of their shoulders. "We're together," he said. "It's a start."

Pao smiled for real this time, basking in the feeling of being a trio again. It helped fill the hole where her shining future had been.

"So . . . which way do we go to get back to camp?" Dante asked her.

"There's no more key," Pao said, shrugging. Dante and Emma looked confused, but Franco's eyes snapped to hers.

"You found it?" They were the first words he had spoken.

Pao nodded. In some ways, she'd had it all along. "It was destroyed when I went through the rift."

Something settled in Franco's expression, and for a moment, Pao could see the hundreds of years he'd lived, even though his face still looked sixteen.

"It's all right," he said at last. "I know the way."

As they headed toward the Niños' camp, Pao couldn't help but crane her neck and look at the sky, wondering where Ondina and her mother were now. Where Bruto was. What would happen to them next? Even the pearl in all its infinite power and wisdom hadn't been able to tell her that.

Maybe it's for the best, she thought. She'd already seen enough impossible things for one summer. Probably for a whole lifetime.

Compared to the route Pao had taken, following the flashlight beam with all its twists and turns, Franco's sure steps were almost anticlimactic.

Pao and Emma walked behind the boys, shoulder to shoulder, taking comfort in each other's presence. Dante seemed to understand, and besides, Pao could plainly see how much he wanted to emulate Franco.

It makes sense, Pao thought. *Franco is basically the soccer captain of the cactus field.*

She would keep the joke to herself for now, though. Surviving the ghost-and-monster-filled underworld deserved at least an hour of cease-fire.

Beside her, Emma's brow was furrowed, her lips drawn in a frown. There was so much Pao wanted to ask her, about the details of her disappearance, about Franco, La Llorona, and Ondina, and about how Emma had ended up in the glass palace. For once, though, she decided to let her curiosity rest.

"Are you okay?" she asked, simply, and Emma's face relaxed.

"I am now," she said. "For a while I thought . . ." Emma swallowed hard, her gaze on the horizon. "I thought I was never going to get out of there."

"I never would have stopped until we found you," Pao said,

and it was true. As terrible as the ordeal had been, she would have gone through worse for Emma. She would have done anything.

"That's what I kept telling the ghost lady," Emma said. "I think she put me under glass because she was sick of hearing about you." Her tone was teasing, but her eyes were still haunted.

Pao flashed back to Emma in the prism, unconscious, helpless. Pao had been so close to letting her down. To letting them all down.

"Hey," Emma said, bumping her shoulder into Pao's. "It's over. We're okay. Thanks to you."

Pao smiled gratefully. She'd missed this. The way best friends knew just what to say.

The noises of camp drifted toward them, and Pao was suddenly apprehensive. She had escaped from the Niños, who had left her tied to a bed. What kind of welcome would she receive now?

"Franco?"

Three boys emerged from a knot of cacti—friends of Sal's, Pao remembered—looking like they'd been in a scuffle. But whatever had caused the ripped T-shirts and dirt-smudged cheeks was forgotten when Franco took a step toward them.

"Is it really you?" one of the boys asked.

When Franco grinned, Pao got a glimpse of what all the fuss was about. He had a kind of magnetism, a rakish, irreverent joy that was peeking through the layers of fatigue and stress.

"That depends," he said. "Who won the fight? I only reveal my resurrected form to winners, you know."

The boys ran at him then, whooping joyfully, tackling him and almost taking him down.

Franco was exhausted, but he grappled with them anyway,

laughing and tousling their hair as they peppered him with questions.

It was like this, with ecstatic boys hanging from his arms and shoulders, that the presumed-dead former leader of Los Niños de la Luz made his entrance.

Pao realized quickly, arriving in his wake, that she'd been silly to worry about her own reception. In the tail of Franco's blazing comet, she was nothing but a chunk of dull space rock. He was a true hero, and Pao had never been so happy to be nobody special.

With his famous weapon and reputation as the boy who'd gone down fighting for Naomi, Dante was getting his share of adoration, too. He stood slightly apart from Franco by the massive firepit, looking sheepish but pleased with himself.

For once, Pao wasn't jealous. He deserved this moment.

She and Emma—whom no one here knew—stayed at the fringes, shoulders still touching, watching it all from a distance.

"Pao?" Emma asked after a few minutes had passed.

"Yeah?"

"It was my fault."

"What was?" Pao turned to face her friend, who was worrying her lower lip with her teeth, a telltale sign that something was bothering her.

"Everything that happened to us. I wasn't . . . just taken. I went with her, the ghost girl—your friend. I went with her."

"Ondina?" Pao asked, nonplussed. "What do you mean?"

Emma took a deep breath. "It wasn't the first time I'd seen her. But I thought she was just a girl from Mesa on a family trip. She and I made plans to meet before I was supposed to join you guys. I was going to show her the river, but when I got there, things got . . . weird."

Pao, processing the words, didn't answer right away. But Emma could never let a silence stretch very long, and she spoke into it too quickly.

"She started talking about souls, and I thought she was just a weird hippie, but then *he* showed up." Emma pointed at Franco, now slinging his arm around a thunderstruck Marisa. "He told me not to trust her and started asking questions about my ring, and by then I just wanted to get out of there, but all these ghost zombies or whatever showed up and dragged me into the river and—"

"I don't understand," Pao said, feeling dizzy. "Why would you arrange to meet a girl from Mesa who was on a family trip?"

Emma's cheeks went pink. "Oh. I don't know, she was at the club after tennis practice, and she said she wanted to see the Gila. I told her I knew a place. . . ."

"And you didn't tell me?" This seemed like the least of their worries right now, but for some reason, it was the thing that stung Pao the most. Emma had been making other friends without her?

That the friend in question turned out to be the ghost of a drowned girl looking for a matching soul was beside the point.

"Pao, I'm so sorry. I should have. I just . . . I'm sorry."

Pao felt her temper start to rise . . . but then she thought about her river dreams, and the strange boy-girl whatever that had been going between her and Dante lately. There were things she hadn't told Emma, either.

She exhaled slowly. "It's okay. Ondina would have done anything to come back to life," Pao said. "And Franco was looking for a key to get him into the rift. It wasn't your fault. Just an epically bad wrong-place, wrong-time situation."

"So, you're not mad at me?"

Pao shook her head, and she meant it. "Just . . . no more secrets, okay? From now on, we tell each other everything."

"Deal," Emma said, sticking out her hand. They used the special handshake they'd made up in drama class last year, ending with a double pinkie swear.

"I have about six million questions to ask you, though," Pao said when they'd finished.

"You wouldn't be you if you didn't," Emma said, shaking her head and linking her arm with Pao's.

At last, the knot around Franco and Dante began to loosen, and the Niños noticed Pao.

Sal approached her first, and she found that despite everything she had gone through, despite the emptiness still lingering in her chest, her smile came easily. Maybe that's how healing worked—a little at a time.

"You kept your promise," he said, and Pao felt her smile grow bigger.

"I did my best."

Sal put his chubby hand in hers and squeezed before smiling shyly at Emma.

"I remember your bike," he said to her. "Purple, right?"

"Purple," Emma agreed, smiling back.

Naomi took Sal's place when he scampered off to examine Dante's club. Her expression was unreadable as she sized up the two girls, giving Emma a nod that almost passed for friendly before turning to Pao.

"Guess I underestimated you," Naomi said after a long moment.

"Sorry I ran off."

"Sorry I tied you to a cot."

"Yeah, that was kind of rude."

They both laughed—the soft laugh of two kids who had seen too much.

Together, Naomi, Pao, and Emma looked toward the fire, at Marisa. She had tucked herself under Franco's arm, her hair loose and wavy, her smile positively radiant.

"We all thought he was dead," Naomi said, her voice hushed and almost reverent. "Seeing him now . . . it's . . ."

"A miracle," Pao said, reaching over to squeeze Emma's hand.

"Complicated," Naomi offered, shaking her head. "What was he doing down there, anyway?"

Emma turned to her. "*She* wanted to use us. Our souls. To bring her daughter back. Franco could have escaped. He was captured trying to save me. . . ." Her eyes were more solemn than Pao had ever seen them. "I'm sorry," she said.

"It's not your fault," Naomi said, no trace of thorniness in her tone. "We've been fighting the rift for a long time. It's insidious, and Franco knew what he was up against better than anyone. Believe me, he didn't do anything he didn't decide to do."

"He didn't know La Llorona was still a threat," added Pao.

"La Llorona . . ." Naomi echoed, shaking her head. "I can't believe it was her the whole time."

"Never underestimate a mother with a grudge," Pao said darkly, looking at Franco. Did he feel bad for his mistake? For his role in creating the monster La Llorona became? How much would he tell the Niños about that?

Naomi smirked, then asked in all seriousness, "What's next for you?"

"Home," Emma blurted out. "And soon. My parents must be going crazy with worry." She nudged Pao's shoulder with hers. "I'm gonna go see if Dante's almost ready, okay?"

Pao nodded and stayed with Naomi, who was considering her with a different kind of expression. . . . Could it be respect?

"You know," Naomi said, "you wouldn't be the first kid to walk into the cactus field and never come out. We could use someone like you."

"But La Llorona is gone—" Pao started.

Naomi dismissed her words with a wave. "That doesn't mean there won't be other threats. There's still work to be done. For instance, we don't know what the rift's closing means. We need to do research, conduct experiments and stuff."

Pao smiled. "You know how to sweet-talk a girl."

"Yeah, well, you're not that hard to tempt."

For a minute, like she was holding the pearl again, the future spooled out in front of Pao. She could live here, wear the black patchwork uniform of Los Niños, study the rift and the effect of its closing on the cactus field, the Gila, and herself.

She could stay almost thirteen forever, and train, and fight, and be around people who understood what she'd been through, who had felt the rift pulling on them and decided not to run from it.

Naomi watched her like she could read the thoughts swirling behind her eyes.

"I went home once," Naomi said, her voice sounding ancient and weary. "Or I tried to, anyway."

"What happened?" Pao asked.

Naomi shrugged. "Didn't take. After everything that had

happened to me here, sitting in science class felt like I was living a life that didn't fit anymore."

"What about your family?"

Was it Pao's imagination, or did a shadow flit across Naomi's face at the question? In any case, it was gone before she answered. "They were better off without me," she said simply. "Even if I'd stayed, I wasn't the daughter they'd lost. I wasn't the daughter they wanted back."

Pao didn't know what to say to that, and Naomi didn't seem to expect a response. But her words wormed their way somewhere deep into Pao, and she knew she wouldn't forget them anytime soon, no matter what she decided.

She had more questions for Naomi, but Dante and Emma returned then, the club mercifully returned to its foldable chancla form and stowed in Dante's back pocket. Some of its shine was still in his smile, though, and Pao thought it probably always would be.

They had all changed. But what would they do about it now? Could they resume their ordinary lives at the Riverside Palace and the country club?

"Ready to go home?" Dante asked, slinging an arm around Pao's shoulders, unconsciously mirroring Marisa's and Franco's poses across the fire.

She almost shrugged him off, embarrassed in front of Emma, but there was no need. Emma's smile at both of them was so bright, it blasted away Pao's worries. Pao had chosen the right future—the one full of friends and family. And no matter what else it held, there would definitely be more comic-book and junk-food fests. That was enough certainty for now.

"I've never been more ready," Emma said. She *would* be the daughter her parents wanted back, of that Pao had no doubt. "Pao?" she asked. "You ready?"

"No way!" Dante yelled, dropping his arm.

Pao followed his gaze, wondering what could possibly be more important to him than going home, and seeing nothing at first.

Then a black bundle of fur and teeth and too-large paws barreled lopsidedly toward her through the desert dust.

THIRTY-TWO

Just the Beginning

"BRUTO!" Pao shouted, tears springing to her eyes.

She ran toward him, taking in the way he was limping on his injured leg, and the way his black tongue lolled out of his mouth as he beamed at her. "Good boy!" she mumbled when they reached each other, letting him lick her face all over, not even minding the slobber.

He looked different, she realized when he finally settled down. The green protrusions on his back were gone, and his eyes were black instead of green, but there were still patches of scales among his fur, and something vaguely reptilian about his face.

She couldn't scientifically explain why he had transformed, or how he had escaped the rift to reunite with her, but Pao, for once, didn't care what science had to say about it. All she knew was that, for the first time since the river had coughed her out, she felt whole again.

Marisa offered to accompany them to the border of the cactus field, though Pao could tell she was reluctant to let Franco out of her sight.

"I'll be back," Pao heard her whisper to him before kissing him on the cheek.

As they waited for her, Pao looked at Dante, remembering when he had kissed *her* cheek. Had that just been a *Here you go, 'cause we might die* kind of thing? Did he even remember doing it?

She shook herself mentally as Marisa joined them. Pao had much bigger problems than that. Like what she was going to say to her mom about Bruto.

Or, you know, any of this.

"Thank you," Marisa said to Pao as they set off. "You were true to your word, and you went farther than any of us. . . ."

Pao could tell the older girl was still reeling from the fact that her world had been turned upside down and right side up again within a matter of days.

"A friend once told me I was relentless," said Pao, remembering Ondina with a pang.

"In some people," said Marisa, "that's a good quality. Franco's the same way."

Man, this girl has it BAD, Pao thought.

"Will he be the leader now?" she asked.

"He says we'll share the responsibility, which will make things easier on both of us," Marisa said. "Life will be better all around, thanks to you." And then, to Pao's total shock, the former terror of the school lunchroom stopped and gave her a hug.

After that, it was time to part ways. Pao remembered the haunted look on Marisa's face when she'd spoken of wishing she could forget her family, and it stopped Pao from asking if she'd return home. Maybe homecoming looked different for everyone. Maybe Franco and the Niños were Marisa's home now.

Pao, Dante, and Emma walked the rest of the way to the boundary in contemplative silence, and Pao realized that each of them, in their own way, was getting ready to reenter a world they'd left behind.

"What do I tell my parents?" Emma asked quietly, coming up beside Pao.

"What do we tell any of them?"

"You get to tell them you were a hero," Emma said, her voice small. "That you saved me. I have to explain that I went willingly to meet a stranger who turned out to be . . ."

"A snarky, slightly psychopathic ghost?"

Emma giggled, covering her mouth. "A *reformed* slightly psychopathic ghost."

Dante overheard only part of the conversation. "Oh, is Pao finally admitting to being psychopathic? I've been waiting for this moment."

"Dante!" Emma and Pao said in unison, but they all laughed.

"I'm just saying, putting food coloring in my fishbowl? Only a psychopath would have done that."

"I was seven!" Pao said, her cheeks flushing. "And it was just an experiment! I didn't know it would kill Bubbles, okay?"

This time, even Bruto—trotting obediently along at Pao's heels—seemed to laugh.

The sun was setting when the Riverside Palace came into view, and Pao, despite how much she'd always hated the apartment complex, felt her heart leap at the sight.

Next to her, Dante stiffened, as though afraid of once again encountering the green mist that had forced them to leave. But it was gone, along with the ghost woman who had wielded it. Nothing was going to stop them from getting back home.

"So remember," Pao coached Emma, "you got lost in the cactus field, it got dark, and you got tired, and you'd heard that you were supposed to stay in one place when you were lost. Dante and I *idiotically* decided to go looking for you, and we got lost, too. We finally found our way out, and we're very, very sorry for being so reckless and irresponsible."

Emma nodded, her lips a flat line.

Dante looked pale, but determined.

"It's not a bad story," came a heavily accented voice from behind them. "But I bet the real one's more interesting."

The four of them, a little jumpy from the past few days, whirled around as one, Bruto growling and Dante's hand already on the chancla in his back pocket.

Señora Mata's wheezing cackle told them all they needed to know about how ridiculous *that* looked.

"¡Abuela!" Dante went from weapon-wielding hero to relieved grandson faster than La Llorona had transformed. He threw himself into her arms despite being a head taller, and she clung to him for dear life.

For about a second.

Then she said, "Okay, okay, heroes, get inside, rápido, before anyone sees you." She looked down at Bruto with thinly veiled disgust. "La criatura stays out on the fire escape."

Bewildered, exhausted, and utterly out of fight, Pao did as she was told.

Inside Dante's apartment, things had returned to normal. No green light, no weird candles, no corporeal mist. Señora Mata ushered them onto the sofa and brought out a plate of empanadas—still warm, as though she'd known they were coming.

Pao was far more curious than hungry, but the look on Señora Mata's face told her, in no uncertain terms, to shut up and eat.

So Pao bit into one, glowering. When she did, she groaned out loud—it was that good.

"You did me proud," said the old woman, beaming from ear to ear. "I knew that maldita fantasma was no match for my chancla. But now give it back."

Dante's mouth, still full of empanada, fell open. "¿Cómo?"

"Give it back, hijo! You think you get to walk around Silver Springs with an Arma del Alma?" She laughed, a short, barking thing. "When I wouldn't even let you have a pocket knife?" She muttered, "Tontito."

When she snatched it out of his pocket, Dante looked mutinous.

Emma giggled, a bell-like sound that momentarily cleared Pao's empanada-clouded brain.

"Where did you get it, señora?" Pao asked. "And the flashlight?" Just then, it dawned on Pao that she'd arrived home empty-handed. "Uh, sorry about losing your shopping bag. The Florida Water came in handy, too. How did you know?"

Dante's abuela rolled her eyes, a gesture Pao was very familiar with after a lifetime of asking too many questions.

"Impatient girl. You think you're the only one who ever met Los Niños de la Luz?"

"But . . . when?" Pao asked. "How?"

"To you I've always been an old lady," she said, shaking her head. "But I was young once, too. For a hundred years, I was young. And then it was time to come home."

"A hundred years?" Dante asked. Like Pao, he was shell-shocked, and Emma didn't look much better off.

"Wait. You're saying you—"

"No more questions, niña." Señora Mata cut her off, perhaps

sensing the eight billion more of them that were percolating behind Pao's eyes. "Not for now. For now you have worried mothers and empty beds."

"This isn't over," Pao said.

"Por supuesto. This is just the beginning," the señora assured her.

THIRTY-THREE
Florida Water, Anyone?

When the doorbell rang, with just twenty minutes to go before the SpaceX launch, Pao let her mom answer it.

It had been three days since they'd returned home. Pao didn't think she would ever forget the look on Mrs. Lockwood's face when she'd arrived at Dante's apartment to pick up Emma. The blood had left her cheeks, and she'd nearly collapsed. (For the record, her reaction had nothing to do with Bruto—he was still out on the fire escape.) Emma had rushed to give her mom a hug, propping her up in the process. And then Pao's mom had come in, and nothing else in Pao's world had mattered.

Their story about getting lost in the cactus field had passed muster without much examination. It didn't hurt that it was corroborated by Señora Mata, who told of her own girlhood mishap in the same field, winking at Pao when the two moms weren't looking.

Pao hadn't seen her friends since that night. Their guardians (especially Emma's) wanted to keep them close, even though all three kids had gone stir-crazy by halfway through the first day and sworn up and down they'd never go near the cactus field—or even any *cactus*—ever again.

After many phone calls, the trio had been given furlough for today, because it was a special occasion. Pao was hopeful the parental paranoia would wear off completely by August.

Today, Pao's mom opened the front door, ushering Emma inside, hugging her as she whispered a few words over her head that Pao knew were supposed to be for protection. Mercifully, no candles or incense had been lit that morning.

The moment Emma sat down on the couch next to Pao, Bruto curled up at her feet. To Pao's enormous surprise, her mom had loved the creature, scales and all. Maybe miracles *were* real. Pao had certainly seen enough evidence this week to believe there was more to life than met the eye.

"The launch starts in five minutes!" Emma said, bouncing up and down on the cushion. "Where's Dante?"

Pao smirked. "Probably putting gel in his hair or something."

Emma giggled, but secretly, Pao was eager for him to get here, too. She'd missed him more than she cared to admit.

On the news broadcast before the launch, the anchors were still talking about the incredible return of Emma Lockwood. *"Warning signs about the danger of wandering in the cactus field have been posted in the public parks along the Gila,"* the anchorwoman said.

Apparently, getting turned around in the desert was a real hazard.

Pao tried not to roll her eyes.

When photos of the kids who were still missing scrolled on the screen—Marisa's and Naomi's included—Pao grew more somber. Her mom was at her altar, picking up tiny pieces of dried rosemary with her fingertips.

"Maybe we could . . . light a candle for them?" Pao asked, trying to ignore the way her mom's eyes got wide, her mouth soft around the corners. "For the kids who haven't come home."

Pao still dreamed about them, the ahogados, their faces serene as they floated up toward the water's surface. And of Ondina and her mother, the infamous La Llorona, finally letting go of their anger. Finally moving on.

Pao wondered if, one day, she would tell her mom what had happened to her in the cactus field and the river. All the things her mom had been right about. Señora Mata had advised against it, saying it was best to let people hold on to their illusions sometimes, but Pao had never been great at following orders.

Still, she wasn't ready to recount it all, not yet. She wasn't even sure how she felt about it yet. Or that she completely understood it. Maybe someday she would.

For now, she took the matchbook from her mom's hand as Dante knocked too loudly on the door and Emma and Bruto got up to answer it.

"It's a lovely idea, Paola," her mom said, straightening the wick.

When the flame caught, Pao imagined it expanding into a protective bubble of light that surrounded the Niños and the ahogados. And Ondina and her two brothers as well. Even La Llorona, who Pao hoped was at peace and wailing no more.

She closed her eyes and held the vision for a few seconds, just like her mom had taught her when she was only a little girl.

Her concentration broke when Dante threw a piece of popcorn at her head.

Laughing, her mom ruffled her hair. "Go on," she said, "I've got it from here."

Pao kissed her mom on the cheek before turning back to her friends, thwacking Dante on the head with a cactus throw pillow before settling down a little closer than normal to him on the couch. When they bumped elbows by mistake, her stomach swooped a familiar swoop.

Pao reached out for Emma's hand on her other side and squeezed it. "Good to have you back," she said.

"Good to be back," said Emma. "All thanks to you."

"Hey, what about me?" Dante said.

"You did make a pretty good caveman," said Pao, mimicking him wielding a club.

"Better than a stupid plastic flashlight," he shot back.

"Don't forget the stinky Florida Water," Emma added.

"Does someone need Florida Water?" Pao's mom asked from the kitchen.

"No, thanks!" all three kids chorused, then broke into peals of laughter. Even Bruto smiled.

The countdown began, the Falcon Heavy rocket pointing skyward, and Pao felt a rush of gratitude that was almost enough to blot out the memories of all she had experienced.

Maybe she hadn't seen what her *real* future would bring—the one powered by her and not the void. Would she go into outer space someday, or make important discoveries and contributions to science? She didn't know for sure. She'd just have to have faith in herself and be okay with not knowing.

At least for now.

ACKNOWLEDGMENTS

Like most people in the world, I have been a fan of Percy Jackson and his gods and monsters and adventures for a long time. In so many ways, getting the chance to add to Rick Riordan's enduring and hopeful canon with characters and stories that feel like home to me is an absolute dream come true.

With that in mind, I'd first like to thank absolutely everyone at Rick Riordan Presents:

Tío Rick himself, for building his beautiful sandbox of mythology and inviting other authors to play in it, for his hilarious and insightful contributions to this story, and for his unwavering support of Pao and me at every step.

My editor, Stephanie Lurie, who found things lurking in the shadows of this story that I didn't even know were there and encouraged me to chase them. Without her help and guidance, this book would have been a shade of itself.

All the other authors at Rick Riordan Presents, who were so friendly and welcoming to me as the new kid on the block, and whose stories inspire me every day.

The unstoppable force that is the Percy/Riordan fandom, for

receiving my ghosts and me and making us feel right at home.

Next, I want to thank my agent, Jim McCarthy, who never laughs at my dreams, no matter how big they are or how fast and furiously they come. He told me early and often that my stories were worth being told, and he has been steadfast in his encouragement.

I am so, so grateful to every single reader, teacher, librarian, and bookseller who has picked up one of my books and shared their thoughts and feelings with me or a friend or a patron or a customer. You are literally the reason I sit down at my computer (almost) every day. You make it all worth it.

This book (and my whole life, let's be real) would be nothing without my three best friends and critique partners. These are the fiercest, most badass women to ever pick up pens and make magic with them and I love them with all my heart:

Lily Anderson, who is a genius in so much more than IQ. Nina Moreno, who has more magia in her pinkie finger than the rest of us could ever dream of owning. Michelle Ruíz Keil, whose heart is bigger than the sun, who made room for me when I needed it most.

Then there's my family, in all their messy, beautiful, patch-work glory. Thank you for giving me enough inspiration for a lifetime of books. For reminding me where I come from and how much higher I can soar.

Alex, my love, how can I even find the words? I do all my best research about what crushes and butterflies and falling for your best friend feel like with you every day. Thank you for finding me just in time.

And of course, I couldn't have done this without my little

A, the love of my life. Thank you for telling me how cool scary mermaids are when I'm not sure, and reminding me what's funny when I get stuck. You are my biggest champion in all the places it matters. This is for you, querida.

Don't miss Pao's next adventure!

PAOLA SANTIAGO
AND THE
FOREST OF NIGHTMARES

ONE

There's *Almost* Nothing Worse
Than Meat Medley Pizza

If it hadn't been for the dream she'd had about her estranged father the night before, maybe Pao's bonding time with her mom's new boyfriend wouldn't have been quite so awful.

But her luck never worked like that.

Six months ago, Paola Santiago had walked out of a collapsing magical rift after defeating the legendary ghost turned god, La Llorona, and freeing the spirit of the Weeping Woman's last remaining lost child.

Pao had tamed a chupacabra.

She had even earned the respect of the girl who had tortured her in sixth grade.

And yet, she still didn't have the power to turn this guy into dust? Ideally right now, across the sticky table of this pizza place?

Maybe if she glared at him a little harder . . .

Pizza Pete's was full tonight, with chattering families, screaming kids, and illuminated arcade machines trying to trick dads into digging deeper for quarters. GHOST HUNTER 3! one of the games flashed in acid-green letters.

No way that's *realistic,* Pao thought, narrowly avoiding a scoff. Like a series of zeroes and ones blinking on a screen could ever get close to the real thing. Binary code was incredibly versatile, of course, but Pao had learned firsthand that there were some things that math and science couldn't fully capture.

Pao's mom looked at her like she had heard the almost scoff. Pao stared back insolently, tempting fate.

Ever since winter break had started three days ago, Pao had been prohibited from scoffing. Also scowling, smirking, stomping, and swearing (even using mild words like *stupid* or *jerk*). The message was clear: There was no room for sullen Pao when *Aaron* was around.

To be fair, though, it didn't seem like there was much room for *any* version of Pao. So why couldn't she mope to her heart's (dis)content?

Because moms were unfair, that's why.

In the arcade, three boys a little older than Pao were hurtling full speed toward *Ghost Hunter 3*. "I hear it's, like, actually scary!" one of them squeaked.

"Yeah, Sully said the guys that made it went to *real* haunted houses and, like, *slept* in them and *saw* things."

"So cool! They're like *actual* experts!"

I'm so sure, Pao thought, returning to her scathing inner monologue. Like a bunch of white guys with phone cameras in a tourist trap knew anything about real ghost hunting.

But the truth—and Pao's terrible secret—was that she would have given anything to be fighting real ghosts or monsters right now. She would have been thrilled to see a terrible hairy Mano Pachona, or a full-grown slavering chupacabra. Anything to prove that last summer had been real. That she had actually been through something.

That she wasn't just a freak who no longer belonged in her own life.

Across the table, Aaron shifted uncomfortably in his seat, grinning goofily when he caught Pao looking at him. No one had spoken a word in nine minutes and forty-three seconds. So much for bonding.

Her mom was looking desperate now, and for a second, Pao almost felt sorry for her.

But only for a second.

After Pao's disappearing act last summer, things had improved between her and her mom. For a while. But Pao had quickly realized that accepting her mom's differences, as she had done while trapped in the endless throat of a magical void, was actually a lot easier than getting along with her in real life.

Especially now that her mom was dating Aaron.

Pao tried to ignore him, thinking of her dream the night before instead. Even a nightmare was better than this guy. She'd been walking through a dense pine forest, a weird green light filtering through the trees. The road she'd walked was long and straight, and at the end of it was a silhouette she'd somehow known was her dad.

It made sense, Pao thought, that she hadn't seen his face. She hadn't seen her dad in real life since she was four years old. Her mom never even talked about him. But in the dream, Pao had run toward him anyway, like he was coming home from a long absence and she couldn't wait to throw her arms around him.

Of course, she hadn't made it that far. Just before she'd gotten close enough, the ground had opened at her feet. A massive crack in the earth took Pao with it as it gave way, leaving her father shouting from the cliff above.

After waking from a nightmare like that, shaking and sweating, was it any wonder Pao didn't wanted to spend the evening fake-smiling over greasy food with a total imposter?

Across from her, Mom and Aaron chewed in silence, exchanging an awkward look between them.

Pao could have made it easier for her mom, she knew, but right now that was the last thing she wanted to do.

Why would she want to help someone who hadn't even noticed that her daughter was suffering the aftereffects of one of her notorious nightmares? The kind she had experienced ever since she was little and had led her to enter a magical rift to fight a legendary ghost.

Her mom was supposed to be *highly* attuned to this stuff. She always had been before. . . . But tonight she'd just told Pao to get a handle on her hair and wear a clean shirt. Like it mattered how Pao looked for this totally inappropriate ordeal.

Mom had met Aaron, a firefighter, at the bar where she worked and within *six weeks* had decided that he was meet-the-kid material. But impulsive choices were kind of the norm for Maria Santiago. Even Bruto the chupacabra puppy had given them an *isn't this too soon?* look as they'd left the apartment tonight.

For about a month, Mom and Aaron had lied about him coming over to "fix the TV" or "drop off a book" or "look for a stray neighborhood dog" (Pao's personal favorite excuse). Last week her mom had finally come clean, and now they all had to play nice.

At first, Pao had been offended by the lying—she was almost

thirteen, she could handle the truth!—but an hour into forced bonding, she found herself wishing Aaron really *was* just the guy "redoing the shower grout."

The boys in the arcade were fully enthralled by *Ghost Hunter 3* at this point. The screen showed one of those cheesy paranormal-activity videos, all shaky camera and blown-out colors and vague, pixelated shapes.

Pao remembered a time when it would have been her and her two best friends, Emma and Dante, crowded around the machine. Dante would have been effortlessly good, Emma hilariously bad, and Pao in the back, refusing to play, mocking people for believing in ghosts.

But she'd barely spoken to Emma in two months. And Pao and Dante were pretending things were normal between them . . . but then why had she told her mom that he was too busy to tag along tonight when he really wasn't?

Not even science held her in the same thrall these days. Her microscope lay unused on the dusty top shelf of her closet. And she hadn't bothered entering the fall science fair at school.

Everything had changed. And Pao didn't know how to change it back.

"Ooh, that game looks scary!" Aaron said, snapping Pao out of her moody thoughts. "I'm not sure I could play it. Probably give me nightmares."

This time, Pao really, really couldn't help it. The scoff took over. It used her body as an unwilling host, like rabies in the brain of a raccoon, and a *pfft* sound escaped her lips. All Pao could do was hope no one heard it. But of course, her mom had laser-focused on her the moment Aaron had said *nightmares.*

And in terms of death glares, La Llorona had nothing on Pao's mom.

She smiled at Pao, a kind of snarly smile, all her teeth showing. A *don't screw this up or I'll take away that phone you just got* kind of smile. "Paola, why don't you tell Aaron what you're working on in school?"

"Invisibility," Pao said after a beat, pulling a pepperoni off her pizza and rolling it up into a greasy little tube. Her mom hated when she did that but wouldn't dare say anything in front of "company."

"Sounds pretty advanced for seventh grade!" Aaron said earnestly. His blond hair fell into his eyes, and he pushed it back. His face was that healthy-looking kind of tan that white people get when they go skiing or something. Pao wanted to wipe pepperoni grease on it.

"It's more of a social experiment than a scientific one," Pao clarified, watching her mother's eyes narrow even more. "You know, camouflage, deflection, that sort of thing. Luckily, I'm getting plenty of practice at home."

Pao had always distrusted people who smiled all the time, and Aaron's ski-catalog grin never faltered. She matched it with something akin to a grimace, knowing she'd pay for the comment later but not caring.

"Well, middle school is a tough time," he said, leaning down to look her in the eye. "I'm sure things will get better. Hey, only a year and a half until high school, right?"

"Yeah," Pao said. "Because high school is historically easy on freaks."

"Mija, you're not a freak," her mom said, waving a hand.

"You're just advanced for your age—the other kids are probably jealous."

Pao would definitely have rolled her eyes if her mom hadn't snapped her head to look across the room right at that moment.

"Oh! Isn't that Emma?" She waved, not noticing that her only child was ready to sink into the floor. "Emma! ¡Mija! Over here!"

It was noisy, and Emma was sitting at a crowded table with at least five kids from school. Pao kept her eyes on her plate and hoped that Emma didn't hear her name being called.

"Who are those kids she's hanging out with?" Mom asked, craning her neck. "They sure have . . . interesting hair!"

Emma's new friends dyed their hair in bright colors and wore jean jackets with patches and pins all over them. They kept up with current events and sometimes participated in protests. Across Pizza Pete's, they all laughed loudly at something, and Pao glanced up reflexively, just for a second. Emma didn't look their way.

"The Rainbow Rogues," Pao muttered, trying not to sound sarcastic.

It didn't matter anyway. Her mom was back to talking to Aaron, and Pao was back to being invisible.

Her eyes drifted over to where Emma's blondish-brown hair (complete with a new purple streak) was just visible over the tall back of her seat.

In September, when Emma had decided to come out to her parents, Pao had been with her—via speaker phone—for moral support. Emma had been nervous, but after all the worry and wondering, her parents had been nothing but supportive. Mrs. Lockwood had even bought a LOVE IS LOVE sticker for their SUV.

Emma had confessed her secret to Pao just a week after they'd returned from the rift, and together they'd plotted the best way to tell her parents. After Emma did it, Pao was so proud of her best friend she'd thought her heart might burst. The next day, they'd eaten every flavor of frozen yogurt in one giant cup to celebrate.

Pao had known this meant Emma could finally stop hiding. At last she'd get to be her whole, shiny self for the world to see. Pao had even convinced her to go the first yearly meeting of the aforementioned Rainbow Rogues, Silver Springs Middle School's LGBTQIA+ club.

They'd both been surprised by how many openly queer kids went to their school, and Emma had walked out bubbling with excitement and plans to go back.

But the more time they'd spent with the Rogues, the more out of place Pao had felt.

There were plenty of kids in the club who weren't ready to decide how they identified yet, and even kids who just called themselves "allies," so it wasn't her lack of specified queerness that made Pao feel left out.

It just seemed like most of the kids who were comfortable enough to be out at school were, for the lack of a better phrase, rich and white. Their parents drove them to and from the meetings in their fancy cars and sent them to school with organic lunches. They bought their kids unlimited poster board and, like, the *nice* markers in every color whenever they wanted to make protest signs.

Pao, with her bus pass and her subsidized lunch, couldn't have the Rogues over to her small apartment or chip in for supplies. They never made her feel bad about those things, of course, but the way they were *overly* nice about them somehow made Pao feel even worse.

And then there was Emma, who was *so* focused on making sure Pao had a good time that sometimes Pao felt she was holding her back. There was no reason for Emma to be the odd one out. She fit in perfectly, and Pao wanted that for her.

So the next time Emma asked Pao to join in—they were protesting a new Starbucks going in across from a locally owned coffee shop—Pao had made up an excuse. After she did it enough times, Emma had stopped asking.

Pao knew it was normal, people growing apart. But that didn't make it any less sad.

She pushed her plate away, her appetite suddenly gone. "I have homework. Can we go home now?"

Aaron had just taken another slice of "meat medley." The worst pizza variety ever. Sausage, ham, *and* pepperoni? What was it trying to prove?

Her mom opened her mouth, undoubtedly to chastise Pao for being rude, but before she could form the words, Pao's drinking glass exploded in front of her, soaking her space-cat shirt in all thirteen types of soda she'd combined from the fountain. It left them a whole different kind of speechless than before, which Pao couldn't help but enjoy just a little.

There were glass shards on her lap and all over Aaron's slice of meat medley. Next to the glass, a quarter was spinning like a top. It must have come from one of the kids playing in the arcade.

After taking a second to recover from her shock (and to make sure Emma and her cool friends hadn't seen), Pao glanced at her mother, who looked murderous.

"Come on!" Pao said. "You can't possibly think this is my fault!

It was a freak accident! Look!" She held up the quarter, which had just stopped spinning and fallen onto its side.

Tails, Pao noticed, then shook herself before she went down a probability-and-statistics hole.

Her mom, thankfully, had turned her withering glare onto the kids shrieking in front of *Ghost Hunter 3*. "Honestly, where are their parents?" she asked, looking at Aaron to check his reaction. When he nodded, she continued. "Throwing quarters around, breaking glasses? So irresponsible."

Pao bit her tongue. Her mom had left her unsupervised (or in the care of their elderly neighbor, Señora Mata) for the greater part of her childhood. Now that Aaron was around, she was suddenly Suburban Susie of the PTA?

Not that she was judging her mom for how she'd raised Pao. It was hard to juggle a kid and a more-than-full-time job on your own. But why did her mom have to pretend to be someone else just to impress this guy?

Wasn't that, like, the opposite of what she always told Pao to do?

As the two adults chattered about bad parenting, Pao tried to soak up the soda on her shirt with two paper napkins, only to end up leaving little bits of wet pulp all over it. She was almost too lost in thought to notice.

"I'm going to the bathroom," Pao said, standing up abruptly.

No one stopped her.

At least this nightmare is nearly over, she thought.

She should have known better by now than to think things like that.

TWO

The Bad Kind of Boy-Girl Weirdness

In the ladies' room *(gendered bathrooms, how archaic)*, **Pao** skulked against the wall waiting for a frazzled woman to herd three sauce-smeared little kids into the accessible stall. The other stall was out of order.

Maybe if Pao stayed in here long enough, her mom and Aaron would forget about her. She could live here, in the Pizza Pete's bathroom. Get all fifteen top scores on *Ghost Hunter 3* at night when no one was around.

She took an environmentally irresponsible amount of paper towels from the dispenser and began to daub her shirt again. It was already tie-dyed, so maybe the weird splotches would just blend right in? Old Mom never would have noticed. New Mom probably had opinions about children with stained shirts.

The woman finally emerged from the stall, looking much worse for wear as she took out sanitary wipes and cleaned the squirming kids from head to toe.

Pao knew her mom was probably getting impatient, but she just wanted some time alone. To steel herself for the last few minutes with Aaron. And to get rid of the feeling inside her that something weird was about to go down.

"Sorry," the mom said when one of the kids blew a raspberry at Pao.

"It's fine." Pao smiled. A more genuine one than she'd managed for Aaron.

"Never have kids if you prefer going to the bathroom alone," the mom said, but she tucked in the little boy's shirt and smoothed down the baby's hair, kissing the oldest one on the cheek before ushering them back outside.

Moms have it rough, Pao thought. And given that she'd seen (in the crazed eyes of La Llorona) arguably the *worst* one in history, Pao was reminded that she should be more patient with her own.

That is, if she could get her away from Aaron long enough to try.

Now walk out of here with a smile, Pao told herself. She would try harder with her mom, even after this awful bonding experience. She would not, no matter *how* funny it might be, crack a joke about how sometimes, in chemistry, a bond between three elements was so unstable it caused an explosion, or a deadly poison. . . .

Seriously, she wouldn't.

Despite Pao's resolution, the long walk home with her mother was uncomfortably silent.

Aaron had ridden his bike back to wherever he lived after the world's most awkward good-bye. Pao knew her mom hadn't forgotten her subpar performance at the pizza place. She was probably brewing a lecture like a strong cup of tea.

The Riverside Palace loomed ahead. The moment they walked through the apartment door, their tense silence would blow up into something too big to control. Pao stopped her mom under the broken streetlamp and looked up at her.

"If it's another snarky comment, Paola, I just don't know if I can—"

Pao cut her off by hugging her tight. They were almost the same height now, and Pao's forehead rested against her mom's cheek.

"I'm sorry, Mom," she said, humiliated to feel tears pricking her eyes. "It just feels like everything's different since I got . . . lost." To Maria, Pao's life-changing ghost hunt last summer had been a simple case of getting lost in the wilderness around the Gila River while looking for her friend. Dante's grandma Señora Mata was the one who'd advised Pao not to tell her mom the whole truth.

Pao stepped out of the hug and noticed that the lines around her mom's eyes looked softer than before.

Pao sighed, stretching for something genuine she could say to her mom in this moment. "I just . . . don't want things to change so fast," she said finally. And despite its lack of ghosts or void beasts, that really *was* the truth.

"Mi amor." Her mom sighed and pushed the too-long bangs off Pao's forehead. "We can't stop the world from changing. But this?" She gestured between the two of them. "This is forever. No matter what else is different, this will always be the same."

Pao nodded, not trusting her voice, not knowing if she could even trust the sentiment, but vowing to try. Yes, her adventure last summer had been amazing, and maybe she was having a hard time fitting back into this life, but it was the only life she had. She would have to make the best of it. She remembered what she'd learned in the throat of the rift about forgiveness.

"I love you, Mom," Pao said.

"I love you, too, mija."

They walked the rest of the way home with their arms around each other's shoulders, tripping and laughing through the parking lot. At the base of the stairs, they ran into Dante, who was just getting home.

"Hey, Dante!" said her mom. "We missed you at pizza tonight!"

Dante's eyes darted to Pao's, and she raised her eyebrows in the universal signal for *please lie to this adult*.

"Uh, yeah, Ms. Santiago. Sorry. Soccer practice, you know."

Pao looked at her shoes, avoiding his eyes.

"Well, I'll give you two a minute, hmm?"

"Uh, I have a lot of . . . homework," Pao said, but her mom had already slipped through the door of apartment C and closed it behind her.

"You know I hate to miss a pizza party," Dante said, not quite meeting her eyes and not sounding sorry to have missed it at all.

Pao felt her face heating up. "Just sparing you," she said. "Bonding time with mom's new *boyfriend*." She said the word like it was something gross before she remembered who she was standing in front of.

Not that they'd ever used words like that, which were too embarrassing even to utter.

Cheek kissing and hand holding were one thing when your life was on the line, but in the hallways of middle school, physical displays of affection were something infinitely different. And Pao wasn't at all sure she hadn't liked things better before, when they were just friends.

But she couldn't say that to Dante.

"I didn't know your mom got a boyfriend," he said, his gaze falling to the ground.

"Yeah, sorry. She just kind of . . . dropped it on me. I figured dinner would be awkward enough without turning it into some kind of—" Pao stopped herself before she could say *double date*, but Dante's face turned red like he had heard it anyway.

Pao knew she should talk to him. Tell him about Aaron the Awful and her dream about her dad. The old Pao-and-Dante would have discussed it all. But things weren't the same between them these days.

As if to illustrate the point, the now Pao-and-Dante shuffled their feet, looking anywhere but at each other. Did he know things were different, too? Pao wondered. He had to.

When they'd started school again, Pao was sure their friendship was unshakable. It had survived for years, after all, and gotten them through their confusing, terrifying, out-of-this-world shared experience. Pao was convinced they'd always fit into each other's lives as effortlessly as they had in the cactus field.

It was just seventh grade. There was no way it could be harder to navigate than a magical rift filled with supernatural monsters and a bloodthirsty all-powerful ghost, Pao figured.

She'd figured wrong. It wasn't just hard—it was impossible.

RICK RIORDAN PRESENTS

MORE MYTHS, MAGIC, AND MAYHEM!

NEW YORK TIMES BEST-SELLING SERIES

ARU SHAH AND THE END OF TIME
ROSHANI CHOKSHI

NEW YORK TIMES BEST-SELLING SERIES

THE STORM RUNNER
J. C. CERVANTES

NEW YORK TIMES BEST SELLER

DRAGON PEARL
YOON HA LEE

PURA BELPRÉ WINNER

SAL AND GABI BREAK THE UNIVERSE
CARLOS HERNANDEZ

NEW YORK TIMES BEST SELLER

TRISTAN STRONG PUNCHES A HOLE IN THE SKY
KWAME MBALIA

NEW YORK TIMES BEST SELLER

RACE TO THE SUN
REBECCA ROANHORSE

PAOLA SANTIAGO AND THE RIVER OF TEARS
TEHLOR KAY MEJIA

CITY OF THE PLAGUE GOD
SARWAT CHADDA

THE LAST FALLEN STAR
GRACI KIM

@READRIORDAN

Disney • HYPERION